Rising Ashes

Harvey Oliver Baxter

RISING ASHES

Paperback ISBN: 978-1-7395208-5-4

Ebook ISBN: 978-1-7395208-6-1

Hardback ISBN: 978-1-7395208-7-8

Cover and interior illustrations by Harvey Baxter (@topazsunzart on Instagram)

Hardcover case art by Ksenia Kholomeva (@milirine.art on Instagram)

To Arlo

Author's Note

This book contains themes I feel necessary to address before you begin:
- Manipulation and possession (loss of autonomy)
- Implied child abuse (nothing on page)
- Bloody violence, death and murder
- Cannibalism
- Vomiting blood
- Poisoning
- Suicidal intentions
- Self deprecating thoughts
- Self mutilation (not relating to mental health)

"If I am the chief of sinners, I am the chief of sufferers also."

— Robert Louis Stevenson, *The Strange Case of Dr. Jekyll and Mr. Hyde*

PROLOGUE

In a land where leaves whisper you to sleep and the sky is lit only by stars, a shadow lies in wait.

The road leading to the house is gated and alarmed with sensors buried within the oak trees weaving up the gravelled path —not a leaf too brown, nor a stone too sharp, and no branches out of place. No uninvited visitors—everything is always pre-arranged. Each day, access is carefully timed and precise. It's impossible to penetrate without being seen.

Well.

In the blackened pitch of night, the shadow looms by the entrance; detectors undisturbed. It glides as swiftly as the scythe of death up the asphalt drive towards the house. It knows this routine, and now it's finally time to finish things.

A startling flap of wings sounds as a bat bursts from the trees, hovering above the roof for seconds before vanishing. Tracking its every move, the shadow waits for the return of silence before dragging itself towards the front door. A pale hand lingers over the polished oak, noting the ripples of stained glass in the oval windows. It hesitates before knocking, noting the blackened claws protruding from its fingers, bleeding into its skin like ink. It pulls away.

Instead, the shadow works its way around the back of the house, slipping through the gate, fainter than air. It expects the triggered light when it steps from the gravel onto the patio stones. Of course, the conservatory is alarmed, but only a fool would miss that.

That won't be a problem tonight. The door is unlocked in seconds, and the shadow slips inside the glass-walled kitchen before stretching to full height.

The shadow takes a deep breath and closes its eyes beneath the pale moonlight that paints its face in an ice-cold glow. But the silence is soon broken, and the shadow's head snaps down at the faint sweep of feet across the laminate flooring.

A golden puppy pauses to look up at the shadow, drinking it in. And three, two, one... *bark*.

The shadow lunges, dropping elegantly to its knees before the now silent puppy, her tongue lolling out from her mouth. She appears to take in the sight of the shadow, its heavy coat, teeth, and wings. A human in costume, perhaps? Humans can be weird.

"Shhh." The shadow gently lifts a finger to its lips, maintaining eye contact.

She gulps and continues to pant in silence, her tail wagging.

"Good girl." The shadow lifts a hand and lightly strokes the puppy's head. "Sit." It scratches her chin when she obeys.

The shadow rises, consuming the room once more, and makes its way out into the hallway leading to the master staircase, glancing back at the animal to ensure she does not follow.

It's a pretty home, but one built on wealth and hushed secrets —its banisters carved from ignorance, and the ornate frames cover the lies and deceit buried within the walls. The shadow shakes its head ever so slightly as it ascends the stairs, its feet sinking into the brass-barred runner.

The landing is the heart, rugs leading to each room like arteries. Warm light pools between the gap in the bathroom door, blessing the occupied bedrooms with a beige glow.

The shadow looks to the left first. Each child's room is shut tight, their names hanging from slate plates. It breathes in deeply again, cracking its neck on either side before kissing its fingers and placing a sign of protection on each door. They'll never need to know what is about to transpire.

To the right, the shadow turns, lowering its head. With so many secrets hidden in the master bedroom, it's unusual how seldom the lock is used. Trailing through, the shadow casts its gaze upon the bed in the centre of the empty room; too much space for two occupants.

Only one soul lies in the bed this evening, however. The only one who matters.

The shadow takes in the scene and seizes its shoulders in preparation, filling its lungs to capacity for the third time. In the bed, the figure stirs—the disturbance is hopefully enough to wake him.

Though not quite.

Slowly, the shadow closes the door, its edge grazing the carpet, then waits at the bottom of the bed.

He wakes.

It only takes him a moment to blink and notice his visitor. He startles upright and rubs his eyes at the outline of wings and wavy hair. He believes it's his son at first, until realising this person is much larger. An adult.

"Who are you?" he demands. "Is this some sort of prank?"

The shadow's wings twitch.

"Answer me! WHO ARE YOU? What are you doing here? I'm going to call the police." He jabs a finger at the unfazed shadow who simply sighs—disappointed.

The man lowers his finger in defeat, his body trembling. He makes no attempt to reach for his phone.

"Who are you, and what are you doing in my house?"

Still, no response.

"Do you know who I am?" Ahh, there it is—the entitlement.

The shadow finally speaks. "We both know who you are. We both know what you've done."

It's a boy's voice, the man thinks. He huffs.

"You will get the fuck out of my house this instant," he demands with a new wave of confidence. A child can't hurt him.

The shadow shrugs. "Why do you think I'm here?"

Silence falls as the man pauses, the cogs turning, rust flaking away. It does not take long for the thought to enter his mind. The man gulps—his palms sweaty; head heavy.

"Are you the devil?"

Another shrug. "The devil isn't real. Well, maybe he is. Maybe he's you."

"What do you want? How much? How much for you to leave? To drop this? I can get you anything you need. Everything is just a phone call away. Name your price. Do I know you? Did I—"

The shadow raises a hand to silence him, its claws visible beneath the silver glow of the moon.

"I don't want your money." The shadow glides over to the side of the bed, leaning down close so that the man can see its full face. Its teeth. "What do you see?"

"Fear."

"Do you have anything to say?"

"I don't know what you want me to say."

"Oh, that's unfortunate."

IF THE HOUSE was not so ostracised from its neighbours, so proud to be a secret, one may have witnessed what happened that night, or heard the muffled cries as the reaper made his move. The police may have been called while concerned citizens broke down the doors.

But with privilege comes tainted pride, and a house can take care of itself.

. . .

IT IS A SWIFT DEATH; he had little time to scream.

The Star takes his life, the untraceable murderer.

Ridding this world of one more sickness—one more evil.

As he lies there, body cooling, his blood seeping into satin, he looks up at The Star as a metallic smell fills the room.

"Your children are safe, by the way. Glad you cared enough to ask. They won't miss you after they find out what you did."

Act 1

He's Not Home

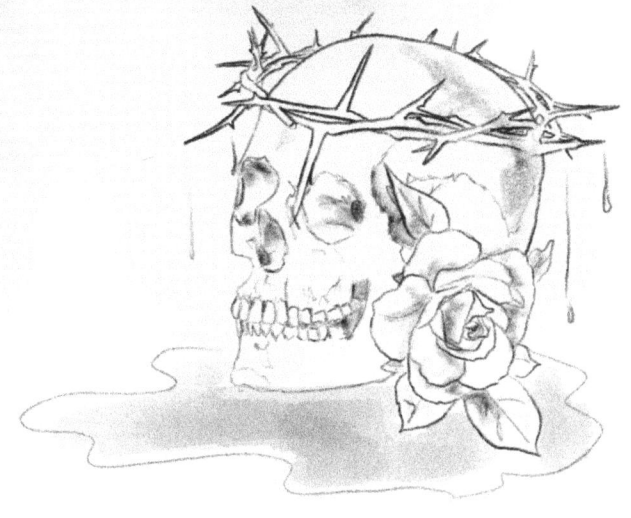

3rd May 1749

I thought I'd outgrown the need to keep a diary, but alas, it appears I have not. I am, after all, no longer a child, meaning my duties have become much more serious than the petty pages of a wandering mind, however, Grandfather passed away this morning, meaning his entire estate is to be inherited by my father. We will be moving to Yorkshire in a matter of weeks, and not only that, but my older sister Adeline is now betrothed to her unfortunate suitor, Christopher Munford, and they are to be married this summer. She will be leaving the Ashtown household and leaving me to care for my ever-annoying younger siblings, Nicholas and Dorabella. I love them dearly, of course, though I am now seventeen, and they are but twelve. Our interests do not align. Dorabella spends her days in the meadows making jewellery from flowers, with her head in the clouds and melodies on her mind, while Nicholas spends his time indoors, reading or playing with his hand-made puppets. Upon the rare occasion father is home, Nicholas becomes his shadow and copies his footsteps like a grown man accustomed to wealth might. I am often glad father works away for most of the week because I much prefer to see my brother playing his games—he is a master of story-telling—but he and Dorabella require my attention much more now that Adeline can no longer fulfil the role of the eldest sister and, well, I am not sure I am ready to be that for them. Is that selfish?

I have no doubt once we are settled in Yorkshire, mother and father will find me my very own suitor, one whom I must marry and bear children with. How disgusting. I have never thought myself capable of being a mother, and I am perfectly fine with that being the case. I do not have that luxury of choosing though, do I? I must marry into equal wealth, if not greater, and I must follow mama and Adeline as all good women do.

I am most displeased with the changes that are to come, but what can a girl do?

I am writing this with the hopes that some higher being will come across these pages and grant my wishes.

I do not want to marry. I do not want my life to change any more. That is all I ask. To be happy, and for my brother and sister to be equally content with their lives.

I do not like that I am aging.

17th July 1749

I resisted the urge to return to these pages. My previous entry was born of fresh frustration and ripe anger. I do not feel that way all the time. Well, I do feel some disdain for marriage, although Adeline seems rather happy with the decisions made for her. Since moving to Yorkshire—which is much more pleasant now I am growing used to the surroundings—Nicholas and Dorabella have grown more attached to me, and I no longer find spending time with them dull. I enjoy the meadow and running in the forests with Dorabella; it is most freeing, until mother shouts at us for not behaving like proper women. It does not stop us. And Nicholas has seemingly grown tired of Father ignoring him, so has now turned his room into a toy museum, where he puts on plays and performances for the porcelain dolls and makes his own models to use as props. He is extremely talented, and I admire his determination to be the world's greatest toy maker. Father does not approve of his hobby, which I understand, though I never want Nicholas to give up. He will travel the globe sharing his stories and bringing joy to all generations and I will protect him from the familial expectations as much as I am physically able to. The Ashtown legacy is so very crushing.

The house itself is much grander than our previous home, and at night it feels a little too big with all those empty rooms, but I know I will not be living here long. The search for my husband is talk of the village.
I hate growing up.

7th January 1750
This will be a quick entry to announce there is to be a ball next week, and I am to be introduced to Gabriel Johnstone, the man my parents want me to marry.
I do not care for him. I have not even met him, but I just know I do not want to belong to him.
Dorabella wants to meet him. She can't wait until it's her turn. The thought of my sister being married off to anyone in the future boils my blood. I will protect the twins from this world for as long as my lungs have air.

I must keep this entry hidden. I think mother has been going through my room.

14th January 1750
I do not like Gabriel Johnstone. He is not unpleasant to look at, but there is something about his... how do I say it? Manner? It is not his personality. He is well spoken and polite, everything a man should be, but there is something about this man that feels almost wrong. *I cannot figure out what it is, I just know I am not comfortable with this. I must speak with mama, if she will listen.*

16th January 1750
Dorabella adores Gabriel and is already asking for him to be invited to our home. I don't think she quite understands that this will necessitate my moving away. She was never as close with Adeline.

Mother and Father believe this man to be my perfect match. Of course they do. He has money. This is an Ashtown-Johnstone partnership. There is no love involved—this is business. The only person who shares my same dislike is Nicholas. I spoke with him while we painted one of his puppets' faces. He agrees with me that there is something not quite right with Gabriel, saying there is a peculiar energy about him. He also told me, very proudly, that he refuses to marry once he is old enough. I smiled at him. At least I am not alone in this. We continued painting his puppets until the sun went down.

19th January 1750

I hate this place. I want to move back to Lincolnshire. I refuse to marry this man. Why must it be this way?

—Taken from the diaries of Marianne Ashtown.

CHAPTER ONE

Mars
Now

The arm is wonky. I can't get the perspective right, and I threw my colour wheel under the cabinet over an hour ago. Taking a step back does nothing—if anything, it makes it look ten times worse.

They say the best thing for a creative block is to put it away and return to it with a 'fresh pair of eyes'. I tried that, but then I just got impatient. I don't like waiting.

I've not been able to complete a full composition in nearly six months, maybe more. Definitely more. I'm not really keeping up with the days. It's summer, I know that, but the weeks all blur as one.

I've always been pretty lazy with my bigger pieces; they take too long, and life's too short. You know, despite the fact I'm meant to live forever. Ha. It's ironic, really. But yeah, bigger pieces. I've done a handful in my life, always in the aftermath of something really depressing. So, I thought now would be a great time to get my 'let's produce a masterpiece' brain on. You know, since we're all falling apart. I'm not even being dramatic.

I blow out the candle. Fuck the ambiance.

The piece can wait, I'll find the motivation one day. I need to take a walk.

THE HALLS FEEL SO MUCH COLDER NOW. Irony loves me I guess, but it's true. I don't see people the way I used to. There was a time where you'd never get peace and quiet in these god-forsaken walls, and now the wind through the cracks deafens you. Not even a quarter of us remain now. The Thorns are virtually no more.

I don't blame people for leaving. If I was anyone else, I'd have done the same. I'm not a soldier, a guard, or a saviour. I'm a fucking thirty-year-old vampire who wears the same four outfits on rotation and cries when they see a butterfly. I'm pathetic.

But I've seen enough.

To be honest, I envy those who had the guts to leave. I hope they're happy and safe and *free*. But unfortunately, you can't live the life I've lived to just 'move on' like that—not after everything I've seen and lost. This is my life now. *Now*? Who am I kidding? It was inevitable from the moment I blindly stepped out onto that motorway, headphones on, my mind away with the fairies. That truck just swerved out of nowhere.

Cut the violins. I sometimes wonder what she saw when they peeled my body from the ground. I wonder why she was there and why she saved me. But that's the first thing we all ask when Marianne brings us back into the world. When we wake in a foreign room, our heads pounding, throats dry, craving blood—our minds grasping for answers.

Why did she choose us?

What makes us special?

Didn't I deserve to die from my own stupidity?

Christ, I need a drink.

.   .   .

I MEET with Lawrence a few hours later; we share a rabbit in the woods then let our legs carry us to a nearby cocktail bar where alcoholic drinks are very quickly acquired and consumed. We've somehow made it a thing, the two of us, meeting in various bars for various potent liqueurs, talking about the utter crap on our minds. We never set a date or time—it just happens without us realising. We always seem to be available at the right moments.

We're not getting back together. Nope. Never. We're both on the same page there, but what happened *that day* drew us all together in ways we would have never expected. We were the ones left behind.

I've not seen Casper in nearly a month, nor Francesca, for that matter. The future of the band is still up in the air, but I don't think any of us care now. I doubt we've even thought about it for more than thirty seconds before we picture his smile, his eyes, and his beautiful, beautiful soul.

Ben.

"You're zoning out again." Lawrence places his crystal tumbler onto the glass counter, and I shake my head to focus on his face. The evening sun frames the sharpness of his cheekbones and highlights the blues in the grey of his eyes. He crosses one leg over his knee, and the dramatically high pleat of his skirt catches on the buckle of his boot for a second, exposing a large portion of his bare thigh.

"I didn't even realise this time." It's becoming a regular thing now, me daydreaming without even noticing. It's hard to tell what reality is when yours is so violently upheaved.

"It's okay. I didn't say anything important this time."

I figure he's joking; he normally is. Lawrence just doesn't have the ability for sincere humility.

I take another sip of my cocktail, and the lingering aftertaste makes it abundantly clear it's not going to get better after the fourth sip.

"I'll get you another drink." Lawrence is quick to notice my distaste and is already on his feet, ready to go to the bar with his own empty whiskey glass.

I bat my hand at him and irresponsibly swig the rest of the drink in one go. I wipe my mouth, squinting at the bitterness. "I think I'm done now."

He shrugs and reluctantly slumps back down into his chair. "Heading off soon, then?" He twirls the dregs around his glass as I nod, the liquid drowning my stomach, making my head fuzzy.

"We should get an early night for once."

His right eyebrow raises into his fringe. "We?"

I take a deep breath and pinch the scowl at my brow, forgetting for a second that I still have my bridge piercing. I didn't mean to say that. *Did I?*

God, why can't I ever think straight anymore? It shouldn't be hard. But it is. It always is now. It's like I'm living in a simulation, waiting any moment to remove the headset to learn this was all a test, just a game, and everyone's alive and well.

"We," I say again, more confidently this time. My vision momentarily blurring.

He just nods.

LAWRENCE THRUSTS my back against my apartment door the second it clicks shut behind us, his warm hands scrambling under the hem of my top.

I tear his white blouse over his head and scoop him into my arms, tracing the familiar scar under his collarbones with my lips. He tips his head back in release, gripping onto my arms with force as I let my tongue follow the path of the scar vertically down his chest. Gasping, he pushes me back against the wall to unzip my leather vest.

We pick up the pace, eager, ready, and stumble onto the unmade bed, collapsing into the sheets, our limbs entangled.

Despite the time, the sun hasn't quite set yet, and the dying light paints a cold glow into the dim room.

All I can hear are his rapid breaths as his body undoes itself in my arms.

I straddle him, pressing kisses across every inch of his skin. My hair sweeps over my shoulder and weaves into his. We're pressed together so tightly, it's as though we are one.

He says my name, sweat beading on his brow. He directs my hands down to our usual routine, and I feel like it's the first time I've been alive in weeks.

We find our rhythm, his skin slick and damp from our movements. The room fills with the final remnants of amber, casting golden-cased shadows along the paint chipped walls. I want to freeze the moment—inject the release into my veins and *breathe.*

After an eternity, my limbs grow numb, the ecstasy liquifying my very bones. I'm out of breath; he moans, and we...

I'm in the woods.

Blood trickling down my cheek.

The most guttural scream pierces my core, and we all turn.

He crumples to the floor.

Chatterton painted a morbid red.

The sun breaks through the frost-bitten branches, and everything falls silent.

When I turn, I see *him*, rising from the ashes of dawn.

Bloody sclerae and thick black nails break through the tips of his fingers, talons shredding skin.

Muddy wings raise in the morning glow.

An angel of death.

He looks at me, but he doesn't. He looks *through* me. He's not home.

He tears her into tiny pieces; he obliterates her.

He's not home.

Blood.

He's not home.

Poppy.

He's not home.

Tell me I'm right.

"He's not home."

I abruptly pull back, and my eyes grow wide. I've gone again.

"What?" Lawrence pants, pulling himself out from under me and propping himself up on his elbows. The room is almost the blue of night now, but I can still make out the curves of his cheeks, and the scowl on his brow. How long was I out of it?

I open my mouth, but my throat closes up until I can barely even breathe.

"What did you say?"

"I..."

He tilts his head to the side in what seems like disappointment. As though he can read my mind. Like he already knew what I was thinking.

I've done this before. This whole sequence. Gone for a drink with the band's guitarist—who is supposed to be my ex—then let the alcohol take me and cloud my rational thinking until we spend the night together. But it's never the night we expect. Because every single time I try to let go, the thoughts start. I can't get past them. They're so vivid.

My mind freezes up entirely. I'm so numb. I can't feel my body at all. I reach for the duvet and begin to slowly crawl over to the other side of the bed. Lawrence lets me, watching as I turn to my side and bury myself completely beneath the sheets.

"I think I need to sleep now," I say, my eyes glued to the wall. I'm shivering.

I don't expect him to respond, and he doesn't. I only hear him sigh before the weight on the bed shifts and he tucks himself in beside me.

I don't sleep.

I can't.

Every time I close my eyes, all I can see are his red eyes burning into me. The wings.

Arlo.

I need to find him.

THE THING IS, what Arlo did—what happened to him—it scared us. No matter how you want to look at it, or who you choose to pin the blame on, it terrified us all. We all thought being a vampire was bad enough, but up until those final moments in the forest, we still believed we were the only other beings like this on earth. We lived in denial, refusing to accept the theories until they dangled themselves in front of our faces. It only hit us once we finally saw him *transform*. Arlo had been running from something we couldn't even comprehend, and we fed him to the beast. He was so vulnerable, and had been since the day Lucy took his life, but how could we have known the true extent of what was coming for him? What maybe had him all along...

What is there left for us to do? Hunt the invisible threat? Sharpen our stakes and pitch-forks and wade aimlessly into the night? I already said I'm no hunter, and the others even less so. We're so far out of our depth, it's almost comical.

The training hit us all hard—almost destroyed us before we even made it to the forest. We were just following orders. Arlo was in danger, and Lucy, that damn *bitch,* was coming for us. We did all we could. We strained our minds to the maximum and threw a few punches. Measly, really. And now Ben is dead, Arlo is missing, and the rest of us have either gone rogue, blocked all contact, or left the city entirely.

I'd be lying if I said I didn't blame Marianne. Well, that's not exactly true. I don't think it's *all* her fault; she was as much in the dark as we all were about Arlo's creature, but she was supposed to be our leader. The one to protect us. She has hundreds of years on all of us, and yet she still wasn't good enough for what was thrown our way. I know she was frightened—she'd seen the power of a

Dumont first hand, and it shattered her trust, but it was almost like it broke her completely. The realisation that Lucy was Isiah's brother made her mind just stop, as though she were a young girl again. She acted rashly and made mistakes. She couldn't save us. But now she barely shows her face.

She won't speak about it. I don't know if she thinks the silence will make it all go away, but it feels like I'm the only fucking person who wants to find Arlo. Skies, she's not even been to see Ben's grave. She's not mentioned him once. It makes me want to scream. To go up to her and violently shake the words from her lips, triggering her back into existence. We need guidance. We need protection. We need her.

LAWRENCE IS GONE by the time I properly wake up. I check the clock and realise it's noon. I must have had at least a few hours of uninterrupted sleep. I don't know why we keep doing this. Why *I* keep doing it. I don't love him. I don't think I ever did. We just know each other's bodies well and are easily persuaded to fuck at the slightest inconvenience. Lawrence is attractive, and he knows it, but we're not meant to be together that way. We're never going to move in together or live happily ever after in fields of daffodils. Our conversations often end in arguments, and the ones that don't only don't because we'll have already reached the bedroom by that point. It's a vicious cycle we're in, and one of us just needs to be the bigger person and cut it all off before one of us actually gets hurt.

I've never spoken at length with Lawrence about his preferences, but he doesn't strike me as someone who will settle down romantically with anyone. He's not bothered about the technicalities of pillow talk or who's cooking dinner. He seems pretty content with that, too. He adores being immortal. He adores the fact he died so young and will forever be seen as a perfect little prince with porcelain skin and frills. He adores his freedom and remakes himself every day.

He doesn't like being told no, but he's like that for a reason, and I know time will drag that out of him. He's been on the run from reality since the age of seventeen, and he never wants to stop. He's endured more than most of us will ever understand, but he just gets on with it. With life. Nothing slows him down. He knows perfectly well what he wants, and he'll make sure he gets it. For better and for worse. Forever.

Back in the main hall all those months ago, with Marianne forcing us all to weave into each other's minds, I could have strangled Lawrence for approaching Arlo and sending him to his knees. I was genuinely close to snapping his neck and throwing him into the dark corners of the room to suffer for hours before his bones forged back together one painful crack at a time. I wanted him to think about the consequences of his actions and beg for forgiveness. But as I'd approached, I saw little Matthew in the shadows behind him and knew. I felt it. Lawrence wasn't trying to Manipulate Arlo or take advantage of him. He was that high on whatever substance he'd taken that day, he'd opened himself up to full Manipulation from that little *bastard* and was being used just as much as Arlo, if not more. Matthew had latched onto what he thought Lawrence was like and used that assumption to corrupt him. It wouldn't have been hard. In his own way, Lawrence had a thing for Arlo. I think a lot of us knew, and he really tried to apologise to him. His inner voice was always too loud, and his pride too strong to admit he'd let a 'child' infect his drunken brain. I doubt he was even aware of what he actually said that day, but Arlo wasn't interested, regardless.

And that was my advantage. I wanted to get close to anything linking back to Arlo. Lawrence has been a constant in my life for a long time now, but this time, I wanted him for different reasons.

So, if I'm being perfectly honest, I want to cut things off before *I* get hurt.

I'm using him more than he's using me. He makes it known he doesn't 'catch feelings'. I'm just taking liberties with that fact and sleeping with him because...

Well, isn't it obvious?

I love Arlo.

Oh, fuck.

I sit at my apartment window with a mug of stale coffee—a reheated cup, one I presume Lawrence made himself earlier on. I dropped a spoonful of fox blood into it, but I got the balance wrong, so it tastes pretty vile.

I'm staring at the wall in front of me. A slither of sunlight shines down beside the table, highlighting the floating particles of dust.

I pick at my pyjama bottoms in a trance. I'm a mess. I'm always a mess. Urgh.

I think I'm pretty set on my plan now. I need to work out the logistics properly, but I'm sick of waiting. I've travelled the country, blindly searching for him, but it's time to really focus.

I'm going to call Rani. I've not seen her since that day in the forest—that was my choice, though. I've known where she is for a while. I just... well, talking to her would be like talking to Arlo, and I still don't know what I'd say. So, I kept my distance.

Marianne sent her and Carmen away for a while to keep them safe, but then I noticed they'd returned. I spotted Carmen's car around town before catching sight of Rani walking into a university building with a file sheltering her head from the rain. I nearly stopped her then, but I took too long to decide, and before I knew it, she was inside and out of sight. All I could do was sigh.

I went to see Marianne that night. She was cheerier than usual, but still reserved during our conversation. I asked her the question I already knew the answer to, but I needed to hear it from her mouth. Could Rani remember what happened that day? She shook her head. Didn't even open her mouth to answer. I was about to snap and throw something at her out of sheer frustration, but her gaze stopped me. As she looked up at me through her brows, I recognised her for what she really was. A tired woman.

"She hasn't forgotten him, if that's what you deduced," she said, sighing.

That was exactly what I'd *deduced*.

"She knows everything she knew until that point. She just believes Arlo dropped out of university. She might be a little bitter he hasn't texted her in a few months, but she'll move on in time, if she hasn't already."

I don't know what outcome would have been worse. That Rani could have forgotten about him completely or the belief he wants nothing to do with her. I don't know what I would have done, but I wouldn't have taken him away from her.

Maybe I would have told her the full truth. She deserved that, at least.

So that's exactly what I decide to do now.

I'm going to call Rani, and I'm going to tell her everything I know, everything I saw, everything I believe, and we're going to find him.

We're going to find Arlo and destroy that creature inside him.

We're going to bring him back to us and restore everything to the way it once was.

We're going to save him.

We're going to bring him home.

14th August 1753

Once again, I thought I would never return to these pages. But I have the ever-growing need to document my life as I am feeling it. It has been a while since my last full entry, the past few years summed up in a few pages I scattered into the fire so no one can ever read them.

I am now a married woman. It was inevitable, I knew I would never escape this. They would not stop hunting on my behalf.

I did not marry Gabriel. I believe he was the last man I mentioned in this diary.

No, my husband goes by the name of Richard Parish, and he is seventeen years my senior. His last wife recently passed away, God rest her soul, but he was in need of a new partner. Enter, me.

Richard is too much at once. He is too sweet, too polite, too charming. It makes me sick.

But he is perfect for the Ashtowns. He comes with a great fortune, and his age is a positive attribute for my parents. He has experience; he knows the world.

He took me to his—our—bedchambers last night, and we spent the night tangled in each other's arms. I have never used my body that way; it made me feel as though I was not quite myself when his hands touched me.

How does anyone enjoy this?

I am not talking about his age, for he is clearly very experienced and looks after his body well. No. I'm talking about the act in itself. Is there normally no emotional feeling or connection? I do not want this, but not just with him. I never want to do this again with anyone. If a god fell from the sky, I would refuse him. I will not bear children with this man. With any man. There is something wrong with me. But if I tell anyone, or if anyone finds these papers, they will send me away. A sanatorium. I will never see my family again. That is what they do with women who do not behave.

17th September 1754
I am still childless. Fortunately, Richard does not require much from me, so in the rare occurrences when he desires me in bed, I oblige. Our times have grown shorter and shorter, and I have learned to block it out of my mind. I am still childless. And that I will remain.

9th October 1754
Father has fallen ill. I have moved back home to be by his side for the winter. Richard says he understands and will give me the time I need. He visits when he can, and I will admit I have grown accepting of his company. Perhaps things will be okay for me now.
I missed spending every day with the twins. They are the age I was when Adeline left now, no longer the children I wish to remember them as. They had, of course, visited me a handful of times, but it was never the same. I hold them close to me now. I must never forget the importance of family.

19th October 1754
Father's illness is growing stronger and stronger. I am fearful he may never recover.

21st October 1754
I do not know how this happened; he has been kept apart from us, but now Dorabella is showing symptoms of the same illness. What can I do? I am scared, so very scared. Men expect women to fear most things, we are the fairer sex after all, so I suppose sitting in my childhood room by the window, with tears watering the vines outside, is natural.

I hold no shame though. You cannot show me a man who has not mourned his father.

23rd October 1754
Father did not wake this morning.

25th October 1754
Richard travelled to stay with me at our family home. I thought I would be happy to see him after all that time, but something feels different. He does not talk to me with the same love in his tone. What happened while we were apart?

26th October 1754
I have not left Dorabella's side. Nor has mama. We will not let Nicholas near her, despite his screams and wails as he bangs on the door. He wants to be near his sister. But mama refuses to let him close. If he catches this, if he dies, that will be the end of our family.

—Taken from the diaries of Marianne Ashtown.

CHAPTER TWO

Mars
Now

Saying you'll do something is not quite the same as actually doing it, unfortunately. I spend a solid hour sat wallowing in self-pity before I get dressed and charge my phone. Rani will have completed her first year by now, and she's probably already travelled back home to her family. But it's worth a try, I tell myself. No more waiting.

I decide to call her once I'm outside, so I can breathe and react properly to her response. I take a grand total of nineteen deep breaths in and out before I hit the call button, a sick feeling brewing in my stomach.

It rings five times before she picks up, but then I hear nothing.

"Hello?" I say.

Silence follows. Then: "Mars? Is that you?"

Skies, it feels good to hear her voice again. To hear the safety in her tone.

"Rani."

"Oh Mars, I thought I was never going to hear from you again.

I've been losing my mind. All my contacts disappeared, and I thought that was it."

She sounds relieved, but frustrated too. *How far did Marianne go?*

"I think we've all lost our minds a bit lately." I can't help but joke the minute my mind goes blank in panic.

She mumbles something through the phone, and then the line fuzzes a little. I hear a distant voice—her mother, perhaps, asking something in Bengali.

Rani mutes the call for a second before returning.

"Sorry, my mum likes to poke her nose in my business. She thinks I'm on the phone with a boy, even though she knows I'm with Carmen. I've told her three times, and she's literally cooked dinner for her."

"She'll always be looking out for you, bless her soul," I say with a chuckle.

"Have you seen Arlo?" Rani immediately jumps in with her question, her mouth close to the receiver as a door slams shut.

"Oh, I..." I don't know what to say. This wasn't how I'd planned to start the conversation, but what did I expect? This is why I called. Of course, she'd be beside herself with worry. Even after living her normal life for all these months, she cared about him more than any of us. She was the other half of his conscience —his anchor. No matter how much I thought I knew Arlo, Rani knew him tenfold.

"Mars?" She needs my response, her voice tinged with obvious concern.

"That's what I wanted to call you about."

"Good. Because I don't think I can go any longer with no one having the decency to tell me what's going on," she finally snaps. "It's been months. I go about my life every day feeling like someone has cut out a chunk of my back. I told myself I'd get over it in time, that whatever happened was maybe for the best, but how could you all just abandon me? Abandon us! Carmen! After everything we learnt? Carmen lived with you all for years. No one reached out—not once. No explanation or indication of why we found ourselves far from the city with memories that didn't even make sense or add up. It took us weeks to snap out of it and move back home."

I don't interrupt. I can't.

"Nothing seemed like it had changed. The city was like it always was, but something felt off, and whenever I thought hard enough about trying to figure things out, I'd find myself in a loop of forgetting my original thought and just going about the rest of my day thinking about completely unrelated things. It was like living in a dream, but one of those reoccurring fever dreams where you can't tell what's real or what's fake. Whatever we're missing in our heads has been brushed under this giant rug of deceit, as though we'd just move on and forget about it." She inhales sharply then swallows close to the receiver. "I know you lot have done something to me, made me forget something—something big. And I know it involves Arlo. At first, I thought he didn't want to speak to me for a while, but let me tell you, time must wear down your little mind game magic because the longer it's been, the more I realised Arlo would never do such a thing.

"You know I had to find out Ben died through Wikipedia? I had to Google the band because that was the only way I'd find out *anything,* and I learn Ben is *dead* from a... what was the lie you all made up? A short illness? Vampires don't catch diseases. I don't need a fact file to know that. I've seen enough movies."

I never thought about that. I was so caught up in thinking about how she felt about Arlo, I never even considered that she wouldn't know about Ben either.

"What happened? Where is he buried? Why has nothing made sense since the new year? I've probably failed my first year because I had more tabs open on my computer about mythical creatures and missing persons than I ever did study notes. I'd open my laptop to all these weird conspiracy sites, and then forget why I was searching them. I'd laugh it off, only to refresh the browser and continue searching."

This was so much worse than I thought. How ignorant of me. I don't speak yet though, I need to let her vent.

"I lost track of days, thought about seeing a therapist, but I held on. I held on, thinking that *maybe*, maybe one day soon, someone would call me. Maybe Arlo, maybe you, but someone would reach out to let us know we could return and fill in that missing weight on my shoulders. To justify why we were left in the dark for so long. I held on and told myself I would never stop." Rani stops briefly to take another deep breath and clears her throat. "I have these dreams; dreams I couldn't have fabricated all on my own. I know how insane the brain is at coming up with stuff, but these weren't just caffeine-induced visions. Arlo was in danger. I wake up saying that a lot. Carmen says I say it in my sleep. Help me, Mars. I don't want to give up, but I don't know what I'm chasing, and I'm scared. I'm scared I'll never escape this and I'm going to lose myself entirely."

Damn you, Marianne.

I scrape my heart up off the floor, a tear dripping onto the pavement. "Rani, I'm so sorry. I can't apologise enough. I didn't want this to happen. None of us did. Marianne wanted to keep you safe—"

"Don't talk to me about Marianne. How could I trust her? She's not the person I thought she was."

I don't know if I can trust her either.

"I'm so sorry. I'm so very sorry." I sense the desperation creeping into my voice. "But Rani, I need your help. I need you."

"You... you what?" She sounds breathless.

"Rani, I'm calling you because I need your help to find Arlo." There it is. I said it.

"But you... You don't know where he is?"

I hate this. "No... we don't. None of us know. Ever since you... He's gone."

"Well, he's not gone."

Her words catch me off guard, her confidence radiating through.

"What?"

"You're acting like he's dead. I know he's not dead. I know he's also probably not himself. One of the last things I do remember is that something has a hold of his mind, like a possession of some sorts. I'm not dim, Mars."

"Oh. Wow. Right." I'm still lost for words.

"So, are you going to tell me what you know so we can get started?"

God, I love this woman.

"Right. Yeah. Well... I can fill in the blanks."

We speak at length about every single detail the pair of us can share, reliving all of our emotions and thoughts from the past year. It's a painful call, but by the end, she tells me she'll be on the next train over. She doesn't need any convincing or persuading. Everything I said she knew was true. Confirming her nightmares.

Now comes the wait.

I DECIDE to head back to my apartment to put together a proper plan of where we'd begin. It's not going to be easy with just the two of us, but it's a start.

I'm surprised after spending an hour on the phone with Rani that I think about telling Marianne of our plan, just for an extra level of protection—something I still hope she can give us. But then I think twice and figure she probably already knows. She has a way of figuring stuff out. She has eyes in every crevice and around every corner. It's only a matter of time before she comes after us and demands an explanation. I wonder where she stands with this. I know she thinks about it. She has to. I know she can't just let things play out this way forever... But why hasn't she done anything yet? She, of all people, should have figured it all out by now. What has Arlo become, what was after him, and where has he gone? She must know *something*, so what is she so afraid of?

I'm about to pull out a pen and paper when there's a knock at my door. Who the fuck could—

Lawrence.

"Ahh," I say as the door swings open and there he stands, in the same clothes he wore last night, holding a paper bag.

"I brought pastries." He holds up the bag and grins, though it's overly fake and forced. It's definitely not the usual expression from the man who prefers to brood and sulk.

"Lawrence, now's not a good time."

"It never is." He lets himself in. I don't have the words to stop him.

"Raisin or chocolate." Lawrence sits himself down at my kitchen table and flops one leg over the other with the confidence as if he lives here. He more or less does.

I remain standing and begin to pace, my clammy hands on my waist.

I think back to the night before. The thoughts, the visions— the conclusion I came to at five o'clock this morning while seeing orbs in my cracked ceiling.

"Lawrence, honestly. Now really isn't a great time for pastries."

"It's always a great time for pastries," he says through a mouthful, chocolate flakes smattering his front.

I guess I'll take the raisin one then.

"Is that all you came for? To bring me an unnecessary snack and make a mess on my kitchen floor?"

Lawrence flashes me a cheeky grin before rolling his eyes. "No, of course not."

"So... why are you here?"

"I just came for a chat." He cocks his head and dusts the crumbs off his laced maxi skirt.

"A chat." My tone lacks enthusiasm; I'm already stressing about what he's going to say. Lawrence doesn't *chat*.

"Do you not want to chat about things? To talk about, you know... where we are, what we're doing... Where you see things going."

I gulp. I notice how he's picked up on the fact that this *thing* was always one sided, at least regarding the long-term outcome.

"Wanna take a seat, my love?" He points to the seat opposite and drags it towards me with his foot.

I have no choice but to sit. He watches my every step with an unreadable façade.

"Look... Lawrence," I finally say, resting my elbows on my knees. I've been on edge all morning and this conversation could have waited for my anxiety levels to drop, but hey, sometimes you've just got to get things over with quickly to move on, right?

"I think I should start, then you can tell me whether I'm right or not. Sound good?"

I chew on the inside of my lip but nod.

"Okay. Great. Well. I came because I wanted to call things off between us—for good this time. Believe it or not, it's not because I don't like you. I understand our history can be described as rocky at best, but I genuinely do like you, and I'd let this thing between us continue forever if we wanted, but I know it's not right, and so do you. There's something hanging between us every time we get too close, and it's like a countdown to an explosion, but no one knows when it's going to detonate. I know it's getting closer and closer—it's so loud it's deafening. I don't get attached like that. Romantic feelings don't just come to me in time, no matter how long it goes on for. I know what I want. I figured that out a long time ago, but that's not you. You're not like me. You need someone to settle down with. To grow old with, if you excuse the terrible irony."

I barely breathe a sound as he speaks. I just stare. He's right. I just hate that I let it get to a point where he's the one to point it out.

He continues. "We both know the main reason why we let this start back up again. I thought I had a chance with him, and you're in love with him, and so here we are, blindly and madly fucking while we both think about where the hell he could be and whether he's even still alive."

I wasn't prepared for Lawrence to be so blunt with his analysis, but he's still not wrong.

"Arlo," is all I say. All I need to say. The words come out so densely, it's like he's here in the room with us, silently shaking his head in disappointment.

Everything is happening at once, and it's suffocating me.

Lawrence lets the realisation ride for a little while longer before adding, "I'm right, aren't I?"

"Of course you're fucking right." I lean over to grab the greasy pastry bag and pull out my croissant, not even caring about the mess I'm making.

"So, we're on the same page then?" Lawrence asks a moment after we've both finished.

"We're on the same page."

"Good." He stands and dusts down his skirt again, readying to leave. "You're a terrible manager." He smirks.

"I don't think anyone can manage you." I'm not flirting.

"That... may be true." Lawrence grins, then fake salutes. "I'll love you and leave you then. Say hi to Rani for me when she gets here, will you?"

"I... *what?*" *How the heck...*

"What? Has no one ever mentioned you talk in your sleep?"

RANI ARRIVES early afternoon the next day, and I meet her at the station. As it's mid-week, and it's only a small connecting train, there aren't many passengers, and when she gets off, I almost don't recognise her. I'm stunned when she waves over in my direction. She's cut her hair into a bob and now sports a fringe and thin wired glasses.

"Mars," she says my name like it's a sigh of relief.

I give her a hug, and she drops her bags to return it.

"It's like I never left," she says into my shoulder before pulling away. "The second I pulled into the station, I just felt like I should never have gone home."

"Don't say that. You're not tied here like the rest of us. You can go wherever you want." I know she knows that, but I feel the need to remind her anyway.

We walk back to my apartment, and I take some of her bags to help. I ask general questions on the way to keep the energy light. I ask about Carmen, who's also made herself sparse after the ties were cut with Marianne, both willingly and unwillingly. She's been staying with Rani as much as possible.

"Carmen is fine. She's a little testy sometimes, but I mainly think that's because of Marianne. She was like a mother to her, and legally was—still is—so I don't think she's been able to wrap her head around why she'd send her away for reasons even I wouldn't understand. I might've lost Arlo in all of this, but she lost her only parent."

She continues before I can give my input. "I know she did it for a reason. She wanted to protect us, yada yada, but it's not right. I've had a whole day to dwell on what you told me, and honestly, I still don't care that we're human and easily susceptible to the Manipulation or whatever. We were just as much a part of this as you all were, and yet we're being treated like we're naïve little children. Too young to understand." She has a point.

"Anyway. Carmen's staying with her aunt in Cornwall now, so

you couldn't have rung me at a better time. I'm not sure she's ready to face things yet."

WE DROP her bags off at my apartment, but Rani says she'd prefer to do the talking in a more public setting. I panic at first in case she's worried and feels unsafe being alone with me, but then I think back to how she acted around Arlo. How she refused to leave his side, no matter what happened. So it wasn't that. Maybe I shouldn't dwell on it.

We pick a café we're familiar with and get comfy.

I've already told her everything I know, having apologised until my tongue swelled, but I do it again anyway, just so I know she's heard me say it in person.

"You don't have to keep apologising, you know. Arlo was bad enough at doing that. I don't need you to start." There's a slight hint of humour in her tone.

"You're right; I just want you to understand—"

"I know. I understand. It makes perfect sense. I knew Arlo wouldn't just leave us all like that. I'm just relieved it wasn't something I did. Gosh, I sound so silly and full of myself for ever thinking that could be the case. Even now you've explained the gaps in my memory, I still keep forgetting the world's a lot bigger than I thought. Vampires are just the start of it all. Are you even like actual vampires or do they not exist? I went on some deep dives on the internet. It's a very scary place."

I laugh a little. "We're the closest thing you're going to get to Carmilla and Dracula, and all those tales. I think so anyway. I've never actually read Dracula." I can't help but joke. I don't know what to think anymore.

"But Arlo's not quite that anymore, is he?" The mood shifts to one more solemn.

"No. I don't think so. We..." The images come flashing back. "We don't grow wings and talons or bleed... black."

I watch her face switch to horror. She never saw what I saw, and I'm glad.

"He's alive, though."

"As far as I'm aware."

"That wasn't a question. I'd know if he wasn't."

I nod at her surety. "He's alive."

"Where do we start then? Any leads?"

I wish I had more answers. All I know is he isn't in the city, otherwise I would have seen him. Sensed him. I must believe that. So, he's not here, and call it a hunch, but I don't believe he left the country. He's probably not alone, either, but launching searches for them would be futile because they'd be hiding in plain sight, with no wings or visible otherness to detect to the average onlooker. Virtually invisible. I say *them* because the creature he talked about will be with him; I just know it, even if I never saw anything. I keep having dreams that there was something else in the woods that day. Sometimes I believe it's my consciousness reminding me of things I hadn't really absorbed at the time, but in reality, I wasn't sure what I saw. I was never really focusing on anything other than Arlo. I could have just made it all up. After all, I'd hit my head. I don't discuss that with Rani, though. Not yet.

But from that possible memory, I somehow deduced that Arlo may not have been the only one the creature picked. My Catholic upbringing and school studies has taught me that things generally come in threes, and if we were going to pursue this hunch, then it would be ignorant to rule out the possibility that there isn't more of them.

Whatever wanted him, and got him, needed him for a reason. I just can't for the life of me figure out *what* reason.

"He won't be the same, will he? Even if we find him. We've got to save his mind as well." Rani plays with the handle on her chai latte.

"By the way he last looked at me, you're right. Whatever has control of him is strong. Arlo knew it too, and he tried to run for so long but just couldn't manage it. I don't think any of us would have been able to. This thing had him under control for months, and he didn't even realise until it was too late. None of us did." And I kick myself every waking moment because of it.

"He's vulnerable," Rani adds.

"We made him the perfect bait." It disgusts me how right that statement is.

"No, but he's not... I know he's shy and awkward, but it's more than that. People take advantage of him, anyway, never mind this supernatural influence. He sees the world a little differently to the rest of us, and not many people want to accommodate for that. My brother is autistic, and Arlo is so much like him, and people don't seem to understand that. I do though, and the thought of him being out there, alone and scared and not being able to explain himself. I... He's..." Rani flaps her hands, exacerbated.

"No, I know." *I know.* Which is why I hate that it took me this long to pluck up the courage to break away from my duty as a Thorn and do this without Marianne's guidance. I'm wading into the drowning tide, but I've got no other choice. We'll soon learn who—or what—was after him and see the consequences. The outcome could be catastrophic. This might not be just about saving Arlo. This could be about putting an end to everything—all of this that might have started even before I was born. I'm trying not to jump to dramatics to avoid losing focus, but the more I think about Arlo and the state he was in... I'm preparing for the end of the world.

Rani looks at me, concerned. It's a heavy topic for us both.

"Where to first, then?" she asks, finishing her drink.

"We go back to the church. The forest. Look for signs, anything pointing us in the right direction." It wasn't like I hadn't been there a million times before, but I felt that having Rani with me would help. She knows Arlo the best. She has insights on Arlo that could potentially offer solutions I never could have thought of. I had considered the danger of this excursion, but I can't prevent Rani from coming. I refuse to Manipulate her—she doesn't deserve that, never did.

She's already on her feet. "What are we waiting for, then?"

We get about as far as the front door before my eyes widen when I see who is approaching the other side of the glass. I stop dead, as does Rani, and I don't need to turn to know her expression.

Marianne.

The door swings open, and we stagger back. I don't know why my arm snaps out to hold Rani behind me. She's not going to hurt us...

"You're going to want to sit back down," Marianne demands, flustered. I've never seen her in such simple clothes before: an oversized hoodie and running leggings. She's pulled her hair back into two tight plaits, with golden wisps kissing her face. Bags circle her eyes, and she looks spaced out.

"Well, hello to you. Fancy seeing you here. What a coincidence." My tone is bland and sarcastic. This was, of course, no coincidence whatsoever. She's been following us. I knew this would happen. I knew she'd finally show her face when it was convenient for her. What's new? *Maybe I wanted this.*

"I know what you're thinking, but please hear me out. You're going to need my help." Marianne sounded exhausted and in no mood to start an argument. She normally dominates a conversation, but this time, it's me who has the upper hand. She looks so small in front of me.

"You know what we're doing?" Rani pipes up, pulling herself around me to face the Thorns' leader.

"Yes, and I'm going to help." She's so drained.

I look at Rani with concerned eyes, and we silently agree to listen to what she has to say. I know Rani is waiting for Marianne to address what she did to her—to explain.

Once we've sat back down, Marianne pulls out a notebook and

slams it down onto the table; papers and tabs stick out of the side. "This might help."

I'm a bit stunned and unsure of what to say. She's been hiding away for months, not leading us, not helping us, and now suddenly she wants to do her job again? Just when I decide to take matters into my own hands? Just when I finally make a decision of my own.

"I do care about Arlo." Marianne looks at us both. She might as well have just read my mind. I can't think of a response. After a beat, she sighs, crossing her legs and biting her lip, nodding as though aware of her animated actions. "I'm sorry about these last few months. About not being there for you when you needed me. I do care, though. I care so much."

Her desperate plea is... believable. There's no scent of Manipulation or persuasion. She just looks so tired.

"So, what have you been doing then, other than wiping memories? Mars filled in all the blanks for me, by the way." Rani's voice is quieter than earlier. She's trying to keep calm.

"This!" Marianne gestures to the notebook. She removes the elastic and opens it up. "I expanded my research from before, using that morning as my catalyst and guidance. This time, I searched for anything and everything that could even remotely link to what happened. I was lazy before and never got very far—my mind was too crowded with finding our killer and believing it all connected. I thought finding Lucy would answer all my questions, and that it would all slot into place and make sense. That it would give me the tools to put an end to what was after Arlo. But I was wrong."

It's not often Marianne admits her faults, but I know it eats her up. Hence why I'm prepared to hear her out now. She's allowing herself to be honest. Rani adjusts her chair and folds her arms, eyes pinned to the woman before us.

"I convinced myself that Lucy and Arlo's creature were potentially the same, despite telling you all otherwise. I led you all down the right path, then took a different route myself. I let it get too personal and confused myself. I was selfish and blinded by my own history to ever expand upon what I understood about *our* history and things never discovered." She looks down at her hands. "I found Lucy because I was adamant she connected to me somehow, but that alone consumed me. My job is to look after you all, and I failed. So, I needed to change my perspective and try a different avenue."

I'm about to say 'finally' but stop myself, thinking that would be unfair. I make sure Rani is still comfortable listening by nudging her foot, and she looks at me, flashing a focused smile.

Marianne swallows almost audibly. "I needed to understand this world to its roots and come to terms with what we were dealing with. I didn't hide from you all. I know it may have seemed that way. I just couldn't let myself get distracted. I learned more about our kind. I absorbed folklore and myths and legends and all those old wives' tales from across the globe. I learned to understand everything I possibly could about what took Arlo, and I wrote it all down in here." She pushes the book towards us both and we lean in to read the articles and clippings.

After I've somewhat absorbed the extent of her actions, I look back at her with different eyes. I sigh.

"You've been doing all this?"

Marianne nods and sucks on her lips.

"You do care," Rani says. The whole tone of the table shifts after she speaks.

Marianne almost chokes up when she says, "I do. I always did."

"And you do want to protect us," Rani continues.

The Thorns' leader slowly bobs her head, closing her eyes in tired relief. "Rani, I need you to know that what I did was—"

"To protect me. I know. You don't have to explain. I don't and won't forgive you, but I know why you did it."

"I understand that." Marianne still flinches at Rani's words, though I admire Rani standing her ground. I'm growing to understand why Arlo spent so much time around her, especially in the past few hours we've been alone. Marianne shouldn't have done what she did, at least not in the way she did it, but I'm glad Rani was able to confront her.

We sit in silence, flicking through the pages and pages of articles and reports and handwritten notes. Then I speak to Marianne. "So, what do you think we should do first, then? You're going to help us, right?"

"I doubt I'll be able to persuade any more Thorns to, but yes, I'm going to help you. The three of us will begin to look for Arlo and try to put an end to this whole mess."

"We *will* put an end to this," Rani says surely.

"Yes. We will." Marianne looks at her sympathetically.

"We were going to need you," I admit to her and myself.

"We need each other," Marianne corrects. Then she sighs.

"Everything okay?" I ask, a tad confused at her sudden shift in mood. I thought we were getting somewhere.

"Yeah. Sorry. Grand." Marianne smiles, but it looks fake, like she's holding something back.

Rani appears to be on the same wavelength as me. "Is there something we should know?"

Marianne's smile wavers. "It's just... before we begin, there's something I need you to understand. Two things, actually. Maybe more as we progress. I just need to get them off my chest before I explode."

Neither of us speak. We just wait for her to continue.

Pulling her chair closer to the table, Marianne leans into her elbows. "All this research got me to revisit a lot of things from my past; memories I shut away and tried to forget. Some things I even forgot naturally, but everything always circles back to the memories we want to move on from." Her expression is bitter and her arms flop down across the table in loose fists. "There are some things I should have remembered vividly, things that may have helped during those months Arlo was with us, but I never even considered them, and I... huh. I could have blamed my two-hundred and eighty-seven-year-old memory, but it wasn't that... it was—"

"Please just tell us!" Rani shouts out in a slightly harsh and unsympathetic tone.

"Sorry." Marianne closes her eyes for a moment. "There's stuff in there"—she points towards the pages—"about a cult, and other-worldly, potential god-related stuff. Then there's my history and the people I knew and... well, for starters, I think I know who Arlo's father is."

My face scrunches. "Arlo never met his father, but he knows who he is."

Marianne looks shocked. "He does? I thought—"

"Yeah. I saw a picture of him once. Tall, skinny white dude, covered head to foot in freckles. He has the same innocent eyes as Arlo, but there's nothing innocent about a guy who leaves his partner while she's pregnant and never contacts her again. Jeremy? Jerry? Jerry, I think his name was."

"Jerome. Jerome Mair." Marianne's face has gone white.

Lucy mentioned Jerome.

"You know him?" Rani and I ask at the same time.

Marianne thrusts her face into her hands before dragging them down her cheeks. "It makes no sense," she mutters. "Our kind can't reproduce... we've got the parts and functions, but it doesn't work. We're not alive in that way. It's not possible."

"Arlo's dad is a vampire?" Rani shouts this a little too loud, and I know the people near us hear.

I turn around and mouth 'DnD' to an alternative looking person with pink hair, who grins and nods as if they understand us perfectly. The luckiest situation I've ever found myself in.

"He's... I don't know. He *was.* The last time I saw him." Marianne is shaking at this point. Whoever he is, this *Jerome,* it's clear he's fucked up more than just a handful of lives.

"When was the last time you saw him?" I ask.

"1989." She knows this event perfectly, it seems.

"Oh." The year I was born. Thirty years ago.

"Maybe he had a blood transfusion or something. That's possible, right?" Rani adds the very relevant science fact that I never even considered. We look to Marianne for an answer.

She leans back. "Well, in theory, I suppose so, yes. It would be highly experimental, like it came from the mind of Mary Shelley herself, but it probably could work in the right environment with the right resources. But why? Why would he want to be human again—oh. Unless..." Marianne's mind drifts, her hands gripping the table's edge. "No. He wouldn't have." She shakes her head. "He loved nothing more than his immortality. His vanity choked me... he was... Oh I hate this so much... why must it be this way?" She looks like she's about to be sick.

"What's the other thing?" Rani butts in, seemingly to stop Marianne from losing focus on the original conversation. This stuff can wait.

"What? Oh." Marianne pinches the bridge of her nose. "Well, it's... the cult stuff. I was thinking it's about time I told someone about my brother."

28th October 1754

Nicholas broke into Dorabella's bedroom last night and spent the night by her side. He refused to let go of his sister's hand, even as mama and Richard pulled him away with force.

Mama hit me for the first time in my life today. Slapped me right across the cheek. She blamed me for leaving the door unlocked, even though I did not. She blamed me for being a bad influence on Nicholas. She blamed me for everything. I know she is upset; it has been a horrible time for her, but it was as though she had held these words in her mind for a long time, just waiting for the right moment to trigger them. I screamed at her, and I have never felt such hatred towards someone I loved. It is the most terrible feeling.

Richard dragged me away as I kicked my feet in protest whilst mother dealt with Nicholas.

Then we spoke, just the two of us, for a long time. He managed to calm me and soothe the redness in my face with a damp cloth. He told me stories to take my mind off things, but all the while he was speaking to me, I could not help but notice how different he sounded. Colder. Less... human.

It is absurd, I know. But perhaps my mind is corrupted now, after all I have seen.

29th October 1754

We buried father this morning.

Dorabella has not spoken a word for over a day. She is barely awake.

I am terrified.

30th October 1754

Nicholas coughed up blood this morning at breakfast.

Mother hit me again.

31st October 1754

There was a terrible storm in the early hours of this morning. Something loud crashed in the garden, but none of us had the energy to check.

31st October 1754

Before I begin, I would like to say I want to make this my final diary entry. I will make no attempt to hide these pages, and I hope they are found, so that I can get the help I need. Please—

This is my account of what happened on the night of the 31st of October 1754.

My name is Marianne Ashtown. I am twenty-two years old, and I am a monster.
All my life I have felt different. Like there is something wrong with my soul.
Mother's tales of angels comforted me as a child, until they stopped.
Until I realised I was not human. Not truly.
Everywhere I walk, misfortune follows me.
First it was Adeline moving away, then it was grandfather dying and us having to move away.
Then it was Nicholas and Dorabella losing their childhood.
Then I was married off to a man I did not love, and I cursed everything.
Now my father is dead, as is my youngest sister, and Nicholas is sick.
And a few hours ago, I learned my husband was the devil, and it did not alarm me—that is the worst part.
He took me up to our bedroom as tears stained my cheeks. Dorabella had stopped breathing. He brushed his gentle knuckles over my face and told me not to be afraid. Then he

told me he never wanted to lose me the way I lost Dorabella.
He explained that when I was away, he met a man whom he
could only describe as a god-like being, who gave him the gift
of immortality.
I did not believe him at first, but at my curiosity and not
fear, he showed me, dismantling my doubts entirely.
He bit my neck, his sharp teeth digging through to my very
bone, then I fell unconscious.
When I awoke, he forced me to drink his own blood, and he
explained everything to me. I believed his every word, for I
too am a monster. It makes sense now.
'We will bury Dorabella, and she will be at peace,' he said.
I pleaded with him to save her, as he did me, but he slapped
me, denying my request with fury. He only wanted me to
live forever with him. Just the two of us.
He told me I will move on and learn the importance of my
immortality. My family will live and die as humans are
expected to, but I will live on with him. We would be free
together.
I do not want that. Not at all. He did not give me a choice in
this life.
No one takes me from my family, not even the devil.
I do not know where my aggression came from, but I—
I stabbed him with my hairpin, then I hit him and hit him
and hit him until his face was bloodied beyond recognition
and he grew still. My strength frightened me, but a life with
him now felt worse.
How dare he. How dare he. How dare he.
His death was not permanent, though, for it would take
much more to murder an immortal, it seemed. He rose and
threw me to the ground with my neck tightly gripped in his
boisterous hands.
He had a face of terror and death. His eyes were wide and
dripping blood.

I thought he would kill me first, but then I kicked his feet out from under him and managed to push him backwards. He hit his head on the bedpost and fell to the ground again. That was when I grabbed the vase and slammed it into his skull.

I smashed and smashed it against his head until it shattered into a million pieces, and I could see the bone in his cheeks and brow.

Then the blood cravings began.

My name is Marianne Ashtown, and I am the devil. I licked his face clean. Then once I decided I had killed him, that I had murdered an immortal, I rose to write these pages. I am a monster. I need help. I am free. My brother is all I have left of love. He is the only person whom I care about.

I will save his life and make him like me. We will live our lives the way we always wanted. He will be a toy maker and bring light and joy to this cruel world. I will live as I so choose, with no man to tie me down. I will have my life back. I am insane. I have lost my mind. I am free. Free. I know not what...

I hope this diary finds you well. I will be long gone from this building before you find it.

—Taken from the diaries of Marianne Ashtown.

Chapter Three

Mars
Now

I stare at this woman in disbelief.

I'm not shocked she had a brother; families as old as hers often parented multiple children. I'm guessing he was a younger brother, and perhaps the youngest. That makes sense. Finally, a boy to carry on the family name.

Marianne never mentions her family or much of her past pre-Isiah. I've come close to asking her once or twice, but sense gets the better of me. I know to never push with Marianne. But now, it seems we're finally going to learn the truth. I'm just not sure I'm ready to hear it.

"Your brother is like you?" Rani asks.

Marianne nods. "He is. Or he was. I genuinely don't know if he's still alive or not. I turned him when he was on his deathbed, and we ran from our old lives. We spent the first seventy years or so just living our lives to the fullest. We learned how to use our new traits and abilities to get away with everything. We lived on the streets and in mansions. He was so talented. He used to make puppets and toys and dress up and perform for whoever wanted to watch. I followed him, and he followed me. I lived my life the way I wanted. I never married; I never settled down with annoying men. We were invincible."

Marianne's face lights up with a brightness I've not seen in months. As she talks, she beams. These are happy memories for her, and she's finally sharing them. I glance towards Rani who looks as if she's trying to think of what to say. Processing it all.

"It wasn't all easy, of course. We left our old lives in such a dramatic fashion. He missed his sisters, and the comfort of our home and family, but he knew he would have died if I'd left him. He never wanted to marry a woman, as I never wanted to marry a man, or anyone. Our only option was to live our lives as we pleased."

Neither I nor Rani speak a word still. This is the most we've heard her talk about anything other than The Thorns, and we definitely don't want to cut her off.

"That's not really the important part, though." Marianne's tone settles a little, and she leans back into her chair again, her face growing more serious. The joy was nice while it lasted. "I think it was around the reign of George IV in the early nineteenth century when he started having these dreams—reoccurring dreams that plagued him quite severely. We all have weird dreams, but these really affected him.

"He would tell me about 'The Rising', this thing that kept showing up in his mind when he slept. It was the idea the world would end, but not in the way religion tells it. No, this was the end of human autonomy. Humanity reborn. 'The end of old times and the beginning of the new.' At first, I brushed it off. I thought it was his conscience fighting the fact he wasn't fully human anymore. We had exceeded mortal age and had the power to Manipulate. Maybe it was guilt. Maybe he'd done something that sat heavy on his mind. But he kept insisting it was something different."

The whole time she's speaking, I'm trying to picture what her brother would look like. What his personality was like. Whether he'd be like his sister, kind and caring but fearless, or something else entirely.

Then it sinks in. I know what she's leading up to, and I'm hit with a much darker feeling. A guttural burn in my chest.

"He started running off for weeks at a time and returning less and less sane over the years. We weren't attached at the hip, you know. You must understand that. We did most things apart, but we would always meet again and reconnect. But by the time Victoria came to the throne, my brother had, in my estimation, grown completely insane."

Rani is frowning now and she's started picking her cuticles, completely unconscious to it. Rani has brothers, I wonder what she's thinking.

Marianne rubs her forehead. "He would only speak about 'The Rising'. He'd say the words in his sleep. How three entities would unite from the 'ashes' and bring about the end of old times. End all suffering and lies and deceit. I tried to dismiss it as a newfound religious interest of his. I thought I was misinterpreting what he meant by the loss of autonomy, for until this point, we'd said all but goodbye to religion since we left home. But before long, I knew I was losing my brother. I was losing him, and for the first time in almost ninety years, I didn't know what to do."

"You can't blame yourself for turning him and what happened to him, he was his own person, you..." I'm making things worse by saying this, I realise too late. I just needed to try and lessen the guilt rising in the air. But all I've done is interrupt her flow. *Nice one, Mars.*

Rani remains silent, fingers still working.

"Please let me... I need to tell this story, to get you to understand." Marianne grows restless. *Seriously, great move, Mars.*

I nod to her in apology and let her settle back into story mode. How long has she been bottling this up?

"He... My brother, he began bringing strangers to our house

and I would hear them at night, chanting and praising his words. Soon after, I joined one of his meetings. I stood at the kitchen door as I watched his friends light candles around him and bow to him like he was a king. I knew immediately I was not welcome. I was not to be part of The Rising. It frightened me to no end." A waiter brushes past Marianne's chair, knocking into it slightly and apologising, but it's as if she doesn't even feel it, her eyes locked between mine and Rani's.

Marianne's tone settles for a moment, severity enveloping her words. "It had taken me almost a century to figure out that I was not mad, delusional, or crazy, and my brother had truly lost himself."

A cult leader. Marianne's brother is a cult leader. Was. Who knows? Like all those documentaries you watch and think 'oh, that's insane'. She saw this first hand. Oh, Marianne.

"What happened? What did you do?" Rani was clearly intently listening, taking Marianne's brief pause to make sure this story did not get lost. The complete opposite of what I almost did.

"He followed me out and slammed the door behind us, throwing off his ruby robe and holding my shoulders tight, promising me everything was okay and that he would explain everything in time. But it didn't matter. I'd lost my brother and it was all my fault." Marianne turns her focus solely to me as she states her admission. Her eyes full of history unspoken.

"Marianne—"

She doesn't stop. "I ran upstairs and locked myself in my room. He tried to explain the next day. He told me he needed people to talk to about his visions—for that's what he'd started calling them. Not dreams, *visions*. Premonitions. He told me he knew I didn't understand, and that was fine, but these people believed him and wanted to prepare for this Rising. I shouted at him and reminded him these were humans, and he was not. Then he told me they would join him soon. I knew exactly what he meant."

I look at Rani now, her eyes as wide as mine as we take in the story.

"He turned them?" I ask, fearful of the answer.

"We'd done so well at hiding our identities until that point. We blended into society perfectly, but this cult stuff broke him. It changed him. The night he told me he planned on turning them, I ran away to the nearest village, afraid of being caught, and went into hiding. But then the following evening, one of his followers came running into the square, shouting and screaming. She was wounded and had lost a lot of blood. She collapsed into the fountain, and a bunch of people went out to help her. She looked so young, twenty at the most. I watched from a basement window as she wailed about fanged creatures and the whole village rounded up in a matter of minutes as she pointed toward our home." Marianne's hands are shaking, but she hides them quickly under the table when she catches me staring. "I didn't stay long enough to find out what happened. I ran as far as I could, then caught a carriage to London. I never saw him again."

"You've not seen him since... when?"

"1853."

"When he initiated his cult," Rani adds.

"And you left before you found out if he escaped," I say.

Marianne nods. "It was a horrifying sight. Something you'd see in a movie. They were like animals, chanting with sharp sticks and axes and... he was my brother. My sweet baby brother..." Tears form in her woeful eyes, and she turns her head to hide them.

"You didn't tell anyone because you didn't want to seem like a coward," Rani observes after a moment of heavy silence.

Marianne's head snaps towards her, but her expression softens. "It would be easier to say you are correct, because I know that would have been the reason... if I *could* remember."

"What do you mean?" Rani asks for the both of us.

Marianne sinks her front teeth into her lower lip. "What, you think I hid the truth about my vampire brother from you all on purpose? After everything we've all witnessed? No. I hadn't thought about my brother in decades. Somehow, I'd blocked away anything relating to Nicholas beyond our childhoods, until that one day six months ago. I woke that night, startled and dripping with the memories that all came flooding back. If I'd been conscious of them before, I might have been able to draw the conclusions I have now. I may have been able to save Arlo. But I just didn't *have* these memories... I..."

"Maybe you didn't want to remember the sad parts. You've been alive a long time; you've had plenty of happy memories to replace them," I suggest, but as I absorb her final words, I begin to think of something else, and I know Marianne is too. *Manipulation.* She'd had these memories stripped from her for a reason. To prevent her from getting ahead... from understanding.

But by who? For how long? The idea of something being powerful enough to control Marianne is something I'd rather avoid. My breath grows heavy as the thoughts develop in my mind.

Rani clears her throat, breaking the tension.

Marianne smiles painfully, wiping her eyes, going back to her story to change the turning subject. "That village still stands, and you can read about that night, but the tale never extends past rumours. Mass hysteria. Like I said, we were very good at hiding our nature. The house was burned to the ground, but no bodies were ever found."

I'm stunned by everything she's shared, but it has not changed my opinion of her. If anything, I understand her more; it justifies every decision she's ever made, whether or not she was aware of it. She may have forgotten about her brother dying, but it made perfect sense why she turned to saving everyone she could. Why she killed Isiah instead of running away. Penance for her past sins, conscious or not.

But now I also see the bigger picture. Marianne believes her brother was predicting the future and that his visions were true.

"I wish I hadn't forgotten about him." Marianne interrupts

my thoughts. "Whatever happened in the end was painful, but it was just me and him for almost a century before then. The two of us against the world. I must have gone looking for him so many times. He's probably long dead. I think I deduced that at the time, yet I continued searching. If the village didn't get to him, his cult would have killed him, eventually."

"But now you believe he was right." Rani steers the conversation back on track for the third time, veering back to the links we'd all made by this point. Links to Arlo. *Three entities.*

Marianne doesn't need to speak to confirm our suspicions. Rani is right.

"I believe my brother was telling the truth about his dreams being more than just dreams, and there's a reason I'm remembering only now. I don't necessarily believe in the supernatural, but I do believe coincidences are never just incidental. My brother was not insane, but we grew apart in our beliefs. For the past six months, part of me wished I'd see his face in an advertisement for a pantomime or a puppet play at a vintage fair—that's what he used to love—just so that I'd know I still have family. But now all I can think about is 'the end of old times'. My life is a burden of coincidences, and I believe Arlo was taken by and became something to do with what Nicholas predicted. I have to be right."

"Arlo is a part of this?" Rani asks, biting her lips, her brows tense in a bid to understand.

"One of the three," I add.

"I don't know what to believe, but my hunches are normally right. That night in the forest triggered my memories to return. That has to mean something. It's all connected."

"So, what do you suggest we do then? To find him and put an end to all of this?" Rani leans forward, and I sense the quickening beats of her heart.

Marianne's words sink in. I'm trying to figure out what I think of all this. I believe every last drop of her story, yet I struggle to accept the scope of it. The Rising could be a potentially world-altering event, with Arlo right in the middle.

"We're going to need more of us. Eventually. When we find him," I say, the understanding hitting me as I eye the size of the notebook again. "Lucy outsmarted us. It was such a simple trap, too. She nearly killed you, Marianne." I glare at her scar, which she always keeps hidden beneath a turtleneck or a velvet choker. Today, it's exposed. "She tortured Ben beyond belief. Her brother was the reason for the death of Carmen's parents, and she was right under our noses for months, without ever leaving a trace. And now we're after... well, let's not beat around the bush, these are essentially *gods* you're talking about. Things that have the power to reshape worlds for the greater good or the danger of hell. Things that transcend religion."

Rani makes a small noise and I look at her now, forehead aching. I try to soften my voice. "This shouldn't be real, but it is. And Arlo is slap-bang in the heart of it all. He very well could *be* the heart of it all." *And the three of us are going to just do what, save the day? This isn't a comic book or the blockbuster movie of the summer.* "We're not cut out for this."

"Of course we are, this is Arlo we're talking about," Rani interjects.

"But we are quite literally nothing compared to what we might be up against. We might as well just give up now and say goodbye to our precious earth. Make the most of our final days. I dunno, book a holiday?" I've lost control of may voice again, the two of them just stare at me. I go on. "Where have you always wanted to go? Seven wonders of the world. Or are there more now? Who cares! They won't be here much longer, anyway. Why don't we just—"

"So that's it? You're giving up? Just like that?" Rani snaps, her eyes squinting.

I take a deep breath. "What? Fuck no. We're already behind." I stand up and grab my jacket. "Let's go and fucking save Arlo."

Chapter Four

The Star
Six Months Ago

They bury the boy's body under clouds of snow, and I watch from a distance with my Sun by my side. Arlo is here—just. I feel the last drops of his conscious pain trickle down my cheek, and I let it happen.

My Sun looks at me, wiping away my tear with the tip of his nail. He understood the full conversion would be hard, and that he would continue to break through occasionally, but we both know The Star is finally here to stay.

Arlo
Six Months Ago

I WATCH as they lower Ben's coffin into the ground. My friend, who I will never see again. He's dead because of me. Because Lucy chose me to die, and Michael chose me to rise. Then they used me, and now I can't even move on my own. I am not my body; I cannot act by myself. I watch through the eyes of a stranger as my friend is buried forever, and there's nothing I can do to undo it all. I wanted to help; I thought I was helping. I thought I was doing the right thing. But I was a fool, and now I am dead in every way that counts.

After the funeral, Michael tells me he wants me to meet someone. I don't want to leave my friends again; I want to reach out to them and be with them, but my body nods and my legs move as Michael holds my hand and walks us back through the gravestones and down the road, all the way down to the cathedral. We enter through a door I never even realised was there.

We walk deeper and deeper into the heart of the building, through passages the public can't possibly be aware of. He tells me to wait near a doorway for a moment before he introduces me, and though *I* panic, my body obeys.

I cannot see who he is talking to, nor do I understand what's happening, until he raises his voice. "I promised, and I shall deliver," he says. I catch sight of his wings spanning from his back in a crack of light as he bows, as if on stage.

My chest lurches in fear, but my body does not budge.

"Have you finally brought them?" the other voice sounds out. It's deep and husky, the tone tired, but not unkind. It almost sounds cautious.

"Arlo, come now." Michael turns back to me and ushers me into the candlelight. *Arlo? Why did he say my name? For the first time since I let go...*

My body follows his guiding arms, and I stumble through the archway. I am still too thin for the weight of the wings now hanging from my back. I will always hate how they feel.

I step forward until I can make out the other figure. I'm drawn to the deep red wings first, then to the rings on the person's fingers that grip the arms of a throne-like chair. Then I look up at his face as he turns to face me.

I stop dead, and for once, my body stops in tandem with my mind.

I know now why Michael called me by my original name now.

Because before me... stands my father.

Jerry.

My dad.

The Star screams internally as I push forwards, my eyes becoming my own once more. I can feel all my limbs—my body. I can feel it all, and it's too much.

"Dad?" I cry out, my legs giving away entirely.

"My... my son." He leaps from his throne to catch me in his arms. I cannot move a muscle, but it's of my own accord this time. I don't know how to work my body anymore. It's been weeks since... Gosh, my head hurts.

And here stands my father. My own flesh and blood.

"My boy." He kisses my head over and over. I flinch, but then I forget how to do even that. I can't help but cry out for him again. My dad. My father. He is with me. He is alive.

I'm not even angry. All I can think about is how happy I am to see his familiar face, one I dreamed of all my life, just never admitting to it.

He pulls my head to his shoulder as I force my arms up to wrap around his back, catching his feathers. The sensation is too much to bear, so I pull back.

"How touching," Michael says. My father lets go of me and stares at Michael with a look of anger and pain. It appears he is about to open his mouth as his hands ball into fists, but Michael's words stop him. "The Sun, The Moon, and The Star. Reunited at long last."

My father is one of us. He is like me.

"We are going to change the world."

. . .

I BLACK OUT NOT long after that. I remember my father stepping up to Michael, matching his height. He glared heavily at the blonde man with an expression I can only describe as hurt. My father is himself as I close my eyes, just as I am *myself*.

Me. Arlo. Stay...

But then my eyes close fully, and when I wake, I'm lost again.

The Star
Six Month Ago

ARLO GAVE into this body the moment he realised he no longer wished to feel. Humans are too complicated.

I can always feel what he is thinking, though. I know he conceded to become something grander and more powerful to prevent his friend's death from befalling others. He will, of course, grow to understand our purpose is so much more than that. We are here to bring the world to new times. To erase all the lies and violence and evil. To teach humanity the error of their ways.

It will be glorious.

7th March 1854

I must stop running from this.
It is eating me alive.
I don't know how much longer I can hold onto this lie.
I'm not human.

20th March 1854

~~Maybe it's time to embrace the monster I am.~~

12th May 1854

I just killed a woman. I drained her right there on the street.
I normally only take enough to quench my thirst, but not this
time. I thought I would feel nothing—I was beyond that
now, but I was so hungry.
I only feel shame. And sadness. And guilt. Does this mean I
am unsalvageable? Am I truly the devil I always claimed to
be? Is this my destiny?

19th May 1854

~~I can't~~

29th May 1854

~~Who am I?~~

15th June 1854

———————

29th June 1854

Burn these pages, just like the last. But only after you reread
them as penance.
You are a murderer. A taker of lives. Why did you ever
believe you were better than those around you?

31st August 1854

I am free, am I not?

I choose my own life.

I can start again! Reinvent myself!

23rd March 1855

I have done it again. I fed like an animal.

I just wanted a friend, someone to talk to. Why must it be this way?

I cannot sleep. Cannot rest. I only hear her scream.

I lose everyone who grows close to me and it is all my fault.

I am a monster.

I am the devil.

14th May 1855

~~Burn it. Burn it all.~~

~~They will come for me.~~

~~They know what I did.~~

—Taken from the diaries of Marianne Ashtown.

CHAPTER FIVE

Mars
Now

Marianne leads us back to the hideout, charging ahead without checking we're behind.

"How have you been? You know, since every-thing?" Rani asks me when we finally fall in line with Marianne. It's a bit of a loaded question, but probably the only thing she could ask at this moment.

I feel guilty once again at how we'd treated her; we've had very different months whilst still suffering the same loss. I'm not sure how best to answer. It's been awful, like a part of the world has just been ripped out in a solid and painful chunk. I've had Francesca and Lawrence to talk to, but Casper has barely been back, and none of my friends in The Thorns have returned—they're not even answering my calls. The studio, my mam's house, and the bar are the only places I've felt at ease—especially the bar, getting drunk and making bad decisions with a band member I'm supposed to be the manager of. Life's a blast, honestly.

"Surviving," is my best response. I don't know what else I can throw at her. It's not fair. Rani nods a little and sucks in her lips.

Marianne doesn't speak to us the whole way, though I don't expect her to. She mutters a few things under her breath but I gather they're not for our ears. She doesn't properly acknowledge our presence until we arrive at her study, the corridors still dead and cold. It's been a while since I've set foot in this room, but she really has been busy since then. Photographs and newspaper clippings cover the walls from head to toe. Her notebook must have just been the highlights—the best of, as it were. It's like we're detectives in the centre of a serious investigation. I almost laugh.

The dark circles and hollow cheeks make perfect sense now. Has she slept at all?

"Did you pin these up especially for us?" I attempt to make a joke, only to free my mind from the absurdity of it all. Rani stays silent.

Marianne doesn't have to open her mouth to answer, she just sucks in her lips.

"Sorry," I say. Perhaps not the best time for comedy, though it's all I have to offer.

"I'll get to the bottom of this. I will find answers." She's already sitting cross-legged on her desk, disregarding the perfectly suitable chair beside it. Her muddy shoes crease the papers beneath her.

Rani takes it all in, walking around the outskirts of the room and tracing her fingers over the pinned-up pages, scanning them all. "You've been doing all of this for six months?"

"Before then. I'd been keeping notes and researching, but I never got very far. Some of my early notes helped me capture some of the city's killers from last year, but obviously I had no real leads until after what happened near the church. So, then I needed to immerse myself in my findings. It was either that or let my mind consume me, which wouldn't have helped anyone."

Rani just nods slowly, looking around.

I walk over to one wall and dust my hand over a section of multiple large pages, stuck over the top of each other. I lift a loose piece to reveal a map underneath. Some of these documents date back decades. I even notice yellowed pages and gothic font hidden under a photograph of Stonehenge. A Victorian age clipping. Hmm, interesting.

"The last mention of the cult I found was about forty years after I left the village," Marianne says behind me, appearing like a phantom. I look back at her, waiting for her to continue. "That article." She points back at the wall where I was looking just a moment ago.

I lift the photo and take in the article.

It's from a Coventry newspaper, dated in the late nineteenth century. The article details an interview with a young woman from a so-called 'insane asylum', explaining how her mother followed a 'god' who knew when the end of time was coming. It's ripped, and the ink is smudged, but I read enough to understand that this very well could have been the cult Marianne knew.

"Your brother..." I start, but I don't know how to finish the sentence.

"Oh, he's long gone." There is an air of certainty to Marianne's voice now as she wafts her hand dismissively.

"You don't know that though," Rani interjects. "You said they found no bodies." She's standing with her arms folded, her heart rate slightly raised. She's afraid of Marianne, but she's trying not to show it.

"It doesn't matter now either way. He was right regardless, and now it's my turn to finish things. Once and for all. Huh. I say that a lot, don't I?" Her tone is bittersweet.

I walk back over to Rani in the centre of the room and stand beside her, hoping to ease her discomfort. "Now we know what we're up against, though. Some god-like entities masquerading as winged humans, trying to bring about the end of the world so they can—what? Start again on their terms?"

"That's what Nicholas always used to spout, though he never mentioned wings. I don't think he was actually visited by them, but he would always refer to three beings and would relate them to astrology." She taps her fingers on the desk. "The more I break apart the memories, the more the words sun, moon, and star ring a bell. He'll have most likely used his imagination and picked names that best fit. I don't believe in astrology to determine power, but perhaps that's because I never took the time to understand it." She now lifts the top sheet of paper from a pile beside her and scans it as she speaks. "As far as I'm aware, these entities sound completely alien to the world. Maybe they are truly from outer space. Ha!" She drops the paper with a forceful grip in both hands, almost ripping it. "They're not vampires, but they got to my brother, meaning they must have pretty strong Manipulation techniques, which then gets me thinking about *our* origins. I wonder if they're somehow connected, even slightly."

"You know our origins?" I ask, my interest piqued. It's a taboo topic we learned early on to never ask, but with everything coming out on the table now, I feel as though I'm well within my right to push the subject finally.

Marianne shakes her head. "Sadly no. Not yet anyway. Rumours passed down generations about the 'creatures of the night', but I can never decipher what's fact and what's fiction. I've been trying to learn what I can over the centuries, but we're remarkably secret as a race and a lot more uncommon than we may expect." Marianne swallows loudly. "Humans have such a bloody history, anyway. I'm pretty sure anyone could have been a creature of the night if they were drunk and out late enough."

"No accounts of Manipulation?" I try. I've never got far with my own research. The best I got once was a diary entry from a maid from the early twentieth century, stating she saw the master of the house drink blood from a porcelain cup. But that was it. No photographic evidence or corroborating stories. Just a young woman claiming a man she likely loathed drank something red. I believe her, but it still gets me nowhere.

Manipulation is also a hard one to catch. Again, all accessible accounts can be explained away. Love, obsession, moral panic, herd mentalities. There will be stuff that doesn't add up, accounts that slipped through the cracks, and they most likely fill the entirety of Area 51.

I hope I'm joking.

"Speaking of Manipulation..."

I sense Rani's fear before the words leave her mouth. Marianne looks at her in sorrow. She knows exactly what Rani is about to ask.

"I want to remember everything, not just from what I've been told."

Marianne nods immediately and doesn't sound inconvenienced when she says, "I figured you'd ask that."

"So, can you do it? Can you unlock my mind, or however it works." She's shaking ever so slightly, her arms still firmly folded.

"I can encourage you to remember, and bring forth the things buried in the back of your mind, but are you certain you want to fully relive those events?"

Rani's eyes widen in fury. "Of course I want to remember. Why do you think I came back here? For a nice little holiday?"

I've never known her to speak so sharply. I'm impressed.

Marianne takes a deep breath then strides closer, standing eye to eye with Rani.

"It will feel quite unpleasant."

"I don't care. I want to remember. Everything. Every little detail you've taken from me from the moment you knew I existed to right this moment. I want it back. All of it."

I know Rani doesn't realise all she's lost, and that was, of course, the whole point, but her wording brings me back to the story Marianne told me about the morning before the concert. How whatever was inside Arlo took over during one of their training sessions and he nearly made Rani rip the skin off her face. I'm only glad I wasn't there to witness it. But Marianne was, and so was Carmen. *She's going to need her memories back, too.*

I turn away as Marianne lifts her hands to cup Rani's face. The pungent scent of such strong Manipulation remains a vivid memory, and I recall how it feels from our training, like sharp tendrils creeping into every crevice of your mind.

"Do it quickly, please. I'm scared," Rani says.

It takes a few moments. The pressure in the room intensifies as Rani lets out a small whimper. But then moments later, her whole body calms, and I turn to see her on her knees, resting her head on Marianne's shoulder. Her eyes are closed, and her grip is tight on Marianne's arm, but she looks at peace.

"Rani?" I say, just to make sure I've read the scene correctly.

Rani looks up towards me slowly, opening her eyes as a tear leaks down her cheek. Her brow tenses.

"It was in my head," she mutters. The tear drips onto her upper lip. She's looking at me, but she's addressing us both.

It. Not Arlo. The thing inside him.

"Arlo didn't hurt you on purpose," I say.

Rani nods ever so slightly then releases Marianne's hands and stands for herself, looking between us both. "He's in so much pain."

"He was," Marianne responds, her tone half questioning, half confirming.

"He saved my life. He snapped a vampire's neck in front of me."

"I didn't want you anywhere near that battlefield." Marianne grows bitter, shaking her head.

Rani ignores Marianne's statement. "And Ben, he... oh, that poor man. Oh, Ben. Casper and... Arlo did what he did to save us. He saved us all."

"He did," I agree, stepping closer and leaning in for a hug. Rani comes to me with open arms, and when she holds me, her grip tightens, and I feel her shaking as her heart thuds against my chest. I sink my chin into her shoulder.

"We will save him," I whisper.

"We have to."

ONCE RANI SETTLES and gets everything else off her chest—a truly therapeutic experience to watch, seeing as no one has confronted Marianne so intensely in a long time, let alone a human—we discuss Marianne's findings and plan how we're going to pull this off. Rani holds out Marianne's notebook and flicks through the pages. Marianne seems reluctant to share that much initially, but ultimately decides she trusts Rani enough.

"If we're going to run with this theory, which is really our only option, I've managed to narrow down the arrival of these so called 'entities' or gods, or whatever you want to call them, to the last sixty or seventy years." Marianne has now opted for her desk chair. "From what I can recall from Nicholas's ramblings, they weren't ready to rise yet. It seemed like it was still a future event, but not so far off that it wasn't worth forming a cult over."

"He intended to turn his followers, as you said, which suggests he expected this event to occur well beyond a normal human life-span," I interject, keeping on her wavelength.

Marianne nods, swallowing. "Exactly, hence why I added about ninety years from that date, looking at the oldest people alive from that time. The earliest these entities should have appeared is the mid-forties, or early fifties perhaps. But from there, there was no time frame. Did they appear together as three fully formed beings, or did they stagger their arrival? How did they arrive?"

"They take human hosts, with Arlo being one. They might not even be able to survive on their own," I intercept again.

Marianne chews her lip. "Good point, so if that's true, then one of them took Arlo either the day he was born or the day he died."

"The day he died. It must be. I knew Arlo before, you didn't," Rani says, placing the book down. She has returned to her normal self now, at a form of peace with her new memories. "All this stuff started when he became one of you." It almost feels like an accusation, but she has a point.

"That's more likely. Maybe they take dead hosts? Reanimated corpses, for want of a better phrase." I'm just firing out my thoughts as they come.

"Vampire hosts specifically?" Rani suggests.

"Or just dying. Arlo was alone when you found him, wasn't he?" Marianne looks to me for clarification and the memory stabs me straight through the chest. He was just lying there in the alleyway, heart failing, blood everywhere... *Not helping.* I shake out of it. "He was, we didn't chase anyone off, but yeah. It's possible something got to him first."

"And your brother, you said you saved his life by turning him, right? So what if something got to him too?" Rani adds. Marianne's eyes widen, face changing. "No. Nicholas wasn't like that. He wasn't possessed he—"

"We still know very little about these entities, he may not have been a host but he was very much involved. An essence perhaps?" I suggest. "An attempt to test the waters, see if this world was compatible?"

Marianne looks even more horrified now, eyes reddening. "He was just a boy..." her voice gives out.

"And so is Arlo!" Rani shouts, pacing back and forth with speed. He's only nineteen! Whole life ahead of him! Neither of them asked for it!"

Marianne looks as if she's been slapped, but then the three of us fall silent. We're at a dead end here, we still know virtually nothing; who they've taken over, or what their roles are. Is one more powerful than the others?

Rani speaks again, standing still and holding her hips. "Look, Arlo may have only been the second, the first was the thing after him, but then that means we might have enough time to find him before the third is chosen." Her optimism is a saving grace in this conversation, I only wish I shared it.

"Or he's the last, and the third entity was just lying dormant and could have been chosen a while ago." Marianne states this so matter-of-factly it's unsettling, but I agree with her.

"How do we even begin to figure this out, though?" Rani is growing frustrated again, returning to the book, eyebrows raising.

"Well, let's roll with it. At least we know what the first two look like. The first showed us its face when it stood beside Arlo in the forest." Marianne says this so nonchalantly; she's oblivious to the fact we have no fucking clue what she's talking about.

"I'm sorry, what?" I shake my head as if I've misheard her. Rani also looks seriously confused, and a tad concerned, flopping the book closed.

"What on earth do you mean?" she asks, looking to me in shared confusion.

Marianne strains her head back in defence, looking at us the way someone normally would when they're outnumbered. "The first entity, the one who'd been after Arlo... He wasn't there long but surely... He reached out to take Arlo's hand—"

"Yeah, no. I think I'd remember if I saw another fucking *angel* on the scene," I cut her off. *What the hell is she going on about?*

Dreams, Mars. Your dreams.

"Guys, stop playing with me. You all saw him. Long blonde hair, grey wings, piercing light blue eyes. He was about Arlo's height and build; they literally ran off together... I didn't chase them because my fucking neck was sliced, and I could barely breathe, never mind stand up. You have absolutely no idea what I'm talking about, do you?"

We both shake our heads, eyes wide with concern.

You should have listened to your dreams. You did see something, you must have, you're just not meant to remember.

"Oh. Well. Fuck." Marianne sits back in her chair and appears to contemplate.

"Well, you'd already sent me running away by that point. Gosh, you're strong. You reached me from where you were? Woah that's..." Rani shakes her arms out, "not important right now. This is something that clearly only showed itself to you, and we need to find out why," she asserts.

"I was literally by your side. I'd have seen what you just described," I add, forcing myself to fabricate the memory. *Did you see it too? Really?* I could never picture anything clearly but... I thought they were just dreams...

"Is he someone you may have seen before? Another Lucy from your past?" Rani drops the notebook on the desk and grips the sides of the wood with her hands, leaning forward.

Marianne looks stunned again, and it's clear she's now thinking of a million reasons to try to explain why only she saw the second entity.

"Marianne, why didn't you tell us this before?" I ask, too impatient for her to respond to Rani's question.

"Because I thought you knew!" she snaps. "I thought everyone saw it! When we talked about the creature after him, I thought we were all on the same page! We just... I—"

"Was that really the reason, or is this another thing that came to you in your little dream memories?" Rani's voice is bold and calculated.

Marianne breathes heavily for a moment, looking from side to side as though her mind is reeling back her thoughts. "No. No, this was always there. I saw them leave. I'm sure of it." She's *not* so sure. Her brows knit together. "You didn't see them leave?"

Now it's my turn to think back. And as I do so, I realise something I never would have considered.

I didn't actually see Arlo leave the forest.

Despite being right there.

I knew he must have left, but my memories from that day are

so choppy, and once Marianne regained consciousness, her neck clotting and healing, our sole focus was getting Ben's body back to...

We were all Manipulated. Every single one of us.

The first entity.

9th September 1855

I find myself in France these days. I needed a change. I've never left the country before; I wasn't sure what to expect. I could maybe settle here, start again. Once again.

14th November 1855

I crossed the borders all the way to Italy, never settling in one place for more than a week. I wish I could speak every language fluently, to understand their happiness and joys. The little things in life.
I am so alone.

20th December 1855

I am a free woman. I must always remind myself that. I can do and say and go as I please, and no one can stop me. Who am I to have ever deserved this privilege?
No one can ever gain power over me. I am in full control of my life.
And so I must live it!

—Taken from the diaries of Marianne Ashtown.

Chapter Six

Mars
Now

"Well, this sure is revealing a lot of things, isn't it? Are our brains even big enough to handle any more of this?" Rani claps her hands on her mouth and stares into space. "Three entities: one inside Arlo, one in the mysterious figure who only Marianne saw, and a likely third that already exists, knowing our luck now. Oh, and these entities are probably from some alien planet—or maybe they're just sentient floating orbs that crash landed..." Her eyes widen. "I wish I wasn't being a hundred percent serious here, good lord." She almost laughs. Who wouldn't, given the morning we've had.

Switch back on, Mars. I shake my head intensely. *Clear your head. Take a step back.*

"Okay. Right. So..." I take a deep breath. "We're gonna have to unpack our memories later. You know what the other one looks like, so we can go from there, right? We'll start an image search. You've got CCTV contacts across the city. Just describe him as best you can and we'll start. This is good. We have a lead."

Marianne had this lead for the past six months, yet got nowhere with it. *Don't let your mind stray. Keep to the topic. Keep focused on your idea.*

"You don't think I tried that already?" Marianne's hands form fists as she thuds her head hard against the table in defeat.

"Come on, wrack your brains. There has to be some connection," urges Rani. "This person, thing, whatever, allowed you to remember for a reason. Who would only show themselves to an over two-hundred and fifty-year-old vampire?"

"Someone from your past," I answer.

Marianne looks ready to throw one of us into the wall, but instead, she sits back, tapping her nails on the arm of the chair.

"It has to be," Rani says.

"No, no, no! I've been through my memories. I've spooned out my brain with a deep scoop many, many times, and I've tried. Oh boy, I've *tried*. There's a lot in there. I've met a lot of people. You know how many faces I've had to remember? Do you know how hard it would be to recall every single person I met for the past two hundred and eighty-seven years?"

"Yes, but you weren't listening. Now you know no one else saw him, meaning my theory is likely correct. If he let you remember him, then he has to have known your previous meeting was significant, no matter when it may have been. So, think. Think *hard.*"

Oh, Rani's good...

Clearly, Marianne doesn't expect to be spoken to that way. It's likely been a very long time since someone has asserted dominance over her, and it's fascinating to watch. Rani drags over a footstool from the corner of the room and parks right beside our leader before she's even processed what Rani asked of her. We watch her get comfortable.

"Right, so. In the last seventy-five-ish years, what was Marianne doing? Who was she meeting? Which countries was she visiting?"

It's like I'm sitting in nursery school, or a rehabilitation centre, being forced to recall things I've learned in the lesson... or session. Since when was Rani this feisty? *Since always, you idiot. Catch up.*

"Rani, I can't just..." Marianne's voice is distant, too soft. This dynamic shift is astounding. I'm just watching it all in awe.

"Right." Rani slaps her knees in frustration. "We've all had memories taken from us, okay? We just established this, but we move on. Sitting and wallowing in self-pity isn't going to get us anywhere. You've spent six months doing this, so make it count. We need to find Arlo."

Marianne then looks at me as if *I* hold all the answers.

"Rani has a point," I say, shrugging. Rani briefly smiles at me before returning her focus on Marianne, resting her hand on the sides of the stool and leaning in close.

"You must have done something. You didn't just lie in a coffin until the turn of the century."

"No, I... I'm trying Rani, I really am." It's like she's about to cry. Marianne lifts her hand to rub the scar on her neck. "I did a lot, and I remember a lot. But I can't pinpoint... nothing is standing out, I can't focus..."

In this moment, my leader seems so small, so vulnerable, help-less... worn out.

Realising you've had memories taken from you is probably one of the most crushing and dehumanising things that could ever happen to you, and you're left doubting everything you've ever learned, done, or seen. It breaks you down to a shell of your former self, forcing you to rebuild from scratch.

Marianne has been through a lot—we all have, but what I've experienced only scratches the surface of Marianne's life. I take pity on her, and I know Rani does too, though in her own way. Rani's also right... we don't have time to think about this. We're running against the clock here.

Marianne sniffs, then bends over to pull open the top drawer under her desk. She dabs her eyes before pulling out a bunch of brown leather pouches, rummaging through the contents.

"What's in there?" Rani asks.

"Stuff. Everything. Nothing. Don't..."

Marianne snaps her arm out to stop Rani from beginning her own drawer search. I round the desk and join the pair, stooping at Rani's side to assess the unorganised mess of papers in the top drawer.

"I don't want you going through my life like this."

Her words make me feel guilty. I'd hate someone doing this to me, but unfortunately this has to be an exception.

"Marianne, please. Whatever we find won't leave this room, I promise," I try to reassure her. She throws me a reserved look.

Rani moves to sit on the ground and slowly reaches for the lower drawer again, and though Marianne tenses, she doesn't stop her. The drawer sticks on its hinges before Rani manages to yank it open. This one is packed even tighter, brimming with documents. I wouldn't even know where to begin.

"You make a lot of notes, don't you?" Rani observes.

"I have to. I've been alive for too long. My brain is still at human capacity. There's no way I'd be able to recall every last detail of the last few centuries.

Rani chews on her nail and pushes her glasses atop her head for greater focus as she rummages through the disorganised folders, muttering to herself. I eye the middle drawer, which I'm hoping is better labelled than the other two. I have no idea where to start, though. We're going to be here for days at this rate.

The three of us flick through the mess in silence for a minute or so before Rani comes out with another bombshell. "Were these the years you spent with Arlo's dad?" she asks. She doesn't look up as she does.

Marianne makes a small noise at the back of her throat, and I look up at her as she speaks. "Yes," is all she says. That one word seemed to sap all her energy.

I'd almost forgotten about this. Marianne knew Arlo's dad, who is also a vampire, or at least he was, until Victor Frankenstein got his hands on him and made him a *reluctant father figure? Jesus Christ.*

We'd have to cover this soon, as well as Lucy sharing her knowledge of Jerome in the woods; the mention of his name seemed to become Marianne's Achilles heel.

Was it all linked?

Do I hope it's not?

"So, Jerry—*Jerome*—may know this person? Any chance you have his contact details still?" asks Rani.

"Rani!" I snap, stunned at her casual tone.

"What?" Rani turns to me, her hands raised in confusion. No regrets at all.

"No." This time, Marianne's voice has enough power to remind me of who she is again, recovering her dominance. "I don't have any contact at all with *him.*" She spits out the final word like venom.

"Okay, okay. Just asking. I'm the only one trying right now, it seems." Rani goes back to the drawer in spite, and I sit back and close my eyes. A headache is forming behind my eyes.

We sit there for a little while longer as Rani proves her word. She's the only one actively rummaging, scattering sheets all over the floor and making a terrible mess.

I'm about to resume mindlessly searching the middle drawer—mostly filled with trinket boxes of little use, when Marianne abruptly stands and pushes back her chair. She heads over to the wall towards a giant painting of sunflowers and lifts her hand gently to the side of the frame. She pulls it forward, and it swings on its hinges to reveal—

Of course. She's got a *fucking huge* safe, of course she has.

From the floor, we watch, awe-struck, as Marianne bends down, inserts a key, then turns the dial until it clicks. When she pulls open the metal door, dozens of shelves glint under the light, full of tightly packed notebooks, each row labelled with—I squint my eyes—*dates*. Diaries.

"Oh, *fuck off*," I hear myself say. Rani is on her feet, but Marianne doesn't turn. She's actively pursuing a specific book, with specific dates—memories.

I stand closer now. Her journals begin in childhood, but many are damaged, with some missing covers, and others looking like pages had been torn out of them, judging by the dents near the spines. Yet they're inaccessible, locked behind glass.

Marianne focuses on the lower shelves, her fingers light as they filter through each binding.

"I've been through these before, many times," she mutters, almost to herself, as she pulls one out and delicately dusts the cover.

Rani comes up beside her. "You kept diaries."

Marianne responds with a simple 'hmm' as she opens one of them and flicks through the pages. By the time I join them, she's been through half the diary already, but I realise it's because each page only contains photographs.

"In the aftermath of the war, I kept a bunch of travel diaries in the fifties and sixties. We travelled all over the world."

"So when you say 'we,' you mean..."

"Jerome. Yes." Although Marianne's tone is still bitter, she knows she can't hide this any longer.

"You were really close?" Rani asks with calm curiosity.

Another 'hmm' from Marianne proves she's not ready to unpack it all, so I change the subject as she continues to flick through the pages. Yet Rani peering over her shoulder helps little with the tension.

"You ever remember having weird dreams? Like Nicholas level weird?" I ask.

Marianne stops turning the pages to look back at me. "Nothing I'd be able to remember. I wish it was that easy, but premonitions didn't run through the family." A hint of malice enters her voice, formed mostly from frustration.

"Just a suggestion. I'm trying." I wince, stepping back slightly.

Rani stands to full height, reaches for an accessible shelf, and pulls out a book before Marianne can stop her.

"That's too far back. You won't find anything that helps in there," Marianne says, dropping her current read to track Rani's next movements.

"You never know, you might not think so, but a fresh set of eyes might find something. You've been holding yourself back."

At this point, Marianne looks as if she's given up entirely. She relaxes her shoulders and steps out, sarcastically gesturing with her arms as if to say, 'be my guest.'

Rani looks at her reluctantly before deciding to ride with her suspicions. She unwinds the leather ribbon binding the pages together. It's from the late eighteen hundreds.

We both watch in silence as Rani skims the script. Marianne watches out of spite, while Rani persists out of stubbornness.

"You've got pretty handwriting," Rani notes, turning a page.

I know Marianne is uncomfortable. Her own private diaries are being exposed to strangers—a human, no less—but she appears confident enough there's nothing in those pages that will help.

"You picked a dull year," Marianne spits, crossing her arms over her chest.

"Somehow, I struggle to believe any moment in your life was dull, Miss Ashtown." Rani doesn't look up, but it's almost like she's... *flirting*?

"Come on, that's enough. I really don't know why you..." Marianne steps forward and holds out her hand for the notebook, but Rani turns away.

"No, hang on! You just mentioned Jerome..." I can't see Rani's face, but I know she's grinning.

"Give it back!"

I snatch the still open photo album from under their legs,

saving it as Rani steps back to hunch over the book, and Marianne leaps at her shoulders, clawing for it.

"Rani, stop this. You've had your fun, now pass it over! This isn't going to help!"

Rani giggles, then turns back around, the book held tightly in her arms.

"Rani! Please!"

Okay, now I think Rani should probably just drop it. Fear burns in Marianne's eyes. This isn't going to help our search. We're pulling ourselves apart before we've even started working together.

"Fine! Fine!" Rani finally gives in. "I'm sorry. I know I shouldn't pry. I honestly wasn't really reading it. I was messing with you. I just—urgh, sorry, that was wrong of me, I know. I just saw the name and I... here." Rani holds out the book to Marianne, who accepts, trying to control her breathing. She appears embarrassed by the ordeal. As the exchange is made, though, a sheet of paper flutters out. It's a sepia print of some sorts—a photograph.

Rani bends down faster and turns it over, her eyes going wide.

"Ooh, who's this handsome chap? He looks dreamy. Ooh! Very 'Corpse Bride'." Rani turns the photograph over. "Julian Wats—"

"Don't!" Marianne tears the photo from Rani's hands, causing a rip in the image. Gasping, Marianne staggers back, holding her mouth.

"Oh, I'm sorry. I'm so sorry... I didn't think! I got carried away." Rani immediately drops the staged ego. Fear blooms in her eyes as Marianne presses the damaged photograph to her chest, panting for breath. Fire burns in her face.

"Marianne, please. Forgive me. I don't know what came over me. I shouldn't have..."

"Don't ever..." Marianne bends to pick up the notebook again to slip the photo back inside. She flattens out the crinkled photograph with a light touch, placing a hasty kiss to her fingertips and pressing it onto the page. I look away. It's too much for me. I'd hate for anyone to even touch my diary if I kept one. I know Rani meant no harm, but she went too far.

"I—I—I'm so, so sorry. I don't..." Rani steps back and rubs her hands over her face. "I should go," she says, letting out a long, concentrated breath.

"No. Stop." Marianne's voice halts her from turning.

What? I pause at the calmness in Marianne's tone.

"I'll come back tomorrow. Too much has happened too quickly. My mind is pretty scrambled, I was up so early."

"And that's my fault." Marianne steps closer, slotting the notebook back in its original place.

"No, don't take the blame for—gosh, Arlo used to do that all the time. Are you *all* like this?" Rani shakes her head and purses her lips.

She's right. Arlo had a tendency to immediately take the blame for every situation, whether or not he was right to. But in this instance, maybe Marianne is right. Rani had been overloaded with a lot of information at once—months and months of shifted and altered memories. I know it would mess with me; it would mess with anyone. Maybe that's just it.

"It's been a long morning for us all. I've got a lot to answer for still. Sorry I lashed out like that. I just didn't want to have to relive any memories I'd rather forget."

"Oh, no, Marianne. Please. I was in the wrong. I shouldn't have pushed you like that. It was uncalled for." Rani stands up and turns towards the door.

"Stay. Please. It's... It's okay. That's what friends do, right? They wind each other up, share secrets, and tease each other about interests and relationships." Marianne sounds desperate, but when she smiles in such a bittersweet way, it makes me sad. I suddenly wonder how much of a normal childhood she had. Something tells me she didn't get that at all. Even if it was nearly three centuries ago.

"Is that what we are? Friends?" Rani's brow lifts in reluctant confusion at Marianne's quick and drastic change in demeanour.

"We can be. And we probably should be. There's not a lot of us in this situation right now." She actually laughs before wiping her eyes.

"You can say that again."

"I'm sorry," Marianne says once more.

"I'm sorry too. I promise I'll never do that again. That's not what friends do." Rani still sounds a tad uncomfortable, but her body language seems relaxed.

"It's not?" The hopeless confusion in Marianne's voice is one I never thought I'd learn the sound of. She's missed human interaction. Spending so many months detached from reality must have driven her mad.

Rani should have never gone through Marianne's things like that, and Marianne should have never taken her memories.

Dear god. I feel so awkward in the middle of all of this. Looking between them both is giving me whiplash. Marianne is running on so little sleep it's scary. I don't know whether I'm coming or going, but then again, I've felt that way for the past year, almost.

I look down at the photo book in my hands and flick through as Marianne and Rani continue talking, hashing things out. I try not to listen in anymore, so I stare with glazed eyes at the pages, flicking through a bunch of black and white landscape pictures and mountains and...

Oh.

"Hey, Marianne. What did you say the guy looked like again?"

Both Marianne and Rani turn their attention to me. I sense them move, but my eyes are fixed on this one image.

Holy fuck.

"Long, almost snow-white wavy hair, clear blue eyes that look almost too clear to be human. Bunch of thick necklaces, and—"

Shit.

Marianne scrambles over for the notebook in my hands and

pulls it from my lap. She grips firmly to its edges as she stares down at the page.

"What? Guys, what is it? Have you found him?" Rani asks, panicking.

Holy shit.

Marianne is muttering things under her breath so fast I can't decipher them. She ignores Rani.

"Marianne!" Rani shouts. Marianne looks as if she's about to look up for a second, but then she continues staring deeper, mumbling and rubbing her mouth in distress.

"Woodstock," she finally says, gaze fixed.

"What?" Rani is still confused. I sit there, unable to blink. The image burns into my mind, and all sounds turn fuzzy around me.

"Woodstock." She turns to face us both now, her eyes wide. "August. 1969. Sunny."

"The festival?" I question.

Very slowly, Marianne nods, her mind miles away. Then her face falls.

"Hill... day two... sun."

"What about it? Marianne, please stop dropping buzzwords."

"It's him." That's all she needs to say.

Rani comes up to her shoulder and looks down at the image before us. I've not turned back to it yet, still staring into space. Most of the image fades until only one detail remains. The most important part.

Marianne rips the polaroid from the book and holds it up against the light on the ceiling.

I'm gonna vomit. I feel actually, physically ill. That's not normal. Vampires don't get sick...

"That's Arlo's dad, isn't it?" Rani says.

What the fuck is happening?

I finally glance back over at the photo still in Marianne's hands. I take it in properly this time, suppressing the sheer fear rising in my stomach.

It's summer in the late sixties in America. In the centre of the photo stands Marianne, grinning in a cowboy hat and a mini dress patterned with swirls. They're standing on a hill, with a stage in the far background and a grassy field filled with people, all standing and sitting at varying distances. A slim, white, red-haired man sits at her feet, holding onto her arms, which are casually draped over his shoulders; his hair is braided into one thick plait that hangs down one side of him.

Jerome.

"That's Arlo's dad," I confirm.

"You *really* knew him, didn't you?" Rani asks, and I look at Marianne, who stills, reaction-less, her gaze distant.

"I glossed over so many of the photos with him in it because I just couldn't bring myself to think about him. That's why I missed this. *Stupid, stupid.* After months of searching, I missed this clue because I was too stubborn," she sighs. "I'm going to have to get to that eventually, but I'd like to talk to Arlo about it first. That's only right," she says, somewhat calmly, while also choking up and dropping the photo onto the floor.

"I understand. You don't have to explain yet. What has this photo got to do with the entity, though?" Rani asks.

"You didn't spot it?" Marianne looks at her, her brows furrowed.

I did, of course. Straight away. Right in the photo's corner, there's something half a second away from ruining the photograph entirely.

A man, with his body angled to the side. He looks like he's about to walk towards the pair, but his face is caught in the frame enough to show his eyes. Those ghost white eyes. He's mostly blurry, and nowhere near as clear as the rest of the image, but what we can see of him is enough.

I knew it was him. I just *knew*. It's like he spoke to me through the image, with his mouth quirked into a mocking grin that sent an icy dagger down my spine. Like he's already in my head.

"Oh," Rani finally says, holding the photo herself now, finally seeing what the rest of us had.

"That's him, isn't it?" I say.

"It is." All of Marianne's former energy has left her body. She slumps back onto the floor and stretches her legs out.

"He did this deliberately. He wanted me to remember. But only now. He wanted me to know he's coming. It's him. He's known me this whole time." She's stares at the ceiling, and the tremor in her voice is unlike anything I've ever heard before, not from her. She's terrified. She clutches to her legs and tucks them up to her chin.

"Okay, okay. Right. So, we—what does this mean? What's the next step?" Rani tries. She seems the most detached from this situation out of the three of us.

"He's planned this from the beginning. And to think I told myself to forget him. He was a nobody! I've met thousands and thousands of people in my life. He was nobody significant!"

Marianne's thoughts play out in the open before us; her filters and guards are fully down, and the gates are wide open.

"Hey, hey, Marianne." I grip her shoulder, trying to pull her back from the memories. We need to keep her present, even if I'm also scared beyond belief. I can't even see the photo anymore, but it's like he's still there in every corner of my mind. The image twists and warps, but his stare remains the same.

I'm not sleeping tonight, or ever again at this rate.

"Arlo looks so much like his father," Rani says, trying to dampen the situation. I don't know if bringing up *Jerome* again will help right now, but I'll take anything other than... *him.*

I wonder how long Marianne suspected he was related. Had she taken one look at him and known, or was it only over time after observing his mannerisms and personality? I know nothing of this Jerome, except for the fact he left Arlo's mother before their child was even born and he did *something* to Marianne. Something life altering.

I'm not sure he's someone I want to learn more about.

But Rani is right. Arlo did have a look of his father. Ever so slightly. The moles, the stature, the smile.

I miss Arlo's smile. I miss him so much.

"That guy came up to us at the festival." Marianne sits up and brings herself back into the conversation with a much more solid tone. Good. She's okay, for now, but she stares at the wall the whole time she speaks.

"He was Dutch, I think. Or possibly Scandinavian. I can't remember exactly, but he didn't speak much English. I remember thinking he was offering us drugs or something. I turned them down and tried to move away from him, but he charmed Jerome. They walked off together, and when Jerome returned, alone, about ten minutes later, he acted a bit funny with me. But it was nothing out of the ordinary, so I moved on. The only thing I remember being off was his heartbeat—I couldn't sense it at first, so I presumed he was a vampire, and was drawn to us specifically because we were like him. But I shut a lot of that trip out of my head. I occasionally stumbled across vampires over the centuries, so it really was nothing to dwell on. It beat though, very slowly. He wasn't like us."

I don't know what to say next. I'm trying to piece together the scene in my mind, but I've still got so many questions, clouding over my vision.

"So that's it, then. We know who he is now. He wants you to remember him, and now you do. We'll find him in no time," Rani says after the short silence. That's the simple approach to this, I suppose. Glad to hear at least one of us still has somewhat of a level head.

Marianne stares into the void as she says, "I wish it was that simple."

"So what now?" I start.

Marianne rubs her face again and stands with a pained sigh. "Now I need a mug of blood and a good night's sleep."

19th January 1856

~~Hello there, it's been a while.~~
~~No, hello. Good evening? Why can't I start this.~~
~~Okay.~~

I suppose it was inevitable I would begin writing again. It appears it is woven into my nature. I am a writer, a documenter, a storyteller.

So much has happened in my very long life, but I have recorded it all in my other diaries, now locked up far away from me. Maybe one day I will forget where I buried them. For now, I am to start my life anew. A fresh, clean slate.

I am staying in London for the time being, just off St James' Street. I have become well acquainted with the Alston family from the north. They recently moved here and were on the search for a full-time maid to tend to the children as well as house duties while Mr and Mrs Alston are away.

Their children are such delights. Mary is seven, and Henry is five; they are the brightest and kindest children you could ever hope to meet.

I convinced them to hire me, and a week later, I was living with them.

I could get used to this. Being a free maid, coming and going as I please. My rules.

This is what I should have always used my ability for, blending into human society. Being happy. Forming natural connections and bonds.

To never be lonely.

This could become my life forever, and I think I might just be content with that.

2nd February 1856

Last night I awoke with a terrible fever. Not illness, no, the fever of memories.

I had dreamt I was sat in a field, flowers for far as the eye could see. Their petals softly stroking my skin as I reached out to pluck one for Dorabella.

I can no longer picture her face. She came to me like an animated doll—alive, yes, so very alive—but I could not see her face. Could not remember the colour of her eyes.

Green. Yes. Green, they were. The brightest green with bursts of gold and brown. But I couldn't see her in my dream, not the way I longed to.

Nicholas I do remember though. He was not present in the dream, but it was as if he were there, his essence framing the scene.

My baby brother. Whom I tainted for eternity.

~~Does he still live?~~

Henry and Mary oft remind me of my siblings. It was inevitable from the moment I met them—two bright young children, full of life, minds entirely free from the dangers and horrors of the world.

I wonder if I can help them. Nurture their passions and interests. Ensure they go on to pursue their dreams.

I hope they get to live long and happy lives, for those who could not.

—Taken from the diaries of Marianne Ashtown.

CHAPTER SEVEN

Mars
Now

Four years ago, I lost my sister. My only sibling. My world fell apart, and I thought I'd never recover from it. Nine months ago, I saved a boy to prove I could save *someone*. Then I lost him too.

Ever since that day, I thought we were chasing a dead end. No one had any theories or leads; it seemed like no one wanted to do anything to help. Now, I'm back where it all ended, or began, depending on how you look at it. I take in my surroundings—the trees, the tall grass brushing my bare calves, and the church ruins in the distance. My mind whirs about angelic beings, vampire cults, and thoughts about the end of the world. Marianne had been made to forget all about her brother and his cult predictions by that *creature*. The monster only she saw. Why?

Maybe he's the devil, or something of the sort. He very well could be, though I don't really believe in that stuff anymore. Seeing is believing. *Hmm.*

The three of us agreed to return to this site, although Marianne and I had individually visited many times over the past few months. We'd never set foot in the church though, so she suggested we returned as a three to see if we could pool our knowledge and piece together all the missing parts of the puzzle. After all, if she was the only person who saw the thing that took Arlo, who was to say *we* didn't notice something she might not have? I don't know, I really don't. But it's worth a try.

Rani treads lightly over the mud, focusing on her feet. I keep looking back to make sure she's keeping up, while Marianne storms ahead as always.

"How many people died here?" Rani finally asks. I stop to take in the question.

Marianne takes a few extra seconds to process it, then she turns to us. "Technically, no one. No one on record."

"Except Ben," Rani adds softly.

"Yes. Except Ben." Marianne takes a deep breath, and my chest constricts.

I listen to the wind whistling through the trees, and above, a bird soars. It's a hot day, but the shade is still cool. I shiver.

I still have nightmares about this place. I still remember Casper's scream. I only glimpsed Ben's body before the rest of The Thorns shed jackets and scarves to preserve his dignity, but it was enough to scar my brain forever. Lucy's guard *tore his guts out.* Casper had held him together like a rag doll, but the damage was too much to repair, the stuffing gone—body empty.

I nearly lost my right eye and couldn't focus on the chaos. And then, after it all, the phoenix rose from the flames. *Fire* burned in Arlo's eyes. His bird-like wings looked too heavy for his thin frame. When he turned to me, it was as if the world had stopped. But *he* wasn't behind those eyes—he looked straight through me. A cold, inhuman gaze.

I'm aware my thoughts are drifting so I shake my head to bring myself back to the present. This isn't going to help any of us—my wandering mind. Marianne glances at me briefly. She knows what

I'm thinking. But then she turns away and heads over to the church, crossing the old battlefield.

I never saw the inside of the ruins. The front door was rotting away, held together by blackened iron bolts. Decades of vines and ivy made it almost impossible to access without catching yourself. I think the last time Marianne was inside was on that day with Isiah.

It's like a ghost has passed through her; her face drops as she pries apart the branches and slips inside, turning back to us both. She doesn't speak a word.

I mimic her steps, though I'm far less graceful. I've never had the best coordination.

"Can you get past?" I call back to Rani, reaching out a hand to catch her. She's the last of us to squeeze through the vines.

"Just about," she says, struggling. She falls through the rest and catches her forearm on a thorn, wincing at the welling blood.

I stare for a moment, suppressing the mild hunger rising within. When she meets my eyes, I feel only guilt. Silence follows. Then, with a damp finger, she wipes the scratch and shakes her arm out, dismissing the incident.

I take in the building's scale to distract myself. A handful of windows remain, the forest has swallowed the others. Only a few pews still stand intact; the rest are trashed, crushed under stone and moss. There's something particularly eerie about abandoned buildings of faith, but this one especially holds the secrets of so much pain and suffering.

I already know where Marianne is headed. She pauses at the altar, just in front the wooden panels that once covered the pit where Isiah proudly hid his work. A remnant of yellow police tape lies torn under a shattered tile—another echo of the pain caused that day. All those families Marianne had to find, all the lies she had to feed the police, all to preserve our existence. Isiah went down with the ship, she would say. She made it known who he was and pointed everyone in the direction of the 'murder/suicide' theory. In the end, an enquiry never took place. I believe she even convinced the county to authorise an unmarked grave. No one will ever be able to find his body.

It was obvious Lucy knew of his history; she'd chosen this place to take Ben for a reason. I'm trying not to picture him trapped here. We'd tracked his scent here six months ago, almost immediately, but she was always one step ahead, so we never caught him in time.

I trace my hands over the remaining furnishings, yet carefully watch my footing. Light filters through the holes in the roof, illuminating the bright green grass dripping in dew from last night's rain.

"Do you think Lucy knew what was inside Arlo all along?" Rani pipes up from behind me.

Marianne snaps around from the altar, aligning herself perfectly with the stained-glass window above. The light outlines her silhouette.

"Yes, of course," Marianne answers like it's obvious. "She more or less admitted it in the letter."

"She might not have known to begin with. Her goal was to wipe out The Thorns because of what we did to Isiah. That has nothing to do with Arlo or these entities—this was plain old revenge," I shout up to Marianne. Then I pause, processing her last admission. "Wait, what letter?"

"What do you mean?" Marianne's voice carries as another drip of water echoes beside us. "Her letter to Arlo—you read it. Lucy mentions Arlo met her friend, which I think is the person I saw outside. So, two separate people. She made it very vague and didn't really share anything useful, but I literally watched you read that letter over Arlo's shoulder. Don't tell me you don't remember that either..." Marianne's tone becomes more frantic as she watches my expression contort with the second realisation of the day. I was Manipulated not once, but twice. Maybe even more. Whoever these entities were wanted Marianne to know about them, teasing her bit by bit, while the rest of us had no fucking clue.

"Rani, the notebook. It's folded over in the pocket at the back. The one marked with a red tab." Marianne directs Rani to open her book, and Rani scrambles to find the right sheet. We both step down to meet her as she slips into the light and opens the letter wide. Marianne reaches to take it before either of us can read it.

She begins reading it aloud.

"Sweetest Arlo, how is death treating you?" It starts. But as Marianne speaks, and I follow the words in her hands, her words no longer match the writing. Lucy gloats about an unnamed friend, one who doesn't appreciate Lucy being Arlo's sire. We wouldn't have been able to make that connection at the time, but that was never what I read. I remember her message being about the two we captured. About Jade. How Lucy made a fool of us. My veins chill. *We read what they wanted us to read.*

The last part is a direct address to Marianne herself and reads exactly the same. But the first part? How many versions are there? Is Marianne's version even the same one Arlo read?

What did Arlo know?

Once Marianne finishes, she stares at the pair of us, wide eyed. "I just spoke gibberish to you there, didn't I?"

I nod, blinking hard and shaking my head. Rani lets out a distressed 'huh' sound.

"What did you read?" I ask her, and she laughs.

"What?" I ask again, confused.

Rani continues to laugh, though it's clear she finds no humour in the situation. It's a despairing, hollow kind of laugh. "It's a shopping list," she says, covering her mouth.

"Oh, fuck," I say, rolling my eyes. Marianne must be thinking the exact same as me.

"Arlo could have read literally anything, and none of us would have had a clue." Rani points out, clearing her throat and looking up at the broken roof in defeat.

"That bastard," Marianne tuts, presumably referring to Lucy, or Arlo's captor—whoever imbued the letter with their Manipulation. *I can't smell a thing.*

It wouldn't make sense to be Lucy, though.

"What, you think that's her doing?" I almost shout this as the realisation hits me. "Marianne, you wouldn't be that susceptible to her Manipulation. You said she was strong, but we all know you would outmatch her. This isn't Lucy's doing. That's the fucking Sun, Moon, rising sign, or whatever the fuck those things really are. Aliens! She knew who they were. Oh my GOD!" I'm on the verge of screaming as I pace the mossy floor. I'm losing my mind. My hair suddenly agitates me, so I tie the rest of it up.

"The guy with the wings. The one I met. He must be in charge. The Sun," Marianne declares after a moment of silence.

"The leader whom the others revolve around," Rani adds.

"The Dutch or Swedish or Norwegian junkie from a sixties Hendrix set," is my contribution. Marianne glares at me, but she knows I'm deadly serious. I find it necessary to add, "I'm just finding it's a lot to absorb at once."

Marianne sighs, stepping into the shadows again, navigating through the debris. "I know," she whispers. "That letter is another dead end for now, then." She wanders off.

Rani stays put for a while, seeming deep in thought, before she heads off in the other direction. I'm left in the middle of the building, having to decide who to follow. I choose Rani.

"You sure you're okay doing all of this?" I ask Rani once Marianne's out of earshot.

Rani kicks at some stones blocking the side chapel entrance before hurling herself through the archway with a huff. I'm in the room when she responds. "Why would I not be? You think because I'm human that I'm not capable?" she scowls at me, and I'm stunned.

"What? No, that's not what I meant—"

"Sorry," she sighs. "You can probably tell I'm a little on edge —I can't hide that. I just wish this was simpler, so we could bring Arlo home." She unties her over-shirt from around her waist and puts it on, tying it in the middle. While this room is closed-in and damp, it's surprisingly the most intact. Some graffiti marks the interior stone, but it's a salvageable project. I don't know why my mind wanders to that, though. This place should have been torn down a long time ago. *Maybe that would have changed things.*

"I'm scared too," I finally admit. Stationed in the doorway, I watch Rani explore the nooks and crannies.

"You can't die though," she mutters.

"I can." I gulp at the harshness of her words.

Rani explores the underside of the bench before looking up. "I didn't mean it like that, not like..."

Ben. Not like Ben.

"I knew what you meant, but it doesn't change my fear." I try to lighten the conversation. "I died before, and it fucking hurt. I'd rather not get myself or anyone else in that situation again."

"How old are you, Mars?"

"What, like actual age or body age?" I don't mind answering either. It's like I *want* to talk about myself, which is out of character for me. Huh.

"Both." Rani confirms.

"Nineteen. And thirty." I swallow hard. This feels a little like an interrogation now with the way she stares at me, but again, I'm not sure I mind.

"Hmm," she says, picking at some flaking wood from a fallen beam. Then she smiles. "So, you're technically the same age as me. Forever."

"Forever is relative, but yes, *forever.*"

Rani's entire manner softens. "Will you ever get bored?" No malice underscores her question, but it does take me by surprise. She sits on one of the remaining benches and looks at me in a questioning way, as if to invite me over. I hesitantly move to sit beside her, her eyes still fixed on mine.

"Maybe." It's my honest answer. No one has ever asked me that before, but it feels like the truth as it spills from my lips. Rani is, after all, Arlo's best friend. If I can trust anyone now, it's her.

"But you're happy with who you are?"

"That's a loaded question."

Rani smiles and shakes her head. "As in, being immortal and the choices you make. And, well... no, never mind."

"No, what were you going to say?"

Rani blushes, and I sense her heart betray her panic. "It's nothing. I don't know why I'm asking all this, to be honest. I'm getting ahead of myself. My brain is scrambled."

"Do you want to ask me about my identity?" I suggest.

Rani's head jerks a little, but I know I'm right.

"You can ask me anything. Not everyone is like that, but I don't mind. Go ahead."

She looks at me for confirmation before asking, "You're queer, right?" Having prepared for something a lot more personal, I almost laugh.

"Yeah. I'm very queer."

"And you like more than one gender?" She's getting more comfortable already.

"I like any and all," I say. "Are you going to ask me for relationship advice? Because everyone always seems to think I'm some sort of queer guru, and while I appreciate the confidence—"

"No. Not really. Well, yes, honestly. Sorry."

I grin. "No, go ahead. I'm joking. I'm also quite decent at advice-giving, apparently."

"Okay. Promise you won't tell anyone about this discussion?"

"Of course, I promise."

"It's kind of useless asking an immortal this, but you're really the only person I'm comfortable enough to ask about this stuff, so can you pretend you're human? Just for now?"

I smile. "I did date before all of this, so maybe I can help."

She inhales again. "Okay, so, mortal Mars... Did you ever wish you could have had experiences with all the different types of people you could have potentially been attracted to before you settled down with just one person?"

I chew my lip in thought. "You mean like polyamory?"

Rani squints a bit. "Maybe, but not really. I'm pretty sure I'm monogamous, but it's just... I love Carmen, I love her a lot, and I can see our future together, but she was my first proper relationship, and I know I'm not just attracted to one gender. But now, I just feel like I'll never know what..." She bats her hand and huffs to herself. "It just sounds so stupid when I say it out loud. You're literally immortal now. You can live however many lives you want with however many people. Gosh, maybe I do wish I was one of you after all."

"You've thought about that?" I pinned Rani as the stubborn mortal, something I always admired her for.

"I don't want to die. I don't want to deal with the stuff you all have to, but I just... man. Only having one life really does suck. I just feel like there's not enough time to do or try everything, and it stresses me out. I don't want to be tied down by anything and have regrets.

"Is Carmen tying you down? Do you want to break up with her?"

Rani's eyes widen. "What? No! That's not what I'm saying at all. I just... honestly, I don't know what I'm saying anymore. I can't think straight." She drops her head into her hands. "Forget I ever said anything. Let's get back to looking for clues." She stands up and dusts off her trousers.

"Wait." I reach out to hold Rani's hand, and she looks at me in mild panic. I let go. "I know what you mean."

"You do?"

"I do."

Rani sits back down and waits for me to continue.

"I think that's a perfectly normal experience for humans, especially queer ones." I smile when I say it, and Rani grins back.

"I dated before my accident. I dated this boy. We were together for about two and a half years. I loved him. We were madly in love as teens and had the whole world ahead of us. But I could never quite shake the feeling that something was missing, that something wasn't quite complete in our timeline. I'd known a while I wasn't straight; I'd had crushes on girls and would always wonder what my life would have been like with them, and then I started questioning my gender, which opened up a whole can of worms. But I loved my partner. He was mine, and I was his—forever, just like we promised each other. He had already planned our wedding and where we'd move to, but I was never sure if that was what I wanted. Then I felt guilty for being selfish, so I swallowed it all down. He was everything to me. He supported me through thick and thin. When I reintroduced myself as Mars and told my family, he was there through it all, but then we started to grow apart. This stuff happens. It sucks, it really does, but we just have to remind ourselves to be strong and try to push through it.

"You know, less than a year later, I was hit by a truck coming down the wrong side of a motorway, and then I was given the miracle choice of really reinventing myself. I never saw that coming, not in a million years. That could have been it for me, but it wasn't. But the point is, I thought I was going to be with him forever. And that scared me, and I never knew why. But now, I realise it was because I had hopes and dreams that I never thought were possible while I was with someone who had *different* hopes and dreams.

"This feeling of wanting to experience more and understand yourself—it's not selfish or greedy. It's life. It makes us human. It's you. It's perfectly normal to feel these things! You're still so young and have your whole life ahead of you. You're happy with Carmen now, and you might be for the next sixty or seventy years. Or things might not work out. You're not dating to marry, nor to break up. You're dating for however long you're compatible. Being in a relationship doesn't have to be the end of your dreams. Your life will work out how it needs to. Regret nothing, because you made every decision for a reason. Being queer will always complicate these feelings because we're not the default—we're something a lot cooler that not everyone can grasp, and we don't always get to talk about our feelings with others like straight people can. But don't worry about any of this. Just live your life. We've learned now more than ever not to waste our time on small things, because even us immortals can die, Rani. Just look at Casper, he... skies. Sorry. No. You know what I mean, though... we just have to—"

Rani hugs me and pulls me in tight, silencing my words. I breathe in the scent of lavender and nature in her hair; keeping me grounded.

I realise then that I've never actually opened up about my death or life before until this point; I've never let myself be this open. But in this moment, with Rani being so vulnerable and trusting, it's like some strange kind of human manipulation. *No,* it's empathy, I realise. I'm feeling empathy. And I want her to know she's not alone.

"Thank you, Mars. Really. Thank you so much."

I'm about to reply when a clatter sounds at the entrance. Marianne appears, waving something grey in her hands.

"Bingo!" she shouts, shattering the moment. Rani pulls back abruptly and wipes her cheeks with a sniffle.

We both stand and stumble over to see what she's holding.

It's a feather.

But not just any normal bird feather—it's easily triple the size of any bird you'd find in England.

"The Sun." Marianne grins. "Gotcha."

CHAPTER EIGHT

Arlo
Four Months Ago

When it slept for me, I was in an ocean. Alone. Floating face up with my ears muffled and senses skewed. I dreamed about my life and every moment leading up to my surrender. Letting it consume me.

I'd wake up in the cold stone room, briefly disorientated, until it stirred awake, too. It used my eyes, my mouth. It breathed for me and would stand, walking over to the window, and dressing itself in clothes I did not own. I quickly grew used to it; I had no choice, but those first few weeks were excruciating. Every time it spoke for me, it burned. My head split, and I couldn't breathe. I wanted to scream, but I didn't have the power to.

They buried Ben's body. Ben was dead. I'll never see him again. Those were the only thoughts swimming around my mind for weeks. I clung onto them as tightly as my mind would let me. I wanted to move on, but those memories were the only things keeping me grounded. Keeping Arlo alive. If I could cling onto the reason why I did this, then maybe, just maybe, I might prevent more death and suffering. I'm doing this for them. A necessary sacrifice.

The morning after the funeral, Michael came into my room and asked me how I'd slept. I told him I was well rested, and he smiled. He had a cold smile. One as sharp as ice, but I didn't have enough autonomy to do anything other than smile back.

"I will let you sort yourself out, then you will meet me in the next room to begin your assignment." He reached out to stroke the waves at the back of my head before pulling my head towards him. I could *feel* it, and I wanted to flinch. But I wasn't me anymore. I needed to remember that.

When I entered the room, my father sat to one side, framed in the only beam of natural light. His hair shone like an autumn morning, his manner calm and relaxed. When I entered, he sat up slightly. My gut sank.

He looked as if he were about to say something, but then Michael appeared from the shadows behind him and squeezed his shoulders, addressing us both when he said, "I've found your next target. There was a robbery last night. The victim is an old woman. The culprit is notorious for targeting vulnerable people and getting away with it. I want you to make sure he never does it again."

I was stunned, rooted to the spot, but then I thought about all Michael had told me before. About the work we did. I couldn't remember, but I must have done his bidding before. We were using our ability for the greater good, I reminded myself. I began to ask for more details, but then my father stood slowly with a sigh. "I'll do it," he said. He didn't look at me directly, but I felt like he wanted to. Maybe it was wishful thinking. I was still processing the fact he stood before me, after nearly twenty years. I wanted to talk to him—alone. But there was no time for that.

Michael did not seem pleased with my father's proposal. He glided around the chair and came to stand between us. "Arlo, this is yours. I want you to go alone." *He's using your name as a test. Never forget that. He doesn't see you as...*

He gave me an address, and I nodded, letting my body speak for me.

I left the room before I saw the look on my father's face.

I DON'T KNOW what Michael made me do before, but from this point on, I could remember everything. I snuck into this man's apartment and Manipulated him. Fed him with kindness before leaving him on the floor to regret everything.

It was a simple task, with no physical harm done, and I left feeling a tad lighter. I helped people.

I could get used to this.

When I returned an hour later, Michael patted me on the back. "Good boy," he said. My father was nowhere to be seen.

The next day, I had another task. This time, a boss was over-working his employees. I watched him write out his notice.

The following task was slightly further afield, but I returned knowing I'd helped people once again. And none of them would ever know I existed.

EVERY TIME MICHAEL called me by my real name and told me how hard I was working—how impressed he was—I felt my hands release the ropes, and I'd fall further inside myself as that *thing* took over. But I was okay with it. It had to be done. A necessary sacrifice.

I truly believed I was a hero.

After one of my tasks, the rain came down hard, forcing me to drag my wings through the muddy fields on my return. My shoulders ached, and I was shivering. As I stood in the shelter's doorway, below the cathedral where we hid, Michael stared at me and asked, "Another job well done?" He leaned back in his chair with a grin.

He was alone, as usual. I didn't know where my dad was. I didn't care.

"All went to plan," my mouth said.

He washed my wings and massaged my shoulders as the storm blew over. I thanked him for his kindness. My Sun.

I CONTINUED THESE TASKS DAILY. The act got easier and easier each time. Michael provided my body with his blood to satisfy my undead nature. Michael was proud of me. He thanked and rewarded me, and before long, when my body moved or spoke, I was no longer in pain. We were working as one.

I rarely saw my father, but Michael said he had his own work to do. We were making a difference. I let go of my thoughts about Ben, because I knew I was doing what was necessary. I was doing this for him.

But then, the nightmares started.

Each night when I went to sleep, I was back in that ocean. But this time, I was drowning. My lungs filled up with water, and my arms stopped moving, forcing me to sink. I began hearing voices— echoes, chants, wails and cries. And a huge weight dragged me down.

Then, I'd awaken, drenched in sweat, and I'd instantly forget.

Two months passed, and we moved away from the city, travelling further down south to York to recommence our tasks.

Michael occasionally accompanied me, but my father always made himself sparse. I'd not spoken to him at all yet, but I only seemed to care about his absence in those few moments I wasn't working. When I wasn't fixing the wrongs of the world.

Michael said my next task would be the biggest yet; he promised I was ready for it. He knew I was strong enough now, and I was ready to make real change.

He sent me to kill a man.

I followed him to work, infiltrated his daily life, thoughts, and emails. Manipulated him. Threatened him. I learned all about his twisted and truly evil pastime, sickened by how long he had been allowed to get away with everything—how many people covered for him.

I learned his routine, fuelled with hatred and anger, and planned his death to a fine point. It would be swift, and I would save so many people because of it. I needed to end his life. It was the only way. His mind was too far gone for me to uncover the root of this evil.

IT MAY HAVE HAPPENED QUICKLY, if not for last night's events.

I was sitting on my bed, my wings outstretched and resting behind me, ready to wind down, when a gentle knock came at my door.

It was my father.

Every time I laid eyes on him, my whole body collapsed in on itself. My mind overpowered everything.

"Dad," I addressed him as calmly as I could.

He took in a deep breath before speaking, ducking slightly through the doorframe to step silently into the room.

"Son. I need to talk to you. I need you to listen to me."

I didn't say anything at first; what did he need to say?

"Are you there, Arlo?" was the first thing he asked, since I was yet to speak.

I nodded.

"Really?" He came to sit beside me cautiously, keeping some distance.

"Of course."

He didn't seem satisfied. I wasn't sure what else to say.

"Is she okay?" he asked, and I scrunched up my nose.

"Who?"

My dad closed his eyes and bit back what looked like a

displeased smile. He turned away, looking out into the dark room. "He's in your head."

I just looked at him, unsure of the meaning of his words.

"Michael. He's..." he cut himself off, clenching his fists.

"He's guiding us. We're changing the world," I said.

"No, no, Arlo. Please. Listen to me." He grabbed my arms with warm and clammy hands. He looked into my eyes with desperation.

"Arlo. He's using us. He's manipulated us. He's fooling us into doing all these simple, heroic tasks to get us to believe we're doing the right thing. To get us to come willingly. To let *go*. He's made me do this for years, but I know now... you helped wake me up. I—"

"Shut up!" I shouted, cutting him off.

"No, no, please, Arlo. You need to listen to me. Please. I'm begging you, my son, please. It's me, your father. Jerome. *Jerry.* I went by Jerry. Is that what she called me? You *must* listen to me. He's trying to take your morals—to twist them. To get you to do anything he desires..."

I grew frustrated with him. This was all he had to say to me after over a month apart? "I need to do this. Why don't you under-stand?" He'd avoided me for so long, and now he wanted to stop me? From saving humanity? He made no sense. Why was he being like this? This was not what we were made for.

"Arlo." His tone grew more concerned when he realised I'd stopped engaging. "My son isn't a killer." He gulped, his eyes searching mine.

"You don't know a thing about me," I spat. Then I shouted for Michael. Calling my Sun.

Standing up in a panic, my father waved his hands frantically. "No! No, no, no! Arlo, stop. Don't do this! You have every right to hate me—" He backed towards the entrance, looking between the door and me. In the space of a single heartbeat, the door flew open and there stood our leader, tutting. He grabbed my dad with brute force, almost choking him and bringing him to his knees. My father's eyes were wider than I'd ever seen them.

"Now, what have you been feeding our Star?" Tutting again, Michael shook his head, muffling my dad's mouth with his hand, while the other reached forward with a black filled syringe. As if he had already prepared it. I watched in silence as my father thrashed and grabbed at Michael's much stronger arm, pushing the plunger deep into his chest like a dagger; his body fell slack a moment later.

Michael hauled my now calmed father to his feet and forced him to stand. "I knew there was a reason why you kept running from me." He patted my father's cheek in disappointment, then looked at me. "Good work. I knew you'd listen. I chose well. Now, get some sleep. You've got a big day ahead of you." Then he left, with my father in tow, who followed our leader like a sullen shadow, no longer speaking, and never turning back.

The nightmares were the worst last night. I thought of my mum. Then I thought of Rani and Mars and Ben.

WHEN I WAKE in the morning, I brush it all off. **_Silly little Arlo._**

I KNOW when best to strike. I take the life of evil, just as planned, and stay focused on my purpose. I block out the thoughts of my father from last night, though they do try to corrupt my mind. _What did he mean?_

But then, as the life of this man begins to fade in my hands, and I say my last words to him, I do something unplanned. I should have just left, stuck to the script and let him die slowly and alone, but a shockwave of anger surges through my body. Without a further thought, I turn back around and bend down to breathe in the scent of blood still sat in his veins.

I tear at his neck.

I drink and drink, and then, when I can't get enough, I tear at his body and feed straight from his still beating heart. I drink and drink and bite hard on the flesh to consume every last drop of his body. I devour so much I lose track of everything I've eaten. I'm so *hungry*.

Then the body becomes *her*. Lucy. Her green hair matted and snapped. I left her unrecognisable, but I was so proud of my work because she deserved it, but this person deserves it more, don't they? The power to destroy, to eradicate, to *win*, feels incredible.

I rip away everything that makes this body human and watch the guts spill out, painting the duvet like a canvas, with every piece perfectly positioned. How fascinating it is that the human body can hold so much blood.

I laugh, wiping my bloody hands over my equally messed up mouth before licking my fingers one by one.

He deserved it. My Sun will be so proud.

So pleased with the work we're doing. So...

That's what he wants you to believe.

I WAKE FASTER THAN LIGHT.

Truly. Awaken. Arlo. Back in my body. Just like that.

I startle backwards, taking in the horrific scene. The mess I've just made. The insides out on the bed, dousing the entire room in red.

When I blink, the body is Lucy's again, only this time, I'm not in a room. I'm in the forest, and the snow is falling. Everyone stops to look at me and what I've done. I see the horror in Mars' eyes as they look between me and my work. The work of my own bare hands.

I'm a murderer.

Then I see Ben, his body cold and torn. I look down at the claws tipping each of my nails, and I...

I RUN BACK to our house, tearing through the hallway and up the stairs to my room.

What have I done? What have I done? What have I done?

I'm shaking, my wings too heavy, my nails too sharp. There's blood on my hands. Blood on my hands. My hands. Blood.

I vomit, bringing up everything I'd consumed moments before. I stagger back in fear of *everything,* and then I scream, breaking down and collapsing to my knees, clutching my skull and tearing at my hair.

I scream and cry until my throat tears itself in two.

What have I done?

My father's words hit me. He knew all along; he knew what Michael was, what he was planning. He knew, and he tried to tell me, but I didn't listen. I fed him back to that monster.

He was free. He freed himself. I don't know how—I don't even *know* him—not really. I've barely seen him at all, but he tried to save me last night, and I lost him before I'd even properly found him.

I want to speak to him now. To be with him. To apologise.

But maybe he's long gone, hidden in the depths of his body, just like I was. For months. I was a fool.

And now I've fulfilled my prophecy.

I have become a monster.

The very thing I thought I was freeing the world from.

I WAIT for Michael to find me. To soothe my mind and make things easier. To climb back inside my head.

No one hears my cries, though.

There's no one in the house.

No Michael.

THE TEARS NEVER STOP, but after an eternity, I look up and breathe in my surroundings. The house is silent, the pipes creak, and the wind whistles, but it's silent.

No one's home.

I'm free.

I run.

14th November 1856

This may perhaps be one of the most important entries of my life. Hopefully. Maybe. Do I want it to be?
I am not alone.
And I do not mean the Alston family. I love those children with my whole heart, as my diaries clearly show, but there will always be something that separates us.
They are not immortal.
But I'm not the only one who is.

I had just finished bathing the children and tucked them into bed before I went on my usual evening walk. I manage quite well throughout the day, but by evening time I must feed.
I wandered towards the pub I tend to frequent at this time of year, searching for a drunken, rude, rich gentleman to drink from. I never kill them, just take enough to sate me, then send them on their jolly way. I find I am quite at peace with my decision to feed this way. No one gets harmed, not really, and I feel a little better about myself afterwards. I am a lady in a man's world. I do what I must, gifts aside.
I completed my business, ensuring no one witnessed my feed, then set myself on the path home. But my travels were quickly interrupted by the strong stench of blood. And not from my own doing. No, this smell was emanating from an unlit alley straight ahead of me.

I found him feeding off a man, almost to the point of fully draining him. His victim was limp and unconscious in his arms, and I did not even hesitate when I dove for him, jabbing my safety blade into his shoulder. He turned to me, elongated canines bared and bloody, and I jumped back in shock, falling on my behind. He strode towards me, and I pushed myself back, pausing at the entrance to the alleyway so I could be seen, but I felt his attempt to control me. Using our gift.

He made no attempt to raise a hand to me. He just wanted to make me forget what I had seen. I had just stabbed him, though he did not want to return that pain. Instead, he backed up in surprise, catching his breath, then he withdrew the blade from his back and threw it at my feet. He looked scared but waited for me to stand before he spoke. 'You're like me,' he said.

I thought I was the only one left.

I told him not to run, and that I could help him. I actually had no idea what I was planning to do, but I just needed him to stay.

He was dressed in clothes from the slums. Workhouse clothes, ripped and worn. I asked him where he lived, and he told me nowhere. I am not sure if he was telling the truth but it did not matter to me.

I promised him I could get him nicer clothes, and he agreed to let me take him back to the house.

His name is Jerome. He has not spoken much yet but I must give him time.

I am not alone anymore.

—Taken from the diaries of Marianne Ashtown.

Chapter Nine

Mars
Now

"It's not real." Marianne is back at her desk, having just got the test results back from the feather. (That poor lab assistant will be none the wiser.)

"As in fake, or not human?" I ask.

Marianne just looks up through her brows.

I close my eyes with a sigh and correct myself, "As in, not of this *earth*. You know what I mean."

Marianne throws me a half smile, then swings her legs around her chair and stands up. "It's made of elements quite literally not in existence. It shouldn't exist. It makes no sense."

"Oh." I don't know what else to say.

"So, what does that mean, exactly?" Rani stands at the doorway. She must have followed me in.

"It means, well..." Marianne chews at her nail. "It's alien for sure, but it could also be a fabrication, like most things lately. The wings are just for effect. They don't actually need them, and I don't think they'd be able to fly with them, either. They're not *real* that way."

"You're literally holding the feather," Rani observes, scrunching her brow.

"I know. I know. They're visible, yet probably just to those with a strong resistance to Manipulation? I don't know. If that was the case, then you wouldn't be able to see it, Rani. No offence. Urgh, none of this makes sense at all." Marianne drops the grey feather, frustrated. "I think they just like to mess with us like they did with the letter, which I keep bloody staring at, hoping it's like one of those blasted magic eye books where the 3D image just *reveals* itself when you look hard enough. It's never that simple, though, and I know that. I'm just running out of options."

"They wanted us to find the feather, just like they wanted us to read different things, to wind us up? Cos they've done a brilliant job at that so far," Rani deduces, sucking in her lips.

I feel like I'm on a waltzer. I pinch the bridge of my nose. "So, this form is purely... what? For the aesthetic?" I theorise, moving my hands to my hips.

"Probably. As they seem to need a host, they likely haven't got a functioning, corporeal form to walk this earth. But out of the probable three, two of them are at least *human* hosts, so these are intentional additions..." Marianne chews the inside of her mouth. "Nicholas never mentioned their physical form. He just mentioned them as 'powerful beings', so with that logic, the wings and claws are likely for *fun*. To make them other. Adapted. *Better.*"

I just laugh, maybe slightly too unhinged sounding. I don't know how else to react, though. Everything is just absurd. "Of course! Why not. *Why. Not.*"

I'M LYING in bed feeling sorry for myself. A common occurrence as of late. I'm frustrated that nothing we discover or learn has been of any help yet. Marianne saw things we didn't. We all read different letters, no one has the same memories, and we're none the wiser about *where* Arlo and these other entities are, what they truly plan on doing, and *when*. In fact, the more we figure out, the more confusing it all gets. It's just a game for these entities. They're just having fun playing with us all.

I think about Arlo a lot—I'm not ashamed to admit it. I think about his smile, his face, his heart, his worries, his insecurities, and fears. I think about how lost he always seemed. How we failed him.

Where are you, Arlo?

I sit up on the side of my bed, facing the window overlooking the city. The cathedral, the castle, the distant train station, and bridges.

Where can I find you?

I hate feeling useless. Like I can't do anything to assist. I can't be there for anyone. It just never works. It's like I'm cursed to doom everyone around me, and I don't know what I'm doing wrong.

I don't know what compels me to go to my drawer and look for my photo album, but I do. Like I said, I'm feeling sorry for myself.

I rummage through the shit I've crammed in there over time and finally retrieve the battered, leather-bound album my grandfather made. He left his stamp on the side. I stroke the cover in reminiscence, then untie the leather strip wrapped around it.

Most photos are from Caloocan, where I lived with my whole family. My grandparents lived just outside the centre of the city, where it was a little quieter and more open. I'd spend hours and hours running around in the backyard with my sister, burning in the midday sun. Poppy would follow me everywhere. I would move heaven and earth for her. Always.

Then we grew up.

And I failed my sister.

I knew these thoughts would start again.

I thought I could keep them at bay with my art and reading and all those things people tell you to do to take your mind off things, but sometimes the thoughts are too strong—too overwhelming.

I pull out my favourite photo of us sitting on the porch steps of my grandparents' house: me, Poppy, my mam, and dad. I blinked mid-click and wished they'd retaken it, but the rest of my family look so happy and joyous. I can almost *smell* the photo. It was a weekend, and my dad finished work early for once. Mam surprised us by making her best version of fresh lumpia for a snack, which always tasted nicer than my dad's. Probably too much salt.

We were happy.

Sometimes, I wonder what my life would have been like if I'd stayed in the Philippines. I know why we moved, but then *everything* happened, and I just wish I could have kept my simple and naïve childhood. No deaths. No immortality. Poppy might still be with me, though I never would have met Ben or Casper or the band. No Marianne. No complicated feelings. I know I still would have had struggles back home, but I just can't help but wonder how different things might have been. Hindsight is a wonderful thing.

I don't regret meeting these people—I really don't—I just...

I hug the photo to my chest and fall back onto my bed, closing my eyes with a sigh.

Why does everything have to be so hard? Why can't I figure out how to fix everything?

I MUST HAVE DOSED off because I wake up to heavy rain outside, and the sky has darkened. The photo has creased on my chest somehow, and I curse myself for being so clumsy. They're

Polaroids. We didn't take digital photos much then, so I need to take great care of what I have.

I look back down at the photo and stroke my sister's face with my thumb. I know I should see my parents more, they don't even live that far. I've been getting lazy, and my priorities have slipped. I need my family sometimes—they mean so much to me. *So much.*

After the almost daily wave of guilt for Poppy has subsided, my pain migrates to Arlo again. Everything always does now. I saved his life because I couldn't save Poppy. I wanted to prove I was capable, and that I'm not a bad omen to those I love.

Love.

I love him. I fucking love him so much it hurts. I know he doesn't feel the same way—or didn't, whatever—but I can't fight the feeling. I need him in my life, regardless. I need him to be okay, to be alive and well and wholly himself. I need...

I'm on my feet and out the door before I can think any further. I stride through the rain in nothing but a t-shirt and cargo shorts (stupid).

I'm running back to the forest.

Back to the church.

I need to find him.

CLAMBERING through the entrance we'd made earlier, I immediately regret not bringing a torch; the space where the light shone through before is now a dull grey, dripping with streams of water. It feels more like a cave now—an echoing cavern. I try not to trip or slip on the moss and weeds as I follow the path Marianne took to find the feather. She said that was all she could find—the only sign—but if *that* was left behind, then surely there was something else.

I can just about see my feet as I enter the side room where Marianne went. We didn't go in here yesterday; we were all too eager to determine where the feather was from, so blinded by that minute discovery.

It looks like it's only just become accessible because of the fallen interior wall, though that's hardly reassuring, seeing as I'm alone and no one knows where I am. I didn't give myself time to inform anyone; I just knew I needed to find *something*.

What I didn't acknowledge before was a wooden board on the floor, as if, up until recently, it had acted like a makeshift door. My heart sinks. Ben had most likely been hidden away here at one point.

It now makes sense why Marianne very subtly steered us away from this side of the building. She must have quickly figured that out.

I thank the dying daylight for my limited view as I enter the room. I need to keep my mind clear. I can't bring myself to question the horrors that poor man experienced. I'm making myself feel sick just scratching the surface of the visions.

I enter the room fully, realising how much it has decayed. This side of the building has been reclaimed by nature so much more, with the oak trees practically forming the far wall, their branches as rafters. It's almost impossible to tell what this room will have been used for all those years ago.

I stand for a bit, catching my breath, then I go searching for any possible link to these entities. I doubt Arlo was ever here, and I hope he wasn't, but everything must link. Something is drawing me here for a reason. It's like my mind knows we missed something. The brain is funny that way.

I get like this sometimes, blindly driven by my desire for answers. I think little about logistics or facts when I have these urges. I just want to find results as quickly and easily as I can.

I leave no stone unturned, quite literally. I'm tearing this place apart. My hands are filthy, and I catch my shoelaces on objects, trapping my feet under the lips and dips of the uneven floor. I pick things up—small grains and plants—and hold them up against the last remaining light seeping through the cracks. There are indistinguishable fibres and vinyl-like shavings, but nothing conclusive.

I trip over a brass-framed painting of Jesus, then just laugh. He was no help.

I'm at the point of giving up when something drops behind me. I startle and stand fully, preparing myself.

"Hello?" I shout; my voice echoes out into the main room, where the rain still gushes through. The weeds flop and wave in the breeze, but no further sound follows.

It's an old building, so of course I'm going to hear these things. This church is so remote, it's been protected from the ravages of time—more than most things. People don't care enough to trek out here.

I think for a moment that it might be Marianne or Rani, who have either followed me, or chosen to return individually for more clues since we found the feather.

But they would have shown themselves the second they heard my voice, so after a further twenty seconds, I pretend I heard nothing and resume searching. It won't be long before it's pitch black in here, and I'll have no choice but to leave it for another day.

I continue on, my hands caked in moss and mud as I throw and tear at damp stone. Nothing of interest reveals itself. I feel like I'm going crazy. Of course I wouldn't find anything here. The feather was a tease, probably been there months. Why am I wasting my time?

I'm at the point of giving up when I hear another sound. This time, it alerts me as more than just a falling tile or heavy rain drop. Someone—or something—is inside the ruins. I'm finally a teeny bit afraid.

"Hello?" I shout again. I need whatever it is to know I'm not afraid of it. "Who's there?" I make sure I say it nice and loud in the hopes it's just an animal that will run at my voice. If it's a human, or something else... I'm hoping they leave too. *Hoping*.

I step back over towards what remains of the doorway, wary of peering through in case someone is there with a knife or some other violent weapon. Hey, I watch a lot of action movies. I know how these things play out.

"If anyone's there, I'm armed." I'm not. I would die first in an apocalypse.

Still, there's no voice, which makes me think it was just a fox or something. It's the woods, animals are free to roam. But then something shuffles to my left, and I grow faint.

I don't have the courage to shout out again. I'm well and truly terrified. I knew I shouldn't have come here alone, especially in the dark. This is classic first-victim behaviour.

I peer around the corner into the shadows of the main building to find nothing but dark mounds of stone and a broken table. I can't make out anything unusual. I vaguely remember what things looked like in the light, so I'm calmed for a brief moment before something shifts and stretches. A black mass moves and contorts, reforming into something bigger and more ominous. I nearly screech and run, but then I realise what I'm seeing.

Wings.

"Arlo?" I try. I hope to the high heavens my eyes aren't failing me.

The mass makes a moaning noise, but one of pain.

My legs carry me forward without thinking. I nearly give out at the sight before me. I wonder if I'm being delusional—surely I am?

But I'm not.

I'm really, really not.

I see browns and beiges and the soft skin of his bare shoulder. Then, I see his hair, a warm, white-gold, messily cascading down to his shoulders. His head is lowered, cradling something by his side —his shirt, I realise. It seems to be covering something protruding from his lower torso. His legs are outstretched and covered in what was once possibly corduroy, but has now worn down to a thin canvas.

He's hurt.

"Arlo?" I cry out, clambering through the archway. His head snaps up, his eyes piercing mine.

I stoop to his height. *He's home.*

I want to reach out and hold him, to find out what's hurting him, but I know he'd hate it. Arlo always hated physical touch, especially skin to skin. And then every single memory floods back —from the moment I found him in that back alley, right up until he turned to me for the final time on the battlefield, his eyes bloody and distant, and his mind elsewhere.

But I know. I *know* that by some miracle, by whatever odds, that the person in front of me now is Arlo James Everett, son of Melissa Everett and Jerome Mair, and he's... *bleeding.*

Shit.

I instinctively reach out to stop the blood, but he cries out and jerks backwards, dropping the rag of his shirt. His wings snap back against the stone with an awful crack.

They're real.

"Oh, Arlo." I'm trying not to cry, but I'm failing miserably. He's alive. He's here. He's home.

He's like a deer in headlights. I can't properly see his eyes, but I know they're wide and likely bloodshot. "Let me help you, Arlo. You're hurt." I try to reach out again with a much gentler approach. He flinches, but then eases back towards me, seeming to relax slightly.

"Arlo, can you understand me? Are you in there? Please tell me you know who I am." The rain grows heavier, and the ground is sodden. He'll freeze if I leave him here. "Please," I beg, staring down at the piece of wood piercing his abdomen. Dark blood seeps around it. "You need to pull it out. Our bodies can't heal if you leave them in. We're not the same as humans." I hoped his body was still the same as mine. I couldn't discern the shade of his blood, but I knew it wasn't red anymore. Parts of it coated my hands now.

"Arlo." I barely breathe this time, on the brink of giving up.

Maybe he's not there anymore. Not himself.

"It hurts," he finally rasps, his words breathless and strained. I bite the back of my hand at the sound of his voice. I feel it right down to my core. His beautiful voice. Arlo.

"Oh, I know, I know. You need to remove it, please. It will sting for a moment, then you will heal. Our bodies are magnificent. It will begin to close in a matter of minutes. Please, Arlo." I'm hovering my hands over his body, scared to touch or frighten him. He looks so afraid. I yearn to ask him where he's been and what he's done and seen. I need to ask him everything, but first, I need to get him somewhere safe. I need him to heal. We can talk later.

"Arlo, we need to get you somewhere to rest. We can't stay here; it's not safe. If this rain continues, there's not going to be much of a roof left. You'll need some fresh clothes, a dressing to cover the wound, and maybe something to drink." I stand and offer my hand to him, though I don't know what else to do. He hates the touch of bare skin.

"I... I can't," he rasps, tilting his head slightly to look at me. His hands return to cradling his injured side.

"You can. I'll help you. You can rest at mine. We don't need to tell anyone you're here yet." I don't have a phone on me, anyway. We'd have to wait until the morning before we did anything, like notify Rani or Marianne.

He doesn't speak, but I watch his head shake from side to side. He doesn't try to move.

"Arlo? It's me, Mars. You remember me, right?" *I love you and would do anything in the world to protect you.*

"Mars," he mutters, so softly it's barely audible. He sounds so tired.

"Yes, it's me! You know me. I—I saved you once!"

Silence again. The rain is growing torrential and seeping through every single crack and fissure. Droplets of water fall onto his body and head, yet he doesn't seem to feel them.

"I know who you are. I remember everything."

His words shatter my heart. I knew he was himself. I just knew it. *Meaning he's definitely alone.*

"Arlo, can you stand?"

"I can," he confirms, before letting out another yelp as he adjusts himself and the wood inevitably shifts inside him.

"I can help, if you want. Hold my hand. I know it's cold and you don't like it, and I'm really, really sorry about it, but I need to help you get to shelter. We can walk to mine, if you can manage. I'll get you something warm. We don't have to speak yet, or ever. I just need you to be okay."

A moment of silence passes before he looks down at his wound. "I need to pull it out, but I'm scared." He sounds so young, so vulnerable. How can I have let anything bad happen to him?

I take in the scene and fully absorb what lies before me—the creature he has become. All because we were too blind to help him. I stoop to his level again, and this time, I turn around so I can sit beside him, correcting my position on the sharp stone to avoid touching his side or sit on his wings.

He watches my every move, wheezing. Oh, Arlo.

"It hurts," he says again, looking down at my side.

How did he get here? What happened? Did he know I'd be here right at this very moment? Is that why he came? Did he follow me? *Stop thinking you're important to him, Mars.*

"I can remove it for you, but I'm going to have to touch your skin," I say.

He inhales sharply. "My bag," he says, then his left arm lifts as he points into the pitch darkness.

"Your bag? You have belongings with you?"

"There are gloves in my bag," he croaks before moaning again and leaning into his injured side.

I understand what he means. He wants me to help, but only if I wear gloves. *He needs me.* Staggering into the dark, I feel around for a fabric that would resemble a bag, searching blindly until my fingers rest on a soft fabric with buckles over the front. I stick my hands in, suppressing the twang of guilt for going through his belongings, and find a bundle I presume are gloves, and then close the backpack back up again, trying not to think about it.

"I got them," I announce, trying not to slip and fall over his body as I return to my place. "I'll try to be gentle."

I think he nods. It's hard to tell, but I ask permission to place my hands on him, and he grabs my hands to guide them.

My gloved fingers reach the ripped flesh around the wound. I almost flinch but compose myself, trying to keep calm for him. His breathing hitches and his hands tremble over mine. "Pull it out, please," he almost cries.

I take in a deep breath and assess what I can from the entrance wound in the faded grey light.

I think through the plan in my head, then sharply inhale. "Okay, deep breath. I'm going to pull on three. Make as much sound as you want, and then it will be over," I say, letting him grip onto the gloved hand at his side.

"Okay," he barely whispers.

"Okay. One, two, three..." I close my eyes and pull as hard as I can, falling backwards onto the rocks as he wails out in pain, his voice carrying around the building.

I want to cry for him. I open my arms to discard the wooden splinter and scramble back to his side, pressing my hand against the seeping wound. He looks like he wants to push me away, but then his hands find my t-shirt and he pulls me closer, panting for breath as his limbs tremble from the shock.

"Thank you," he whispers in my ear. "Thank you, Mars. You always save me."

I want to pull him closer and kiss his crown, to hold on and never let go. But I know I can't. I can't and won't—it's not fair to touch him like that.

"Press your shirt to the wound; it should close up in no time."

I grab for the two separate, discarded ruins of fabric, and notice the shredded holes in the back, where his wings must have torn the shirt in two.

"Thank you, Mars." He sounds sleepy now, like he's about to faint.

"Stay with me, Arlo. I'm going to get you to my apartment." I'm about to place my hand around his back to help him stand as my arm brushes the soft feathers of his wings. He jerks away, his head flitting to mine.

"No," he says, his tone dark.

"What? It's not far. We can't stay here—"

"No! No, Mars. I'm not leading him anywhere that could put you in danger. He can't know anything, or he'll use it against us. I need to move on soon."

"Who's 'he'? The guy who came for you that day? Is he... Arlo, we need to move. It will just be for a night, and then we can go somewhere else in the morning."

"Not we. We can't. I need to leave."

"Why did you come here? How long have you been here?"

"I needed to—ah." He winces again at the pain in his side.

"Arlo?"

"I shouldn't have come here, I just needed, I..."

"You what, Arlo? Are you okay?"

I hear his quick intake of breath before I realise he's crying. I want to reach for his cheeks and wipe away every drop of tears. I want to, but I can't.

"Were you trying to reach out to us? To me?" I try.

"I just wanted... I don't know. Mars, I don't know what to do."

I want to burn down the world for him. Seeing and hearing him like this is torture.

He can't have been in the building long. He must have arrived after I got here. Maybe the noises were him injuring himself? But he has a bag with him, which means he's running, running from— "The Sun. Is he who you're running from?"

"What? How do you..."

So, that's it then. The Sun. That's the name he's using.

Nicholas really did predict this.

"I don't know a lot, but we're trying to find out everything we can. We're worried about you. We want to help you, Arlo. Please, come home. Stay. Tell us what you know so we can put an end to it all."

"You can't," is all he says.

"What? Of course we can, Arlo. With your help, we can—"

"You can't. He's too much. They're coming." His voice clogs up with sobs as his head droops to one side.

I look back at the wound, which has now started to thicken and seal itself. The entrance is nowhere near as big as it first appeared. He's healing.

I look at him in despair. "Arlo," I say.

"Mars."

"We can't stay out here."

"I know."

"At least let me help you into that room. Some of the roof still remains. We'll stay dry in there. We can wait for the storm to pass." I'm trying my best. I don't want him to leave my sight.

He seems reluctant at first, but then he sighs, "Okay."

Okay. We were making progress. *Stay calm, Mars.*

I stand up and head over to the room I was in earlier, ushering for Arlo to follow.

Slowly, he rises, until I can see the extent of the elegant wings on his back, expanding and stretching as he stands to full height.

"They're beautiful," I say, looking up at the angel before me. Looking at Arlo makes me question if angels really do exist. I'm not really one with religion, but these past six months have really made me reconsider things. I genuinely don't know what to believe anymore.

"They're too heavy," Arlo replies, his tone far from comical.

I say nothing else as I guide him into the room. He grabs his bag and limps behind me. He's unsteady on his feet, even with his boots on. He ducks into the room, his wings trailing behind him, and I wander over to the windowless wall to find a spot for us to sit. The thin slits between the stone allow the last slithers of light to slip in. "Here," I say, reaching with my still gloved hand to catch him from falling, despite his towering height.

"We can wait here until the weather eases, and your stomach heals." Arlo sits first, dropping his bag to the side, and stretching his long legs out before him. I join his side, but keep my distance to avoid touching him.

"Thank you," he says again.

"You never have to thank me," I reply, trying not to think about how deeply I mean it.

We'll likely freeze to death here, but I can't make him leave with me. He won't. This is the best I can get him to do. I'm just so happy to see him, to know he still lives, and that he's still himself—after everything.

"You don't happen to have anything warm in that backpack of yours, do you?" I try to humour my tone, yet shiver as my wet hair drips onto my shoulders and sodden t-shirt.

He reaches in, rummaging through the backpack, before pulling out a scarf. It's hard to tell, but it looks familiar. I think it's one of his old ones, the one he had when...

"That will have to do," I half joke, but I accept it anyway, feeling guilty *I'm* the one asking for warmth when he's here, wearing nothing but worn away trousers and battered combat boots.

The rain seems to have eased, and the light of the moon seeps through between the tree leaves and crumbling stone, kissing the side of his face in silver. I can just about make out the two moles under his right eye. His lashes hang low as his gaze falls.

"I've got these," he says; his wings flutter out, as though they have a mind of their own. His tone is lighter, almost like he's trying to make a joke. I smile in the dark, and I believe he smiles back.

Then the unexpected happens. He tells me to lie down, and as I do, I look at his face, feeling the soft feathers of his right wing land on top of me, sinking over me like a shelter. They're so warm.

They're part of him. They're real.

"I'm tired," he says, shielding his body with his left wing. His hand shuffles out until his fingers brush mine. I uncurl my hand to let him settle his in mine; the sharpness of his nails press against the glove.

I don't dare move.

I have so much I want to ask him. So much to learn to save him from his fate. But I don't. I can't find the words.

I fall asleep not long after, tucked up under the infinite expanse of his wing. The last thing I remember is the rise and fall of his chest as his breathing returns to a normal rate. Then, sleep takes me.

I awake the next morning to sunlight burning through the branches of the wall of umber. I sit up, my eyes squeezing shut against the dazzling pain. My spine aches in more than one spot and I'm confused at my surroundings for a second, but once it all comes back to me, I leap up.

I'm alone.

Of course he's gone.

Maybe he was never really there, and it was all a dream. That would make sense. Last night didn't happen.

But I see the blackened bloodstains.

I find the wooden splinter discarded in the rubble.

Arlo is alive.

And he can't have gone far.

They're coming.

CHAPTER TEN

Arlo
Three Months Ago

I'm a murderer.

And not just by accident. I killed and maimed because I enjoyed it. Because that *thing* in my head wanted it, which made *me* want it. I thought I was saving the world, making it good again by eradicating all the liars, cheaters, and evil in the world. I knew what I was doing, and I was too weak to stop it. A cruel hypocrite.

It's still there—The Star—crawling in like ivy every second I switch off and leave my mind open. It's pulling me back down every waking moment, and I'm running out of strength to stay afloat. The nights continue to torment me, making me want to crack my skull open and scoop its presence out of every crevice. Tear it apart. But I can't. It's woven into my soul. The day I died, it was planted there, and now I will forever be an immortal host for an ungodly power.

A little over a month has passed since my escape, my head a mess of turmoil and guilt. I've not stopped running. I escaped York as quickly as I could, hopping onto the first train available and letting it take me anywhere.

I spent a week roaming and hiding in Lancashire, foraging for animal blood while hiding in the shadows. I made my way further south without a true destination. The only thing on my mind was making sure *he* couldn't find me, meaning I couldn't go home or back to anyone I cared about. He always seemed to find me. I've been on watch every time I breathe.

I cannot bring myself to steal, though I could hide myself if needed. I wore the same clothes for weeks until I found ten pounds on the ground and replaced my shirt in a charity shop. I also bought a small backpack to store my findings. I killed people— hurt them, and got inside their heads—so who am I to think I deserve anything? Who am I to crave and want and *feel* after what I did?

Eventually, I found shelter in an abandoned church among the rubble of what appeared to be a former hospital in a great state of disrepair. I can hide here, undisturbed, with shelter from the weather. I should move on soon, but I'm just so tired.

When night-time comes, it waits by the door of my mind. I cry myself to sleep on the dusty, rotten pews, hopeless and afraid. I use every ounce of remaining strength to keep it at bay. I catch my reflection in shattered mirrors, and a monster stares back at me. A fallen angel, with claws as black as night, and inhuman wings protruding from my shoulder blades—sent to earth to punish and be punished. I deserve punishment for what I did and what I allowed to happen. I only wanted to save my friends. It's not a good enough excuse though, is it?

My friends. Rani. Mars. I wonder how they're coping with Ben's death. Did Rani go back to uni? Is she happy? Is Mars still painting? What about Casper? Is he okay? Does he have people with him? Marianne knew there was something inside me, yet there was nothing she could have done. Carmen knew my nature, she really knew, but no one listened to her. Why did everyone treat me like I was harmless?

I'm a murderer! A bringer of death, doing 'righteous' deeds and removing the vile scum of the earth, but I am not a god. I should not possess the power to decide who lives or dies. I am no judge or jury of humanity—I am just Arlo.

And I just want to be Arlo again. Forever.

I throw a rock at the shard of glass opposite me and thrust myself back against the ground; my back collides with the wooden pew, my wings cracking and sending a jolt of pain down my spine.

Abomination.

I'm terrified. He will find me, I know he will. He'll bring out The Star, like he always does, and I will once again do his bidding to alter the very fabric of the world.

I let him get my father, my parent by blood. I fed him back to the beast—*I* did that. My father had broken free, and I didn't listen. I'm so weak. Useless. Pathetic. Fool.

I've thought long and hard about what I'd say to my father, if I ever get to see him again. If there's a chance he's still in there, somewhere, under The Moon. I've thought about forgiving him and allowing him to tell me his side of the story. Why did he run?

Would I want him to meet my mum? Probably, though it would hurt her. But what's worse? Me *never* telling her or never seeing her again because I can't bear the thought of putting her in danger? She can't see me like this, but I don't want to hide from her. What would she do when she finds out I killed people? Manipulated them, took away their autonomy? Does it matter that they were bad people? *I'm* a bad person now.

I have no way of contacting anyone, and I must keep it that way. I just want to hear their voices again and see their smiles. I want to undo everything and start again. But that's not possible—it never will be.

I want Rani. I want Mars. I want my mum.

I want Ben back.

"I know."

I'm startled by his voice, head yanking up and looking out towards the stained-glass windows to my side. Ben stands solemnly in the fading light, wearing the same clothes he always does: a white shirt and black dress trousers. The clothes they buried him in.

This isn't the first time he's visited me. The day I gave my father back to Michael, the day before I murdered and *ate* that horrible man, he appeared vividly in a dream. Ben told me to stay calm and to never stop fighting for myself.

I didn't see him again for weeks after that, until he started appearing nearly every day, sitting in café windows, waiting at bus stops, looking for me. He's spoken to me a handful of times and always says the same thing. To keep fighting.

I know it's all in my head, but he's the only person I have right now. I need his company, no matter how fictitious he may be.

"You need to stop throwing things. Someone is going to hear," he says jokingly, crossing over to sit beside me in the rubble.

I turn to look at his face. While he never looks at me directly, I know he's listening. I take in his *realness*—how whole and weighted his body is. He's so close to me I can feel his breath and the heat of his skin. *Like he's alive.*

"I never meant for any of this to happen," I tell him honestly. It's not like he's real.

"I know that too." Ben has little moles on his neck like me that I'd never noticed before. Maybe I'm just hallucinating, making all of this up—seeing what I want to see.

"I can't ever show my face to them again. They'll want nothing to do with me after they find out what I've done," I say, tucking my legs in.

"I don't think that's true, Arlo. They know it's not you; they all know the real you." Ben promises, his voice as calm and kind as always. *I wish you were real.*

"But I still did it. I gave in. I let it take over."

"But so would any of us. It was too powerful for any of us to overcome! I saw how strong you were at defending your mental guards. This has nothing to do with giving in," Ben assures me. His face tilts to almost face me now, a smile of pity settling into his gentle face. A fleeting image: Ben in front of the church in the forest, his eyes tightly bandaged, his fingers snapped and torn, fresh scars on his body.

"Stop thinking about me that way." He turns his head, facing away from me now.

"Sorry," I say, looking straight ahead in shame.

The church breathes for a moment, then I feel his eyes on me again. I know if I turn, he'll look away, so I stay facing forward.

After a moment of silence, Ben says, "I let Lucy inside my head. I thought I was too weak."

"You weren't weak, Ben." *How dare he think that?*

"And neither are you. Arlo."

"But I am. I became a monster; I let it happen very easily."

"Stop it, Arlo. The monster took your mind, but look at you now! You broke free. After all you did, and how far gone you thought you were, you fought back, and now look at you! You're feeling guilt and fear, and you're *crying*! This is the most human you could ever be! You're winning!"

"I don't think I know how to truly win this." My words slip out.

"You do. I know you do." Ben smiles when I look at him, though I'm lost for words. My throat closes up, and tears well in the corners of my eyes.

We sit in the quiet church walls for a long time. I'm just happy he's with me, and I'm not alone. He's breathing and living. Existing. *He's not real, Arlo. He died months ago; you watched it happen. His insides spilled out onto the grass and mud; his neck was severed and his heart slashed in two.*

"Please, for the love of god, Arlo. Will you stop picturing me that way? It's really off-putting." He's in my head. "I don't want to be remembered that way. Please." Ben's tone shifts to one of embarrassment and shame. *I'm sorry, Ben.*

"It's hard to stop," I admit.

"I know, but surely you remember nicer things about me? I know we didn't know each other long, but hopefully I was a little bit more interesting than a gutted corpse."

"You were."

"Good. I'm pleased to know that."

You were amazing. I was so jealous of your talent and your love for other people. I wished I could be as cool as you and as caring. I wished we could have played piano together, and I wish I could remember the name of the bands you recommended.

"Clan of Xymox. They were my favourite."

I'm crying.

"They're probably not your style, so don't worry about remembering that name. I was just excited to finally have someone else to annoy with my interests." Ben laughs a little, but there's a sad lilt to his voice.

I smile at him, holding back tears. "I promise I will."

Ben shakes his head. "And if I could, I'd read those books you gave me. Maybe you could read them to me some time. Once this is all over."

"You think this will end?"

"Oh, I know it will. And you'll be the one to do it."

I have no idea how he can be so absurdly optimistic, but I desperately hope he's right.

"You were amazing."

A smirk crosses Ben's face, but I can't figure out what's funny. "That's a bold statement. I didn't do much in life—I didn't change the world or anything—but thanks for the ego boost."

My chest aches. I don't want him to ever leave my side. I dread going to sleep, terrified he'll be gone when I wake up. I need him because he is the only person who won't judge me for what I did, because he's dead. And I let that happen. I wasn't quick enough; I gave up. I thought I was doing all of this for him. But he's told me time and time again he doesn't blame me for anything, and though I know it's just my mind talking, I'm starting to believe him.

I drift off, and in my dream, Ben is on stage performing my favourite song of theirs with the band. He glances back to grin at Casper, and then winks at Lawrence and Francesca, before waving down at me in the front row. Rani and Mars are by my side, beaming with excitement, and for the first time in over a month, The Star doesn't come.

CHAPTER ELEVEN

Arlo
Two Months Ago

I was on the run again the morning after I spoke to Ben. I had stayed in one place for too long, making myself an easy target. Michael is looking for me—I know it. Maybe our entities are more connected than I first thought.

Somewhere in the west of the country, I stood on a train platform, with just a worn backpack holding a handful of clothing I'd gathered over the weeks. It had been a few days since my last shower, which I'd taken at a 24-hour gym I found. It's difficult removing clothes now I have my wings. I felt dirty, but then again, I always did. Maybe it wasn't just to do with my hygiene concerns. My soul was dirty.

The next morning, I arrived in Manchester. Casper had once said this was where Lawrence was from, who had been homeless for a time here. I rather stubbornly thought that if he could do it, then so could I.

I made sure to stay out of the city centre to lower the likelihood of being spotted, I'm not exactly a small person anyway, but sometimes the Star's power overwhelms me, causing me to lose control of my Manipulation and attract weird looks from strangers. I could maybe pass the wings off as a costume, but the attention alone makes me uncomfortable.

A week or so has passed since then, and I'm now standing in a doorway somewhere in the Peak District, I believe. It's raining, and I'm freezing cold. I don't know how much longer I can do this for.

I've been thinking about contacting Casper to see how he is. I don't know whether he'll want to see me, and I would understand if he didn't, but I don't think he's with the others, and it's worrying me. I'd never seen two people more deeply in love than Casper and Ben.

Then I think about contacting Mars, but I know they would be with the Thorns, and I can't risk hurting anyone else.

I'll keep Rani and my mum out of this as much as I can. I will die before I let anything so much as touch them.

But then my head splits, and I fall to my knees. The Star.

Come on. Give up. Are you not tired yet?

I can't let it in. I can't.

"Excuse me, mate, you got a lighter?"

Stunned, I stand as a man approaches, his hood large enough to cover his face.

I shake my head and turn away slightly, but he stops and looks up. At first, I think he can see past the illusion, recognising the devil underneath, but then his eyes fall. "You alright, mate? You need some money?"

Yes. Please. Help me.

Let go.

My hands clench into fists and my claws pierce into the flesh of my palms, drawing blood.

"You on drugs or something, mate? You need help?" The man persists, and my head is on the verge of exploding.

Let. Go.

I cry out. It's all too loud. My legs buckle, and I slump in the doorway, yet the man is quick to dive and break my fall.

Strange arms hold me. Cold hands. Burning every inch of me. He grabs the back of my head to lift me up, while his other hand brushes the overgrown fringe from my sticky forehead. Too many sensations. I need new skin.

"Hang in there, mate. What have you taken?" He pulls my arms out and rubs his fingers over the crooks before checking for my pulse; his fingernails brushing over my neck and wrists. I've run out of energy to squirm away. My mind is aflame.

"I'm gonna call an ambulance, okay? You hear me? Just hang in there, mate." Then to himself, he mutters, "Kid's gonna die."

He's frantically grabbing at his pockets for his phone as I slip out of consciousness, breathing desperately, but when he lets go, the last thing I see are his eyes growing wide. He stumbles back in sheer fear, his phone clattering to the ground. I don't hear him fully, but I think his lips mumble one word—*devil.*

I come around slowly, blinking hard before I can make out my surroundings. I'm in someone's living room: a heavily decorated, Victorian-inspired drawing room more like. Porcelain ornaments clutter the room. Heavy, floral-laced curtains, tied back with bows, reveal the warped, leaded windows overlooking the inky blackness outside. The living space of an eccentric recluse, perhaps. I don't panic yet, though. I'm still too exhausted. I glance below me. I'm sitting on a deep leather chair, my arms outstretched against the uncomfortable fabric. I jolt them away in discomfort, and the sticky leather material squeaks as my skin peels from it. Shivers rush down my spine, my wings aching.

Despite the weather, there's a fire on, and there's a Persian rug on the floor beside it.

I look up and notice the figure opposite me; her eyes are glued to me intently as a grin forms across her face. Her wiry grey hair is tied loosely behind her, cascading in waves over her shoulders, and resting against a crimson silk robe. Her heart beats slow and steady. A human.

Shit.

I go to stand, but a rope binds my ankles together, knocking me back into the chair with a slump. I'm trapped.

"Don't be afraid, my angel. I am blessed to be in your presence." Her voice is high-pitched but delicate, like something from a fairy-tale, a wise old grandmother in a secluded cottage. Perhaps I'm dreaming again.

I go to speak, but I choke instead. The Star lies dormant, tormenting my control. I sense it laughing at how I'm barely able to stay conscious.

The stranger continues to stare, her gaze wandering across my whole body in what seems like admiration.

"I apologise for binding your feet. I feared you would leave before I could speak with you. I will pray to Our Father for forgiveness, but I am sure He will understand. It is not common for a human to have the privilege of saving a child of God."

I'm not an angel. I try to speak, but The Star seems to find this amusing. I barely make a sound when my mouth opens.

"I hope you don't mind but I washed your torso and redressed you in nicer clothes. You have been through a struggle, have you not?" The stranger continues, stirring the spoon in her China teacup.

I thought my body felt different. I look down at the plain white shirt I'm in, freshly washed and ironed. My trousers are the same, as are my boots. The thought of a stranger touching my body at all makes me want to vomit. *I need new skin.*

"I must say, it was most unexpected to learn you do not possess a heart. I thought I would be able to sense its divine beating, the purest gift from the Lord, but it appears you are designed differently. May I ask how you breathe?"

I want to scream. I need to get out of here.

"Where's my bag?" I manage to ask.

The stranger's face falls. I didn't answer her question. I wasn't planning on it, anyway. *Why am I still breathing?*

"Your bag is by your feet. Please don't leave me yet." A plea enters her voice.

"Let me go," I demand. The Manipulation drips from the tip of my tongue.

The stranger stands too quickly and steps over to unwrap the rope from my feet.

I feel too weak to stand again, paralysed by the buzz of all these sensations. All I know is I need to get out of here—fast—and I need to erase her memories.

Hungry.

I scream. The stranger jumps back, and the rope falls to the ground. She backs into her chair and falls to her knees. But it is not fear etched across her features, but a look of astonishment. She's in awe.

"Beautiful. Beautiful." She sounds as though she's about to cry.

The Star bites down on my control once more, urging me to feast on her. But I can't. I won't. I squeeze my eyes shut.

Something else washes over me then, a cool wave of release. I open my eyes and there, standing beside the stranger, who is still on her knees, is Ben.

You're saving me. Even though I couldn't save you. Why, Ben? Why?

"Breathe," he says. The woman does not react, proving he really is just in my head.

I look up at him. His gaze is ever so slightly angled away from my eyes. "I can't."

The woman's eyes widen. "The Lord! You are conversing with Him!"

Ben's face morphs into one of pity. "I'm definitely not The

Lord," he says; his tense brow loosens, and his frown turns into a slight grin.

"Please," the woman looks at the space where Ben is standing, though I know she can't see anything. She isn't looking at his face when she begs, "Please, Lord. Forgive me for forcing your messenger to stay. I only need to know one thing. I need to know if my son is safe with you. My Percy. My dear baby boy." She's on her hands and knees now, and Ben looks down with a stunned expression, mirroring mine.

"She's lonely," Ben observes. He looks back at me.

I think of his mother, who I never met properly. I recall the way she fell to her knees in the cemetery, clutching onto her Rosary. The pain she carried with her as she wept the loss of her only child. This woman is hurting. She means no harm. She's alone and grieving. Now, I feel guilty that I can't answer her question.

"Please," she begs, practically kissing the carpet at Ben's feet.

I can't stop thinking of Ben's mother now.

"He's safe," I say, wholly myself. Ben's face snaps up in shock, and slowly, the woman turns to face me, her eyes red. She takes her time to process my words.

I didn't want to lie. I don't know if God is real or not, or if there's a place after death. I don't want to confirm something I have no way of knowing, but this woman has already seen my wings, my hands; she has already concluded what I am, and it feels better than Manipulating her. Maybe I could get away with leaving her to remember me. I don't know if I'd be strong enough to work on her mind that deeply, anyway.

"He's safe, and he's loved." I look at Ben as I say these words. He looks me dead on for a split second, his green eyes glassy.

"Oh, my boy," the woman begins to cry again. I worry I took it too far.

"Thank you, thank you, thank you," she says repeatedly,

coming to a stand. I stand too, towering over her. She looks up at me with sincere gratitude.

"Thank you, my angel."

I flinch at the term, but The Star is once again at bay, and I can see clearly. "Thank you for looking after me." I smile.

"Please stay. Just for a while longer," she asks.

I must leave, but I no longer feel like I'm in a hostile environment. I know I'm safe here, for now.

"Okay." I decide.

Out of the corner of my eye, Ben walks away into the kitchen —I don't get to see his face.

The lady lets me sleep in her guest room and moves the bed away from the wall to make room for my wings. It's small, and just as overly decorated as the living room. Cobwebs hang from the fringed lampshade, but it will do. I'll be safe tonight. While I'm not religious, this woman's faith and devotion brings me a sense of comfort I haven't known in ages.

She leaves me to settle for the night and says she will be sleeping just down the hall if I need anything. She continues to thank me, and never asks more of me. She's just grateful her prayer has been answered.

I do let the thought linger, though, as I turn off the light and sit on the edge of the bed. What gave me the right to pretend to possess such power? Who do think I am?

Then the air fills beside me, and the mattress dips as an extra weight joins me on the bed.

Ben.

I squint as he speaks. "I wouldn't have agreed with what you just did when I was alive, but I understand why you did it. You've helped that woman a great deal. I know my mum would..." his voice fades, leaving his sentence unfinished. I open my eyes to the darkness, making out his features in the dim light.

"Ben?" I need to make sure he's still there.

He doesn't speak, but I can still sense his presence. "Ben?" I call out again, my hands wandering to where I think his right leg is. My fingers meet the bottom of the duvet, and my chest constricts. "Come back, please," I mumble into the dark, a plea into the void. I grip the covers with might, my nails almost tearing through the fabric.

Nothing happens.

"Please." *I need you,* I almost whisper, but I shouldn't waste my breath. I know he's not there.

THE NEXT MORNING, I wake much later than I'd hoped. A kettle squeals on the hob downstairs.

I stand, suddenly aware of my hunger. I have not fed in almost twenty-four hours. While I can last a lot longer than I used to be able to, I know I must feed in the next few hours. My stomach growls, and a headache forms behind my brows. The Star, however, stays silent. *How?*

I struggle down the stairs and assess the front door. I could leave; I could feed then return. I could—

"There you are, dear. Are you well rested?" The woman's gentile voice travels out from the kitchen and into the living room, where I stand near the door. She is holding a cup of tea, and I realise it's for me. "I'm sorry if I woke you, but it's almost noon!" She smiles and gestures for me to take the cup and saucer.

I can last a few more hours, I suppose.

I let her lead me into the kitchen; the old cottage doorway is too low for my height, so I duck slightly to fit inside. It only adds to my otherness, and I try not to dwell on it. At least I can relax my mind here. I don't need to focus on pretending or anything. She sees my true form, and she's not afraid.

She doesn't know what I've done, though. I shudder at the thoughts.

"Did you sleep well?" she asks.

I nod and sip my tea.

"Would you like anything to eat?" She's analysing me again. "Do God's messengers need to consume mortal food?"

"No, thank you. Sorry." I don't really know how to respond.

"Is there anything I can do?" She continues to ask me questions to ensure my comfort, though I do not like being treated so delicately.

With a prolonged silence and an empty teacup, only one request comes to me. I made up my mind last night while lying alone in the dark. I know what I must do next.

I ask to use her computer.

"Why, of course! Do what you must!" I think she's still too stunned by my existence to ponder the fact a winged creature with claws is requesting the use of her electronic devices, but I'm grateful for her lack of questions on that matter.

I load up the ancient brick of a desktop in the corner of her living room and begin searching.

I need to contact Casper.

I thought about it all night, ever since Ben disappeared. I need to speak with Casper. I need to see him and ground myself. I need to talk about Ben. I need to *know* him.

I know he travelled home after the funeral; he left before the wake to catch the quickest flight he could. Even if he's not there now, I can reach his brother to ask.

I search up record stores in Alexandria, Louisiana. I even search nearby cities just in case. I remembered Casper mentioning Jesse worked in one, so I note down all the phone numbers, and then search my bag for all the loose change I collected. I have enough for three calls from a phone booth. I jot down four contact numbers on the inside cover of the book in my bag.

Then my stomach growls, louder this time, and my vision blurs.

I need to go. *Now.*

I grab my bag, and then I'm out of the door and down the street without looking back. An apology on the tip of my tongue.

I never even caught her name.

I RUN to the closest patch of greenery and feed on whatever I find first. I'm remote enough to know I've not been followed, but the hills are so *open*. I always try to block out the details of my animal catches. I'm not proud of them, but I must feed. I can't afford to lose myself again. I need to stay afloat.

Once I figure it's late enough in the day to contact the other side of the world, I find the nearest working phone booth and try to figure out which store to try first. If my heart still worked, it would have been in my throat. I need just that one pinch of luck. I need this plan to work.

I dial the number of the first store. It rings three times before a sweet and heavily accented voice answers. Clinging to the phone with trembling hands, I ask if Jesse Murphey works there, and after a very brief pause, the voice tells me they don't know the name.

My hands are clammy as I enter my next few coins. *Please be the right one.*

The second call rings five times before it's answered; a deep voice picks up this time. "Good morning, Carter's Records. Gene Carter speaking, how can I help you?"

I forget to speak for a moment, then after the second hello, I ask for Jesse. The wait is excruciating.

"You wanna speak to Jesse? Sure, give me a second."

I can't believe my luck. My stomach flips.

Now comes the hard part.

"Hello, Jesse speaking."

I'm going to vomit. He sounds so much like Casper. It's definitely him.

"Erm, hi. I..." *Speak, Arlo. This can't be all for nothing.*

"Hello? Who is this?" Jesse's voice grows more stern.

"My name is Arlo, I need—"

"Arlo? Casper's friend?"

Casper's friend? He's mentioned me? Jesse knows who I am?

"Yeah," I say hesitantly.

"Oh my god. Arlo? Where are you?" He sounds overly concerned, like he's been looking for me... *oh.*

"I need to speak to Casper," I go for it. I can't waste any more time.

"God, sure. You need his number? He just left a few days ago, he's gone back to Durham. Are you in Durham? Are you..." His voice muffles for a few seconds, and I think I've lost contact, but then he returns; a piece of paper crinkles in the background. "I'll get his number. Please let him know where you are as soon as you can, he won't stop talking about you."

I'm lost for words. All I can say is thank you.

"Don't thank me, I'm just glad you're alive. Hell, I've never even met you, kid, but you must be important to him if your name is the only one he's mentioned besides the band. He's not himself, but... sorry. I'll let him talk to you. I'm just so relieved."

I hang up after he gives me the number. I can't bear to listen anymore. It's too much. I don't deserve this concern. I was stupid not to contact any of them sooner. The second I ran away, I should have gone straight to them. I...

I couldn't risk it though, could I? I can't bring Michael to them again...

I use my last coins to call the final number, taking extra care to make sure I dial correctly.

The phone rings and rings. It's going to cut out. It's not going to work. I've wasted all this time for nothing...

"Hello?"

Casper.

"Hello? Who is this? If this is another prank call, I'll report—"

"Casper."

He goes silent.

"It's me, Arlo. I need to meet with you."

21st November 1856

I cannot believe the situation I have been blessed with.

I should have written more to document the week I have had, as it has truly been a delight, though I do not believe I would have had enough paper.

Jerome intrigued me from the start, of course, and though my initial doubts in his morals were valid, I truly do believe finding me saved him. Will continue to save him.

We talked and talked about our lives, sharing more and more over the days as we grew closer and I feel like I can breathe again.

We are going to leave. Leave the house, move away.

Live! Ha!

I do not want to leave the children, but Jerome helped me understand it would be for best. They will always be safe.

17th February 2019

~~Jerome.~~

~~Oh, Jerome. Who are you?~~

18th February 2019

~~Let's try this again.~~

~~What do I remember about you? Before you became who you are now?~~

~~Have you changed at all?~~

~~I should have killed you when I had the chance.~~

19th February 2019

~~We had a good life, didn't we? What we did?~~

~~Why did it end that way? What did I ever do to make you think that was the only option?~~

~~Why, Jerome?~~

~~Urgh. What am I doing?~~

25th February 2019

We pretended to be siblings, remember? We spent a decade building up our fabricated life. Decided on our entire story and helped each other along the way. I kept your morals straight, and you allowed me to grow more comfortable with myself. Before long, I'd practically forgotten all about my previous life, because we were moving forward. Living for our futures. All I wanted then was what we'd invented.
I liked our little life. We opened businesses for the working class, opened a food bank, travelled the country striking deals with businessmen. We shot our way through society. Sure, it wasn't all fine and dandy, but we managed! I was able to put my Manipulation to good use to keep myself safe, and not just as a vampire, but as a woman in a man's world. You never spoke for me or took control, we were in it together, and it worked so perfectly. You'd been around a lot longer than me and were left to your own devices for far too long. You'd been on track to losing your humanity, but you told me I'd helped you. When you said we were unstoppable together, I believed you.
Why did that change, Jerome?
What did he do to deserve what you did?
What did I do?
~~*Jerome? Please. I need to understand.*~~

9th March 2019

~~*Why did I leave those children?*~~
~~*Why did I ever listen to you?*~~
~~*Was it all an act from the beginning?*~~

—Taken from the diaries of Marianne Ashtown.

CHAPTER TWELVE

Mars
Now

I don't bother going home. It's past noon, and there's no more time to waste. I'm aware I look like I've just crawled out of a cave—*thank you strangers for your excessively prolonged stares*. I'm walking through the city centre, looking like I just escaped a plane crash in the Amazon, with only one destination in mind. If I can reach Marianne before anyone else to tell her what happened, I know she'll believe me. Anyone else, bar Rani, would just laugh in my face. Or worse, they'll tell me to get lost. I know what the remaining people think about Arlo.

After narrowly escaping an 'are you okay, darling? Can I help you?' comment from an old bloke, I make it to the hideout and barge through the corridors into Marianne's office. It's empty. But I notice the coffee on her desk, steam still emanating from it—meaning she can't be far. The hall, maybe?

I don't pass anyone on the way there—I never do these days—but the closer I get, the more a feeling develops that I may not be entirely alone. I can hear voices, raised tones mixed with mumbles, and as I round the corner, I note the door is wide open, and...

Oh, *fuck.*

"Where the bloody hell have you been?" Lawrence shouts towards the door. I stand still, taking in the scene before me. I couldn't have run if I tried. There, in the centre of the room, stands Marianne, with Rani, Carmen, Lawrence and Francesca forming a circle around her. They're all staring at *me.*

"Hi," I say. It's the only word I can think of.

Lawrence storms over to me, his skirts billowing behind him. "We've been trying to reach you all morning. Your phone kept going straight to voice mail, so I went to your apartment, and you weren't there, but the flaming door wasn't even locked! What the heck have you been up to? You look like shit." He gives me a once over then grabs my arm, though not aggressively. He rubs at the dirt, possibly checking they aren't wounds. Lawrence looks worried, and I flinch at the intimate gesture. The whole room still has their eyes pinned on me.

"I was out." I'll get to the truth eventually, but I'd like to settle into the group first. I've clearly missed something important.

"Out," Lawrence repeats quietly, like he's already given up.

"Well, at least you're here now," Marianne pipes up and indicates for us to join the group.

"What did I miss?" I try to stay calm and settle my thoughts about last night.

"Marianne brought us all together so we can start looking for Arlo and the entities," Rani says. She seems pretty calm, with Carmen close by her side, giving me the evils. She's always so tense. It's easy to forget I've known her since she was ten years old —she always seems to be stirring up a storm or something. I know she hates Arlo, and by process of elimination, I deduce she's only here to support Rani. Great girlfriend, but terrible resting face.

I'm being unfair. She's been through a lot, and has every right not to trust nor like Arlo. I just wish she'd stop staring at me like I just ran over her pet cat.

I take it Marianne returned her memories then.

"Since we established we're going to need a lot more force on our side, I brought everyone together so we have a bit more hope at executing a plan," Marianne continues, gesturing towards us all. All *five* of us.

"This is all you could get? Three humans, and a..." I'm about to insult Lawrence, but I stop, absorbing everyone's shocked expressions. "Him," I finish. I'm so disorientated and stressed; I didn't mean for it to come out quite like that. "No offence, I just..."

"None taken." Fran shrugs. "I don't really know what's going on; I'm just gonna be the guy in the chair."

"This is all I could get. No one else responded. I couldn't get hold of Casper—" Marianne's voice strains at his name.

Oh. There really was so very few people who cared about Arlo.

"But what about what your brother predicted?" I ask, pausing briefly before I accidentally announce her secret. But then I think, *fuck it*. Secrets will get us nowhere at this stage, and it turns out, she's already divulged this information with the room anyway.

"Ahh yes, the secret unhinged sibling no one knew existed. Sounds familiar, doesn't it?" There's malice in Lawrence's voice as he speaks. He does have a point though, despite Marianne not having had the ability to remember what happened with him, let alone make us aware of him.

"If I'd been allowed to remember, I would have told you all," she says. I wasn't expecting her to be so blunt, but I guess we've passed the point of pretences. "I believe my brother most likely died well before any of you were born, even before your grandparents, and great-grandparents for that matter. I needed to pull together all my memories and lay them out in order before I started spouting theories. I needed to be sure of his claims. And now I am." She doesn't even take a breath, yet her gaze is sincere.

Fran and Rani nod along with her, while Carmen's face is stoic as usual. I can't read her, and her heart gives nothing away.

Marianne continues, "I try to forget a lot about my past all the time—to live in the present. I believe it's the only way to survive immortality. While these memories were taken from me, they probably would have driven me insane eventually. I've been around a very long time, and I've done a lot of things I'm not proud of. I've made mistakes, losing more people than you can imagine, but now, I need you all to trust me so we can work together to stop all of this." She takes a deep breath and I notice how intently everyone is listening.

I trust you, Marianne, I want to say, but I hold my tongue.

"I've been under some sort of Manipulation from one of these beings. This person entered my life decades ago, and for all I know, he's been controlling me since then. Meaning the plan, however they intend to execute it, has been set in motion for a while."

"That person or creature wanted you to see him that day." Rani asserts, the thought clearly at the front of her mind. Carmen sighs quietly.

Marianne shrugs a little. "It worries me how far ahead they could already be because of that. However, I believe I have all my memories back now, and my brother's insane ramblings have helped me in my attempts to figure out what these creatures want and when they're going to act."

She feels like our leader again. Even more so now than before. Her honesty rings out across the room.

"We don't have time to argue about morals. Nicholas predicted the end of the world as we know it, so yes, it may seem pathetic that only a handful of us are willing to do something, but a lot of The Thorns are very afraid right now. I'll work on them, but for now, we need to get started. No more waiting around."

Everyone stays silent. Sod it.

"I was with Arlo last night," I say.

No one opens their mouths. Then Lawrence scowls. "You *what*?"

I look at him, then everyone else, worry weaving into my features. "I saw Arlo. In the flesh. Not a dream, not a hallucination. I went back to the church, and he was there." I almost choke on the words.

"He's here?" Rani asks, her eyes wide as she stands.

I nod and suck in my lips. "He *was*."

"But he's not anymore?" Carmen questions sharply.

I shake my head. "I don't think so."

"With all due respect, Mars—*why*?" Lawrence's brow is still contorted, and his question holds a thousand meanings. So, I try to answer them all.

"I went back to the church because I wanted to find more clues. I was there for a while, then I heard noises and went to investigate. He was injured and alone, but it was him—the real Arlo." *Don't cry, Mars. Keep it together.* "I don't know if he followed me or whether it was a pure, wild coincidence. But I spoke to him, and he's frightened. He's running from The Sun—that's what he calls it—and he refused to come back because he was worried The Sun would be following close by. He was gone by the morning. I came straight here to tell you." I direct the last part at Marianne, whose expression is indistinguishable.

No one speaks again, and it's excruciating.

Then Carmen says, "You know, Mars, if you were anyone else, I'd recommend my therapist. But I believe you." I want to say her face is kind, but I'm still on edge when she looks at me.

"I believe you too," Rani agrees, nodding intently. She throws me a look of understanding.

"Me too," Fran adds. "Though I'm still very confused about most of this. I really do try to keep out of this world."

My eyes flick between Marianne and Lawrence, waiting for them to speak. I refuse to feel relief until they react.

"Do you think he'll come back?" Marianne asks, as if I'm the most knowledgeable one out of all of us. *I suppose I am at this point.*

"I don't know. I don't think he'll risk it. He was after something, but he couldn't tell me what. But he looked like he'd been on the run for months. He was terrified."

"We need to go to him then, don't we?" Lawrence finally speaks. He looks at me solemnly, and for the first time in a while, I'm reminded of how young he seems sometimes.

All I do is nod.

⁂

IT'S NOT long before we're back in Marianne's office, getting somewhat comfy on various parts of furniture dotted around the space. Nobody is really themselves right now, but I think it will be a long time before any of us return to normal. Everything is changing.

I'm just glad everyone believed me.

"I've put the letter from Lucy through every test I can think of and I still can't decipher what it said, but because of that, I believe it indicated something about the entities. This is one of my only leads, and it still might get us nowhere." Marianne waves the paper above her head in defeat.

"I was going to attempt reading it, but I can't even protect myself from you lot half the time, so my input is useless." Lawrence shrugs, sinking back into his chair.

Fran sits staring into space. I only look at her for a second before turning my attention back to Marianne. "You know who The Sun is now. Have you managed to get hold of any CCTV footage or anything? Sometimes we make slip ups with our disguises."

"The Sun isn't a vampire, or at least he wasn't when I met him.

I don't know what these entities have in common with us other than Manipulation, but I'd put good money on them being way more powerful than any of our kind can even fathom. He got into my head without me even realising—"

I blink a few times in her direction.

"Sorry, yes. I checked as much CCTV as I could from the area. The feather is our best lead, though it's relatively nothing. Planted to mess with us, I reckon."

"But we're in agreement the three entities will unite to cause some sort of change in the world, possibly something to do with mind control or whatever you like to call it. *Manipulation*." Rani starts to pick her lip as she speaks.

"I think they want to control us all and make the world some sort of perfect paradise. It makes sense, based off what Nicholas would hint at."

"Like an apocalypse?" Carmen suggests.

"A mind apocalypse. The end of autonomy as we know it."

"Well *shit*." Carmen grimaces.

"So, let me get this straight." Lawrence tilts his head in contemplation. "You met this mysterious guy at a festival in the sixties, completely forgot about him, and then saw him again that day reaching for Arlo's hand before disappearing into the aether with him?"

"I believe I did, yes." She doesn't bite at his bitterness.

"Jerome met him too," Rani adds, her voice soft.

"Yes." Marianne avoids eye contact with us. "He did."

"So, this *has* been in the works for decades," I confirm Marianne's earlier statement, just to make sure we're all on the same page.

"Can I have a look at the letter?" Fran pipes up suddenly, shocking and confusing us all, derailing the conversation.

"What, this one?" Marianne holds up the sheet again, and Fran nods subtly.

"Us humans can't even read it as a letter, Fran. I don't know why—" Carmen is cut off as Fran stands.

"Can I please just read it?"

Marianne shrugs in defeat and passes it over. Francesca holds it close, skimming the page. We all watch in silence as she reads.

That's not a grocery list.

"Well?" Lawrence's tone is patronising as he crosses one leg over the other and angles himself to face her, chin in his palm.

"The Sun is called Michael, and he's working with The Moon to enact his plans. Arlo is the final puzzle piece. Lucy didn't seem to have a clue what Michael was actually doing. She just knows his name, I think—well, *knew* his name, ha. Bitch. Good riddance."

You could hear a pin drop.

"What the fuck." Lawrence snatches the sheet from Fran's hands and tries to read it again; his fists crumple the sides as he realises none of what Fran just said is in his version. "What the actual fuck, Fran? Why did you make up some bullshit? You know how serious this is? God, I can't believe you—"

I'm watching Fran's face as Lawrence shouts, as is Marianne. We're thinking the same thing—I know it.

Fran just read the real letter.

For whatever reason, she is immune to this Manipulation.

What if...

Marianne clenches her jaw then a pungent smell follows. Carmen and Rani both look at their watches and phones simultaneously while Francesca keeps her eyes fixed to our leader. Even I reach for my phone to tell her the time before pausing. Marianne used a really strong piece of her mind for that, yet Fran didn't even flinch.

"What... the... fuck." Realisation strikes Lawrence moments after me. His eyes widen as he slowly looks back up at Fran, who is just sat there chewing loose skin from her lip.

"You weren't making that up," he says, though it's not a question.

Fran shakes her head, then turns to Marianne. "I'm sorry. I should have told you sooner. I was only ever about eighty percent sure anyway. I just thought I'd test it..."

Carmen and Rani look a bit lost, but they'll catch on in three, two, one...

"Are you really human?" Carmen shouts across the room.

"She is." Marianne answers before Fran can open her mouth to reply. I can almost see the whirring mechanisms in our leader's mind.

"Have you always..." Lawrence's question trails off, as if realising he has no idea what to ask.

"I used to think it was ever since you tried to turn me," Fran's voice is soft as she addresses Lawrence.

"You did what?" Carmen and Rani ask almost together; their questions vary slightly, but the premise is the same.

I remember the incident. It was about five years ago. Ben and Casper came banging on my door early one morning with Francesca by their side. She had a small bite wound on her neck. Lawrence had tried to bite and drink from her, and she knocked him out before running to the couple for answers. They had no choice but to tell her. The three of them went back to Lawrence's apartment and saw him sitting in a bloody sheet, with blood dripping from his hairline. He apologised and promised he'd never do anything like that again. In fact, Casper even said he looked afraid. But Fran didn't blame him for long. His long-standing fear of Marianne proved he wouldn't repeat such a mistake. Not after what he'd seen her do to The Turned all those years ago. He's only just about gotten over not being able to relax when in the same room as her.

"It was a long time ago; I didn't mean to." Lawrence leans forward, holding up his hands in surrender. Marianne knows of this incident, but he still avoids eye contact with her. "You think that made you immune?" His tone turns serious towards Francesca, who shrugs.

"I *did*, but it's hard to compare it with anything. Before, I never would have known if I was being controlled. I sometimes thought you three were hiding something and grew suspicious of things you got up to without me, but I brushed them off as drink or drug-related, or god knows what else. I never let it concern me." Fran shrugs again, sighing. "It was only after I joined this world that I slowly came to realise I wasn't acting the same as humans. When I observed you and Casper and Ben, I could tell when something felt off. Then earlier this year when you all went looking for Lucy and Ben, none of you told me what you were doing, so I couldn't follow you, but when you came back and told me what happened, Marianne looked me dead in the eyes and told me Ben just *died*. I knew she was lying, but I was too stunned to question it. But it got me thinking about what I'd seen before." She looks up at Marianne, a tear glinting in her left eye. "I know he didn't just *die*. None of you will tell me what really happened, but I think knowing you lied to me makes it worse. I've been a part of your world for years, whether you like it or not. I deserved to at least know what killed my best friend."

"I'm so sorry, Francesca." Marianne sinks into her chair, pain tainting her features.

Fran doesn't seem to listen. "It's a virus, right? An infection? A parasite? Well, what if I'm just immune? What if I'm one of those unlucky few who just can't be affected? That's possible, right? It's still science... biology? I wish I wasn't immune; it would make life so much easier to live in ignorance of the horrors happening around me, but hey! Life goes on, doesn't it?" Fran throws out her arms and tries not to cry. I can sense it—her heart is erratic.

"Fran, please. I..."

"I know, I know. I know you wanted to protect us. You would never have known I couldn't be lied to that way. You were doing what you thought was right, like a mother would." Fran doesn't look resentful, though she seems exhausted suddenly.

"I saw his body," Lawrence adds, staring into the void. "It

wasn't pretty. You really don't deserve the memory of it." His voice cracks as his eyes fixate on the stone floor.

"You are a good person, Marianne," Rani adds, breaking the silence. "We hate that you hide things from us, and we might never forgive you for things, but we know you care about us."

Carmen nods, almost imperceptibly.

"I hate it." Marianne finally says. "I've spent so long avoiding humans, and now I've got you three brilliant, *brilliant* women, and I hate that I have to lie and hide from you—to use you."

"We know," Carmen says.

"I've lied so much to protect everyone, and it's not like I enjoy it."

"We know, honestly. It's okay," Fran pipes up.

Marianne pulls open her top desk drawer and throws a phone across the table. The lock screen flashes, and I immediately recognise it as Arlo's phone. *Why does she...*

"Help me with this then, please," Marianne says.

"What's—" Carmen is cut off.

"I've had it since February. I've been using it to message and update his mother to keep her from worrying. But I'm running out of things to say now. I cleared out his room last month and stored everything up for him; that's where I got the letter. It felt cruel to go through his things, but I needed... He promised her he'd be back by August. *I* promised he'd be back by August. I can't keep extending this made-up trip, and it's eating me up. What do I tell her?"

"He'll be back by August," I say. I talk quickly to avoid overthinking my fury about her entering his room and taking his belongings, his private things.

Stop it, Mars. She's being honest with you all still. Take it. His room needed clearing out regardless.

"Can you really be sure of that?" Marianne asks; her eyes search mine, as though trying to read my thoughts. I know everyone else is thinking the same as her.

"He wants to see us; we want to find him. Now we're aware of that, it's only a matter of time. He can't be far."

"And if Michael finds him first?" asks Fran.

"He won't." I'm not so sure about this, but I don't let that show in my tone.

"Mars, please. We're out of our depth." Rani moves away from her girlfriend and joins my side, locking eyes with me. "What did he say to you? When you saw him, what did he say?"

"Not much, but enough." I straighten, trying to maintain my confidence. "For one thing, I know he wasn't under control. He's managed to free himself, so we might have more time than we think."

"But for all we know, Michael, or The Sun, or whatever, has already found and taken him again. This entity is strong—like insanely strong—what's to say he wasn't swept up while you slept?" I wish Lawrence wasn't so damn pessimistic.

"I just know it, okay? Arlo is free, and I think he has been for a while. He's running, and he's afraid. But we'll find him. We will, I know we will. We'll find him and we'll save him, and when The Sun and The Moon come knocking, we'll destroy them. We'll free Arlo once and for all, and we will win."

I don't realise I'm shouting until I see the shock on everyone's faces. I'm being too loud, too intense. But I can't help it.

They're coming, he said. Arlo is the last entity.

No one speaks for what feels like an eternity. Then Rani moves over to Marianne's desk and begins rummaging through the drawers. Marianne looks close to protesting again, but Rani stops and drops the photograph onto the table alongside the phone. Marianne sighs. It's the photo from Woodstock.

"Call me insane, but if we're really going to do this, like *now,* it might help for us to have a bit more of an understanding of who all three of these entities are. And thanks to the real letter, we know all three of them exist." She's shaking. "This is genuinely a stab in the dark, but based off all these scary coincidences and revelations, maybe it's not as crazy of a theory as it sounds."

"Spit it out," Lawrence demands.

"You said this entity, *Michael*, spoke to Jerome that day, right?" Rani directs this question at Marianne, who nods, her brows tensed.

"They wandered off together, and while there's been some time in between, like what, twenty years? That doesn't matter. My point is, you've not seen Jerome since 1989. *No one* has credibly seen him since 1999, so forgive me if I'm wrong and lead us on a wild goose chase, but, after everything we've learned recently, is it not obvious The Moon is Arlo's father?"

I can hear three pounding heartbeats, and imagine my own.

She's right.

It *is* obvious.

Arlo is The Star, his father is The Moon.

Well, shit.

Chapter Thirteen

Arlo
Two Months Ago

The call cuts out and I stand in the booth, trying to calm my hands, rubbing them dry against my legs.

I look around to see if anyone is watching, but no one seems to be around, until a man rounds the corner and comes into view. My dead heart drops in an instant, but he doesn't even acknowledge me. He's just carrying his shopping bags and minding his own business, like everyone else. *No one knows you're here,* I remind myself.

I'm meeting Casper next week. He made sure he was alone when we talked, so no one would know. He wouldn't stop asking if I was okay, but when I asked him, he said he was fine and deflected the question back to me. He's been through so much, yet he somehow cared about how *I* was. It made no sense.

He told me he was happy to hear my voice and would love nothing more than to talk about Ben. He said he could talk about him for all eternity, his voice laced with pain. But still, he insisted he was fine.

We agreed to meet outside of the city centre to minimise tracking and to visit Ben's grave. I don't want to put anyone in danger, Casper included. I told him I couldn't stay with him long, and he said he understood.

I WANDER over to an old traditional pub, its sloping ceilings, stone floor, and wood-panelled walls ingrained with the stench of stale beer. I feel the eyes on me as I enter, though no one can see my true form. They just see a stranger. It reminds me of a scene from a horror movie I watched with Rani, though I doubt there are werewolves in these fields.

"A pint of tap water please," I ask, and after an uncomfortable stare down, the barmaid grabs a glass.

"Ice?"

"Please."

I take my drink and find a spot in the far corner to observe my surroundings from every angle. *Never leave yourself exposed.* My number one rule plays over and over in my head.

I sit for a while, mentally rehearsing a meeting with Casper. Every possible outcome comes to mind, and I begin to zone out a bit.

"This seat taken?" I hear the voice before I acknowledge the young woman standing over me.

"Oh, no. Sorry. You can take it." I panic a little with my response, caught off guard.

"Great, thanks." She smiles, and I think she's going to drag the chair away, until she pauses and squints her eyes at me. "You're not waiting for anyone?"

I should lie and say yes, but I've just allowed her to take the only other chair from this two-seater table. She'll know I'm lying. I shake my head.

"So, you're just sitting alone, drinking a tap water. That draws attention in a place like this. You're not from around here, are you?"

I really want this conversation to end. The girl looks defeated when I don't reply, but she doesn't leave. Instead, she sticks out her hand and introduces herself.

"I'm Lucy, and you are?"

The name hits me like a bullet to the chest. Now all I can see is green hair, tattoos, and red lips; I feel hands roaming my body, grabbing, pinching, and sliding over my skin like a boa constrictor, closing off my airways until I can't breathe.

I'm outside before I can even process my legs have taken me there. I'm panting for breath, blinded by the sun. I'm dizzy and sick and—

I vomit onto the pavement, narrowly missing the picnic bench. It's all bile and blood and *flesh*.

No, no. I'm just seeing things. I haven't eaten that since—

Someone leaves the pub behind me and looks at me strangely, though I try to avoid eye contact with them, afraid they'll see what I see. Smirking, they just shrug and walk the other way. I slowly turn back and look at the ground again. Just blood.

Just blood.

I'm running again. I need to find somewhere to sleep. Shelter. I need shelter—away from everyone. I'm in a village, somewhere. I can feel The Star eating away at my fear, begging to return.

I'm running and running and running. I can't think straight— I can just see *her*.

Flashes of green haunt my vision; her grin, her eyes... *her body hitting the ground as I tear at her throat, exposing bone and flesh. Blood bubbles out in every direction as she grins and laughs and chokes, then I tear at her limbs and she's still laughing, and I can hear her all around me. It hurts; everything hurts.*

"Arlo, come on. It's okay. It's okay. Breathe."

It's Ben's voice, but he's not here. I'm looking around, and though I can't see him, I can hear him.

"She's gone. She'll never come back, you don't have to worry."

She killed him. She killed him. She killed him.

"Then you killed her. You stopped the cycle. No more deaths."

No more deaths.

I wish I could see him. I can just make out the hills and cottages beyond, with people milling about and minding their business. A dog barks, stunning me back into reality.

"Breathe, Arlo."

And I do. I can see clearly now, nausea fading.

I slow down my pace and listen to a nearby stream. I realise I'm standing on a bridge as the sun shines through the cracks in the trees. I breathe in the clean, pine-scented air.

I'm okay.

I FIND a barn on the outskirts of the village and clear a comfortable spot for myself, moving away moss-covered stones and dust from the dirty corner.

I open my bag and take everything out to organise it properly.

Over the past few weeks, I'd gathered a pair of slightly torn black gloves, a scarf that reminded me of one I used to own, a spare shirt, seventeen pence in copper coins, four blue pens, and a battered, coverless copy of *East of Eden* with the five phone numbers written into it.

I lay everything out. Back home, I used to own a whole bookshelf, brimming with books my mum and auntie got me over the years, then ones I'd saved up money to buy from my Saturday job. I loved reading and writing.

My poems are still probably shoved in my drawer at uni, if I even still have that room. What month is it? May? I should have been doing my exams now. Then moving back home for the summer.

I wonder how Rani is finding things.

I wonder how my mum is.

As far as I'm aware, I'm not a missing person, meaning someone has covered my disappearance up. Probably Marianne. I hope she hasn't confused my mum too much.

I put everything back in my bag, except for the book and one of my pens. I turn to the last few blank pages and write.

I write down everything that comes to mind, everything I want to say, including what and how I feel. I sit for hours until it grows dark. Tucking my book away, I pull out my scarf and fold it into a pillow. I lie in the dark for a while, making out patterns in the ceiling as a spider slowly crawls across the wall in front of me.

When my eyelids grow heavy, I begin to feel the cold. With a sigh, I curl my wings around my body and tuck my legs up, my eyes drooping shut.

Then I fall asleep.

I dream about a forest, though it's not one I ever recall being in. Chirping birds and a flowing waterfall sound nearby. I'm wandering around, then I realise I'm not alone. Mars is walking beside me. They're talking to me, but I can't make out their words. The dream feels like it goes on for hours until I realise their voice is getting louder, and it's suddenly getting dark. Then, they're just *not* there. Something abruptly grabs me from behind, and I spin to face—

Him.

Michael.

"Come back to me," he begs, clasping his hands around my throat. I'm falling through the dark, falling and falling through a bottomless void. He's calling for me, and I can still feel the weight of his grip.

I startle awake before I hit the bottom of the abyss. I can't breathe. Reality is almost as dark as the dream, but I cry out in relief.

It was just a dream. Not real. He's not here.

I'm okay.

"Arlo."

I'm like a deer in headlights. Sounds come from outside as the wooden frames creak with the wind, but there is no mistaking the human voice inside.

I'm angled in the corner, unable to see the rest of the barn. I press my back against the wall and try to control my breathing.

I'm hyperaware of every sound around me, and it's over-whelming. My ears buzz, and I press my hands over them, squeezing my eyes shut to block out the noises. It's no use.

"Are you awake? Arlo? Please don't be scared."

I've been around that voice just enough this year to know who is in the room with me.

Gradually, my hands relax around my ears as I straighten, sitting upright. I'm processing everything at half speed.

"Arlo? Son?"

Son.

He's found me. Michael has found me. They've come to take me away. To bring The Star back. I've failed.

"Arlo?"

The voice is right beside me now, and I startle, making eye contact with the shadow figure. I'm cornered. Nowhere to run. The window space beside me is too high and too small to escape through. I scramble back as far as I can and scream, covering my ears again. I squeeze my eyes so tight it hurts and frantically kick my legs out.

"Go away. Please. Leave me alone. Leave me alone. Please. Please."

I think I start to cry, my throat strained and raw. I wait for The Star to call out to meet its family, for Arlo to be pushed deep down inside, never to return.

But it doesn't.

Nothing happens.

Maybe I'm still dreaming.

Once, when I was much younger, I had a dream within a dream within a dream and believed I was dead. Now I wish I was. I wish I could stop existing, feeling, running.

"Son, please. It's just me."

I can still hear his voice. I pinch myself to wake but nothing happens. I'm too scared to look up. Too scared to move. To breathe.

Footsteps pad across the stone, and I sense his presence drawing nearer. But then, the mass drops, and he's crouching before me.

I can't open my eyes.

He doesn't speak for a moment. Then, he says: "I met her in the summer of 1991. She'd just graduated university, and she was on holiday with her parents in Edinburgh. I was born in Edinburgh. A long time ago." A soft laugh leaves him. "She had the brightest smile I'd ever seen, and she was glowing. She's beautiful."

I sit and focus on my breathing. His words.

"I worked in a pub then; it was something normal for me to do. I watched her laughing with her parents and noticed the light she gave off when they spoke. I couldn't keep my eyes off her. She was so full of life, so *human.*" He shifts a little and I hear myself breath in deep. That's my mum he's talking about. My mum.

"She came up to order a drink, and I asked how her day had been. She told me they'd been up to the castle earlier that day and that she was leaving tomorrow. Said she never wanted to leave, that she thought the city had so many more stories to tell."

That sounds like my mum. She always goes on about how much she loves Scotland. I want to smile but I can't. Not yet.

"That was when I stopped thinking straight. I couldn't shake my eyes from her. So, I asked her out. Right there, on the spot. I was mad to do so. I thought she'd turn me down and make a quick getaway with her parents. Instead, she smiled and asked me what I meant. 'Go for a drink with me,' I said, and then began the happiest eight years of my life."

Something drips in the distance, but it doesn't stop him.

"I'd been human for nearly two years at that point, but I never really understood what that meant until I met her. I'm human now, in a way, and that's all because of her. And you."

He stops speaking. I only hear his shallow breaths. My whole body relaxes. That's my dad. He's alone, and he's... he's himself.

Don't be fooled. You gave him back to The Sun. You watched it happen.

"It's just me, I promise." His voice is soft and... kind. The subtle Scottish lilt in his accent is apparent.

I slowly raise my head and open my eyes. It's so dark, but I can make out his features: his long red hair, his wings, his ringed hands reaching out to the ground between us. His eyes stare straight at me and his face softens as he exhales through his nose.

"Why did you leave her?" I whisper my question.

I watch him close his eyes before he slides his legs into a cross-legged position in front of me.

"I didn't know she was pregnant," he says after a beat.

I want to believe him, I really do. I almost do.

"Why did you leave her?" I ask again, still waiting for my answer.

He makes a sound that almost seems like a laugh, but his expression is dark.

"Thirty years before, Michael found me and spoke to me like a friend. He promised me things he thought a selfish immortal like myself would want. At the time, I thought he was a delusional drunk and walked away, brushing him off, but twenty years later, he found me again. He gave me a choice this time, or so he led me to believe. He was always a walking deception." My dad makes a noise, somewhere between a laugh and sigh. "I'd done some bad things—some really bad things—and they'd hit me all at once, the reality of all I'd caused. I didn't want to live anymore. I'd spent centuries as a vampire, and it didn't take me long to realise I'd become a monster then. There was nothing human left in me. So, he let me choose. He offered me eternal greatness, the life of a god, or he promised to make me human. I had nothing left to give then, and all I wanted was to restart my life. To live as a human, as I'd never been able to before. So, I begged for the impossible, and he made it so."

Breathe, Arlo.

"I watched him drag in a human and told me I could switch places, if I so wished. I don't remember the process, but it worked. I was a man, a real human man. And then, he disappeared. Or so I thought. You see, Michael never left. He knew I'd eventually come crawling back once my body started to age, and I realised my mortality. It scared me, growing up. Then, I kept getting ill—I couldn't do it—I'd lived too long to cope with growing old. But he knew that all along. He wasn't giving me a choice, he was using me, and gaining my trust. He was manipulating me, so I would crawl back to him, like a dog, and beg for my old life back. It was a test, and in his eyes, I passed. I ran away from your mother for no other reasons except cowardice and greed. I wanted my immortality back. So, he killed me, and I was reborn with this *thing* inside me. The Moon, he calls it—I don't know why he chose those names. Maybe it's just something for an English-speaking tongue to grasp. God, I've been given too many chances on this earth." His voice sounds almost pained now, the memories a sharp sting. "He spent nearly two decades trying to use me, and although he succeeded most of the time, I made it a challenge for him, especially at the beginning. But then I started giving up. I spent nearly two decades locked up in my own mind as The Moon roamed freely in my body, constantly at his beck and call. I was all but lost until you came—until you walked into that room. I knew instantly. You look so much like her. Melissa. Beautiful, beautiful Melissa Everett."

I feel the tears before my breath hitches.

Just like Ben keeping away The Star.

"Dad," I finally say.

"Son."

He reaches for me, though I'm hesitant to move at first. I'm exhausted, yet I welcome his embrace. I need him.

I sink into his side as he joins me against the wall, our wings touching.

"How did you find me?" I ask, my voice weary.

"It took me over a month. After he took control of me again, I slowly started coming back to myself in pieces. But you never left my mind. You kept me rooted in this world. You held The Moon at bay. I looked everywhere, but I followed the traces."

"I tried so hard not to leave any."

"You didn't. You've done a remarkable job. I just knew where to look."

"But you don't know me. You couldn't have known what to do."

"I will always find my son."

I don't know what else to say. I sit in silence, resting my head against his shoulder as he wraps his arm around me, pulling me close. He's so much warmer than I am. I lean into his heat.

"He's going to find us," I say.

"I know."

"Does that not scare you?"

"He'll always look for us and try to get into our heads, but we just need to figure out how to outsmart him."

"But how?"

"We've got one thing he doesn't."

"What's that?"

"A reason to live as ourselves."

I close my eyes.

"He will try, but we won't let him get what he wants," my dad continues, quieting his voice. I let my head sink further into his shoulder.

"I'm so tired," I say.

"I know. I know, son. We'll be okay now, though. I'm never leaving your side. I promise."

He lightly kisses the crown of my head before I drift off again.

WHEN I AWAKEN, I'm curled up on the floor, a foreign jacket draped over my body.

I rub my eyes and sit up. Light beams through the doorway to the barn, and there, sat propped up against the wall, sits Jerome, my dad. He's wearing an oversized white shirt, loosely buttoned, with a grey waistcoat over the top. The smart black trousers and polished boots indicate he hasn't lived this month as ethically or as faithfully as I have. He's peeling a fresh apple with a sharp knife.

Then, the night before comes flooding back, and I bolt upright.

My dad flinches at the kerfuffle but chuckles when he looks at me. His wings flutter slightly as a gust of wind travels around the room.

"Did you sleep okay?" he asks.

My throat is so dry.

"We can find you some food. I might not need it anymore, but I lived long enough as one of your kind to detect hunger when I see it. You need a drink."

He sounds different from last night, more relaxed.

"I'll be okay for a few hours," I manage.

My dad shrugs before returning his attention to his breakfast. I don't dare ask where he got it from.

He doesn't look at me when he speaks. "Does she know?"

I swallow the lump forming in my throat. "No," I say, pained by the admission.

Instead of lecturing me on what to do, he shifts the topic, but still focusing on my mum. "How is she? The last time you spoke to her, how was she?"

He's speaking as if he's known us for the past nineteen years of my life.

I'm mad all of a sudden, mad at everything—at everyone. I stand up and grab my bag, letting his coat fall to the floor. "We need to move."

My dad looks up at me, seemingly reluctant at first. But then he stands up beside me, and we're eye to eye. I can see what the people back home mean. He does look like me—slightly. I think it's the nose. Or maybe it's the face shape. The tenseness of our brows. Only now, as the light bounces off his pale face, can I see how vivid and green his eyes are. Just like—

I wonder if I'll ever see Ben again, now I'm no longer alone. I still need him. I want him to...

I stare at my dad and take a deep breath.

"I need to meet someone in a few days. But we need to be careful. He can't follow us here. If he finds Casper, I'll never forgive myself," I say, completely aware of the fact my father has no idea who Casper is.

But he nods. "Okay. We won't leave a trace."

I nod, a silent understanding passing between us.

I'm on the run again, but this time, my dad is by my side.

INTERLUDE

"Oh, hello there! I thought you weren't going to answer. I've just popped around for some tea. A cup of tea? Maybe a nice biscuit or something?"

"You don't know who I am? Oh dear. I wasn't expecting you to know me, silly! I'm a stranger, but I've come for a nice cup of tea. Maybe even a place to sleep for the night? Is that not what you provide? Or do you only help people with wings?"

"Oh, I saw him too. You're not crazy."

"*Did* he now?"

"Well, I may not have wings, but I am going to ask you some questions, and you're going to answer in vivid detail. Does that sound okay to you?"

"Thought so. Right. Can I come in?"

"Interesting. So he's not been back for three days?"

"No, no. I'm not going to hurt him. He's very important to The Sun. Soon, you'll understand."

"Are my followers intimidating you? Would you like me to tell them to wait outside?"

"Thanks gents, I won't be long."

"Interesting. So he never mentioned the end of old times?"

"He wasn't himself, then. Hmm."

"Oh no, that's all I needed, really. Thanks for your help, darling. Can I call you darling?"

"God, this chat has made me rather thirsty."

"Oh no, I don't actually drink tea. I stopped drinking that— hmm, I'm really showing my age now—about two hundred years ago! Wow, how time flies!"

"No, no. I'm not an angel."

"Not quite."

"Oh, I know what I fancy. I know just the thing that will quench my thirst."

"Aww. I'm so sorry. You've been so kind to me."

Act 2

Answers

Chapter Fourteen

Arlo
Two Months Ago

Although we've been walking for a few hours, it feels like forever. I didn't dare risk taking any more public transport—I was too exhausted to maintain my illusion that strongly—so we stuck to empty country roads until we reached the motorway.

We haven't spoken. Well, it's more like I've not responded to him. I don't really know what *to* say. What can I say? I want to be able to act like everything is normal, but it's not, and it never will be. My dad is alive and well, traipsing behind me with his wings and rings. I feel tension building in my throat, and I know I'll snap in a second, but I don't know how else to act.

I promised Casper I'd meet him in five days' time, and that's also eating me up, because not only would I be endangering him, I'm now adding fuel to the fire by bringing *The Moon*.

"I could probably cover for both of us if we got a train," my dad says, sounding slightly breathless.

"We can't risk it. The less people see us, the better," I respond, staring straight ahead.

"So, walking along the side of the motorway is discrete?" He sighs, and I picture him throwing his arms out wide to exaggerate his point.

"A car passing us in seconds is far safer than sharing a space with fifty plus strangers for hours under surveillance." I don't even explain my point, hoping I've said enough.

He doesn't respond.

We walk for a while longer. I have to catch a rabbit, and although I hate showing my hunger, I know I won't be able to continue without any food. I appreciate him turning away as I step over into the field, though. He doesn't comment on anything when I come back, other than telling me to wipe my mouth. We continue in silence.

When the road fills up, we cross over to a disused bus shelter as the rain starts pelting and soddening the map. I protested about stealing it, but dad was in and out of the shop before I could even do anything about it.

I throw my bag in the corner and slump down against the wall, feet aching. The small stone shelter stinks of multiple bodily fluids, but I've stayed in far worse. I'm almost immune now.

My dad just stands and stares at me. It's off-putting.

"What?" I don't intend to sound so harsh, but I'm too tired to correct myself.

My dad sighs. "I really didn't know, you know." His wings flutter out, shaking off the rain. I look down at my feet. "If I had, I would have never left. I was trying to leave before anything like this happened, so I wouldn't be leaving anyone behind."

My head snaps up. "You left her. You said you loved her."

"I did! I loved her so much—I still do. I had our whole lives together planned, but I was selfish. Michael watched from the shadows at every waking moment, and—" He drags his hands up his face and through his hair, cutting himself off.

"You're blaming Michael."

My dad sounds flustered. "No. Well, yes. Sort of. I know it was my fault. I was the one who didn't like aging. *I* was the one who got up and left in the middle of the night. But I never asked for this life. I know that doesn't excuse anything I did, and I understand that so much it *hurts*, but I can't rewind time. I need to learn to accept everything. I am a pathetic excuse of a man. I don't want pity, Arlo. I *know* I'm pathetic." He begins to pace, choking on his words. "I'm sorry. I'm just so... mad. At everything."

I wait for him to continue, not having words to input. I'm still trying to process it all.

"I'm mad at who I was, what I've done. I'm mad at the decisions I made that led me here. I'm mad I let Michael use me for decades, and I listened to him. I'm mad I left the only person I truly loved to raise our beautiful, smart, sweet son on her own. I'm mad I never got to see you grow up, all because of my own selfish wants and desires. I'm mad I left you and put you in danger, leaving you to die just like I did all those years ago. I should have been there to protect you. I'm mad at everything. Every single waking moment I am free from The Moon makes me *sick.*" He throws himself down before me and crosses his legs, holding his knees under his elbows. "I think that's why I gave up. I thought it was easier to just let The Moon take over because then I wouldn't have to *feel* so much."

Outside, the rain lashes down and pelts off passing cars. The floor is damp, but it will have to do. I look out the doorway for a moment before returning my attention to my father, who now sits with his head in his hands.

I sigh. "She misses you," I say, biting my lip.

Jerome's head flits up, his eyes filling up. One tear drips to his cupid's bow as a soundless 'what' forms on his lips.

"My mum misses you. All the time. But she would never admit it."

"I'm sorry. Arlo, I wish—"

"I missed you too, and I never even knew you. Is that weird?"

I think he mumbles something like 'oh, Arlo' as he reaches for me. I don't want him to touch me right now, but he wants to, so I let him. He doesn't know me yet. He stands and moves his weight over to my side to wrap his arms around my body. Holding me tightly, I feel the press of his rings against my ribs. I let him hold me, but I shift in discomfort at the tightness of his grip. He kisses my forehead again before pulling back, as if realising I'm not going to properly return his embrace.

"You don't like hugging, do you?" he asks gently.

"It's not that I don't want to, I just... it feels weird. It makes my skin itchy, and it's like my bones can't breathe—" I startle at how easily I opened up. I rarely explain that to people. My mum is the only person who knows fully.

"Noted. I won't do that again then. I'm sorry. I'll learn." My dad moves an inch away from me, and I take a deep breath, averting my eyes. "Is that—" He stops mid-sentence.

What? I slowly look at him, noticing where his eyes are fixed. I'm playing with the ring on my finger, my hands restless.

I answer the question for myself. Of course this was his ring. I'd long since blocked that memory, convincing myself I only wore it because I liked it. I didn't need my father... I didn't.

"It suits you," he says, like he's in a trance.

I turn away to focus on my breathing. I resort to pressing my thumbs and forefingers together and rubbing them in circles. But with the claws at my fingertips slightly obstructing the movement, I pick the hem of my shirt instead. It's an old band t-shirt with two holes over one of the shoulders, but it's soft. It's manageable.

"Arlo," he says into the silence, trying to catch my attention again.

I instinctively inch away from him, but I turn to meet his eyes as much as I can. His cheeks are still damp.

"I'm never going to ask you to forgive me, you know."

Good. Because I don't think I can.

"Okay," I mumble.

"And when this is all over, I'll understand if you don't want me to be a part of your life. I'd hate to force something so big upon you."

"You think we'll survive this?" I don't.

"You will. I'll make sure of it." His words hang heavy over the both of us.

"I just don't want anyone else to get hurt."

"*We* can make sure of that." My dad promises as the rain gets louder, almost drowning his words.

I pull out the map to escape my thoughts. It's all getting a bit too much and I can't think straight. It's too dark in the shelter to truly make out directions. I sense my dad's eyes on me, watching every move, and I find myself glancing at him every so often to check he's still there. That The Moon hasn't taken over. And though I probably wouldn't notice, I check nonetheless.

"Tell me something about you," says my dad when the road quietens.

I drop the map as he positions himself against the far wall until we're mirroring each other, our feet almost touching.

"Like what?" I don't know what he wants to know.

My dad tilts his head, chewing the inside of his mouth. "What are you studying at university?"

My father really does know nothing about my life. Had Michael hidden everything from him?

"I studied English Literature." *And I don't think I'm going back.*

My dad smiles. "Do you like to write? Is that what you want to do?"

"I wrote sometimes. Poetry mostly."

His smile widens. "I can't wait to read it." He must have noticed my expression falter as he adds: "That's if you'd be comfortable sharing it, of course. I understand you might not want your dad reading your work," he says it kindly and honestly, but his wording strikes me in the chest. *I have a dad now.*

I nod slowly. "Maybe one day."

"When this is all over."

"When this is all over," I repeat.

The wind picks up, forcing me to fold the map up to keep it from blowing away. I tuck it back into my soggy backpack.

Only now I've relaxed a bit to focus on my surroundings and company, do I notice a faint, slow heartbeat. Too slow to keep a human functioning. I look up at my dad and acknowledge his existence again. He's real.

"What else do you do? Any hobbies?" he asks, adjusting his legs again for comfort.

I shrug. "I played the piano a bit."

"Oh lovely!" My dad's face lights up. "I loved playing the piano. I used to play a lot at the turn of the century—last century. No..." He laughs brightly. "A while ago." He clears his throat, swallowing his excitement. "I'd probably have to relearn." His smile stays, though, and it rubs off on me. *I'm talking to my dad.*

I realise this conversation has been one-sided until now, so I ask something I've wondered about from the moment we first met. "When were you born?"

"1566. Edinburgh. Leitch's Close. The youngest of eleven— technically seven, technically three. I only ever knew my two sisters. No one else made it past the age of six." His smile doesn't falter when he tells me this though. He looks happy to finally tell someone the truth.

"Four hundred and fifty-three," I say, having just calculated his age.

"Not quite." He grins. "December."

I nod, letting my brain process. Still, he looks young—too young to claim me as his son—yet creases mark his face and eyes, revealing his age to those who know to look. He'd spent ten years aging normally, which means he must have been *young* when he died. *Like me.*

"I can see you analysing me. I know I don't look a day over four hundred." He winks. I don't know which expression to show him, but he answers my question before I can ask for specifics. "I'm twenty-eight." He clears his throat again and looks up at me from beneath lowered eyelids.

Eighteen.

"My story is a bit too much to get into now, though. Plus, I'd have to remember the order everything happened. But I can tell you eventually, if you want," he promises.

"When this is all over," I repeat, allowing my lips to curve into a smile.

We sit in silence again. My dad even drifts off to sleep for a bit, but he starts nodding when he wakes, as if rehearsing his lines. He takes a deep breath and leans forward, his eyes never leaving mine. "Did she find someone else?"

"No." It's the simplest and most truthful answer.

"Is she happy?"

"I think so. She has our dog."

"And she has you," he adds.

"I've not seen her for months. She doesn't even know if I'm alive." Panic washes over me. No matter what, I always return to that worry.

My dad doesn't look stressed, though. "You must have people looking out for you."

I...

"You had vampire friends, right? They'll have taken care of things."

Will they have? After everything I've done?

"You're not a missing person."

He has a point. That has crossed my mind before, but having someone else spell it out for me makes the reality even more obvious. Maybe they did still care.

"Tell me about your friends. Do you have a partner?"

I startle at the question, but then I hear Marianne's voice in my head.

"I'm not... I don't." I sigh and clear my throat. "I'm aromantic. And asexual. I don't like people that way; I don't want relationships like that, which is fine. It's normal, I—"

"Like Marianne."

"What?" I choke in shock.

"Oh, sorry. My friend. I had a friend like that. She wasn't attracted to people that way. We..." He bats his hand dismissively to try and change the subject, but I'm even more stunned now. The name Marianne surprises me, but then it hits me. He's talking about *the* Marianne; he doesn't know who she is to me. Michael really hid *everything* from him. Did he even know Lucy? Or was Michael making sure they couldn't draw connections?

And then I'm back on the battlefield, facing Lucy, and her words come flooding back. I didn't know my father's full name then.

But she mentioned him. *Jerome.*

Marianne knew Jerome.

Jerome knew Marianne.

Lucy knew Jerome had done something to Marianne, and she used it as a *threat*. How did I never process any of this before? How did I...

"How do you know Marianne?" I ask, wishing I could back up further into the wall.

My dad looks at me with eyes as wide as my own.

"You know her? Marianne Ashtown? She's still alive?" His face is a mix of delight and concern. Maybe even a drop of fear.

"She's our leader. The Thorns... She looked after us all." If I had a heart, it would be pounding right now. I'm in half a mind to run. What did Lucy mean? What did he do? *'I've done some bad things. Some really bad things.'*

"What did you do to her?" I demand answers, gripping tightly to the strap of my backpack until the fabric burns my palm.

"What? She's... oh god. Oh no. Oh Arlo, please. I'll explain. I promise I will. I just... I need you to—I need you to understand I'm not the same person I used to be." His position becomes one of fight or flight, and his hands start to tremble.

What did he do?

I stand abruptly, beginning to pant and heave. "*What did you do?*"

He stands up and raises his hands to explain.

I'm about to throw my arms out to push him away, but then an engine roars to a stop, and a bus pulls up. *Not abandoned.*

Before I even have a chance to consider anything else, I leave.

24th February 1891

I sometimes worry Jerome has forgotten our plan. Our purpose. We are here to help people and use our power for good. He has too much fun sometimes, and I fear it will come back to haunt us in ways we may never escape from. We cannot leave this life behind—not yet, not when there is still much work to do.

Maybe I am just being dramatic. Letting myself dwell too much. Everything will be fine. He just gets like this sometimes. ~~A little greedy.~~

12th March 1893

14th March 1893

~~*Do I worry too much?*~~

It has been a tiring few months, holding up appearances and settling business. We have achieved so much. My previous diary is brimming with things I am truly proud of, but sometimes it overwhelms me. Holding up this façade, keeping that grin as I shake hands with men who are ugly inside and out. Nothing I do will change a woman's role in society, but I can only be myself. Use my gift for good. I say my piece, and they have no choice but to listen to me.

But why have I returned to these pages after months of being away? Because I have had enough. My brother, as he has become to me over the years, is losing touch with our original plan. He does too much, goes too far. We settle a deal, but he returns to it with an ultimatum, an extra demand, turning faces sour. I tell him to stop and take a step back, to leave the deals as they are, but he demands more—always more. I fear he is regressing to his former self, the greedy and lost boy I found all those years ago on a dangerous path to demon-

hood. He wants and wants, yet is never satisfied. What if I truly cannot change him, after all?

Last night, he returned home in the early hours of the morning with a bloodied nose and a cracked tooth. "We're moving," he said, and I simply laughed, though not at the situation—no, that anger would come to me later. I laughed at his tone, because I could sense his attempted control over me, but he was too drunk to work it.

"Sit down, you fool. Do not try that on me. You know it never works," I told him. ~~But what if it did work? No, he would not have done that. This is just an isolated incident.~~ This wasn't his first fight. I had cleaned many a wound for him. I'd relocated his shoulder thrice and forbade him from leaving the house on multiple occasions. He would get blind-sided. Living in his head. 'Pay the workers evenly', we'd agree, before it became 'now gamble away all your assets.' I found it entertaining at first, watching men I despised throw their lives away, but suspicions grew. These men knew too many people, and they were beginning to put things together. 'Who was that man you were with, Barty? I've heard he's a nasty piece of work and convinces men to pay out too much. I even saw one man go mad after dealing with him. He is the devil, I tell you. The devil.' This was a conversation I had overheard between two businessmen after one of our meetings. Jerome was leaving trails, and I was left to pick up the pieces.

"If you are going to convince these men to lose it all, the least you could do is give their abandoned assets to those who will make a positive difference. Pay the workers, then support them with the excess funds. Help them to leave these environments for good by paying them living wages, not just equal pay. Pay them to thrive, to grow to greater things." I tell him. "But these men never learn. Do you not see? They all turn *into each other. No matter how they begin, as soon as you throw money at them, they end up in the same place." He thought he had a point, but I dared to group* him *in that pile.*

"And you are different from these men? Because you live forever? How does that change your nature?"

"It changes a lot. I am not a man. I'm something more."

I slapped him and went to bed, my head whirring with frustration. He appeared in my room a short while later to apologise, begging for forgiveness and admitting his fault. He said he would let me take over entirely, but I pretended to be asleep. He never repeated his offer.

~~Why, Jerome, must you be like this? We had a plan. Everything was working, and we were making a difference, changing lives for the better, using our powers to convince and save. When did you lose that?~~

7th June 1893

I believe I owe myself an update on my feelings. It has been over two months since my last full entry; the others I've torn out and burnt. Many of my pages have met such a fate recently, but I believe this is a positive update.

Jerome has kept himself in line, keeping his position in our dual deal, but taming his desire for watching men fail. Believe me, I want nothing more than to watch these men burn, but if we are to keep up a long-lasting appearance, allowing us to maintain our work in this high society, then we mustn't be so careless in public. We can do our business in private, and that I have, but never in the earshot of another. This past week, I accidentally fed too fast and killed a man for the first time in years. I convinced myself he deserved it, and no one would learn of my endeavour. I would not make a habit of it or relive my darkest times. But when Jerome helped me discard of the body, he picked me up and spun me;

the surrounding flames dancing around us. "We can make this work," he said. ~~Could we?~~

This month, our social standing is at an all-time high. We purchased a grand house in an affluent neighbourhood, then sealed a deal to provide free medical care for workers in the local woollen mill, hiring out our basement as a medical room.

Jerome killed three men that night and brought back the body of the bully for us to feast on, before we drank ourselves into the early morning, singing the songs of our childhoods. Those men deserved it. They did.

I'm not making a habit of it.

I can keep this balance; I have the strength to. I'm not like I used to be. I know how to avoid going overboard. To feed and not kill innocent strangers. Yet this way, we feed, while ridding the world of devils. Balance is all I ever needed.

Jerome has also kept his promise to me. He rebuilt trust in our surrounding communications and dissipated my seeds of doubt.

No one batted an eyelid when Barty disappeared in the end. His wife inherited his empire and did the work for us. She used his earnings to fund the upkeep of an entire neighbourhood, then invited a family of nine to move into the top two floors of her house. She hated her husband. Good riddance. Every man we kill, we convinced their estates to distribute the wealth. We are back on track.

Life is good.

We are saving humanity.

21st June 1893

Our next target is a business we have had our eyes on for a while, the extended company run by a man named Cornelius Watson. He has a history of poorly mistreating his workers in both leather factories, with ties to three of the

harshest known workhouses still in operation in the city. Factories functioning on workers who have homes, but survive daily conditions you would wish upon no one. A brutal man with brutal intentions. Money for eyes and a stomach full of hatred.
He is a difficult man to contact, but he will prove no match in the end. We always get what we want.

24th June 1893
Jerome and I have booked a meeting with Mr Watson next week. Let our work begin.

27th June 1893

——————————

——*Taken from the diaries of Marianne Ashtown.*

CHAPTER FIFTEEN

Mars
Now

J*erome is The Moon.*

The admission has been ringing through my head ever since we split up.

I sometimes feel like I'm the last to catch on to things, but we were all in the same boat this time. I focus so intently on the finer details I sometimes forget to take a step back and look at the bigger picture. To really grasp the basics before I pilot the plane and guess where to land.

Jerome is the third entity—he must be. Nothing is a coincidence in this world. The Sun, *Michael,* found and chose him. Then, they chose Arlo to complete the trinity. What a sick, sick game of happy families.

As I set off back to the church with Marianne, after I briefly went back to lock my apartment and retrieve my phone, I began searching for missing people called Michael, all the way from the turn of the century to the 1960s.

I promised to prove that Arlo had been there, and I desperately hoped he'd return again. Marianne had asked Carmen and Rani to look around the quiet areas on campus, where Arlo used to frequent, while Lawrence and Fran were tasked with infiltrating CCTV cameras around the city, then at bus stations, and the train station. Fran's newfound ability meant we no longer had to protect her from anything, and that she could also see how often we had to use Manipulation in our day-to-day lives. She was probably the safest out of all of us now, though. *Does that mean she'll be safe from the entities' plans as well? Will she be the key to stopping them? It's not a movie, Mars.* But there might be others like her—people who our skills don't work on. There must be. If we fail, will there be enough people left to pick up the pieces? Will humanity know what to do when everyone else is lost? How will they be able to fix things, though, with so few people across the entire globe? There's so few of us right now... *We won't fail, though. Come on, Mars. Don't give up on Arlo.*

I blink hard then return to my phone. Michael—I need to focus on Michael right now.

And skies do I love the internet sometimes.

I nearly trip over my own feet when the article appears.

The link shows a pixilated black-and-white photograph of a tall, blond man in a printed t-shirt of a sun. He's grinning, his arm wrapped around someone I assume was his aunt or some older relative. His low ponytail, and bright, open expression, makes him seem like a normal guy. Not like the eerie, inhuman image of him in Marianne's photograph.

The strange disappearance of Michael van der Meer. August 1967.

It was translated from Dutch, but the article was simple enough to understand. Michael was a twenty-seven-year-old 'failing artist' who had fallen into serious financial debt that his family described as 'the beginning of his decline', whatever that meant. No one knows the exact time he went missing because he had not been in contact with anyone for a good few weeks before someone finally checked on him. He quite literally vanished off the face of the earth, and not a trace or lead has followed since.

He lost his mother nineteen years ago, and his father fourteen years ago. The last time it was reported, his older sister had been moved to a home after being diagnosed with vastly progressive dementia. The van der Meer line ended there.

He was legally declared dead, and the case was closed over four decades ago. A horrible story from start to finish, but that's not even the creepiest part. Blood, his blood, was all over the apartment; splattered across the wooden floors, smeared on the walls, and across a giant unfinished canvas painting of an angel.

So, this was the first victim. The Sun.

I can only picture Arlo now.

Except Arlo has people who remember him—people who want nothing more than to find him—and Arlo is still very much alive.

"That's him, isn't it?" I nearly trip over a stone again when the path steepens. Marianne stares at my discovery.

I only need to hear the slight intake of breath to understand I've succeeded.

I wonder what he looks like now, picturing what Marianne saw that day. Two angels of death.

I google Jerome now. I know Arlo mentioned he also went missing. His article is a little harder to find, but I eventually get there. Jerome was never legally declared missing, though. He seemingly left enough clues to indicate a straightforward case of partner abandonment. He seemed to disappear from public knowledge after a few years, though. *Once The Sun got to him.*

I'm speculating that was the case, but for all I know, The Moon could be even worse.

"What did Arlo look like?" I hear Marianne's voice ahead, breaking me from my thoughts. I pocket the phone.

"Tired," I say. I can't think of any other way to describe him. "More tired than I'd ever seen him." It hurts to admit that.

"Did he have anything with him? Other than the backpack you mentioned?"

I shake my head as Marianne faces me. We'd reached the top of the hill and were about to descend into the forest through a short country lane.

"And you are so sure he was himself?" she asks, firmly placing her hands on her hips and looking around.

"Definitely."

Marianne bites her lip, pondering thoughts. It's a little awkward for a moment, then she throws herself against a nearby tree stump and lands her head in her hands with a sigh before brushing her hair back and looking up at the sky.

"Are you okay?" My tone is wooden—I'm not sure what's happening.

"I'm not doing very well with this," she admits, refusing to look at me.

"The search? Or life in general?" I try to add a lightness to my voice, and she grins a bit.

"Everything, Mars." She looks at me solemnly then. "I honestly don't know what to do anymore. I tried to keep myself together in there, but it's really hit me. We've bitten off far more than we can chew. There's *five* of us."

"Are you giving up?"

"No, I don't think I can ever truly give up on anything. I've lived far too long for all of that. I just feel helpless. I did a lot of things I'm not proud of in my past, and it's starting to feel like the world is judging me for it. Is this karma?" She holds her face again and takes a deep breath.

"It's all very overwhelming. We're all on edge, thinking about what we could have done to stop it, while blaming ourselves and feeling out of our depth. You're not alone here," I state, resting a hand on her shoulder. I've never experienced this dynamic with Marianne; it's always the other way around. Did *I* trigger this?

"I know, I'm sorry." She looks at me now with pity swimming in her gaze.

"We're going to do this, though, no matter what it takes. We know who we're looking for; we know what their goal is—or we're pretty confident we do. We just need Arlo to come to us to explain everything we're missing. And I know he will come to us. He came to me! There's so much hope." I force a smile, yet her expression barely changes, and a flash of anger surges within me. "Don't look at me like that," I say. "Don't look at me like I'm being overly optimistic or too positive or delusional—"

She closes her eyes with an aged smile. The expression of a woman who has seen and experienced more than I could ever fathom. "I just can't help but feel like everything is my fault. Everything links back to me, and I feel like I should have noticed this so much sooner. I could have stopped it from happening. I spent months trying to piece together things that we could have done as a team in a matter of days. I just don't know what I'm trying to prove anymore."

Again, I wasn't expecting such brutal honesty from her.

Marianne bats her hand dismissively. "Ignore my dramatic phrasing. I'm old. Humour me."

I awkwardly sit by her side. "You're talking about your brother, aren't you? You think you've been connected to this since then?"

Marianne nods and closes her eyes.

"But how on earth could you have made any sort of connection, then? Even if you always had those memories, you said it yourself, you thought he was simply mad." *Anyone would have. A man who listened to his dreams too much and took it to the extreme.* "You're a good person Marianne, I don't care what you did for the two hundred and fifty years before I knew you. You've probably lived five life cycles in the time I've barely lived half, but I've been in your life for over a decade, and the Marianne I know is incredible, which isn't even a good enough word for it." She opens her mouth to protest but I don't let her. "You've done so much for us. You protected us for decades. You saved each of us at least once—which is more than most people on this planet can ever admit. You saved my life—you protected Lawrence; you protected Ben and Casper and *Carmen.* God, you took on the role as her *mother* without even batting an eyelid! You eliminated the threats in so many areas, saving countless lives. You stopped Isiah, and now even Lucy is dead—"

I don't let her interfere, not yet. "Lucy was more experienced and powerful than all of us. It's not your fault. We did all we could to find Ben. We all failed, not just you. There was nothing else we could have done."

Marianne sighs, like she expected me to say these things. It makes me a little mad but I understand what it's like to be preached at. She needs to hear this though. I grab her shoulders. "Listen, please. She's gone now, Marianne. She's gone, and Arlo is still here. He wants us to find him and he wants to stop running. He's just too stubborn and selfless to come back." I take in a breath to calm my rising nerves. "We will find him soon, though. I know it. He will take us to this *Michael,* and we'll kill him." It feels a little heartless to refer to him by that name, knowing the real Michael had been trapped inside the mind of this creature and was likely all gone now. But I mean my words. "There, I said it. We'll destroy him so he can't take any more hosts, leaving him no choice but to vanish off to whatever part of the universe he came from."

Marianne blinks, locking eyes with me. "But what about the thing inside Arlo and... Jerome." She looks back away when speaking the name of Arlo's father.

I will admit I haven't let myself ponder that technicality yet. I'm trying to stay focused and avoid overcomplicating things. I won't let any more harm come to Arlo. I'll die before that happens.

"Jerome meant a lot to you, didn't he?" I try to divert the topic from Arlo, but in doing so, I dive head-first into Marianne's past.

It's probably not the best thing I could have asked. Selfish of me, really. I'd just rather dwell on something else other than Arlo.

She nods before speaking. "Jerome Mair. God. That's a name I never thought I'd have to say again."

"Tell me about him." Is that really the right move forward? Probably not. I would make a terrible therapist.

I expect her to deflect, but she gives in. I thought it would be more of a challenge.

"What do you want to know? How we met? The hundred and thirty years we spent together? What he hid from me for a century?"

What did Jerome do?

"Everything." I ask for everything she is willing to give.

Marianne sighs and laughs a bit again, adjusting herself on the stump. The blinding sun makes me sneeze.

"I wonder if he's told his son the whole story. If there's anything left of him anymore," she says, grimacing. I wonder how much of Jerome Arlo has seen, too. I want to know how long Arlo has been running for. Was his father after him? *They're coming.*

27th June 1893

*I attended a meeting this morning in the town hall, one
filled with those advocating for change. Votes for women.
Abolition of free labour. Subjects so heavily avoided by society. With my head down, I entered through the side entrance
as instructed.*

*The hall was set out like a school classroom: chairs on either
side of an aisle, all facing towards the front where a young
man stood beside a blackboard. Many others had gathered
around, finding seats and chatting amongst themselves. A
man greeted me with a handshake, and a woman winked at
me, as if her message was clear. I felt both uncomfortable
and at home all at once. But then I cast my gaze upon the
gentleman at the front again, and when he looked up, his
eyes smiled for him. I felt a flutter in my chest, unlike any I
have experienced before and I maintained eye contact as I
found my seat beside three women. He looked older than me
—older than my body, that is, but not by much. His deep
brown hair was combed back neatly, and he was dressed in a
simple black suit with a high-collared white shirt. He was
tall and of a slim stature, but he carried himself like a boy.
A young man in a world too intense for him. His slightly
hunched shoulders revealed his shyness, and as my eyes
wandered, his suit appeared a tad too large on him, as
though tailored for a much larger man. Perhaps his father?
From where I sat, I could just about sense his heart,
drowning out all other sounds, the unsteady thud enhancing
his nerves. He cleared his throat and greeted the crowd,
silencing discussions. My focus snapped back into the room
and I blinked hard. I was unsure what had come over me.
The man cleared his throat again. His hands curled up to
the cuff of his white shirt, tugging at the fabric.*

He is nervous, I thought. I smiled at him again and hoped he

noticed. *Don't be afraid,* I thought, then his head snapped up
and his eyes frantically searched the crowd. He heard me. I
was inside his head. How did I manage that? No one else
turned or flinched the way he did.

My chest fluttered again, and my cheeks flushed red.

"My name is Julian Watson." A handsome name. "I am the
firstborn son of Cornelius Watson, destined to continue his
legacy."

Then everyone in the room gasped, myself included.
Cornelius was the very man I was due to meet later that
week, the embodiment of evil and greed. And here before me
stood his son. Holding a meeting that would entirely contra-
dict everything Cornelius stood for.

People shouted out with gratuitous anger. The woman beside
me stood and told him to get out of the building, for he had
no place amongst the rest of us. She did not even wait for him
to finish. *Let him finish!* I thought, and I must have thought
it too loudly, as the woman threw herself back on the chair in
a trance and spoke no further. I had done it again.

Julian straightened, his pulse rising far beyond the normal
rate. "There is no man I hate more in this world than my
own flesh and blood, my father. I will do anything and
everything in my power to undo everything he has set up.
And I will succeed."

Pride immediately washed over me. I shot an arm up and
cheered. Then everyone in the room followed suit, and
Julian's face transformed, lighting up—his eyes glistening.
"We will protect the people of this country, improve health-
care, push the freedom of women and fair pay for all, and
we will fight until our dying breaths to do so. Who is with
me?" he said with newfound confidence, then his eyes met
mine once again, fixed in the space between us.

We cheered even louder, then we got to work. We laid out
weeks and weeks of plans, discussing every detail at length. I

avoided Julian for almost the whole session, deliberately beginning conversations with all my other peers, for that feeling in my chest was growing, and I had no words to explain it. It was inevitable I would have to speak with him eventually, but I held back for as long as possible.

He disappeared for a time, allowing me precious moments to relax. I took up a lengthy conversation with a young woman about our roles in society as ladies born into wealth, the role I've had to play for a while, and how that affects the way we see the world. She never shared her name, which was common for meetings like these, because many of us would end up silenced or worse if anyone of notoriety caught on to our plans. We were saboteurs working from the ground up, cutting away at the poisonous ivy in the city and neutralising it from within, so I found it startling that Julian had publicly announced his name. He had no fear of the repercussions. He did not care. He had that much faith, he was doing this regardless of the outcome.

Maybe it was admiration that I was feeling, maybe that was what ate away at my chest. But I felt it the moment I laid eyes on him, long before he introduced himself. ~~Should I hide this book? Do I want Jerome finding it?~~

Julian, of course, returned, but he brought with him bad news. His voice was hurried and frantic as he said, "My friends, it is time we disperse this meeting. I have received word we are not safe here and must evacuate immediately. Grab everything, leave not a trace. Take my card, instructing you to look for signs for the next meeting. I hope you all continue this journey with me, but please hurry out the back door, and do not, whatever you do, let yourselves be seen. For your own protection. Now go!"

We gathered what we could, shoving papers up skirts and into hats. No one dared to speak as we dispersed. I adjusted *my bonnet and folded my papers into my purse. We all ran towards the back door as Julian stood in the room's centre, making sure we all escaped safely. I did not even allow myself a second of eye contact, but as I brushed past him, he reached out to grab my gloved hand; the warmth of his humanity seeping through into my fingers. I turned back as his grip jolted me, meeting his eyes. He lowered his head and gaze, but I heard his words perfectly. "Thank you," he said. Then he let his grip slide, and my body carried me out of the door without looking back.*

I made it home later than Jerome expected, but he wasn't surprised. "Good session?" he asked from the lounge, a newspaper flopped on his lap.

I did not know what to say.

29th June 1893

Today, we meet with Cornelius Watson under the guise of discussing the purchase of one of his tanning factories, the highest performing leather manufacturer in the country, or so he led the public to believe. He seemed reluctant to meet at first, but we soon won him over.

We have that certain charm, you see.

After unveiling the true purpose of our visit—discussing the purchase of one of his private workhouses—he insisted we met in one of his private offices, away from the rest of the 'goings on', as he described it. He was uneasy and asked how we possessed such knowledge. We reassured him we meant no harm, laid out our proposal, and when he scoffed, we did not let it phase us. He is a weak human.

Of course, he lost to us in the end, and we finalised the deal over multiple handshakes, an offer he could not refuse.

We turned down his offer to show us out, spending an hour weaving ourselves through the site, observing the conditions first-hand. We were going to make a huge change here. I could not help but grin.

I bit one of his associates on the way out and drank enough to satisfy my hunger before making him blame it on faulty machinery, of which there was plenty. Jerome laughed, then slung his arm over my shoulder.

All in a day's work.

I looked for Julian everywhere. It was foolish of me. After everything I learned from him in that one short meeting, I knew Julian would keep himself far from his father's work, but I still hoped to see him.

Cornelius looks nothing like his son, and I am glad. Where Julian's lips curl into a natural, soft smile, his father's turn down in disgust.

I must meet with him again. Next week is too far away. I need to tell him what I'm about to do.

He deserves to know.

30th June 1893

We laid the plan out together. We are to keep the factory in Cornelius's name and have his company attached to every aspect of the building. Then, once the workers are sent home, we will set it alight. I will then spend the day after visiting every employee. With the money we have received from Cornelius, we will pay them enough to look after their families for a few years while helping them to find better and safer jobs. The only people left to pick up the pieces of negligence will be Cornelius and his close followers. We gave him false names, you see. We do not exist.

I told Jerome about Julian. All the details I could remember and insisted we could trust him. It was Jerome's idea to bring him in on the plan. I was instructed to inform him of it at the next meeting.

Julian could provide inside details and everything would run smoothly.

I couldn't stop smiling.

3rd July 1893

This morning, I attended the second meeting. There were significantly less of us this time. The location was more secluded and run down, but it would prevent us from getting caught. None of that mattered to me, though. I needed to speak with Julian.

I waited until the end, where I remained seated, and once Julian realised I was not leaving, he sat back down.

"So, you agree with my plan?" he asked, crossing one leg over the other. He held his hands together and rubbed them slowly. I noticed the shift in his once confident manner. His heart picked up, and he itched his neck twice before I answered.

"Oh, I do, Julian. (Not Mr Watson, he was not his father) I agreed with every word you said." I hesitated, my own palms sweating slightly before I stood and held my hand out to him. "My name is Marianne Ashtown."

Julian adjusted himself in the chair, then took in a deep breath, shaking my hand firmly. That familiar warmth from before almost caused me to shiver. "Oh, well. Hello, Miss Ashtown. It is nice to finally get to speak to you properly. I—"

"You're a good man," I cut him off, sitting back down and tilting my head to the side slightly, taking in his reaction. That funny feeling returned in my chest, but I made sure I did not show my mild discomfort.

"Oh, thank you?" He laughed with nerves, his heart skipping a beat.

"There are not many men like you. I'm sure you know that, though." I meant every word. I barely knew him, but there was just something about him—something that told me he was different.

"You really believe so?" He raised an eyebrow in a questioning, yet innocent manner. His hair was loose today, his dark brown waves kissing his temples.

"Oh, I do. Why do you think I returned? I have a lot of faith in you, Julian."

Without responding, Julian stood and straightened his trousers, stepping away and turning his back. He picked up a cane I noticed leaning against a table earlier, but I never remembered watching him use it before. I thought he was about to leave, or that I had made him uncomfortable, but then he walked over to the far wall and started speaking as he looked out of the grime-covered, rotten window frame.

"I was the firstborn son of my parents. You know all about my father, but my mother is just as bad, just as selfish. They are not human, not the way humans should be. I was born into expectation and wealth, and right from the moment I could talk, I learned to argue with them. I was a difficult boy, and I am sure my father thought he could beat it out of me, but I never changed my mind. I knew what he did was cruel, unjust, evil. And my mother just stood by and let it happen. My sisters grew to despise our parents just like me, but my brothers did not. There is no helping them, I'm afraid. They were captured under his spell too young, and I live every day knowing my father wishes he could disown me and kick me out onto the streets. That is the power every first born has, you see. Everyone knows we exist, so we cannot be silenced."

Julian never lifted his gaze from the window, and I never moved from my position. I listened as he told me about the first time he learned about the workhouses, the things he was forced to endure as a child, how he was scolded and beaten into submission. How he had to stop doing things he loved because his legs were too often battered and bruised and in too many places, preventing him from continuing his running. He told me of his mother's forced tutoring, and the meals he was forced to skip as punishment. He lived every day of his life being told he was a disappointment, a failure, a mistake. All because he refused to uphold the family name —the work of his father, grandfather, and great-grandfather. Because he wanted to do something good in the world all by himself. He wanted to break from the life he was forced to have, and doing what we were doing meant that he could. Then, he shared details of a failed marriage he was forced into at twenty-three. His bride-to-be called off the wedding to run away with a man much richer than Julian. She called him weak and pathetic, and his parents agreed with her.

Julian shared so much of his life in such a short space of time. I was in awe. Every last drop of information sunk straight into my bones. He spoke to me as if he had known me for years. I don't know why he poured his heart out to a stranger, especially me, but I let him. Julian was the pinnacle of human potential. How beautiful it is to persevere and believe.

Slowly, he turned and walked back over, resting his left side on the cane. He sat back down before me and winced, then huffed out a laugh, closing his eyes. "I am so sorry you had to listen to all of that. You can tell I do not talk to many people."

My eyes widened as I remained focused on him. "No need to apologise. I wanted to hear it. I'm glad you felt comfortable enough to share it with me." I smiled.

"I barely know you, we are strangers, but I just feel…" He pulled his chair closer, and as he did so, he leaned forward. I

213

caught a pleasant scent of peonies. "Tell me, Miss Ashtown, why do I feel like I already know you well?" He looked at me longingly, desperate for answers.

"I am not sure," I replied. "Unfortunately, I did not know you existed until last week." That was true, though I may have done if I had just researched his father more.

"Unfortunately?" His heart reacted funny for a moment, a grin appearing on his face. I could not read his tone—it gave me an odd feeling.

I fixed my smile. "Unfortunately, because if I had done, I would have been able to share this proposal I have much sooner."

Julian leaned back, his face contorting. "Oh."

To avoid confusing him further, I explained our plan, giving him all the details necessary for him to not only believe me, but to trust me. If he did not already.

He immediately agreed to help and insisted he met with Jerome and myself as soon as possible.

"You've done things like this for a while, then? You and your brother?" He kept rubbing his hands together excitedly, but also to cover up the nerves I knew he still felt.

"I have. We have made it our life's goal."

"How old are you, may I ask?" he asked politely, but he covered his mouth in a panic before I could answer. "Oh, how rude of me. I'm so sorry, it just slipped out. I get too comfort-able very quickly and sometimes I say things without thinking of the consequences. Please forgive me. I cannot believe my impropriety."

I laughed. It is impolite to ask a woman her age, but I have never understood why. "I am thirty-two." The age the current version of myself would be, ten years older than my body, but a hundred and thirty-nine years younger than my soul. It's a complicated thing, immortality.

Julian nodded, relaxing a little. "I am twenty-six, just while *we're sharing personal information. Oh, you must forgive me." His voice sounded almost like laughter, but it was really just nerves.*

"You are closer to my brother's age then."

"Oh, marvellous. I do not feel like such a child then." Julian rubbed his neck under his high collar again.

We talked a little more as the sun began to set and once I found an appropriate moment to end the conversation, I stood and told him it was time I made my way home. He shot up with me, then winced again, banging his leg against the chair. I did not need to see beneath the material of his trousers to know how badly bruised his skin was. The rage of blood swarming around it was almost too much to bear. A wave of hunger swam over me, and I forced myself to turn away to clear my senses.

"At least allow me to hail you a cab home? It would be improper for me to let a woman go out in the dark alone. I would never forgive myself if anything happened to—"

I looked up at him sincerely. "I will be fine," I promised.

His face dropped. "Oh, I wasn't implying you could not look after yourself. I only—"

His personality was infectious. I quickly grew to love the way he panicked and worried. His humanity was almost too painful to witness.

"I know. I will be fine." I smiled, then I handed him an envelope, containing our address and nothing more.

"We will expect to see you at noon tomorrow to discuss this further."

I walked towards the door, but he called for me before I reached it, holding the opened letter for me. "Miss Ashtown, I—I just wanted to thank you again for believing in me, even though we barely know each other. Thank you. I mean it sincerely."

I closed my eyes, my lips tightening into a grin. "Thank you,

Julian. But I am sure we will grow to know each other soon enough."
He nodded, resting his hand on the back of the chair.
"Oh, and please. Call me Marianne. There is no need for formalities after what we're about to do."

And so we meet with Julian tomorrow. Time to begin our plan.

—Taken from the diaries of Marianne Ashtown.

Chapter Sixteen

Mars
Now

My eyes never leave Marianne's as she tells the story of how she met Jerome, all the work they did together to help the local community and beyond. But just as I marvel in awe at all she managed to achieve, the conversation turns. I knew it was coming, but for those twenty minutes of her reliving her life, I switched off my worries and just listened. It was only the tip of the iceberg of her life but it's more than I've ever been given.

When her hands start balling into fists, part of me wants to pull her into a hug, causing me to regret ever bringing it up. Maybe it's better if I don't know... Maybe.

"You don't have to relive it if you don't want to, Marianne. I'm sorry; I really shouldn't have asked—"

"Lucy knew." She cuts me off. "Either he told her proudly or Michael has been watching us this entire time. Either way, it's not my secret any more."

I'm still a little uneasy with this. "If this is not the right time... I can wait." *Can I?*

"No. Now is probably the best time. I need you to know what Jerome was like. To understand why I'm so scared."

Here we go. Marianne straightens up, wiping her eyes.

"We had a friend called Julian. He was, well, he was my best friend. I don't believe in soulmates, but I believe he was the closest thing I could have gotten to one, if life had gone differently." She looks away for a moment.

The Julian from the photograph.

"We'd known him for years; we did business with him, helped him free himself from the expectations of his father and their family name. He was kind. He wanted to help people and fix everything wrong with the world, and I wanted to help him achieve that." She goes on explaining how she met him and all the surrounding circumstances. She doesn't realise she's doing it, but she smiles slightly every time she mentions his name. Her mouth quirks up and her eyes wander. He meant a lot to her. So much.

Then her face sours, just like that.

"I thought Jerome wanted the same. He played along so well, yet he never explained why his face would stiffen every time Julian spoke. At the time, I thought it was maybe jealousy. Perhaps I was spending too much time with this human man. But whenever I came to press him on it, he would call me delusional and change the subject." She tuts and grabs her knees tight. I want to hold her hand. I should. I started this.

"I can't believe I thought they would get along. I was so naïve. They reminded me of each other originally. Their difficult upbringings that shaped them. Jerome never discussed his past at length, but I filled in most of the gaps over the years. I believed Julian's presence would, I don't know, be cathartic for him? I honestly can't explain my train of thought. Julian was twice the man Jerome ever was." Her cheeks are red with anger now, and it's only after I process her reaction that it clicks.

Oh, Marianne.

I piece it all together.

"He killed him, didn't he? Jerome killed Julian."

Marianne looks at me, pity pooling in her eyes. "Oh, Mars. He did far more than just that."

4th July 1893

I <u>must</u> make sure I keep this book hidden, for I am afraid of what I might begin to say. I am no longer just documenting my life, but also my deepest feelings. It is important I remember what things make me feel. I must hold on to these emotions.

Julian Watson arrived at our town house at three minutes to noon. I noted the fresh scent of flowers on him as I greeted him and invited him into the drawing room.
Jerome stood and greeted him with a nod and handshake. Julian tucked his hat under his arm with a grin then complimented Jerome's hair, comparing it to the sunset red of a summer's evening, and when Jerome muttered a thanks, Julian picked up on his accent.
"Ahh, a Scotsman! You did not tell me you were Scottish, Marianne!" He looked at me with pleasant surprise, and I shrugged in apology.
"We moved here as children," I had to lie.
Jerome kept his tone serious, trying to read Julian. "Does that bother you, Mr Watson?" His accent grew stronger than I'd ever heard, as if to make a point. At Julian's blank expression, Jerome laughed and lightened the tone by squeezing Julian's shoulder. "Forgive me. Please, take a seat." He gestured to the chairs arranged around the empty fireplace in the centre, where the brass clock ticked away on the mantlepiece above. We had recently installed a large mirror there, too. I remember looking at myself for a moment as the men sat down. I adjusted my hair slightly. I don't know why.
I ran to fetch the freshly brewed tea and sat it down on the table between them, joining Jerome's side. The conversation was already well under way.
The pair of them got along remarkably well. I observed

many a smile and laugh between them as they discussed our business plan, with Julian offering input where he felt necessary. Jerome withheld some details that I would have perhaps given myself, but I reminded myself this was their first meeting. Plus, I had never shared with my brother what Julian had disclosed with me. I didn't feel it necessary, not yet. I held those in private confidence with my new-found friend.

The plan was relatively simple. A week from today, we were to attend the factory at midnight, lap the site to ensure everyone was out, and then start dripping oil inside the building's perimeter. Julian would keep his father distracted all evening, while myself and Jerome would work around each side of the building before striking the match together and heading straight for the woods. My brother and Julian would spend the week ahead, gathering evidence of the goings on behind the scenes to release to the papers the next morning. Not once did Julian express fear of being caught. Even after all his father had done, he was not afraid of him.

The more we talked, the more I observed Julian. He had come without his cane today, but there was still a slight limp to his step. He still wore his high collar to cover his neck, but his brown eyes were as full of life as always. He has an infectious laugh and filled the room with such ease; it was difficult to look away, and Jerome's unwavering eye contact was a wholly positive sign that the three of us would get along marvellously.

Julian thanked us before arranging a follow up meeting at the Watson offices with Jerome.

Once he left, a swell of happiness bloomed in my chest. Jerome appeared behind me.

"Well he is a bright young man indeed."

"He is wonderful," I said.

7th July 1893

Jerome returned from his meeting with Julian with a body in his arms. I panicked for a fraction of a second, but then I rolled my eyes as I helped him down the back stairs to lay the older male corpse on the slab we kept in the cellar.

I normally would ask what the victim had done, but I recognised this face. This gentleman worked at the factory. I had seen him slap a young woman while lighting a cigar.

I spat on his face, and Jerome took his first bite.

"Old age?" I suggested when he was done.

"Time caught up with the fellow. Such a shame." He grinned through bloody lips; his canines passed over his bottom lip, his pupils blown wide within the bloodshot whites of his eyes.

We buried the body in a disused cemetery in an unmarked grave.

I did not drink that night. I caught a rabbit instead. Jerome made no comment.

8th July 1893

Both Jerome and I slept in this morning, for whatever reason. We were awoken by the doorbell, and I shot up, startled and confused. I heard someone rushing outside my door and watched from the crack. Jerome strode past, buttoning up his shirt as he did so.

We were expecting Julian and had completely lost track of the time.

Nothing much to report for this day. We spoke business as usual then Jerome insisted Julian stayed for some food when it began to rain rather heavily.

I know why Julian wears high collars now. I noticed a large, darkened patch of skin on his collarbone when he angled his head. A mark from birth, it seems. I wonder why he hides what is simply part of him?

9th July 1893

Jerome vomited up blood this morning and blamed it on his catch from the night before. 'Foul blood' he said. I asked him who he killed this time, but he insisted he didn't—he only drank. I didn't believe him. He made a comment about illness doing the rounds in the city, and I suddenly thought back to my childhood. To Dorabella, my father, and Nicholas. My real brother...

It was a long time ago. It just made me think for a moment. Just think.

10th July 1893

One day to go until the fire. I am a little nervous, anticipating the outcome and repercussions. The good we will bring to so many people.

Humanity. We are helping humanity. I keep reminding myself of that.

I fed from a handful of birds today. Jerome finally asked me when the last time I drank from a human was. I told him it was yesterday, and he just nodded before returning inside. That was a lie. I have not touched a human in... well. Since the day I introduced myself to Julian.

We meet Julian for a drink this evening, with Jerome insisting the night was all paid for. He patted Julian firmly on the back and kept calling him 'old sport.' It was a little odd, for Jerome never normally uses those terms, but we were enjoying ourselves. Relaxing. Being human.

12th July 1893

It is done. We did it. Everything went according to plan. The papers have been informed, the sources have been anonymously leaked. This is the beginning of Cornelius Watson's downfall.

Julian has not been to visit us this morning, however, and despite the delight at our accomplishment, I am worried. I must check up on him.

Jerome noted my discomfort earlier and asked me why I looked so upset. I told him my reasoning—perhaps Cornelius had done something, and maybe we had made a mistake by leaving them alone together when the fire started. Jerome seemed to only be half listening as he turned the page of his newspaper.

"Remember, he is only human," he said. I was out of the door before I could absorb his words.

I found Julian in his home, alone, and felt indescribable relief. He was completely unharmed, yet dark circles clung to his eyes. He had slept little, he said, but he was happy we accomplished our plan. He invited me in for a cup of tea and we spoke for a while.

I am just relieved his father has not blamed him. We would have to keep an eye on him over the next few weeks, to protect Julian and ensure our long-term plan was working.

I do not care that he is mortal. He is important—to this city, to this country, to the world.

To me.

14th July 1893

Cornelius is being investigated by the police. The public are learning what he stood for, what he represented. Three of his associates have resigned, claiming to want nothing more to do with the man.

Julian arrived at our home, beaming. I let him inside and he hugged me; it happened by instinct, I could tell. He panicked afterwards and stepped back, looking over at Jerome in the front room, who was staring straight at us.

"I apologise, that was inappropriate. A handshake would
have sufficed." It appeared he was apologising to Jerome
more than me, though.

"It is a good day. We are allowed to celebrate," I said. Jerome
cleared his throat, but I ignored him. He can be so prudish
sometimes.

29th July 1893

Today, perhaps, was not the brightest of days. Cornelius's
criminal charges were dropped on the condition he improves
his worker conditions and breaks no other laws.

Tripe. This is absolutely ridiculous. He cannot be allowed to
go on!

Jerome has already arranged a meeting with him. I'm not
allowed to attend. I have faith he will do good work though;
Jerome was always the best at subtle Manipulation.

I invited Julian for a drink this afternoon, while I awaited
Jerome's return. Julian obliged. Within the hour, we sat in a
public house in a private snug towards the back of the building. I wanted to avoid Manipulating others into pretending
they hadn't seen a well-to-do lady in such a male dominated
space.

We talked for a long time, Julian more so. He expressed his
hatred for his father once again, who would do anything in
his power to get away with his crimes. He was too protected,
too well known in the industry. It would be impossible to take
him down once and for all.

I promised him Jerome knew what he was doing. This was
merely a setback. Everything we had done so far had not
been reversed.

"Jerome is a good man," Julian said, more than once.
"He is."

We washed down our pains with a few more drinks. I had to
Manipulate a handful of gentlemen to leave us alone after

they approached to say this was no place for a 'lady', even in my designated area. It is always the same. I do not let it bother me, though. After all, I can do what I want. I will forever be privileged that way.

When the conversation shifted to more personal matters, I suggested we got a carriage home to continue our chat in a more private setting. Julian obliged and held out his arm for me as we left.

I held onto his arm and immediately absorbed his warmth, feeling the muscles tense under his skin. I cannot explain the feeling it gave me—I have no words to describe it—but as he let me step up into the carriage and followed behind, sitting beside me instead of in front, my chest flipped. I became increasingly aware of every detail of him. The way his hair parted over his eyes, the way his shirt creased under his waist-coat, and the way I could make out the skin beneath his collar, his pulse steady and slightly visible in the hollow dip beneath his throat.

Julian called out the address and shut the carriage door, and whether he meant to or not, he shuffled ever so slightly closer to me.

It was the drink, it must have been. Neither of us were entirely ourselves.

I commenced the conversation, which was currently relating to our siblings. Julian spoke very highly of his two sisters, Beatrice and Isabella. He hopes to earn enough money from his soon-to-be business to free his sisters from the family name. His brothers refused to leave his father's side, even after the scandal. They knew everything all along. I shared about my siblings and tweaked my story to fit with the life I had fabricated. I explained how my eldest sister had moved far away, yet I stayed truthful about the twins. I told him they died young, and Julian expressed his grievances, reaching for my hand. I did not move away. I looked into his eyes, trying to calculate why my chest hurt. He was so alive and present and...

I think back to the feelings I had toward Richard in the early months of our marriage. Was this attraction I was feeling? Was this what it was? Was I attracted to Julian? Was he attracted to me?

I focused on the steady beat of his heart beneath his shirt. It made me hungry. I must have just needed a little extra sustenance, sometimes alcohol has that effect on me. But then Julian looked down at me staring and he asked if I was feeling well.

I startled out of my trance and met his eyes. "Oh, I am quite well," I said, grateful we had arrived home.

Jerome was sitting in his usual spot as we entered, and he was in a pleasant mood for once.

"All will be well, sister. All will be well."

Then he stood up and offered to take Julian's coat. "Are you staying for dinner?" he asked.

7th January 1894

Time has got ahead of me again; it has been quite an intense few months. But here are my updates, simply listed for clarity. I have a tendency to decorate my words.

- Cornelius and his remaining associates were investigated again after new evidence emerged, causing one of his remaining two workhouses to be shut down. The conditions of one of his tanning factories were forced to significantly improve by the new year, which they did—thank you, Jerome.

- Julian came to our home late one evening with a swollen, purplish eye and explained how his father had hit him and blamed him for not helping maintain the business. Jerome said he would take care of it, and it was the first time I

acknowledged his Manipulation at play with Julian. I confronted him afterwards, but his response was, 'I have helped him though, have I not?' And I could not argue with that. It just did not sit right with me. We had never needed to do it before with him.

- Julian set up his accounting business, the subject he was trained in, and hired both men and women to assist. It made front page news. Many called it insanity, but he persevered, and his efforts are proving fruitful. He hired Jerome and I as assistants and advisors; between the three of us, we have made an exceptional start to the new year.

- Jerome has asked me seven times why I have not fed off a human in so long, and every time I give him the same answer: I do not think it necessary. He grew angry with me, saying I needed to look after myself and feed properly, but I know what I am doing.

- And finally, just a note about myself. I have lived a long time, seen many things and experienced many emotions, but ever since Julian has entered our lives, he has reminded me of what it is like to be human, and to that, I am eternally grateful.

3rd March 1894

We enjoyed a lovely meal cooked by Julian and his sisters this evening. He refused to take credit, though he prepared most of it. They are so sweet.

His father refuses to speak to him, and I think Jerome had something to do with it, but I know that it is for the best. Julian deserves some peace.

Jerome said it was the best meal he had eaten in a long time. It looked as if he was exaggerating, but it was such an enjoyable evening, it did not bother me.

Later on, I asked him if he had enjoyed the evening. He looked a little off towards the end of the visit, but once we were in the cab home, he brushed away my concerns and explained he was tired. I did not press him on the matter.

29th July 1894

It has been over a year since the fire now.

All three of Cornelius's workhouses have been shut down, and all workers were dispersed into better conditions across the city. His two remaining tanning factories are still up and running, but with much better working conditions. Three other factories in association with the Watson name have also drastically improved their conditions, too. Cornelius has not spoken to his son in months. Julian is glad of it, and it makes me happy to see he is finally free of his father. He no longer walks with a limp, his shoulders are straighter, and he has gained a healthy amount of weight, filling out his stature so his presence seems larger and more noticeable whenever he enters a room. Still, he is a slight gentleman, thinner and gaunter than Jerome and the other gentlemen we associate with, but I am proud of his improvement.

He is very handsome. Inside and out.

Jerome is beginning to concern me, however. He will get us caught sooner or later. Three ordinary, seemingly innocent people have been reported missing in the local area in the past few months, and I know he had something to do with it, though he refuses to admit it.

I have not drunk from a human in over a year. It has not hindered my life in any way; it has only made me feel more like myself. More human.

I am happy.

5th September 1894

Julian's youngest sister Isabella died suddenly today. She had contracted a fever only days ago, but did not wake this morning. He came knocking straight on our door with the news, and we invited him in, offering him a warm blanket and pouring him a drink.

We told him he could stay as long as he needed, and that we would do anything we could to help him and Beatrice.

I did not need my powers to understand his pain, for I had experienced it all before. The guilt, the what could have been, the anger.

He stayed the night, curling up on our sofa with the fire on, tears glazing his eyes.

My dead heart ached for him.

Jerome pulled me aside before I went to bed, and his face unsettled me. He looked almost... mad.

"Humans die," he said.

I knew that, of course. Yet Julian could still grieve. This was his sister, after all—his family. I wasn't overjoyed with Jerome's tone, and I told him as such.

"I'm just saying." His voice settled. "When you live forever, you learn the insignificance of mortality. You learn to over-come it. Julian will die, just like the whole city and world that surrounds us. They die, and we reinvent ourselves, living on. We cannot let these worries corrupt us."

I scrunched my nose in disgust. "I dislike what you are implying here. Why speak this way?" I turned away from him.

"I'm just looking out for you. I don't want you to get hurt when the inevitable happens."

"What are we doing all of this for then?" I snapped back. "We are helping humans to improve their world, if they are so insignificant, why are we even bothering?"

Jerome scoffed then glanced at me as if I were covered in dirt from his shoe. "I'm not having this conversation if you are going to act like this." Then he walked towards his own bedroom with a long sigh and shut the door.

I am at my desk now. Rain pours down my window, and I can hear the distant sobs of Julian beneath us. I want to go to him and offer comfort, to reassure him everything will be okay. But Jerome's words stop me.

Why am I listening to him?

Why do I always seem to listen to him?

9th November 1894

We moved house last week. Jerome said it was necessary, and I knew he was right. His worsening habits were sure to raise suspicions soon.

I told him to stop killing, that he was becoming the man I thought I saved years ago.

He scoffed and told me I was being silly. He said he never killed anyone who did not deserve it and never went in blind like before. It matters not though. Murder is still murder. I cannot believe I used to take part in that and justified it...
Something has changed in me, and I know it has something to do with Julian.

Am I being too soft? Am I forgetting who I am?

I wish I was human.

Jerome came to my room last night and apologised. He expressed he had gone too far and promised to stop killing. I want to believe him, I really do.

But I said nothing. He needs to prove it first.

1st February 1895

I stopped writing for a time because I did not need to. There was nothing to report. Everything was working out again. Jerome stuck by his word and only drank until satisfied,

*leaving no one in pain or on the brink of death. He stopped
his unbearable tempers and insisted we invited Julian to
more places with us, despite him living quite far away now.
We would meet him in his offices for work three times a
week, but that was becoming the only time we would
connect.*

*I was missing him, which was why it overjoyed me when
Jerome insisted we met with him more.*

"I knew that would cheer you up," he said once.

He was right. It did.

30th March 1895

*Jerome and Julian are closer than they have ever been. It
means a lot to me. They play cards together, meet with other
gentlemen, and have twice returned drunk to our home, with
Jerome shaking Julian's shoulders and calling him names,
and Julian returning the sentiment. Our bond grew stronger
than ever.*

17th April 1895

*"He is still human," Jerome said, despite the months we have
had and the enjoyment we have felt as a three. He closed the
door on our companion and turned to me with blood in his
eyes. "He is so very human."*

*I don't know what provoked this or what shifted for him to
say that. I looked at him, startled and confused.*

*"Oh, stop looking at me like that. I am simply reminding
you to not get attached. We love him—he is our good friend
—but I have seen the way you look at him. You cannot have
him the way you want."*

*I forgot to breathe for a moment as a tear welled in my eye. I
wiped it away before he noticed. "And what way do you
think I want him?" I snapped.*

Jerome's brow quirked. "You want to bed him. You are in

love. I see it in your eyes. I know you too well, Marianne. You cannot hide these things from me, even if you think you can."
"How dare you..."
"I care about you, Marianne. He will grow old, he will ail, and he will die. We will live on."
I stormed away, refusing to listen any longer.
He clearly does not know me very well. He knows not the first thing about me.
I told him as such as I slammed the front door in his face.
"You are wrong." I said, then I wandered out into the night with no destination in mind.

2nd May 1895

I do not know why he did it.
Maybe I do. Maybe it was to prove something. To get to me. You have no idea what I am talking about. Sorry, I just needed to write what I felt.
We were out this evening, the three of us: myself, Jerome, and Julian. We enjoyed a meal as usual, then Jerome suggested a pub. We continued our conversation, laughing and joking with each other, discussing work plans, then life plans, and everything in between. We were there for hours, and I lost track of the time entirely. It was late enough that the bartenders called last orders, and we had to finish our final drinks.
We talked about where we saw ourselves in the next few years. It was Jerome who began the conversation, but I noted how quiet Julian went when he directed the question at him.
"Oh, well. I hope to be as happy as I am now!" he said, lifting his glass to praise. I laughed and clapped my hands before returning them to the armchair. I felt Julian's fingers slide over to mine.
Jerome caught it—I know he did. I saw it in his eyes... disgust.

Was he jealous or something? Was that it? Jealous that I had developed such a deep friendship with Julian... a human. Was that it?

Jerome stood up and raised his glass. "To Julian."

Julian's face mirrored my confusion before Jerome elaborated. "Julian, come here." Julian stood reluctantly and paused at Jerome's side. Their height difference struck me for the first time. Jerome was a tall man; it was always something people pointed out. Julian looked tiny beside him, even though only a few inches bridged the gap between them.

"To Julian, the man who changed our lives and so many others. You are a wonder, my friend. We love everything you do."

Then, he pulled a reluctant but flattered Julian in by the small of his back and kissed him. Firm on the lips. Jerome pulled their mouths together with such force, Julian dropped his glass, which shattered on the stone floor. He held his arms out, wide in shock.

Thankfully, no one was around to witness the act, for we always kept to the far corner, but I stood immediately when Jerome let go, with Julian staggering back.

"I think it is time we leave," I said firmly. Julian blinked a few times before bending over to adjust his shirt.

"Yes, well... I, erm, good idea." He was lost for words, not looking at either of us.

I looked at Jerome, who was still standing tall, a slight grin on his face.

"Yes, sister. Perhaps we have drunk enough. We shall hail a cab." Then he patted Julian on the back and winked at me.

Silence marked our return home until I closed the door behind the two of us and slapped Jerome clean across the face before he could open his smart mouth. He stumbled backwards.

"Oh. Wow. You really are strong. I forget that, you see." His words were slurred and laced with alcohol, but I cared not.

"Keep your hands off him. Do you understand me? I do not know what you hoped to achieve with that little stunt, but if you lay a finger on him again, I will make sure you never forget it!" I screamed. His face went slack with horror.

"I... honestly, sister—" He rubbed his cheek. "It was just a bit of fun. We enjoyed our evening, did we not?"

That was no excuse. My eyes said enough. I'm not his real sister—never was, and I feel it now more than ever.

"Forgive me." He straightened up. "I do not know what came over me." I knew he was lying, though. He knew exactly what he was doing.

I shoved past him to climb the stairs. He followed.

"Marianne, please. I meant no harm."

"Meant no harm? You kissed another man in a public place without his consent. You meant no harm? Tell me that again." I turned to him on the landing, pointing my finger between his brows.

He raised his hands in surrender. "I am sorry. I understand what I did was wrong."

"Do you?" I refused to believe him. He wanted to get some sort of reaction out of me, but why did he choose that method?

"You care too much about him, Marianne. He is not going to be around forever. I keep telling you that."

I knew he deliberately changed the subject to avoid giving a real excuse, but my fury brought words to my tongue that I instantly regretted. "I can turn him. He can live forever, and we can continue our work."

I did not mean it. I would never do that to Julian. I could never burden him with immortality.

"You would do that? With or without his consent?" When his brow raised, a smirk on his lips, I wanted to hit him again. He knew exactly what he was doing.

"I hate you!" I screamed before running to my room like a child. I wanted nothing more to do with the conversation. I needed to be alone.

3rd May 1895
I cried myself to sleep last night as silently as I could manage, my heavy dress weighing me down on the bed.
I thought of Julian all night, of all the scenarios that could arise from the previous evening. What would he say? Would he ever speak to us again?
There was only one way to find out.
I must visit him... alone.
I do not plan on telling Jerome where I am going, nor will I give him the chance to ask.

4th May 1895
I should cut out some details here. I am too ashamed to write it all. What I did. What I felt.
I went to visit Julian at noon yesterday. At first, I believed the door wouldn't open, but it did.
Julian smiled at me.
"Oh, Marianne. I was not expecting you."
Could he remember the night before at all?
"May I come in?"

We spoke for hours. He was not mad in the slightest. He excused Jerome as a merry man and did not judge his preferences, which was most unexpected. I explained I worried it would ruin our relationship, both professionally and personally, but he assured me there was no harm done.
The whole time we spoke, I was in awe at how relaxed and unbothered he was. Julian has this wondrous ability to live life in such a positive way. It almost enraged me how little explaining it took for him to believe me. He would never

*know the anger Jerome made me feel, but being alone with
Julian calmed me in every way.*

*I felt I had overstayed my welcome before long and was
about to excuse myself to leave, but then his hand fell on my
arm, and I sat back down. I do admit I secretly hoped he
would do that.*

*"Stay. Just for a while longer. I miss your company. The two
of us have not been able to speak alone for some time. I am
glad you came," he said.*

*Then my chest did that funny thing again. My mind
emptied as I homed in on his lips, his nose, his eyes.
His heart.*

It pounded so loud, so fiercely.

Was this attraction?

*I thought it must be, especially after letting it build for so
long. I wanted to make him happy, in whatever way he
wanted.*

*"I worry if I stay, I may never leave." I laughed a little,
unable to explain the sensation beneath my skin.*

*"Well, you do not have to. If you want..." He stood before me
then, and his soul consumed me. I looked up and stood,
noting the scent of peonies again. That scent always
surrounded him. Then his arm was around my waist,
bringing our bodies close.*

"I think, I... Oh, I, Julian." I was lost for words.

*Now, I have spared some details, for my brain could not
comprehend what I was doing. But I want to remember this.
I want to record how I felt that evening.*

*"Marianne, I've been meaning to talk with you for quite
some time now. About us, about..." His voice trailed off, and
he leaned back slightly. I felt his heart thundering against
my bodice.*

*"I think... Well, I had quite hoped that I would get to kiss
you, instead. Is that weird? I do not mean for it to sound*

strange, but..." His whole body was tense. I did not know
what to do.

But I knew what to say.

"Kiss me. Kiss me, Julian."

And he did. The passion behind his kiss washed away all of
my other thoughts.

I had not kissed another man in over a century. I had
forgotten how it felt. Forgotten I did not know how to react
and was never quite sure what to do.

Julian drew back and gasped for breath. "Oh, Marianne.
My... forgive me." Why did he always apologise?

"There is nothing to forgive," I said. "Kiss me again." I
enjoyed how he reacted to my words.

He kissed me again and again—deeper and more intensely.
Then he trailed his lips down my neck to the lace of my dress.
It was clear he wished he could linger further when he placed
a ghost of a kiss at the base of my neck.

"I fear I cannot control myself any longer, it is most
improper, but I fear..." He was panting for breath as his
arms tightened around my back.

"Then let go," was all I said. I believed this was exactly what
I wanted, and what I should have done months ago. It was
attraction—I was sure of it—I just never knew how to act
upon my desire.

Julian lifted me at once and carried me upstairs to his
bedroom. I was drunk on satisfaction and the desire for all
that made him himself. Gently, he sat me on the edge of his
bed and undid his collar, his eyes hungry.

"Please, tell me I am not dreaming." I believe he said.

"You are not." I promised, then a wave of confidence over-
came me. "Lie down," I said, and his eyes glistened.

I remained at the foot of the bed as he lay down. The
pounding of his pulse thundered around the space. My teeth
threatened to lengthen, but I refused to let them.

I turned and crawled over to cage Julian, kissing him myself this time. I kissed him and kissed him before undoing his shirt buttons. He looked down at my fingers, grabbing them with trembling hands. "Marianne," he said as I peeled apart the shirt to expose his soft, pale chest.

I leaned back to drink him in. I had not been so close or intimate with a man in such a long time. I stared at him like he were a painting, admiring every brush stroke of his skin. The firm pinkness of his nipples, the rapid rise and fall of his ribs as he scrambled for breath.

"Marianne," he said again, though I was speechless. "Kiss me. Kiss me again," he begged, wholly undone beneath my gaze.

Instead of going for his lips this time, I leaned over his chest and kissed his heart. Once, twice, three times. I kissed every inch of his skin.

Then, as I became breathless, I bent to press my ear against his heart. I lay there for a while as his hands undid my hair. It beat so strong, so fast, so...

Alive.

Alive.

Alive.

Julian.

I awoke the next morning, naked and wrapped in the silks of Julian's bed.

His back was turned, body still in rest.

I followed the pattern of the wallpaper with my eyes to keep myself awake.

"Julian," I called out, though he did not hear me.

I remember every second of what we did last night. And I had no shame, but something still felt wrong.

I am not sure I felt what I expected, or what I hoped I would feel.

But why?

Julian was everything to me. He was the purest mind and heart I had come across in over a century. He cared so deeply about everything. He lived and breathed for humanity. I do not deserve him—I could never have him, never how I wanted. What did my mind want? My soul? I can never explain the way I am. The way I may always be. But there was one thing I was certain of.

I had not taken Julian to bed last night.

I had taken humanity.

19th August 1895

Our business with Julian was back up and running in no time. He exchanged words with Jerome and assured him they would never need to speak about it again. We successfully passed three minor extension laws to improve infrastructure and water quality. Julian's accounting work reached record highs. We celebrated, of course.

Jerome has settled both his temper and tone. He apologised again to me for what he did, and I forgave him, hoping we could all move on. I never told him what I did with Julian, though I suspect he has already figured it out. He is yet to confront me about it though.

I slept in Julian's bed last night again, yet I just lay in his arms, letting his heart beat in place of mine. I told Jerome I was going out and would see him in the morning.

He hummed a goodbye.

I did not dwell on his carelessness. I just wanted to feel something. I thought Julian's body and mind had the answers. I am just not sure if I should be doing this. I feel not quite right. It makes no sense.

21st September 1895

I forgot to celebrate my birthday this year. Jerome and I are past caring about personal technicalities now, but we at least used to acknowledge them.

There must have been a reason it passed me by.

2nd October 1895

Julian's eyesight is worsening quite rapidly. He jokes about it and says it runs in the family, but he is not even thirty. I am worried about him. He tells me not to though.

Jerome said, "It was bound to happen. I warned you. He is getting old."

He is not old. We are old. We're ancient. Why is it we get to stay the same, but Julian must age?

Why were we the ones chosen to live forever?

12th October 1895

I think I understand myself now. And what I have with Julian, I believe it would work.

I enjoy making him happy, I want to give him what he wants, but he demands nothing from me. He does not make me do anything I find uncomfortable or not quite right. I think I love him. Quite deeply so. I love his whole existence. Beyond what I thought I knew of love. This is something different. I am in love with his soul.

I should probably tell him that.

Would he understand?

30th November 1895

Jerome killed again this morning. He's going to be the death of me. I don't know how much longer I can forgive him. His apologies are meaningless.

3rd April 1896

He is only human.

He is only human.

He is only human.
He is human.
He is human.
He is.
Alive.

This morning, Julian asked me to marry him. I woke up in
his arms, and he told me he wanted to ask me something,
something he believed we were ready for, if I would
have him.
He pulled out a ring and got on one knee as we dressed.
My throat closed and my lungs gave in.
I ran.

He is only human. You could never do this, Marianne. You
cannot do this to him.
He will not live forever.
I cannot turn him. I cannot. I will not.
Who am I to dictate his humanity when I am the devil
incarnate?
He can never know what we are.
Oh, my Julian.

He is alive.

12th May 1896

———————————

15th May 1896

———————————

16th May 1896

———————————

19th June 1896
Jerome has changed. I do not know how to describe it. I
cannot. I just know I must leave him.
I cannot stay with him any longer.
He will never be human again.

~~*I'm scared.*~~

20th June 1896
I'm going to bury this book. Or burn it.

Julian. Julian. Julian.

I'm so sorry.

—Taken from the diaries of Marianne Ashtown.

Chapter Seventeen

Mars
Now

I never expected Marianne to share such details with me, but I let her talk and talk. My mouth grows dry as I listen.

"I don't remember those last few months. I went through my diaries, but I didn't document nearly the whole year of 1896. I don't even remember what we did with work or the changes we made. I know now that was all because of him. Jerome." Marianne shakes her hands out as if ridding herself of something. Trying to let go. "The next thing I remember and wrote about were the times we were in France, Belgium, Germany, and Austria. Then, before I knew it, it was the turn of the century, and we were in Eastern Europe, travelling further and further east, hopping from city to city in a matter of weeks. These were the years I never thought about in detail, but I know he undid everything I was growing into. I know I killed again—I know I drank and drank until my belly was full for days. I know we gallivanted around like we were on top of the world."

"Marianne, I'm... I'm so sorry." That's all I can say. Her admissions have shattered my heart into a million fragments.

Marianne wipes her nose, then straightens. She's hurting, uncovering and reliving the worst parts of her life while I sit and listen like a child during story time. I'm a useless comforter. I just don't know how to absorb it all.

"He told me what he did. It was as simple as that. Only it was over a century too late."

Oh.

"I learned everything he'd taken from me in 1989 when he brought me through Highgate Cemetery in London and showed me the site of Julian's grave—the grand mausoleum dedicated to the whole Watson family, and my gut sank." Julian would have hated that, I think. Based off all she's shared, it's almost as if I know him. Like he's sat right here with us.

"I asked him why he'd brought me there, and Jerome admitted he thought it was time he told me the truth, because we were 'so close now' and 'on the same page.'"

I know where this story is leading and I hate it so much. My own hands are clenched into bone cracking fists.

"Have you ever wondered what it would be like to be Manipulated so strongly for nearly one hundred years? I don't know how he managed it; I must have been so weak. He convinced me to never think about Julian or who he was to us. But he didn't just take my memories of Julian; he took away that whole chunk of my life, including all the work we did. I locked it all away. I don't know why he needed to take so much; he must have been so damaged, so angry, so inhuman. I..." Marianne spits on the floor, like she's sick of acknowledging his existence.

"He walked me to Julian's grave and let me read the dates. He was only twenty-nine when he died. Mars, he killed him days after I last wrote in my diary. I worked it out. He..."

"Marianne, oh god. Please, you don't have to..." Bile rises in my throat.

Marianne's tone is frightening. It's making me so angry, so confused, so upset. I'm feeling every emotion all at once, and I'm feeling guilty about it. *She* had to live this. *She* had to experience this. I'm merely a listener to a sordid tale.

She takes a deep breath, then closes her eyes.

"He sent him to his death, then Manipulated me and forced us to leave the city on the very same night. He thought Julian was making me too human, making me care too much about humanity and *mortals.*" She growls the last word. "Told me it was because I was forgetting why we were chosen to live forever, why we shouldn't waste time caring about the tiny lives of humans who will pass us by in a heartbeat. It was jealousy, Mars. Jealousy in its most sinister form. Because he could no longer find his own humanity within himself, and he hated Julian for helping me find mine."

She grits her teeth tightly behind pursed lips, looking at me as if she wants to apologise for her tone. But why should she? She's... *god*, she's so strong I can't fathom it. I can't...

"All the work we did, everything we set up. It made no difference in the end. Everything changed. I had to *research* him, I had to... I wish I hadn't. He was practically erased from time, Mars. His father's name was front and centre in every article I found. Julian was only ever referred to as being his son. That was it. No one knew him like I did, and no one got to know him. He didn't even make it to thirty! He—"

I grab her into a fierce hug, catching her rage. She doesn't resist. I understand her, understand everything: why she created The Thorns, why she saved us all, why she treated Isiah's betrayal as such an unforgivable act—deeming him unsalvageable. Because she'd seen it all before. And she'd been a victim of it for over a century.

Jerome was not even close to being human. Marianne is, though. She discovered how to live. Even after everything, I will always look up to her. No matter what she did, her humanity remained, lying dormant. Pushing through.

But this is the true capability of our kind. The reality of what the parasite does to our perception of life. Morality. *Humanity.*

What we're destined to become.

Maybe we'll all Turn, eventually.

No.

I refuse to let time taint me.

CHAPTER EIGHTEEN

Arlo
Two Months Ago

"Arlo. Arlo, please. Wait! Please, listen to me... I need to explain."

He follows me onto the bus, and I don't try to stop him. It's practically empty, so I'll easily be able to Manipulate the few passengers that see us. I sit at the back, anyway. I hate knowing people are behind me.

My dad follows me to my seat, trying not to draw attention to himself. He sits beside me, and the rain from his hair flicks onto my lap. My own hair has grown long enough to tie back, but I don't have time to sort it. My chin is rough with patchy stubble, too, and I hate it. Too many foreign textures.

I sit with my body as close to the window as I can, trying to ignore him. But part of me is glad he followed. I don't know why.

"Arlo," he says, his voice rough and desperate.

I ignore him, but he knows I'm listening.

"I want to tell you everything, if you'll let me."

My silence is the permission he needs.

"I knew Marianne for a long time. Over a hundred and fifty years. We masqueraded the streets as brother and sister for decades, just living our lives as unstoppable forces. We watched 1860 become 1960 and beyond. We saw *so much*. It was the best time of my life..." He sighs. "We were like chalk and cheese. She was more human than I ever was, but she grounded me and taught me so many things. She stuck by me because we thought we were the only ones left of our kind. We were both lost and desperate and found comfort in each other's existence."

"Why did Lucy mention your name?" I turn to him, keeping my eyes steady.

"Lucy?" he sits up straight, confused.

"Lucy. She knew who The Sun, and The Moon were. She said so in her letter." He must know who I'm talking about.

Jerome shakes his head. "I'm sorry, son. I don't know who Lucy is. Was she a friend?"

"She killed me."

My dad's eyes widen in realisation, but he doesn't speak. Then I watch his eyes grow dark and his jaw clenches. "What does she look like?"

"She had green hair. It was hard to miss." *How is death treating you?*

"Oh."

He knows who she is then.

"I saw her talking to Michael a few times. I thought he was just using her to run his little errands like me... She killed you? She turned you? I'll kill her. I don't care—"

"I already killed her."

My dad's mouth forms a silent 'oh' before he makes a muffled 'huh' sound with his throat—it's almost like a laugh, though more unhinged. "She was his pawn, then. His way to win you over. I had my humanity dangled in front of me. You had her to exact revenge upon. He's smart." My dad's voice is laced with venom. He really is himself.

"I didn't kill her because she killed me. I killed her because she tortured and brutally murdered Ben. He was my friend." *Kill him.*

"Oh."

"But you're probably right. He used us."

"Ben meant a lot to you, then?"

"He did." I don't like this question, but I answer it regardless. "I didn't know him for very long, but we had a connection I can't explain. He was just so kind." I can picture his broken and battered body. "That's where I'm going, to find out more about him. To see Casper, his husband." They never had a chance to get married.

"I'll come with you. If he meant a lot to you, he means something to me too."

At this point, the man in front of us turns around, looking utterly horrified. My dad points to an invisible camera and tells the man to wave, and he does, telling the guy we're filming a drama. He nods, and that's that sorted. I just hate how easy it is. I always did.

I'm aware the topic has changed now, though, and my dad is taking that to his advantage. I won't let him off.

"Why did Lucy mention your name to get to Marianne? She used your name like it had power over her."

My dad sits back against the chair, his wings bending unnaturally. No one else can see that, though.

"Because I killed her best friend and Manipulated her about it for over a century."

His admission hits me like an arrow to the heart. My vision goes blurry, and my hands clam up. I don't like this. I need air.

"What?" The sound of my words almost doesn't leave me.

"I'm sorry. I want to explain, though."

"Explain what? Explain why? As if it excuses you?" *You killed people too. Hear him out.*

"No. No," he snaps. "What I did was inexcusable. I will never expect her forgiveness, nor do I deserve it. I told you I am not a good man. I'm coming close to being half a millennium old. I've been a *monster*. I said goodbye to my humanity, my life, and every-thing I knew a long, long time ago, because I thought my purpose was to be *more*."

Don't listen to him.

"I hurt people, Arlo. My ignorance and blindness hurt people, and the fact I'm still here is my punishment. To suffer with the memories of everything I've done. The fact I followed Michael will be *my* burden to carry for the rest of my days. But you have saved me in ways I can't even describe, Arlo. You are the reason I will never let The Moon take over, why I want to put an end to this once and for all. At one point, I was the worst person you could ever imagine. I just want a chance to prove I've changed. Forever now."

He became human to prove it.

You. Killed. Too.

"I should have kept my gift of humanity, but I was weak, I'm always weak, and I gave into Michael's tempting and all he promised. He latched on to the bad parts still rotting away inside me and fed off them until he caught me again."

I don't know what to say. I'm shaking, and my brain reminds me I'm a bad person too. Over and over. I gave in to Michael. I was weak and easily led. I killed and Manipulated people. Friends. I used my *friends,* and look where it got me.

I didn't kill before The Star, though.

He did. Can I accept that?

I'm nauseous, and I've got nowhere to turn. I want to run again; it's always easier to run.

Hear what he has to say.

"Dad, I—" *don't know what to do.*

"I'll tell you what I did. Every last detail. I *want* you to know. I don't want to hide it. That's not me anymore. I can't hold on to these things as if they'll just go away. That was what got me into this whole situation. I lost all my humanity. I was a machine, with nothing human left inside me. I..."

"You killed." I finish for him, staring straight ahead, rubbing the strap of my bag until my fingers go numb.

"I killed. And I lied. And I hated. I hated humanity, because deep down, I knew I'd thrown it away. Marianne kept it. She always hung on, even to small parts of it, and I took all of that away the night I killed Julian and took her away from our life. That was his name. Julian. Julian Watson. He was... he was human, but the sincerest kind. He represented everything I lost, and it maddened me. I refused to accept I could never be like him."

My fingers burn now, my stomach curling in on itself. I still can't look at him, but I let him continue, letting my eyelids close slightly as I form the scene in my head.

"We worked with him for years, working our way through the business world of late Victorian London. He had a passion for life, sustaining it, improving it. He saved so many people with his work and quickly grew attached to Marianne. She rarely left his side."

I can picture it, quite vividly. I form an image of Julian in my mind, see him smile. Marianne beams too.

"At first, I was just jealous and couldn't explain why. It wasn't romantic love they shared, it was something more. I know that now. She was attracted to his light, his mind, and soul. But then, as time drew on, I grew to hate how human he was making her. I know she was aware of it too, and it sickened me to know she didn't care. She wanted to feel all those emotions and reactions and *morals* she'd once had in life, and she loved it. But I stole that from her."

My dad rubs his legs. I know he's staring at me, internally begging for me to listen. I am listening. I hear every word, but I just can't look back at him.

He continues, "I planned it so precisely. I chose an evening she'd be busy, and I invited him for dinner at our home, just the two of us. We talked for a while, but I remember the first thing he asked was where Marianne was. His attachment to her helped me to justify what I did next even more. I lied and forced him to believe she was unwell. And then I poisoned him. From the moment he took his first sip of wine, his body slowly began to shut down."

I'm going to be sick, my stomach churning with his words.

"He figured out what I'd done, but it was too late, his body was shutting down, there was no stopping it. I told him I was tired of him and he only wanted to know why. Perhaps he'd already accepted his fate. But then he asked me... Oh, I was awful. I..."

"What did he ask you?" I snap my head towards him. My blood boils and sweat trickles down my back. My father's eyes are rimmed red, his lips torn. I don't let his expression distract me. "What did he ask you? As he sat before you, eating his last meal, thinking about how betrayed he was, and how he'd never see his friends or family again, and how much longer it would be before he stopped breathing while you looked at him with pride—*what did he say?*" The words roll out of my mouth like a tidal wave. I don't even have to think about them, I just *speak*.

He looks momentarily lost for words, then his throat bobs, and he swallows and puffs out his chest. There's too much air in his lungs.

"He asked me if I was the devil."

The devil isn't real. Well, maybe he is.

It's coming, it's coming, Arlo. Don't let it... don't...

"Oh, Arlo. I know. I know there is no excusing my behaviour. I made it painful, long, and unnecessary. He was such a wonderful man, he really was. I might as well have been the devil."

Maybe he's you.

"He never asked me for a cure, he only asked me to take him home so he could die in peace. So that he could die in a room he knew, in a bed he recognised, in the hope it would be painless. That should have been enough for me to regret everything all at once, but it changed nothing. I was so far gone; not one part of me wished to reconsider. I just looked at him and promised to grant his wish."

Breathe, Arlo. He's being honest; he's telling you the whole truth. No cutting corners, no softening the blow. He wants you to understand he's changed. Just listen, and it will be okay... You will be okay. He's changed. He's...

"I helped him into the carriage as blood soaked his shirt. His own blood. It was a horrid, horrid drug, churning and disintegrating his insides. I wouldn't use it on my worst enemy now, but that's exactly what he was at the time. My worst enemy—humanity. I hated nothing more.

"I helped him into bed. He grasped for me as everything inside him burned. I watched the light leave his eyes and his chest slow to a stop. Then, I... god, I—I've said enough. You can see me for who I really was. For I was the devil, maybe I always had been. That was my destiny.

"I ran straight to Marianne's room the moment I returned home, knowing she'd be inside by then. I shoved myself so deep inside her mind—something I'd never done to that extent before—and that was it. The next morning, we were on a train to a boat out of the country, and for nearly a century, I made her like me."

"Oh, get over it."

Nonononono. Please. No. *What did I do to let you back in?*

"Arlo?" My dad's concern is sincere. I'm just struggling to find the words to open my mouth, and—

"He was only human. You said it yourself. Don't you realise how insignificant they all are?" *No. Please. Please. Please.*

It doesn't change anything. Doesn't wake up The Moon, not even slightly. *Dad.*

"We're getting off the next stop," he says. My *dad* says. Not The Moon. *Why is this just happening to me?*

I stay clutching my head tightly as I try, oh I try so hard, to keep it away. My head is spinning.

Once we control them all, none of this will matter. The three of us will free this world. Wake it. Make it see.

The bus pulls to a stop, and I'm dragged up—vision entirely blurred. The Star is angry.

We're still on the motorway as we get off, but I can make out buildings a few yards away. I throw myself to the ground, or he throws me, I don't know. I'm just trying to focus and win. I need to stay focused.

"Arlo. Arlo, fight it. You're better than it. It's nothing." I hear my dad yell.

He's waiting for us. Wake The Moon and go back. It's almost time. It's time for our purpose. Wake him.

"My son. Please."

I scream. I scream so loud my voice shatters. I can't even see. Everything is a blur of colour and sound. I can't feel my legs or my hands or anything. I just feel *it.*

I claw at my chest and dig my nails in deep. I must get it out. Get it out of me, rip it, tear it if I must. I can't let it win. I can't. Never. Never. No.

"NO!"

"Arlo."

A voice carries over the crowd in my head and fights against it, forcing itself to be heard. I let go of my raw skin. It's not my father's voice this time.

Ben.

"Arlo, listen to me. You don't have to forgive him. You don't have to forgive your father for anything he's done. You don't. You don't owe him anything. But you know he won't leave your side now. You know he loves you, and you are the reason he's still himself. So let that ground *you* this time. Let Arlo stay, because you know you need to stay for everyone."

I can't see him, he's nowhere. But that was his voice. Ben. My friend.

"Arlo, you know you can do this. I know you can. Breathe, don't look at it; don't acknowledge it. It's hungry. It's starved. It needs you to let it in, and you will *not* let it. Starve it, Arlo. Starve

The Star from everything it tries to eat. Don't let it eat, Arlo. Arlo!"

Ben.

I'm doing this for him.

"Arlo?" My father calls for me again, but this time, I can see him. I feel my body again. Cold air rushes into my throat, my lungs, my limbs. I'm alive; I'm here. And I always will be.

I'm doing this for everyone.

He's holding me tight, supporting my head and my back. I notice my backpack strap hanging over one of his shoulders, resting under his right wing.

"Stay Arlo. We're going to win this time."

I'm staying.

18th July 2006

It's done. I hope.

They're all dead.

~~Who am I? What have I done?~~

Maybe the nightmares will stop now. The images of all those bodies. ~~How long, Isiah? How long?~~

But I've stopped it now, though, right? Now that I've ~~cleansed~~

Cleansed? CLEANSED? Who am I to use that sort of language? I saved The Thorns. My Thorns. I saved so many people from death.

Isiah. He was the reason for all of this.

~~Right?~~

It used to be so easy for me to write diaries, no matter how much was going on in my head. I used to be able to articulate myself.

But I don't know what I'm feeling anymore. I'm so numb.

I started The Thorns as a new life for myself. To remove all traces of ~~Jerome~~ my past. To prove I was never like that. It was all ~~him~~ someone else taking the reins. The Thorns were my chance to lead all by myself, to be who I always wished I could be.

But Isiah... it's like my life is stuck on a never ending cycle. As though my immortality means nothing. I was destined to be fooled and used, and no matter how old I get, I can never escape from it. It just goes on and on and on and I'm blind to it, until it's too late.

I'm not as strong as I thought I was.

I'm not strong at all.

There's so much blood on my hands. It's not coming off.

I did the right thing though, right?

I didn't... killing the Turned hasn't changed me, has it? It won't change me? I've not killed anyone in years. I was just doing what needed to be done to keep everyone safe.
No, because—

Julian. Are you mad at me?

—Taken from the diaries of Marianne Ashtown

CHAPTER NINETEEN

Mars
Now

We're walking again, only this time we're side by side. I absorb everything Marianne told me as we enter the sun-drenched forest.

I wonder how Jerome became The Moon. I know *why*—that part's obvious. He wanted power. I'm in half a mind to think he asked for it.

Arlo never asked. They are not the same.

I think about Marianne's past, and how much more she chooses to hide from the world. I don't blame her for withholding it, though it saddens me to think I'll never fully know who Marianne Ashtown really is. What she was like as a child, what she did in the years she's never mentioned.

I'll never be able to see inside her head.

I hate having these thoughts, but I can't help it. I'm unable to forget her story, and all the other things she might have done before or after, especially under Jerome's influence. Saying you've done bad things as an immortal could mean anything.

"I'm fine with you not trusting me, you know," she says, still keeping in pace with me. I normally walk a little faster than this.

It's like she can see the cogs whirring in my head as my silence fills her with doubt. "I know I keep so much from you. I know I don't like to let you all inside. It's just always been better that way."

"I understand that, you don't have to explain," I say, though I'm merely trying to be civil. She's never shared something so detailed with me before. She's trusting me with it all.

"I wanted to tell you that stuff though, I needed someone to know the story from my perspective." She stops me before I have a chance to ask her to elaborate. "And I want to share more with you, I need someone to know me. It's important. You never know what could happen."

"What are you implying?" I stop walking, and we pause beneath the shade of the trees.

Marianne turns to me with a smile, a tear gracing her rosy cheek.

"Take this, will you?" She pulls out a large, brass key and shoves the heavy weight into my hand.

"Marianne, what is this all about?"

She keeps smiling, but there's no happiness behind it. "There's a reason I needed you alone, and I'm glad you got me talking because this feels *right* now. It feels natural."

"You're scaring me." I step back a little, the key still in my hand.

"Oh, don't be scared, silly. It's only me. I just need to ask you something."

Oh.

"I want you to take over The Thorns."

What? I squint and scrunch my nose. Surely I misheard that? "You want me to what?"

"Take over The Thorns. Be my successor. It's always important to have someone after you."

My brow hurts. "After you? We're immortal!"

Marianne shakes her head as if I misunderstood her. "I'm sorry. I didn't mean to make it sound so ominous. I just..." She closes her eyes and takes a deep breath. "We may be immortal Mars, but our minds aren't."

I feel rather sick, to be honest. Again.

"I don't know who the oldest Vampire is. I don't know if we've ever been studied or explained or anything. But what I do know is that everything has an expiry date. We just break apart extremely slowly."

The Turned. I swallow and close my eyes momentarily. "You think you're losing your mind? Losing control?" I'm completely unprepared for this. *What's the key for?*

"I used to feed off the rich men frequenting bars and businesses of the night. At first, it was because I didn't have a choice, not necessarily because I wanted to. But then I continued. I tried not to take lives but sometimes I slipped. Sometimes, I let Jerome kill, and I'd help him drain the bodies, and..." her voice grows more and more intense as she talks. "I stopped all that. I stopped all that killing a long time ago, but I..." She peers down at the ground.

I know what she's going to say next. I think of how she's acted around the humans since Rani returned. Perhaps I'd been the only person to pick up on it.

"I've started feeding again. And I don't think I can go back anymore. The other blood isn't working the way it did, it's not satisfying me. It's not... I tried to go back, but it's not doing anything." She seems panicked, her voice hoarse with fear.

"How long?" I swallow.

"Just since Arlo and Ben. I'm sorry. I know it's inexcusable. These months have changed me. It's triggered something in me that must have always been dormant until now. I'm meant to be the leader of The Thorns to protect everyone. After what I just told you, you have every right to hate me. I could never become him, but maybe I'm my own special type of monster."

"We can help you go back. It's not been that long. We can help ween you off it. It's just an addiction. We've all fought through addictions in The Thorns, and we won. Ben won, Lawrence is winning. You'll be the same. It's just like that." My voice goes all high-pitched and I sound so naïve. And although Marianne nods, I know she's not listening. "It's not too late for you." *Maybe this really is where we all end up in the end. Fuck immortality, we're all Turned, deep down. It just takes a lot longer for most of us.*

"You're right. It's not. I just need to start putting things in place. For my own peace of mind." She's not convinced.

We stand still in the shade as the sunlight breaks through the cracks in the leaves.

I have to ask. "You haven't killed any humans since you started The Thorns, have you?"

You've killed plenty of Turned though. I've seen you do that. I shudder.

Marianne shakes her head vigorously. "No, no. I promise I haven't."

"Then, everything's okay. We can work through this." *I need to stay positive. Focused.* "Am I meant to use this?" I hold the key up between us. She grabs my wrist with a steady hand.

"Not yet. Just keep it on you."

"What is it?"

"The key to my whole life."

WE MAKE it to the church in complete silence. I'd almost forgotten why we were here until I see the crumbling stone walls, then in my head, I see him: his frail body, the too heavy wings.

I show Marianne the blood trails dried onto the stone, but they're still just as black.

I didn't need to prove my story to her, but it feels better knowing there's no denying what I saw.

She doesn't elaborate on what she told me earlier: the story of Jerome and Julian, her re-found habits, or how she thinks she's losing her humanity once and for all. I think she's just tired, and I'm not childish or dumb for thinking so. At the moment, I am of clearer mind than her. I don't have nearly three centuries of existence to clamp down on or hide away. I've not seen or experienced what she has. I've not been used the way she has. She's exhausted. And once we free Arlo, she'll finally be free, too. She will always have humanity within her, I know it. I have every faith we can return things to normal. Arlo gave me that faith, and I latch onto it.

We wait for hours until the sun begins to set. Nothing happens, though I never expected it to. But I don't want to leave yet, just in case.

I play with the large key in my pocket then grip it tight, visualising the secrets it holds. *'My whole life,'* she'd said. Everything she's ever felt and known, all written down and stored in her room. Is that what it's for? It has to be. I'm worried about her proposal. I just don't know if I'm ready for it all. I don't know why she chose me, of all people, to follow in her footsteps and take on the mantle. I don't even know if I'm strong enough for that, but she trusts me. And I need to trust her.

She paces the room like she's in a daze, not entirely herself.

WE SPEND the two hours or so sitting. Standing. Wandering. The sun moves behind the clouds, and a chill breathes into the crumbling walls.

Carmen texted Marianne's phone an hour ago to say they'd found no indication of him anywhere. Lawrence rang her about thirty minutes later, then messaged straight after saying, "No luck. Fran's still trying though."

"He's not coming," Marianne finally sighs, her eyes wandering high into the rafters.

"I know." I look down at the ground, analysing the moss.

Where are you, Arlo? Please come home.

I wrack my brains, trying to picture anywhere else in the city where he could be. Somewhere that wouldn't put any of us in danger. He's not at the hideout, or the university, or any of our flats.

Where could you possibly be, Arlo?

CHAPTER TWENTY

Arlo
One Month Ago

It's been almost two days since I let go. Since I gave in and lost myself to The Star. My father kept his word and hasn't left my side since. He cares for me, hunts for me—he does everything. He promises me I'm not weak and he knows I'm capable of doing everything myself, but he says because he never gave himself the chance to look after his son before, he wants to help me as much as he can now.

We made it to Leeds without speaking of The Star's takeover. He carried my bag the whole way, never taking his eyes off me.

"I'm proud you're my son," he kept saying. After everything he told me, I found his words grating, but the more he spoke, the more I let the statement sink into my bones. He is my father. He's alive, and he's *like me.*

We've both killed. To any onlooker, we are the same. Devils of this earth.

It's the following evening now, and after passing through York and travelling up into the Moors, he asks me to explain my tether, what brought me back to myself. I know I'm his; he's made that abundantly clear.

I'm reluctant to answer at first, as if admitting it would mean it would no longer work. If I speak too much about seeing Ben, perhaps he'll never return. And our bond would be broken. I already feel him drifting from me, from my mind, but since we're on our way to meet Casper, it makes sense to explain myself.

"I'm quite a lonely person," I start, voicing my first thought. My father nods, not sympathetically, but in a show of understanding.

"I was too. It must run in our blood."

Our blood. Black and rotten.

I push away my dark thoughts. "All my old friends ended up not being very nice. By the time I left school, I only had Rani; she was my best friend when we came to university. She was the only person I had to follow, speak to, and share company with. Then I died." *I never came back.* "Mars saved my life, but Ben welcomed me home."

My dad doesn't speak, but I know he's listening. So, I continue.

"For some reason, Ben is my tether. He's always there, keeping *it* at bay, keeping it so far away. I don't know why he cares so much, or even why *I* care so much about why he's protecting me. I feel like I need to know everything I can about him." *He might just be all in your head.*

"Do you believe in ghosts?"

The kitchen. The tapping. The smile. "I don't."

My dad nods, and we continue walking. "I do. I think he really might watch over you. We'll speak with Casper, and you'll get your answers."

I just wish my relationship with my father was normal. I wish we'd been close for years, so I could trust him through and through. I wish he never shared all he'd done, while also feeling thankful he told me. I'm struggling to process everything, so meeting Casper is the only thing I'm allowing myself to think about.

ANOTHER DAY HAS PASSED, we're closer to Durham now. I feel sick.

My father continues to take care of me.

I don't know why.

I MEET CASPER TOMORROW. I hunch, vomiting out my insides under an oak tree. My father buries the evidence and hands me a dead crow. I look up at him, tears burning my cheeks. He promises everything will be okay.

The Star is silent.

We rest against a different tree and allow our bodies to relax. We've not stopped for days. It's been impossible to think of anything else but this destination.

My father lights a small fire with wood he's collected, and we use our wings as blankets. For the first time since they became a part of me, I hold the feathers between my fingers and pull. I tug and rub my fingertips over all the different textures. I stare at them in the firelight and watch the way the light bounces off them, perplexed.

Are angels real? Or is this all for show?

I look at my dad, who seems to have dozed off, his chest slowly rising and falling, the orange glow reflecting off the necklaces around his neck. He looks peaceful. I wonder how he finds peace after everything he's done and been through.

I don't want the sympathy to crawl over me, but it does.

The sun has more or less set now, and I'm about to drift off myself, until I peer behind the flames. Ben has joined us; he sits cross-legged, wearing different clothes this time. A striped jumper.

He's looking at my father, I think, but the moment I make out his features, he's facing me.

I wait for him to speak, but he doesn't.

We sit opposite one another for what feels like an eternity, listening to the crack of the wood. The stars smile down on us from the opening in the forest's edge.

The trance I find myself in drags my eyelids shut, but my stubbornness refuses to keep them closed. I must stay focused on Ben. Every time he materialises, I think it's going to be the last.

Maybe he *is* a ghost. I don't know anymore. I'm not sure of anything now. It's like I've been born again, plonked on the earth anew, and I must learn every emotion, every sensation, every feeling all over again. I need to understand again.

I'm drifting, and I know I should put the fire out before I fall asleep, but I lack the energy to move. I'm growing delirious. Ben, barely corporeal, stands and steps through the low flames to nestle himself between us both. I turn my head to the side for a moment to catch his face, but I'm asleep before I can focus on it.

The fire is long extinguished when I awake, my father already pacing the clearing.

Today is the day.

I hope I'm not making a huge mistake. Michael *can't* know.

We arranged to meet in a park just outside of the city, the closest and furthest we could get for the safety of us all. My father insisted I purchased some new clothes first—and by 'purchase', he meant steal, because seventeen pence wouldn't get me far at all. I refused, of course, because no matter how awful I looked, I refused to inflict any more damage on humanity, no matter how small an act it may seem. He protested before eventually giving up.

"What time did you agree?" My father won't sit on the bench

beside me. Instead, he paces before me with his hands clasped behind his back. *Is he nervous?*

Perhaps this is his first human interaction in a while. A normal conversation, devoid of everything that has consumed the last twenty years of his life.

"Eleven. Soon," I say, resting my hands in my lap. Trying to stop the jittering.

When I finally spot Casper walking up the path to our left, I consider hiding my true form. But then I feel like an idiot. Casper saw me that day. Casper knows what I am. I shouldn't hide anything from him.

"Is that him?" My dad asks as I stand. My organs liquify as Casper's face comes into focus. His hair is much longer, as is mine, and he's much slimmer than I remember. His clothes are plain, and his face is absent of his former piercings. I hold in my breath, and I sense my father tense beside me. He mutters something under his breath, fast and panicked sounding. I have no time to ask if he's okay because Casper is here, and all words escape me.

He stops dead before us, taking in our forms. My dad must have also relaxed his control, allowing Casper to perceive him as he perceived me. Casper doesn't speak while analysing every inch of us. He keeps his hands in his jean pockets—balled into fists, I sense.

I don't know how to talk or initiate a conversation. I'm on the verge of breaking down with the realisation Casper is real; that he's okay and unharmed. He gulps, assessing my father. Instead of asking questions, he says, "We're going to find somewhere slightly more sheltered to talk, yeah?"

I nod and move aside to let Casper lead the way. We follow him to a path completely enclosed by bushes and vines with a single, unoccupied bench. Here, we can be ourselves and just talk. *If I can find the words to.*

"So," Casper says, clapping his hands together and sitting to rest his elbows on his knees. "Who are you?"

The question seems directed at both of us, but I know he wants to know about Jerome. I promised Casper I'd be alone. It's obvious he's intimidated and confused.

"My name is Jerome Mair. I'm Arlo's father, and unfortunately, I'm in the same position as him. It's a pleasure to meet you, Casper." My dad extends a jewelled hand for Casper to shake, but he doesn't try to engage in the introduction. Instead, Casper looks at me, confused.

"You said you were going to be alone?"

"I was," I manage, my throat clogging. I have to keep my head tipped back slightly to keep my airways clear. "He found me."

"He's really like you?"

"Yes." I don't know how to elaborate.

Casper nods slowly, absorbing everything he's pieced together so far. Then he leans back on the bench and looks up at the trees, addressing the leaves instead. "Before I tell you anything, I want a full explanation. And I mean *full*. No cutting corners, no hiding details you don't think I'd understand. I want *everything*."

I'd prepared for this, or I told myself I had, but it was still hard trying to figure out where to start. Thankfully, my dad begins for us.

The more he speaks, the more comfortable I become with inputting my side and perspective. Casper's eyes widen, and his brows raise, but he listens to everything and doesn't speak a word until we're done. My dad explains his story from the moment he met Michael to the present with no sugar coating. He even shares new details with me. He doesn't repeat the details of what he did with Marianne, though he will have to explain that another time. *Another time.*

Once my father rounds off his story, I explain my own, recalling everything from the moment I rose again. I tell Casper what I did after I fled. Of the lives I Manipulated, the lives I took.

But Casper doesn't flinch.

When we finish, he audibly breathes in, then *laughs*, though I interpret it as more of a reaction to the absurdity of it all. There's nothing humorous about the situation.

"What do you want to know, then? About Ben?" he says it so casually, even my father is taken aback, confused. This was not the reaction he expected, either.

"You don't hate me? Hate us?" *You don't have any questions?*

"Not yet." Casper almost smiles. "You haven't given me a reason to hate you, Arlo," he says. "You killed Lucy. That's all that matters to me. Call me inhuman, call me insensitive, call me what you want, but I believe you. What do you want to know? I've wanted to meet with you for a while. I'm just relieved to know you're alive."

He doesn't quite sound like himself, but I remind myself I've not seen him for six months, and *a lot* has happened. I swallow.

"I just want to know why he's always with me," I say, and the moment I do, I feel Ben's presence appear. My dad's wings flutter, and Casper's gaze wanders, but no one speaks. *Can they see him too?* A breeze picks up, flowing between the three of us. "I want to know why he means so much to me."

Casper's heavy breathing worries me, and I fear I've triggered something. A memory perhaps. He shrugs, and his brow quirks up in worry as he looks at us both. "I was ready to talk about him in great detail, tell you what an incredible human being he was, the impact he had on us all, but I don't think that will give you the answer you're looking for. I think I know why now. I've just figured it out."

"What do you mean?" I ask. I'm not following.

"Ben was everything to me." He's staring just to my side, where I feel Ben's warmth. There's no way he can see him, too. I'm imagining all this, surely. Ghosts don't exist. They don't. He's just a fragment of my imagination, my beacon. He's not really there. He's not.

"He was my light. I followed him everywhere. He changed

everything in my life, and... I'm sorry." Casper's words are silenced with a sob as he stands to face us both.

"You look so much like him," he says to my father. At first, I assume he's referring to me, but then he continues, and my gut sinks to the floor.

"I know no-one else would have picked up on that, but I spent ten years of my life breathing the same air as him. I've just watched you talk and talk, and act out your emotions and feelings. I've analysed every motion and mannerism and tried to piece together why you seemed so familiar from the moment I saw you, Jerome. And then it just clicked. All the pieces fell into place."

I look at Ben before I look at my father, as if he holds more answers. My brain is churning away into mush, and I try to focus on his face. He won't look at me. Why won't he look at me? *Breathe.*

Casper holds his mouth with trembling hands, looking directly at my father when he asks, "Does the name Katerina Martín mean anything to you?" His words are laced with malice, but I don't think he means it.

My head snaps fully in my dad's direction as he staggers back and loses his balance.

Oh.

Oh.

I feel faint.

Casper's reaction to my dad's response is all I need to know.

It's funny, because in this moment, I tell myself it should have been obvious, but it wasn't. I never would have known.

"It does, doesn't it? Katerina Martín. Do you know who she is?" Casper's voice shakes like I've never heard it before.

Ben, look at me. Please.

"Kat. Katie. New York. September. 1990." My dad speaks almost in code, as if he's piecing it together in real time. Everything comes to him bit by bit until the whole picture materialises.

'I never met my biological dad.'

Ben—

"You know who she is?" Casper says again, his voice the firmest it's been. It's not a question; it's a confirmation.

My father nods then falls to his knees, dropping his head into his hands.

"She married his dad six months after she returned because she didn't want the family shame. She was stressed and embarrassed, and he promised to be a father and help her and her son."

Casper's crying, and I can't breathe. I feel Ben's hand hold mine. Tight. It's so real. He's—

"My son."

My brother.

BEN LOOKS AT ME. He's so whole and real. His emerald eyes gaze straight into mine as his brows tense and his grip tightens.

I know why he means so much to me. Why I killed for him. Why he's always there to fight for me. He didn't know, though, did he? He was just so kind to everyone, no matter who they were. *He* was the real angel.

"I didn't know, but I think my mind did. I always felt there was *something*. Maybe that's why I couldn't leave," Ben says, his voice soft and unsure.

"I didn't—" I choke up completely and have to turn away. I feel Ben's grip slip from mine as I look towards my dad and Casper. Casper kneels at his side.

"She didn't hate you. Ben didn't hate you, either, but they just wondered why you never called her." Casper's tone is gentle and strong as he reaches for my dad's hand.

"I didn't mean to." My dad struggles to breathe, and I don't know what to do.

But Ben joins us. He stands amongst us and crouches to their height. He's so close to Casper, and then he wraps his arms around him, and leans into his shoulder. I watch the tears drip freely from Casper's eyes onto the grass. *Is he really there?*

My dad looks up, his eyes red raw. He's cowering like a child in fear. He's not a good person, he said so himself, but he left Ben's mother without knowing, just like he'd left mine.

"I should have called. She left the next day, and *I should have called.*"

My dad was human for two years before he met my mother. He lived before my mother.

He's Ben's father.

"It's okay," Ben says. My dad freezes and stops blinking.

"You didn't know. You couldn't have known," Ben continues, smiling. I might just be imagining it, but Casper looks as if he's leaning into Ben's embrace.

"I'm sorry," my dad says. He says it to everyone, an apology deep from his soul. It's all he can say.

I'm numb.

I built up all my remaining courage to see Casper, to learn more about a man who meant a lot to me, and now I know why. I had never considered this. Benjamín Marco Audley is my brother, and we didn't get to learn that together. I discovered I had an older brother I had always longed for, who died before I got to treat him as one. I only ever caught glimpses of his life, he only ever got snippets of mine. We lived in different cities, grew up in different environments, experienced entirely different things, and all the while, we shared the same father, who didn't even know we existed. We ended up going to the same university and following in our father's footsteps without even realising it. Is this what fate is?

Ben is my brother. He's mine by blood. Now he's gone.

"You're..." Casper starts, watching me from the ground. I zone back into the present. Ben isn't here anymore. Just Casper and my father. Both turn their attention to me.

"I should never have been granted that wish of life," my father says, wiping his eyes. "I ruined it for you both. I was so fucking *blind.*"

Does he wish I was never born?

"You're their father, though. Whether or not you were to blame, you left behind two sons. And now you know. Now you can be their dad." Casper stares at my father, his entire manner calm and reassuring.

"Do you regret me?" I ask. All other thoughts have left me.

"Oh god, no! No, no, no." Jerome is on his feet in an instant, heading straight over to me with his arms outstretched. I don't want him to hug me, but at the same time, I do. I don't know what to do or how to feel. "*Never* think that. You are my world, my anchor. The moment I saw you, you changed *everything.* I am your father; you are my son. I would burn worlds for you and vow to protect you for eternity. You are *my boy.* I love you more than words can say."

He hugs me, and though my arms remain by my side, I don't hate the feeling. I spy Casper watching over my father's shoulder. He sits on the grass with his arms wrapped over his knees, his eyes still weary.

"She killed him. Lucy. She killed my son," my dad whispers into my shoulder.

"She tortured him. For fun. And Michael sat by and watched. He did nothing," I spit. The anger grumbles in my stomach and squeezes its hands around my throat.

My father's grip tightens for a moment before he steps back and lets go. He locks eyes with me. "We're going to end him."

I hear Casper stand behind us. "I want to help," he says, before I can even open my mouth.

My father steps back to let Casper join the circle, just as Ben reappears from behind. The four of us stand in a circle, facing each other. I stare at my brother opposite me. He smiles, the rivulets of tears a permanent stain on his cheeks. He holds Casper's hand, whose fingers *curl* around it in a real grip. Then I watch him do the same with my father, clinging tightly to him.

I'm frozen in place, trying to concentrate on everything transpiring around me, controlling my breathing—blinking away the water glazing my vision.

"You can all see me?" Ben's voice is so quiet, I almost think I'm imagining it. But then my dad responds, his gaze distant.

"I see you, son. I'm sorry."

Then Casper speaks. "I see you, Ben. I feel you. My eternal."

"I..." I'm staring at him. His soft black curls, his freckles, his vivid green eyes. His smile. His light. His life. "I see you Ben, I always will."

"We're going to end The Sun," my dad says. "By any means necessary. We will not allow him to take over every mind, every soul, and burn through humanity. He cannot win this; we are too much for him. Humans. Life. Love. He will never understand. And we won't give him a chance to."

We're doing this. The Star and The Moon have gone.

"I love you, Ben," Casper says, closing his eyes.

"I love you, son." My dad's eyes are also closed now as the pair of them lower their heads.

"I love you, brother. I love you. Thank you." It's Ben. He's looking at me. He's speaking to me.

"Ben," I manage.

"Hurry," he says.

The link fades before I can acknowledge that this really is the last time. He's not coming back. But I feel him now. I feel him deep in my soul. And I will, forever. Forever.

Goodbye, brother.

CHAPTER TWENTY ONE

Arlo
One Month Ago

C asper walks us to Ben's grave. I've seen it. From a distance. But I never had time to see it up close. To touch the stone. To close my eyes and *remember him*.

The cemetery is quiet, as it usually is, but we spot Ben's grave from a mile away because of the endless flowers propped against it. A mix of white and purples. Purple was his favourite colour. I remember that.

My lungs feel weird behind my ribs, and I have to slow down before we reach it. It's a very heavy feeling, visiting the grave of someone you knew whose importance you only realised when it was too late.

My father steps straight over and bends down to grip the headstone. He lowers his head, his hair almost trailing the grass. He mutters things under his breath and stays there for a while. I keep enough distance to take it all in, to read the marble.

'In loving memory of Benjamin Marco Audley. Born 23rd June

1991 – Died 4th January 2019, aged 27. Siempre amado, en la vida y en la muerte. Loving son, taken too soon.'

I understand the Spanish but I wish I'd studied it more. I don't think he spoke it much, but perhaps we could have learned it together. I find myself wishing for many things I can't have now.

"This is the first time we're the only people at his grave." Casper looks at me.

I forgot about Forever Red. About Lawrence and Francesca. How they were loved and adored by tens of thousands of people.

"It's beautiful," I say.

"It is. A beautiful grave for a beautiful soul."

We stand in silence, having our moments alone with him. My father is still at the foot of the headstone.

"I didn't want to come back here," Casper says eventually.

"Ever?" I ask.

He shakes his head. "I nearly moved back to America permanently. I wanted nothing more to do with this place. I thought that was it. Everything was over. Why would I want to stay here day in and day out when he wasn't with me to do the things we always did? But then months passed, and I knew I had to stop running. The Thorns fell apart, Marianne locked herself away, Fran and Lawrence travelled around in their attempts to move on, and the only person left to tend to his grave was Mars. They made it their responsibility. They came nearly every day at one point, and I felt so guilty I'd left them."

Mars. I think about them a lot, and Rani. My lifelines. I never deserved them.

"I'm staying here for a while, I think. I need to get my life back on track. Ben would hate knowing I let his death waste me away. I have reasons to keep me here now."

"Your friends," I try.

"And you."

Why do I matter? "Me?"

Casper takes in a deep breath, then sucks in his lips, facing me.

"You're his brother. Which means you're family, regardless of the technicalities. You're family, and I'm going to help you to stop this." He doesn't reach out to grip my shoulder or playfully fist pump my arm like I expect. He knew what I wasn't comfortable with.

"Thank you," I say. Words cannot express how grateful I am. I don't understand how I'm worth all of this.

Casper huffs a gentle laugh. "You're so much like him, you know."

"I am?" *I am.*

"People say we're a product of our environment, but I believe there are things so deep-rooted among family members. You cry the same." Casper observes this as a small tear snakes its way down my right cheek. I wipe it away aggressively, not wanting to be analysed. But maybe I do.

"What else?" I ask.

My dad is standing again and steps back to join us. "Did he have a happy life?" he asks, interrupting my question.

Casper lowers his head slightly. "He did. Mostly. He had a lot of struggles, a lot of things he kept from people, but he was still one of the brightest souls I've ever had the privilege of meeting. Of being with."

Jerome nods as if he expected this answer. "But you made him happy?"

"I wouldn't say that. I don't think relationships can cure everything, but they can give you a reason to want to search for a cure. Ben was very hard on himself, and it scared me. He scared me a lot, but he persevered through every storm thrown at him."

My dad nods again, looking back at the grave.

Casper moves between us. "Ben and Arlo are the sweetest and most selfless people I know. Their mothers raised them well, but there is something else connecting them, even before the world made its mark. And that's you, Jerome. Even though you didn't even know they existed.

"And to answer your question, Arlo. Sometimes, when Ben told me something about you, or I found out something from Mars or Carmen, I often related them back to something I experienced with him—things Ben would have done, or how he would have acted. Ben was a very private person, he avoided so much, but he was there for every time that mattered. The first thing he thought when he met you was that you were an angel. He felt that connection immediately and insisted he had to look after you. What was the main thing you thought about *him*?"

That he was like me. That he would understand me.

"He was like the older brother I never had." *Truth.*

Casper smiles—a beaming, proud smile. I've missed him.

"There you go," he says.

My dad comes close to my side. "Arlo, can you feel it? They're gone."

I know he's talking about The Moon and The Star. They truly are no longer with us. Dead and buried. Casper seems to understand what we're referring to as well. "You're completely yourselves now, right?"

We both nod. Freedom has never tasted so sweet. "They're gone. Forever."

I hope.

We step away from the grave and walk further into the centre of the cemetery.

"I need to see them. Melissa, Katerina," my dad says as we walk. "I need to speak to them. Not to explain myself—I don't expect them to listen or forgive me—but I just want to see them and let them see me. Is that bad? Am I wrong for wanting this?"

"I figured you'd want to do something like that. I've already been thinking about the best way to introduce you to Kat. I don't know how she'll react. After losing her only son, introducing his father might not be pleasant now. But I know she wonders about you. Ben said so. So, we can try it. I'll go with you."

I think about my mum, how she knows nothing about what's

happened this year. Someone will have kept her up to date, surely. Even if it was a lie, she deserves to be free of worries. I need to see her myself. I know I do, despite the danger. And I want to bring Jerome home.

I want to do this.

He'll find you.

We can make it quick.

He'll come for you both.

We won't let him touch her if he does.

Gosh, my mind is so clear.

So, that's what we do. We put everything to rest, once and for all. A reunion. Before it's too late.

I GO with them to Nottingham first. I haven't been this far south in a long while. I forget how much different it feels—not just the weather. There seems to be this shift when you get half-way down the country when you become aware you're no longer in the north. It's hard to explain but I just feel it.

We ride by train, and the entire journey is filled with the memory of Ben. Husband, son, brother. Invisible words on the marble. Words only the three of us can see.

Katerina knows Casper is coming, and she knows he's bringing 'people', though he didn't disclose who. There's no soft way of saying it over the phone.

My dad vomits on the way up the road when he knows we're close. We have to stop for a while, even though he doesn't want to. He insists he needs to do this.

We invented a narrative where Casper, using the descriptions and timelines Ben gave him over the years, found Jerome in America (we pretended he had lived there permanently for a while). Despite what he said, Ben did want to meet his father, another similarity we held.

Katerina already knew I existed, apparently. Ben mentioned me multiple times before he died, despite only knowing me for just over two months. There's no way to fake the coincidence, even if you tried. Jerome had never set foot in Durham until Michael brought him there. The fact I met Ben at all is a miracle, and I'm not one to believe in them.

Casper walks up the driveway first, and the two of us hold back.

This is Ben's childhood home, I realise. It's a small, suburban sixties build, with a sloping roof and flat windows. Steps lead up to the glass porch from the freshly cut front lawn. We watch from around the corner as Casper slips inside the porch and knocks on the door. Katerina answers seconds later. My father's breath hitches as he moves around the bush. I've seen her once, from afar, mourning the death of her only son. Her long, black, curly hair is woven with strands of grey; her face more aged than I remember. She mustn't be that much older than my own mother. Even through the glass, I sense the tiredness in her eyes.

I watch the conversation transpire. Casper leans in for a much-welcomed hug, then I have to look away for I know it's time. I reach out a gloved hand for my father's. He bought me them—actually bought them—on the way here. A new pair with no holes. "So, you're always in control," he said. It meant a lot to me.

Now it's my cue to introduce myself. We'd planned this order, so it wasn't too overwhelming. Katerina knew enough about me, so meeting me shouldn't be as hard.

I wait for Casper to come down and collect me, and he tells me she's gone back inside to wait and get more comfortable. It makes sense, and it also gives me an extra few moments to breathe.

He leads me up the steep drive and we enter the house. My father waits outside still.

I don't know how to describe it, but the inside of the house looks exactly how I expected: plain but cosy décor. A crucifix is pinned in the hallway amongst frames. I don't have time to analyse them fully before I'm directed into the living room, but I do glimpse Ben amongst the photos.

I walk in and Katerina is sitting by the window, cupping a mug of tea. The size and layout of the room highlights my height, but I don't linger on it as Casper introduces me. Katerina shakes her head slowly, pain washing her features. She surely can't see through the glamour I'm forcing over myself.

"Oh, Casper," she says, still looking at me, absorbing every inch of my presence. "What have you done?" She's not angry, though. She knows the answer.

"Sorry, Arlo. Come, come sit. It's lovely to meet you." She gestures for me to share the sofa with her after clearly acknowledging the panic on my face. I walk over to the window but keep a wide distance between us.

Casper let me borrow some clothes for this meeting. They're not my style, but I couldn't be picky. He gave me an old, plain white t-shirt and a black pair of ripped jeans I had to add a belt to. I could go back to the comfort of my worn corduroy later, he said. I tried to style my hair as casually as I could, despite its current length.

Katerina stares at me, yet her presence is gentle. "You're his brother. Aren't you, dear?"

I look at her and nod. A mother can always tell.

"Why didn't Ben tell me?" she asks Casper, who now sits on the sofa beside us. His usual spot, I presume. Casper's eyes speak a thousand words.

"He didn't know, did he? You did this all by yourself." Again, she doesn't seem mad at all. She's exceptionally calm.

"I figured stuff out," is all Casper says. It's enough.

"But you spoke to him; you knew each other. He spoke highly of you." She's looking at me like my mum does, but she doesn't reach out. *Casper told her, too. He understands me.*

"He meant a lot to me. He helped me a lot, too. I didn't know it, but he acted like a brother." I'm surprised at my own calmness, but she keeps me at ease. I'm not afraid. Maybe I'm just disassociating. It will hit me in a moment.

"Would you like some tea? I made some tea. I can make you some tea if you would like. What do you like?" Her words come out of her mouth frantically now. Maybe it's just hit *her*. She stands before I can speak.

"Tea would be nice, thank you." I smile. *It's coming.*

Her face drops a little as the burst of energy fades. "How do you like it? Ben liked his black with one sugar. Is that what you like?" *Poor Katerina.*

The sudden image of my dad waiting outside throws me into panic mode. It's like a ticking time bomb without the countdown.

"Black, please. No sugar."

"Casper? The usual? Coffee?"

Casper positions himself to stand. "Erm, actually, I'll have a tea, please. Ben's tea." He clears his throat. She leaves with a nod, and I want to leave now too.

"We can't bring him in. Not yet. I made a mistake," Casper whispers, leaning closer towards me.

I agree. Bringing me was bad enough. It wouldn't be fair to her. It's too much.

Casper leaps up to the window and looks out for my father. His shoe and shirt are visible, and he's clearly looking through the leaves. Casper shakes his head and makes a neck-cutting action. All we can do is hope he gets the message.

That calms me a bit more, but it doesn't entirely neutralise the rising nerves within me. I'm here now. The ground can't swallow me up, so I need to accept it. *Come on, Arlo. You can do this.*

Breathe. She's going to ask questions. I need to prepare for that. Humour her. She's been through enough.

Katerina reappears shortly with our steaming hot drinks and biscuits on a tray. Homemade. She places them on the coffee table in the centre of the room and hands the mugs out before returning to her seat beside me. I adjust my legs, straightening them out, then tucking them back in. I don't like taking up too much space.

The little alarm clock in front of the TV is all I can hear before she speaks again.

"How old are you? Can I ask?"

She wants to piece together the timeline of events. I understand. I'd want to do the same.

"I'm nineteen. Born on the second of September 1999," I reply —my chest a heavy weight to hold.

Katerina hums, processing it. "Nice time to be born," she says.

"It makes me the oldest in my year, usually. Unless they were born a day before me." It just comes out. *She didn't need that fact, Arlo.* I'm a little stressed, you see.

Katerina smiles with mother-like pity. "Ben was born eight years before you."

Silence.

"Are you coming back for his birthday? I was going to make a cake." She flicks her attention to Casper, but her gaze returns to me before she finishes the sentence. "I was going to make his favourite, just like I used to when he was a kid. I—" She chokes up then and grabs her mouth, turning her chin away from us both to blink away the tears. "I'm sorry," she says.

Casper is on his feet already and by her side. He scoops his arms around her shoulders, leaning down to kiss her crown. "No, I'm sorry. I should have explained beforehand. I've sprung a lot on you."

Katerina bites back a sob as she nods, then shakes her head, then nods again. She struggles to look at either of us. I feel like I should leave now. I'm making everything worse by being here.

"I just... sorry." She wipes her nose and eyes with her sleeve, and Casper takes the mug from her hands and sets it down. He stoops to her side.

"We'll leave you. I'm sorry, Kat."

But she grabs his arm with both hands, her eyes wide. "No, no. Please," she begs, looking at me. "I want to talk to Arlo. I want to talk about my son, his brother. Thank you, Casper. Thank you for introducing us. I'm just... I get emotional easily." She bats away the sympathy in the room and lowers her head to wipe invisible dust from her jeans. I don't want to move a muscle. I'm still struggling to take a deep breath.

"How did you meet Benjamín?" she asks, shaking herself out of her sadness and bouncing back on the settee, her eyes dry. "He told me you were a student. Were you a fan of their band?" She smiles.

"More or less, yeah. I'd heard of them, but I had no idea where they lived. Meeting them was a pure coincidence." We'd planned this response. I had learned the script by heart. Casper backed me up.

"Arlo was a poor unsuspecting bystander sitting beside Ben on a bench when a fan approached him."

Part truth. It was important we kept the story as real as we could. Not only did it mean we were lying less to a woman who didn't deserve it, but it was far easier to remember. I'm a terrible liar. I just *can't.*

"Oh, Ben mentioned this! So, you didn't realise you were sitting next to him?" Katerina's whole manner has changed. She's lighter, warmer. Happier.

I remember the night vividly. Janie and Beth. I wonder how they reacted to Ben's death. *Gosh, Arlo. Why must you always be so negative?*

"I don't know if Ben told you, but I'm pretty connected to my faith. While I'm not going to preach or anything, I believe this was God's intention. I think He needed you to meet in that moment.

He brought you together. Sorry. Ben would hate me for bringing it up."

Maybe she's right.

"Coincidences only go so far." Casper grins, and by the way Katrina looks at him, I believe he's echoing her words.

"He also said you play piano? Like him? I've still got one of his keyboards in his room. Maybe you could play sometime?" Adrenaline still fuels her voice, clinging to the happiness.

I panic. I hate performing in front of people, regardless of who they are, and now would be one of the worst moments to go anywhere near the keys—

Casper saves me again. "Well, actually, that's what I wanted to play you. Arlo actually recorded some pieces with us, and I was wondering if you'd like to hear them? Ben plays his bass, and Francesca is singing. It's not a final song, by any means. It was just something we put together, but it sounds incredible." He's already pulling out his phone as Katerina nods. Despite the lingering embarrassment, I'd also like to hear it. I wonder how Casper mixed it together.

He presses play, and the three of us listen in silence as the instruments start amongst the recording crackle and muffled, sombre lyrics. The second the bass starts, Katerina shifts beside me again, rubbing her hands together and nodding in time with her eyes closed.

It really sounds amazing.

I almost cry.

Ben is my brother. Mine. He is me, and I am him. Yet he's gone.

I turn away before it finishes. It hurts too much.

"Arlo?" It's Katerina who notices first.

I don't dare look at her out of embarrassment. I should not be the one needing comfort here. But then she calls me 'son' and tells me to come for a hug. I melt into myself. I'm not *her* son, but it doesn't matter. She's the mother to my big brother, she's a protector. She possesses no malice, harshness, or cruelty.

I turn to face her. The pair watch me closely. I don't want to cry—I really don't—but the tears come, anyway. I flop onto my side, resting my head in her lap. She lifts a gentle hand to brush the hair from my face, stroking my temple with soft fingertips. I'm too numb to move. I barely even let my own mother get so close most of the time, but I don't want to move away. I fix my eyes on the pattern on the rug at our feet and let the tears fall. My wings stretch behind me to avoid touching her, but she doesn't even know they're there.

I think she's talking to Casper. I can hear their muffled words, mild and delicate. Words of comfort. Then her hands stop and move to hover over my shoulder for a breath.

"Ben would have loved to have been your older brother. He always wished he had one. You're welcome here whenever you want. Forever," she says.

I've got another home now. Another place where I'm wanted. Another place where I can be safe. Which is when it hits me. It's so dangerous for us to be here.

But if Michael gets even a breath too close to her, I'll kill him, and it will be easy.

I'm suddenly charged with rage and sit up. *If he comes, I will destroy him.*

Let him come. Let him see what I'm capable of.

Casper looks at me with a hint of worry, but I smile—a real smile, not formed of pretences. I know I can do this. I will end all of this.

KATERINA TALKS SOME MORE, asking about my mother before inevitably talking about my father. I tell her the truth; she deserves it. I tell her I never knew him either—narrowly avoiding the fact I know him *now*. She doesn't seem angry or frustrated, though. I think she expected that.

She tells me how she met David, who offered to marry her a few months after they met, so they could start a family together without the questions or awkward stares. She says she wished Ben kept her family name, but in the end, he was just as much David's son as hers. They brought him into the world and were there for every moment of his childhood. She doesn't dwell too much on their divorce, but she's aware of the toll it took on Ben.

"I had to learn to be a better mother, even then," she admits. Ben always said she was the best. Mothers are always too hard on themselves.

After sharing more stories, happy tears, and a plate of biscuits (deliciously homemade), she asks her final question. The one I could tell she'd been holding back.

"Do you know where he is?"

We freeze.

Katerina's face twitches ever so slightly. "I don't need to meet him, if you do. I just—Sorry, I didn't mean to ruin the conversation. I can't help but wonder what he's doing now, that's all: what he looks like after twenty-eight years, and if he's settled down. He was nice to me, but I only knew him for a day." She half laughs. "Gosh. It doesn't matter. I'm keeping you. I'm sure you're both very busy. I can't believe you travelled all the way here to see me!"

Katerina stands to clear the used crockery. I stand too, as does Casper, and we promise to return soon. For Ben's birthday. For cake.

She kisses Casper's cheek politely, and then pauses before me, waiting for me to initiate the hug if I'm comfortable enough. I'm comfortable enough. Just. I hug her, and she holds on tight.

· · ·

I LEAVE FEELING LIGHTER, despite the final tone of the room. I'm glad we visited.

It takes me a second too long to notice my father is no longer standing where he was, though. He's not around the corner either.

"Oh shit," Casper mutters, and I know he's thinking the same as me.

Michael.

I'm ready. I can do this.

Can I really fight him alone and win, though?

A few minutes later, after frantically searching, I spot him. My father. Alone. I let out all the air in my lungs.

He's sitting on a metal bench in the nearby cul-de-sac with a bottle of what looks like expensive red wine at his feet. His head is heavy in his hands. The Manipulation is so strong even I take a second to see his wings. Once we approach, he looks up in a slight panic, shielding his eyes from the sun.

"Oh, hi," he says, completely oblivious to our fear.

"We thought you'd been taken, idiot!" Casper shouts.

"Woah, I didn't go that far. My legs were hurting. You were gone a while!"

"Dad," I say, much softer than Casper. Jerome's head turns to me, and his whole manner relaxes.

"Sorry."

"I thought you'd gone again."

"Never." His tone is entirely serious now. "I promised I'd never leave you again. Did you not believe I meant it?"

I just struggle to trust.

"Don't answer that." He bats his hand and stands on unsteady legs, bringing the bottle up with him. "I'm sorry. I didn't think. Forgive me."

"Any reason for the wine?" Casper asks, almost comically.

My dad raises the bottle to inspect it. He's like a teenager, not my biological father. "Ahh, well. I got a bit stressed and worried I was going to fuck everything up, which I have a great track record for, so I thought I'd soften the edges a little!"

I only realise the bottle is empty when I figure he's *drunk*.

"I think we all need to find somewhere nice and relaxing to get some food. Any preferences? Italian?" Casper takes charge of the situation, and my dad willingly releases the bottle, giving in like a child about to stomp his feet in a hissy fit. It's so absurd, I begin to zone out again.

"I'll find us a nice restaurant, and you're going to sober up and behave." Casper talks to my dad like he talks to Lawrence, another man who enjoys his beverages. But his voice also holds something deeper, like he's done this for many years, not just with Lawrence.

"I'm sorry, I shouldn't have—" A stunned hiccup interrupts my dad, but instead of laughing, like I've seen many people do at this stage, he sighs. "God, that hit me all at once. I'm a lot worse at handling my alcohol than I used to be. Huh. Funny. I'm still learning what it's like being me in this body." He sounds a lot more serious now.

He's not a vampire anymore, not that that affects his tolerance, but he's also technically just a human now. The Moon is gone, meaning his body is just a vessel for his soul. Have I forgotten what that's like? Not having to feed off poor woodland creatures and rats for the rest of my eternal life? I know we can eat normal food if we want, but it's never enough.

Are we even eternal? Who is the oldest vampire? Is that a fact anyone can get hold of? Do we just take a very, *very* long time to age?

Do we go crazy? Will eternity be too much to bear?

Questions for another time, Arlo. My mind tells me.

With his phone in hand, Casper leads us down the road towards the city centre.

It might be a long walk. Enough to sober my father up.

It is.

Casper spends the whole journey talking to my dad about Ben, and my dad asks everything that seemingly comes to mind. He eventually stops hiccupping, and his manner returns to being relatively normal. The bounce in his step simmers and his shoulders loosen. He says he understands why it wasn't the best time to introduce himself to Katerina as he falls into step beside me. He reminds me he never expects forgiveness.

I know, dad. I know.

WE SIT and talk over dinner, which definitely feels weird at first. We devise a plan to stop Michael.

"He needs the strength of all three of us to be powerful enough to get inside *everyone's* mind," my dad says. "And he wants to be somewhere historical and central enough to channel his energy."

I knew next to none of this. I really was just a pawn.

"So, he wants to control us all? Why?" Casper asks. I've always wondered the same. Michael promised me I was destined for great things—to change the world—but he never let me remember what for or why.

"As far as I know, the entities have been overlooking this planet for centuries—millennia, even. They think they've found the flaw in our code, so they chose three hosts to pose as vessels for their existence. They believe themselves to be the cure for this world. To make everyone *perfect.*

"Make us perfect?" I repeat.

My dad nods. "Gods playing gods," he says solemnly.

"But we're—*they're*—not gods. Michael even said so."

"Not the gods of faith or religious texts. Just pure, unimaginable power."

"Aliens?" Casper suggests, and my dad just shrugs.

"If you want to see them that way, I suppose they are. They're not of this earth."

"But why did they choose us? Why Michael, why you and me?"

Jerome shrugs again. "Michael was unfortunate, though I was led by desire no one had ever expressed before. As for you... well. You're my son. My guess is, Michael, *The Sun,* saw how vulnerable *I* was, and thought you'd be an easy target. He was wrong, though, because I'm not half the man you are. He prayed on your vulnerabilities and insecurities, but I only see them as your strengths. He made a mistake with you, and that's why we're going to end it."

All I can do is nod. Nod and absorb it all. I've suddenly lost my appetite for everything, not that I need this food anyway.

"Are vampires connected?" Casper asks, tucking into his pasta and breaking the tension.

He has a good point. The two kinds share commonalities, with Manipulation and immortality being the major ones that stand out. Maybe they are of a similar origin. I never thought too deeply about it until now. I was too caught up in *not being myself.* But now I *am* myself, and I need to know the answer.

"Yes." My dad's tone is unreadable. That's all he says. A confirmation. Then he drops his fork, sits back in his chair, and presses his fingers together, falling into a trance.

"Dad?" I try regaining his attention.

Very slowly, he nods his head, calculating his thoughts.

"I wonder if he knew that too," he says, his eyes still disengaged.

"Knew what? Dad, do you know something about vampires?" *He has been around for nearly five hundred years.*

I swear he grins. "I wonder if Michael knew he'd chosen a first turned."

First?

"Dad?"

Casper remains silent, his eyes never leaving my father.

Finally, my dad straightens and flexes his ringed fingers over the table, looking down. "Okay. It's time I share this then, I think. I don't like to bring attention to this—at all, honestly—but I've got a lot of trust to earn back, so it's no use hiding this from you." He addresses us both.

"The vampire who turned me was a woman called *Clove,*" her name doesn't come easily from his mouth—foul memories. "She told me she was the first and had not been turned. In fact, she fed willingly from the 'gift of the sky'. She never told me what she meant, and before long, I'd almost forgotten her story entirely, but it adds up.

"Around sixty years before I was born, there was a phenomenon in the sky. Small rocks scattered across the globe. At the time, she said there was only one, but in the early twentieth century, I studied and learned they hit as far as Sri Lanka. It was fascinating, but it disproved her theory. If people around the world fed, just like she did, then there could be at least *fourteen* firsts. Fourteen recorded on-land sites. And I may have been *her* first, but there is no evidence to say there weren't dozens and dozens more that came before me."

"Sorry, I'm following, but how is this evidence?" Casper says. I just sit, stunned, which is something I've always been good at.

"Oh, sorry. I got carried away. What I was getting to was the research I found, which is why I said it added up. There was another documented case, the only other documented case of extreme similarity, on the 31st of October 1754. The day Marianne became a vampire."

Marianne. I hold my breath.

"The day her brother died, and she turned him too. The brother who went on to have visions of something he called 'the end of old time'. I only pieced the dates and everything together once Michael turned me, but Marianne's brother Nicholas essentially *predicted* this whole thing. These entities inside me and Arlo must be from the same point of origin. I think The Sun somehow planted some small part of itself in Nicholas that day, making him a messenger for what was to come."

I can't bring myself to look at Casper eye to eye but I have a feeling he's thinking the same as me. I hope he is.

"The Sun, or at least a part of it, landed that day, in whatever incorporeal form it possessed. It didn't search for a host then, but it knew it wouldn't be able to survive long on its own. I believe it shared enough of itself with Nicholas to get a taste of this world before settling on a host. The spying eyes of a creature beyond human comprehension, hidden in plain sight. Nicholas was the first piece of the puzzle, only he lost his mind in the process, started a cult, and then disappeared off the face of the earth." He makes a 'hmm' sound as he drops his head, voice quieting. "I only wish I'd told her what I found when I did instead of trying to always have the upper hand. Maybe we could have stopped things before they even began. Hmm, hindsight and all that..."

Mine and Casper's expressions are enough for my dad to realise this is all news to us both. We finally lock eyes for a moment.

"She didn't tell you about him?"

"Nope." Casper seems a little mad now. I think I am too. *I am.*

"She never even mentioned him?"

"Not once." He's definitely mad. Then Casper slaps the table and just... laughs. "You know, if I wasn't already a vampire who'd seen some *stuff*, I would definitely say that's a great plot for a fantasy novel. But I'm experienced enough to know now that this is very much real life, and everything always has the ability to get weirder. Ben's mom was right. Sometimes coincidences are more than just coincidences."

At the mention of Katerina, Jerome flinches, but he doesn't dwell on it.

"Marianne's got some answering to do," Casper continues, his laughter gone. "She didn't even mention she had any siblings at all."

She must have sensed what I was all along. Didn't she?

"She didn't like bringing him up, in fact she'd sometimes go decades without mentioning him." My dad throws us a soft expression as if to say 'if that helps'. Like he wants to defend her. Like he *cares*.

"You knew what Michael was?" I ask my dad, fighting back tears as I push my worries down. I can think about Marianne later. For now, I need his honesty before I scream at yet another revelation that physically *hurts*. This time, I feel it rip.

"Like I said, I didn't piece everything together until it was too late. Only when I came crawling back to him did it all click into place. I remembered what Marianne told me over a century ago, but I knew in my selfish, weakest, pathetic moments that I didn't want to be the prey. So, I became the predator." It makes sense, but it still hurts. "I told you I wasn't a good man, and I don't want your forgiveness."

I'm too far into this now, though. The closer we get to the end, the more I'm expecting from everyone.

"I forgive you." *And after I speak with Marianne, I want to forgive her too. I have to. It will eat me up if I don't.*

"What?" Casper turns hostile.

"I forgive you, dad. I believe you want to fix everything. I believe everything. I want to trust you. So, I will. I trust you are telling me the full truth. I'm tired of hiding and worrying. We want the same thing now. But if you betray me, I'll have no choice but to kill you." *I'm losing my mind.*

My dad smiles and exhales through his nose. "That's my boy."

I'm numb to it all now. I just need to get to the end.

"You will apologise to my mum, won't you?" I take a bite of my now cold pizza, trying to return the conversation to normalcy.

"I will."

"Then we'll speak with Marianne." I look at Casper. "I think we might just be able to complete the puzzle once and for all."

I just need to get to the end.

12th March 2019

~~I wonder what my life would have been like if I never met him. Where would I be now? Would I still be me?~~
~~Does that make sense?~~

14th March 2019

I'm sorry I failed you, Ben. And I'm sorry it took me this long to say that.
I'm so very sorry.

—Taken from the diaries of Marianne Ashtown.

Chapter Twenty Two

Mars
Now

The key weighs my pocket down as Marianne and I walk back to the hideout. The weight of her admission lingers between us. I try not to dawdle too much as we make our way back down; I don't want her to think she's worried me. She has, but a part of me questions if she's kept things from me because she fears my reaction. She's a strong leader—she always has been—and she has a clear goal in mind: to protect us all. But how long is the lifespan of a vampire really? Are we really eternal or do we still age and die, but over a prolonged space of time? Losing ourselves in the process.

Marianne is nearing three hundred now. She's the oldest vampire I know by a long shot. And she believes she's Turning, I think that's the best way to put it. I won't let that happen—The Thorns won't—that's the whole reason why we exist. To *stop* that.

I wish she'd been allowed to remember Nicholas. But that was the whole point, wasn't it? Her memories were taken so we couldn't intervene. I just wish we discovered this sooner. Marianne had many memories she could have shared with us, no matter if they helped or not, but I suppose that makes her human. Humans hide. Humans lie to protect. She's still human, I know it, even if she doesn't.

Once we're back inside, the halls feel warmer... more active. We're not alone.

We head to Marianne's office, but before we make it, we notice life. There, practically queueing outside the main hall, are close to ten Thorns. Old Thorns. Ones who have come back.

I check the key is still against my leg then let Marianne take the lead.

"Guys?" She's just as surprised as I am.

One of them, Elise, steps forward. "We got your message," she says, and the others nod. Elise, out of all people, was the last person I'd expect to see returning after what she'd been through with our Manipulation practises last year.

"We want to help. We've all got people we don't want to lose. We don't want to stand by," another says.

I smile.

We have a team. We are going to win this.

"Come inside, all of you. I'll catch you up." I know Marianne is smiling, even from my stance behind. She sounds like a weight has left her, and I think the return of other members will remind her of what's important. What she's always stood for.

I'm glad.

I grin and nod at all the familiar faces as we follow Marianne single file down the hall. They wink and acknowledge me back, and it's like nothing has changed. Sunlight streams through the cracks in the walls, and it's last year again, before everything happened.

Before Arlo.

Thinking his name makes my eye twitch just as the last person smiles at me. I try not to let it show, though.

I keep picturing last night.

. . .

I SLIP in last and keep my distance from everyone else, allowing Marianne to explain everything herself—let her share what she wants to and what she deems necessary. She shares more than I expected, but seeing how desperate we are, it's understandable. She explains about her brother and what he predicted. There are a few loud questions of 'why didn't you tell us before?' and 'this is why we left', conveying a general lack of trust in her decisions. But no one leaves. They remain seated, listening intently. Marianne touches her neck a few times out of discomfort, but she doesn't stop. She tells them everything—everything about Michael and Jerome, including why she left him. She talks about starting The Thorns because of what Jerome did, even bringing up Isiah as a contributing factor to her wanting to protect humanity.

If she'd just said all of that in the first place, we could be miles ahead now, I think. She never forgot about Jerome, and that information would have helped us—but would it have? Movies make it look simple: memories resurfacing at convenient times, characters waiting to tell stories at a specific moment in the film, all to move the plot along at a steady enough pace. But this is real life, and Marianne is trying her best.

She's trying.

SHE TALKS for a further ten minutes. I join her side eventually and tell my story about Arlo. As they'd all returned to help, I assumed that meant they wanted to help Arlo too, but some expressions indicate otherwise. They're still scared of the monster he'd become that day. Maybe they never cared about him like I do.

When Rani and Carmen eventually join us, I sense the further distaste, and I know Rani does too. It takes a split second of eye contact between us to tell. The pair of them position themselves at the front, closest to me, as Marianne continues.

Our leader turns to the girls to ask if they have any leads, yet when Rani answers, someone scoffs, disguising their comment. Everyone's attention snaps to them. Before Rani has time to respond, Carmen stands and directs her words at the Thorn—a brown-haired man I've only ever seen a few times before. Tall and muscular, with a bushy beard. Absolutely no match for Carmen 'stares into your soul' Wood, though.

"Let's get one thing straight, before you all explain why you're really here," she says. Marianne looks as if she's about to interfere, but seems to think better of it before allowing Carmen to continue. "I'm human, as you all know. It's no secret I didn't trust Arlo from the second he woke up in this building. But the more I learned about him, the more time I spent around him, and the more people around me cared about him, I thought maybe I'd been too harsh. I didn't know the first thing about the kid. But now I do, and I've spent the past six months with my memories altered, forcing me to forget about his importance and what really happened that day." She steals a quick glance at Marianne, who looks pained by her comment, despite understanding the reasoning. "Arlo needs our help, whether you like it or not. In order to end this 'Michael', or 'The Sun', or whatever stupid cryptic name he goes by—the goddamn God of Space for all I fucking care—we need Arlo, and we need him *fast*. Because I don't know about any of you, but I'm sensing something really fucking big is about to happen sooner rather than later, and I'd rather not have my fucking mind wiped or controlled ever again. I've read 1984. I like my dystopia novels, but I do *not* want to experience it in real life. AI is bad enough. I don't need a god in my brain."

Everyone looks as though her words shot bullets through them.

"Thank you." Carmen stops shouting and sits back down. Rani grabs her hand and squeezes, looking at her partner with proud eyes.

"Are we all on the same page then?" Rani adds, much quieter, but she knows everyone is still listening. Everyone in the room nods, even the guy who started it.

I must admit, I understand what Rani sees in her.

"Right." Marianne recaptures the attention of the room after the moment has settled. "So, as you all know, Arlo might be close by. Given what Mars witnessed, we believe he's running, and he's injured. We believe this means Michael is close, and Arlo won't be free for much longer. Our mission is to get to Arlo before he does, otherwise we might just be, excuse my language, *fucked.*"

I think everyone is in agreement. That's a pretty solid assumption.

"So, what's our plan, then? We found no evidence. Lawrence and Fran have nothing. I'm presuming you didn't find anything, either, and none of these lot have any leads... so, where else do you propose we look?" Rani asks, gripping Carmen's hand.

Marianne sighs. "That's where I'm stuck. I've got contacts across the country and *nothing* has come up."

"No easter eggs left behind in your brother's prophecies?" Someone asks, their tone mildly comical.

"He never mentioned specific locations, but even if he did, Arlo is actively trying to avoid them, so it wouldn't help. We need Arlo—and Jerome—before we can really impact Michael's plan." She takes the question seriously, and everyone remains silent.

We're going around in circles. Just a cacophony of pointless facts, none of which are the right shape to fit the puzzle. Nicolas predicted it. It's been six months, almost seven now, and for all we know, we're already out of time. Arlo could have been taken the very night I thought I'd found him, and things could be starting *now.* In a second, we might all be mindless machines, living out some fantasy of a life. No autonomy, no thoughts, just *impossible perfection.*

That's what Michael wants. What the entities are striving for. A perfect world free of hate and pain and lies. Pioneered by an inhuman hypocrite. *What would that world look like?*

I used to work in a pub when I was eighteen, and every time I smelled gas, I imagined us all just blowing up in an instant, and I wondered how many milliseconds of thought I'd get before I died. I wonder if it will be like that, but instead of being minced into a million pieces, we suddenly cease to be ourselves. I wonder how much of myself I'll be allowed to keep, if any. What percentage of perfect am I in his eyes?

What percentage of all of us will stay the same?

I'm terrified.

Arlo, come home.

"Mars, you're zoning out. Do you need to sit down?" Marianne says. I realise that I'm standing in front of everyone. I'm extremely embarrassed.

"I'm fine," I say, but I sit down, not fully present. I only slightly acknowledge Rani smiling at me.

I close my eyes and sit back. *Come on, Arlo. Please don't let it be too late.*

WE ALL RISE to leave not long after. I feel myself stand to follow everyone out. Rani asks to come to mine quickly to grab something she left behind, but I'm just a walking vessel, my mind trapped in the constant cycle of this impending explosion.

The sun is setting. Carmen is following us, and so is Marianne, heading towards her town house. I think I feel rain.

"What's with the key you keep playing with?" Rani asks.

"Nothing," I reply. I hadn't realised she'd noticed.

"Something for later," Marianne says, overhearing the question.

We walk a little further before turning the corner, ready to part from our leader.

But I stop dead as a figure comes into focus.

"You knew," he says. He's hunched over, with his sodden wings trailing behind his frail body like heavy weights. I see the scar trailing from the waist of his torn trousers, twisting to his ribs. It's a lot bigger than I remember the wound being in the dark.

Rani gasps so loud it's almost a scream.

Carmen tenses.

Marianne doesn't make a sound.

"You knew what was after me." He points his finger at her, panting for breath, his arms unsteady. I can see the purple under his eyes, the paleness of his skin. His beautiful, beautiful, precious face.

Arlo.

You came.

"You knew this whole time."

Then he collapses.

CHAPTER TWENTY THREE

Arlo
Three Weeks Ago

We decide to visit my mum sooner rather than later. I wish I had her number. Although Casper promised Marianne would have taken care of things, I need to speak to my mum myself. I need her to know I'm okay. It would be cruel to continue hiding from her.

We extend our stay in the city for a further few days and promise Katerina we'll be back for Ben's birthday. We decide that as Jerome is going to meet Melissa, then it's only fair Katerina gets to see him first.

Introducing him was never going to be easy, but it's now or never. I really don't know how much time we have left. Or what's going to happen. Are we all going to survive this?

The day before his birthday, we're back at the house. Casper knocks, though Katerina is expecting us. He rang Katerina two nights previously to break the news, and after a tearful conversation, she agreed to meet Jerome. *Her American,* she called him.

Ben's grandmother is already there, kissing and hugging

Casper as a greeting, before assessing me with melancholic eyes and pulling me in for a hug. I let her; she sees Ben in me too. This was their first birthday without him.

Jerome hangs back, waiting for his invitation. Casper had warned us that Edith Martín would probably react abruptly around him. She looked after Ben during his darkest years and will always blame Jerome's disappearing act as the 'root cause'. "She's a little old-fashioned like that," he said. My father understood. He was surprised she agreed to meet him at all. She was there for Katerina the moment she landed back in London: for Ben's birth, his childhood. She saw it all, and Jerome didn't.

Jerome dressed as casually as he could, braiding his hair back and removing all of his jewellery. He could pass as my brother in public. It's... unsettling. He stands a few yards from the porch, and down the steps to keep his distance. But once Casper and I step aside, the four of us wait for him to enter. He looks to everyone for approval, his brow tight with worry, eyes filled with concern.

But then Katerina steps out and walks down towards him confidently, and I see his surprise when she pulls him in for a *hug*. We don't see what follows, Edith is quick to usher us both inside to *'leave them alone for a while'*. I want to know what they talk about, but I don't have a chance.

Edith shows us into the living room and promises to return with the world's best smoothies before shuffling off. Casper looks at me like he's about to laugh. I haven't processed what emotion is appropriate yet.

"Well. Not what I expected," he says, staring out onto the carpet and rubbing his palms down his jeans. "Not at all."

I'm already peering outside the window to look for them, but the angle isn't right. Edith shut the door behind us though, so maybe they'll be a while.

Of course they'll be a while. They've not seen each other for twenty-eight years and he's the father of her *son*.

"You're not allergic to anything, are you, Arlo?" Edith appears at the door, carrying a tray. Casper leaps up to help her shaking hands and places it on the table.

"Peanuts, I think, but I've never been tested."

I know Ben had a tree nut allergy.

"Oh, don't worry. I stopped putting all nuts in my recipes a long time ago. You should enjoy this!" I thank her as she hands me my drink. She seems lovely, and I know Ben loved her. She was like a second mother to him.

She speaks and laughs with Casper before sitting down on the other side of the room with a sigh. I feel awkward again.

"I'm sorry, dear." She looks at me, her face stoic.

"I'm sorry too." I don't know what else to say.

Edith shakes her hands at me. "You have nothing to apologise for. You never met your father or your brother until it was too late. I'm only sorry you didn't get the time you needed." I wasn't expecting her to sound like this, so bold. She scowls then, as if processing things. "That man is not fifty. Not a mark on him. He's playing some game."

"He is. We did a DNA test to prove he was Arlo's father," Casper lies—another one we planned in advance. We decided we'd rather lie like humans than Manipulate. *How long do DNA tests take?* Hopefully she won't pick up on that technicality.

"Perhaps it's his brother, then. He was not Casanova of New York in 1990. No chance."

A stubbornness laces her voice, but she has every reason to feel this way. It makes me like her more. I wish she was my grandmother, though I suppose she technically could be.

"Jerome was born on the thirtieth of December 1971 in Edinburgh, Scotland. We've seen his papers." Casper sounds so American when he says the city, despite living in the UK for many years now.

"He was only eighteen. A child!" Edith thinks about it. "He lied to her about his age!"

I gulp. She's not wrong. But not in the way she thinks. "He did," I say.

Yet assigning him this age seems to soften Edith's anger. She adds the story up in her head. "He was immature." We let her come to that conclusion. She asks my age, and when I tell her she just nods. "He's got some things to work out with The Lord."

That he does.

About fifteen minutes pass, then we hear the door. Katerina enters the living room with Jerome close by her side. It hurts to see them so close, but I try to block it all out. *It means nothing.*

Neither of them speak, but Katerina sits beside me and Jerome next to Casper, a pre-planned decision that puts me at ease. I can sense Edith's tension, but she keeps her face plain. I wonder what they talked about.

The silence is unbearably loud, and I clear my throat to comfort myself.

"I should probably speak now," my dad says. "Since I've got a lot of explaining to do."

"You were a boy," Edith says.

"I—" Jerome looks at her, confused. "I was an adult when I—"

"Mum, please," Katerina shoots a glare at her mother, who sits back in defeat.

"I made a decision back then. I had a wonderful trip, and then I came back and lived my life. I spoke about Jerome, *Jay,* as though I hated him for not calling. But over the years, I came to forgive him. What did I expect him to do? Fly over and whisk me off my feet? We'd known each other for a day—" She stops to look at Edith, who seems highly uncomfortable at the admission she's clearly heard many times before. "Yes, mum. I did my begging for forgiveness, you know I did. But I found peace, and I moved on. Jerome did nothing wrong."

I look at my dad, and so does Casper. We're all probably thinking the same thing. Katerina was never mad at him. She was constantly burdened by guilt.

"Oh darling, I never meant to..." Edith sucks her lips together. "I know I blame people a lot. I'm sorry. I just wanted to protect you."

"I know, mum. I know." Katerina lowers her head.

"You had every right to be mad at me for what I did to your daughter." Jerome sits forward and leans on his legs, pressing his hands together. Katerina leans down too.

"I will probably always be mad. You can't expect a mother *not* to be. But I understand you, and I will learn to grow past my anger in time. Are you sticking around this time?"

"I hope so." My dad nods. It's a loaded statement—we have no idea what's about to happen.

"Will you be coming tomorrow to celebrate Ben's birthday?" she asks.

"If you will have me."

"We will. He is your son, after all."

My dad's eyes glaze over, his voice strained. "He is."

IT'S A WEIRD DAY, but we leave feeling accomplished. Katerina had her chance to speak with the father of her son. Edith had a chance for closure. We talked a lot, asking many difficult questions with even more difficult answers. It completely drained my energy and social battery, but it was necessary.

The following day, we light a birthday cake for Ben. I wish he was here to see how loved he is. I haven't seen him since that day in the park. I don't think I'll ever see him again, but the more time I spend with Casper and my dad, the stronger the feeling is that he's is always with us.

BY THE END of the month, we're heading up the country to meet my mother. We spend the preceding days planning how to do it, seeing as my mum also hadn't seen me for months. I hate how long it's been. She's probably beside herself with worry, no matter what The Thorns did to put her mind at ease. As my mother, she'll always worry about me.

"I want to spend some time with her, do you think she'd want that?" my dad asks on the train to Carlisle. He asks a lot of panicked questions like this. I thought meeting Katerina would have calmed him a little, but he seems to be even more on edge now.

But I know it's different. He knew Katerina for a day. He knew my mum for eight years.

They had a life together. Before me.

Casper spends the journey sharing his music with me and letting me play with the spinning planet keyring from his house keys. I try to sleep as much as I can.

It's been a lot for me—mentally and physically. It's hard to handle when so many things happen at once. But we can't slow down. Michael might find us at any moment, ending everything. Just like that.

I want my mum.

To say goodbye.

No, stop it, Arlo. You're going to be fine.

Am I?

Are we all?

WE WAIT for thirty minutes for our connecting train, but the station is quiet enough to ease me. Waiting for changeovers stresses me out.

"I've never been to the Lakes before. Always wanted to, though." Casper has already picked up a 'Ten Things to See in The Lake District' pamphlet and continues flicking through it.

"It's not like the highlands, but it's incredibly close," says my Dad, speaking with his natural Scottish accent.

"Another place on my list to visit. Ben took me to Edinburgh a few times, but we never had a chance to see anywhere else." I sense his sadness, but he seems to cherish it as a happy memory.

"Did you see the old streets? The Closes?" *My dad's birthplace.*

"Oh I did. Incredible, especially from the other side looking up. Those buildings are so tall."

"They just kept building." My dad smiles. "Filthy, though, especially down my end. If there's one thing I'll be glad for in modern times, it's the clean water and medicine. It would have saved so many of us."

His siblings.

Himself?

"Woah, yeah. I never thought about that. You'll have seen so much, so much change." Casper seems genuinely impressed, and my father grins at him.

"I did."

"What was it like?" Casper turns to my father, fully invested. "Like, growing up and stuff? All those years ago."

My dad looks startled at first, but then his shoulders loosen as he gives a distant smile. "It was a lot. A lot of happy times with my family, a lot of struggles. Where I lived was hard to get out of, despite how hard we worked. But it was all we knew. My sisters looked after me the most, from what I remember."

"Older sisters?" Casper's smile remains.

"Older. I was so lucky to have them. I was a... difficult child." My dad laughs and rakes his hands through his hair. "Bessie and Margaret. They would have outlived me by quite a lot. I think it was the stubbornness."

"Bessie? Bess?" My ears perk up. "Did you—did you tell my mum about them?"

"I did." Jerome's brows flex to mild confusion.

"My dog is called Bess." *That means something, something*

big. My dad was woven into our lives even more than I first thought. He was always present. My dad doesn't speak, but a ghost of a grin graces his lips when he tilts his head away from Casper.

"Bess," is all he says to no one in particular.

"Did you, I dunno—did you ever meet anyone famous over the years? Did you travel?" Casper starts up again.

My dad appears to enjoy our curiosity, despite not knowing where to start. "Probably. I may have never known, though. I was somewhat of a recluse for many years of my life. Until I met…"

"Marianne," I say before he can finish. I predicted the uncomfortable pause and stop it from happening.

Slowly, Casper nods to himself, his face unreadable.

My dad lowers his head as a train enters the station behind us. I cover my ears.

OUR TRAIN ARRIVES a few minutes late, but we're getting closer. The weight of it all hits me when we board. I'm terrified.

We get off and decide to walk instead of waiting for a taxi. While hiding our wings is easy on trains and buses, they're still a part of us, and cars are exceptionally uncomfortable.

It's a sunny afternoon. My mum will finish work soon; she normally takes Bess out before she makes tea. I'm presuming her routine is still the same.

IT DOESN'T MATTER, though.

We're too late.

"FOR PEOPLE WITH WINGS, you move surprisingly slow," a voice calls from behind us.

We all turn, with Jerome pushing himself in front of us

instinctively. I've never seen this person before, so my initial fear of Michael quickly subsides.

But the more I stare at the figure, the more I realise there's only one other person who could see our wings *and* know we were on the run. My dad says it before the name comes to me. "Nicholas."

The figure's smirk confirms it all. *So, he's alive.*

He looks nothing like her.

"Are you not tired yet?" he asks. Two women appear behind him. Vampires. They position themselves and fold their arms.

"You've been following us," my dad assumes.

"That I have. Congratulations, by the way. You're pretty good at covering your tracks, just not good enough to hide from us entirely."

Us. He's working with Michael.

Of course he is. He is a part of him.

I don't have any words to add. My dad does all the talking, his stance now defensive. "Marianne thought you were dead. But unfortunately you lived long enough to more or less be."

Ignoring my dad's comment, Nicholas steps closer. The vampires keep their distance, probably following his command. The Manipulation *drips* from him. He's like a child in men's clothing, a good six inches shorter than us all, despite his imposing body language.

Nicholas steps even closer until he's mere inches from my father. He cocks his head like a puppet. "He's waiting for you," he says, before focusing on me with a nasty grin. "And you, his Star—the last puzzle piece. He's growing impatient. I promised I'd bring you to him. No harm needs to come to anyone else." He pins his hands behind his back and presses his feet together. "The end of old time is near. Be ready to welcome the new dawn of being. True freedom. The light."

He sounds insane. Genuinely insane. His whole manner screams of a man in need of help.

Then I feel it—*smell* it. His Manipulation. We freeze in place, and it's a paralysis I know all too well. I hear a brief grunt of struggle escape Casper's lips, but I cannot turn to look at him. It doesn't work on my dad, though; his fingers twitch. In a blur, his claws wrap around Nicholas's neck, while his other hand shoots out to prevent his cult followers from intervening. *He's so strong.*

I watch Nicholas's eyes bulge and teeth lengthen. I sense him fighting back—this is a strength I've never known. This is aged and *immortal.*

I can't move.

Yet when Nicholas plunges a fist into my father's chest, my father drops him, falling to his knees as a spray of black blood ejects from his mouth. Black. The Moon is still in there somewhere, which means The Star is too.

But as Nicholas staggers back and clutches his neck, I'm free.

Casper and I run to my father, and I look for a wound while he glares deeply at the cult leader. There's no visible injury.

"Still in there, then. Good, this should be easy. He told me about the scar, and how, after all these years, it never properly healed," Nicholas says proudly. We glare at him. "It also made it easier for him to bring you back as his little experiment. His creation. He didn't need to dig as far to find your heart." My father coughs and spits onto the ground, panting for breath. There's blood on his lips, two different shades.

"The Sun showed me so much. He gave me this gift, you know. Or did you already figure that out? I didn't know you met my sister, but he told me *everything,* and I know she wouldn't have held her tongue with you."

Nicholas knows everything. He knows exactly how to play us. I don't have the mental power to outsmart him.

"You told him too much, Jerome, silly man. He told me if you fought back that I should go for the scar in the centre of your chest —just under your heart, and straight between the ribs. He said it's always been your weakness. Ever since she hacked you open and peeled back your skin, draining your chambers dry."

Clove. I'm piecing it together. Just.

"Your father knew you were a devil. He always saw through your lies. He knew she was no healer, despite what your mother claimed. Your mother coddled you too much and would do anything to keep her baby boy alive. Your sisters moved on, and you abandoned everyone when it got too much for you. You enjoy doing that, don't you? Giving up."

My dad wipes his lips and rises to his feet. "You're sick. You know that, kid? You've let him reside in your mind for too long. I can help you."

Nicholas flinches at being called a kid. It hits a nerve. "He was inside my head long before yours. I've had time to meld with him. You're still fighting it. How much effort did it take to dull down The Moon? Was it worth it? Knowing he'd bring it back in an instant? I don't need any help from *you.*" He laughs.

I wonder for a moment what he was like when he and Marianne were kids. How much Michael has changed him.

"Come on, Jerome. And you, Arlo. It's time; you know it is. Come with us and let's start anew. Stop with this pathetic game. It's boring."

I feel my legs moving before I acknowledge them.

"Leave them alone!" Casper screams, but his last word is cut off as Nicholas refuses to let him finish. Casper claws at his throat, grasping for the words he can't find. *How dare he—*

"Take me then!" my dad shouts, overpowering us all.

What? No!

Nicholas frowns, seemingly confused. "You can't fool me. I know what you're doing. He needs you both."

My dad strides over and stares down at Marianne's brother, overshadowing him in every aspect as his wings span wide.

"Take me. I will come willingly. Take my mind, bring The Moon back, and deliver me to him. But you leave the human alone, and you stay the hell away from my son."

It's enough of a distraction; Casper is already running. It's my father's doing.

I want to cry out, but I know it's no use.

So, I run too. I run as fast as I've ever run in my life. I don't look back; he doesn't let me.

I run, and I run, and I run.

I can only hope my mother isn't home yet.

There's only one place for me to go now.

CHAPTER TWENTY FOUR

Arlo
A Day Ago

I never wanted to bring them into this. Any of them. But I had to stop running. I gave in.

It's been nearly three weeks since I left my father—*again*. I plead to a higher power, begging for Casper's safety too. It's all because of Jerome, who sacrificed himself so we could be free. He won't let any harm come to my mother, I know it. Yet my mind lingers on Nicholas and on how little he cares for humanity.

Nicholas is alive. He works with The Sun. He is *part of* The Sun.

The end is now. If they find me, it's game over. *What if they don't even need me? What if two is enough, and this is it...*

I hear Mars before I see them. They're alone, muttering to themself, while running through the forest to where Ben died.

I follow them, keeping my distance and sticking to the growing shadows.

Mars. Oh, how I'd missed them. I almost cry with relief when it hits me I'm home.

The more we walk, the more I watch that day play out. The sound Ben's body made when it fell to the ground, staining the land with his blood. *Hold it together, Arlo.*

They climb and stumble over into the ruins. It would be safer to take a different entrance, so I do. I'm shaking with hunger, despite having taken blood only hours ago. I can barely walk straight.

I wonder how they've been this whole time and why they're now going to the ruins. Are they looking for me? *Don't be silly, Arlo. They'll have moved on by now.*

I wait five minutes before I attempt to climb round the back. But just as I get my leg over, I trip on a crumbling stone and lose my footing, falling down and catching my side on a raw piece of wood.

I feel instantly nauseous. The whole stick, rotten and sodden, comes loose *inside of me.* It's dark now, but I feel the blood drench my hands. I know it's black.

I want to scream as the pain takes hold, but I don't want to scare them.

Sorry, Mars.

I drop my bag and shuffle into the shadows, clutching the wound and lacking the strength to pull it out. I rip off my shirt to stem the blood flow, but it won't stop.

Then they call out.

I try to bite my tongue to hold in the pain. I don't know what to say to them.

Their footsteps near before they come into focus.

Help me, Mars.

"Arlo?" They say desperately, stepping out from the doorway to come into full view.

They bend down in front of me, their pleading eyes latching onto mine. They hold their body as if they want to reach out but think better of it, keeping their hands by their side and clenching their fists.

I can't look at them, not clearly. My eyes refuse to focus. I can't, I...

Their eyes are glued to the wound on my stomach, and before I can register, they reach for the wood. I startle, and the pain grows too intense. I did that myself; I shouldn't have moved. I'm—

I think I'm going to die. There's so much blood. How much would it take to kill me? Would that be safer? Would it save everyone if I just stopped existing?

"Oh, Arlo," I think they say, though my ears are ringing. It's as though the walls are caving in around me. I struggle to breathe. "Let me help you, Arlo. You're hurt." They reach out again with a softer approach, but I can't help but recoil, or at least I try to. I have nowhere else to go.

Rain roars around us. I don't remember when it started raining. Was it always?

"Arlo, can you understand me? Are you in there? Please, tell me you know who I am?" They sound breathless now.

I know you, Mars. I'll always know you.

"Please," they beg. They insist on pulling it out to help me heal. *I won't die. I won't. I'll be okay.* Their next plea is almost inaudible. "Arlo."

"It hurts," I finally say. It even hurts to speak. My whole body aches and shakes. I'm giving in.

"Oh, I know. I know. You need to remove it. Please..."

I drift in and out of consciousness, my body trembling. With deep breaths, I try focusing on their face.

They encourage me to follow them home. To safety, they say. They promise to get me fresh clothes and a proper dressing for the wound. But I can't. I can't ever risk it. I'm causing harm even just being in their presence. I've been too greedy, too selfish. They don't deserve this.

"I can't," I manage, holding onto the wood to alleviate the pressure digging into me. I can't pull it out. I can't move. I'm so frightened. They ask me if I remember them. "Mars." *How could I ever forget you?*

Their eyes widen when I respond. "Yes, it's me! You know me. I saved you once!"

You saved me far more than once.

Everything blurs from there, and it's like I'm floating. I'm outside of my body, watching from somewhere far above. I'm with Mars, my friend. They always know how to save me.

They help me remove the wood. I'm reluctant at first. I refrain from screaming as the jarred edges tear into my muscle and flesh. I pass out for a few seconds, I think, or maybe I choose to block it all out. They keep asking me to come with them, but I refuse with the last scraps of energy I've stored. I think I speak of Michael, though I don't expect them to understand.

It still hurts, but I'm safe. This is good. I can relax. *Relax, Arlo.* But I can't. I think of Ben, my father, everything I've learned. I can't breathe.

"I need to find..." Pain shoots all the way up my side, my wings bending in funny angles as I recoil.

"Arlo?"

"I shouldn't have come here. I just needed, I..."

I need you. I need Ben. I need Rani, my mum, my dad. Everyone.

A tear escapes my left eye, and my world closes around me. Their voice muffles to gibberish, and I squint my eyes shut, trying to focus.

"I just wanted... I don't know. Mars, I don't know what to do."

And I don't. I really don't know what I'm doing, what I should do, or what I should have already done. It's too much.

Then their words inject themselves straight into my veins. "The Sun. Is he who you're running from?"

How do they...

I can't do this. I need to run. *I always run.*
Stop.
Stay.
Stay.
Stay.

They know about Michael.

They understand. They understand me. Why we can never leave this place together.

I'm blacking out again.

I remember trying to stand, despite my aching back that burns with the rest of my body. My wings weigh almost twice as much when I'm back on my feet. I stumble backwards, gravity my enemy.

"They're beautiful," Mars says, taking in the whole of my existence.

"They're too heavy," I snap with unintentional anger.

I remember lying down. Mars beside me. They shiver; I don't want them to shiver. I don't want them to cry. Why do they look like they're going to cry? Don't cry, Mars. There aren't enough tears for us both.

"Thank you," I say.

"You never have to thank me."

Oh, but I do.

I'm so sorry, Mars.

I don't sleep, even as they fall into a deep slumber beside me, wrapped in my scarf under the shelter of my wing. I can't sleep. I can never sleep. He's coming for me. I can't stay.

I'm so sorry.

Chapter Twenty Five

Arlo
Now

I wonder what my life would be like if I'd not gone to university. If I'd stayed at home. Would he have still found me? Would any of this have taken place? Is that my destiny, or did I create my fate the moment I left home?

I can't help but wonder if my path was laid out from the start, or did I create it?

I'M STANDING BEFORE MARIANNE, Mars, Carmen, and *Rani*. Oh Rani, I'm so sorry I dragged you into all of this mess. I'm so sorry.

I'm going to pass out. I'm exhausted. I have nothing left to give. I can't go on like this.

"You knew," I manage. My head weighs a ton, and my legs threaten to collapse beneath me. I point up at Marianne as flashes of the past six months hit me all at once. "You knew what was after me. You knew this... whole... time."

Then I collapse.

Act 3

A Reunion

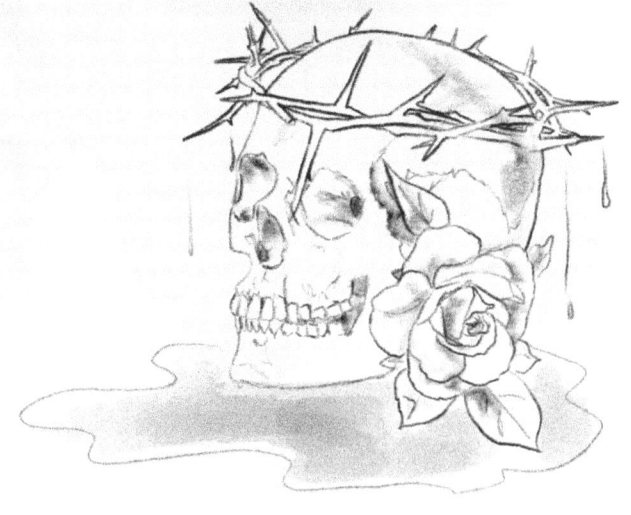

CHAPTER TWENTY SIX

Michael
Now

I t's the truth. I don't know how I came to be—to exist. But I remember before the light, before *all* light.

It was always the three of us; myself, my Moon and my Star. It's easier to call them that when that is what they are to me. The darkness and the light all at once.

We found no purpose, so we searched for one.

When I awoke on earth, I knew my spirit would not last long. It needed a host. I said I found Michael, but that's not the *whole* truth. Two centuries earlier, I planted a small part of myself in the heart of a dying boy and gave him the eyes to see what was to come. He was an experiment that proved to be a success. I would be able to survive inside a human body. So, when I finally returned, with my entry logged as nothing more than a snowstorm, it was time to begin the end of old time. That's when I stole Michael. I used the mildest influence I could muster within the boy to persuade him to let me take control. I'd made the boy follow him for years.

I had nothing to show him yet, nothing for him to agree to,

but it wasn't hard. When he stepped back to admire his work for the final time and took a blade to his own throat, I began again. This time, I became something corporeal, something this world could understand. A human body with the wings of a painted angel and the claws of a stuffed eagle—Manipulated perfectly into existence. Something *more.*

Then, I met Jerome two years later. It's a small world, isn't it? Can you guess who he was with when I found him? The boy's sister of all people! Oh, what a delight. I couldn't hold back my excitement. She was too much; he was just right. I had to hide him then, make sure she didn't figure things out too early.

Then thanks to Jerome, I knew Arlo would be The Star before he even existed.

I BELIEVE we came from the same maker; humans like to call them *vampires,* though I may never know for sure. They had strength, but not quite enough to make a real change. They need our power. This world is so poisoned—so blind—we must start over, with everyone the same. *Perfect.* It's possible, I'm sure of it.

I made a slight error in judgement, however.

I never thought Arlo would be a problem. I presumed he would make an even more willing host, given how pathetic his father was.

Now he's been running for months, and even though Nicholas found me and promised to help speed up the process, I am once again left disappointed.

Hmm.

"Yes, I'm disappointed in you, *boy.*"

"After all I've done, master. For you, for the future."

I suck my teeth. Weird humans.

"You were the first thing I found that was remotely living. You were always just a reserve, so don't consider yourself special."

It's no use, though. I've been part of his mind for too long.

He'll always stay by my side. I should utilise his eyes more, if he lets me in.

"I've spread the word, Manipulating everyone I meet. You have so many supporters. They just don't know it yet. They will be ready, though. I promise."

He's not listening to me. It doesn't matter how many *followers* I have. That's not the point. They'll all be following soon. *Soon.* If I can get my hands on those infuriating Mairs. "You couldn't even bring *one* of them back, never mind both. Do I have to do everything myself?"

I wasted my time thinking he'd even be remotely useful. Again. Tut. Tut.

It was a simple job. We knew where they were, yet when Nicholas scurried back to me, his face was bloodied and arms scarred. They got away—easily too.

I know it's Arlo; he's fighting back and thinks he's winning.

I wonder if I made that mistake because of my human limitations or whether I really did just let the missing stitch go unnoticed. This is the whole reason I need to save this world. Even my own body fails me.

I know where they'll be now, though. No point in waiting anymore; I've done far too much of that.

Nothing will keep them apart or keep them from family.

Time for a nice little trip back to Durham.

17th March 2019

~~I wonder if our paths will cross again.~~
~~I wonder if there is anything in the world that would make~~
~~me forgive him.~~
~~I hate that I miss him sometimes.~~

19th March 2019

What am I doing? I feel like I'm going in circles lately.

21st March 2019

I need to understand my part in all of this.

—Taken from the diaries of Marianne Ashtown

CHAPTER TWENTY SEVEN

Mars
Now

We all did our part in carrying him, his body heavy with the added weight of his enormous wings. I remembered the feeling of them over my body last night, and the difference in temperature from his icy body to the warmth of his feathers.

Now the four of us are carrying an angel, with two on each side supporting his whole body, heading to Marianne's house.

He's drifting in and out of consciousness and tries to walk when he can, but he's too delirious to walk by himself. We lower him onto the couch, careful not to crush his wings. The bones are hard and strong on his back.

None of us even exchange a full sentence. We're speechless. Hurried breaths and panicked mutters escape our lips; we're in a state of utter bewilderment.

What does he know?

·　·　·

OF COURSE, we all refuse to leave his side, even Carmen. Marianne's eyes are erratic, and her hands restless. She paces the room like an ant in a biro circle. He must know about Nicholas then, surely.

He knows everything.

Rani pulls a blanket from the Chesterfield to cover his bare skin, eyeing up the wound and hovering her kind hands over the space above it, wishing she could help. Carmen helps Rani before squeezing her shoulder in comfort. Rani softly brushes Arlo's long hair from his face and plants a ghost of a kiss on the top of his head while his chest rises and falls—too fast.

I stay beside Marianne to observe the scene. "You believe me now?" I say, trying to remain light-hearted, yet I know she believed me from the start.

"He thinks I hid Nicholas from him, and that I knew who Michael was the whole time," she mutters, her wide eyes fixed on his frail body, arms crossed.

"You can't blame him for thinking that though, can you?"

Marianne shakes her head and rubs her chin. "He needs to feed and rest, then I will tell him everything he wants and needs to know. Then he can tell us everything he's seen." She seems so sure of this, like it's a simple matter.

"The Thorns might not trust him," I voice my fear aloud. We're all thinking the same thing.

"They're going to have to." Carmen backs away from Arlo, looking between us both. "I sure as hell didn't want to, but we don't have much choice, do we? It's either his word or blind luck."

That's another way of seeing it, I guess. Carmen always has a point, even if she sounds harsh while saying it.

Rani stays by Arlo's side, rubbing his arm through the blanket, respecting his comfort, even unconscious. "He's going to be okay, though, right? What's the scar from? It looks fresh." She doesn't look at any of us.

"Last night. I think he caught himself on some wood or something. I helped get it out, though. It's healed nicely." I don't know why my voice is so quiet. It's not like anyone else is listening. I suppose I'm just a bit on edge. Stunned.

"I'll get him some blood. Mars, keep watch and tell me if anything changes in his condition." With a nod, Marianne disappears into the kitchen, leaving me and the humans. I sit cross-legged beside Rani, whose eyes are level with Arlo's sleeping face.

My stomach drops when I look at him. His soft lashes, delicate skin, and those cute moles under his eyes. *I love him. I love him. I love him.*

Mars, stop.

I hate when my mind wanders back to that drunken night after we saved Elise. The way his body felt under mine. The redness of his lips after we kissed. I only remember flashes, but I knew I was in love with him then. But he doesn't feel the same. And it's not *me.* He's like Marianne. It's just the way everything aligns.

You'll get over him.

I hope so.

I'm brushing back his hair when Rani's hand hovers over mine.

"I know how much he means to you, Mars," she says, and I almost panic, thinking she sees right through me. Am I that obvious?

"I... I just want him to be safe. Finally." I think that's a good way to voice my concern.

Rani's eyes smile, meeting mine. "I know. It's the least he deserves after everything."

"He's too pure for this world," I say. My voice sounds distant to my own ears as a lump forms in my throat.

"He might just be." Rani turns back to watch him sleep; his eyelids flutter slightly. I wonder if he can hear us and is merely resting his eyes.

Carmen shuffles behind us. I forgot she was there.

"You know I'm not *that* much of a bitch," she announces, and we both spin abruptly at her statement. Carmen lifts her hands with a smile—an *actual smile*. "I know how important Arlo is to you both. Rani, you don't shut up about him. You never have and never will, but I don't mind. I listen to every word, because I always wished I had a friend to care about that much. It's a really special thing, and it's so *rare*. Friendship is such a powerful force you must never let go of. And Mars! You saved his life, probably more than once. In fact, definitely more than once." She sighs.

"But now you think it's your responsibility to ensure nothing bad ever happens to him again—forever! While that's a complicated feeling I may never understand, I empathise with it. You both care beyond words can say, and I'm just caught in the middle because of my major trust issues." She laughs again. "But after getting my memories back, I know whatever is inside Arlo is nothing like Isiah, and I *know* he is a good person. He's himself now, otherwise he wouldn't be here. He's scared. He knows '*The Sun*' is coming for him, so we're going to help him. We're going to be there when it all happens."

I never expected those words to leave Carmen's mouth, and yet they nearly shatter me. It's the most I've heard her care about anything.

"Oh, don't look at me like that. I swear I can be nice sometimes." A soft lightness remains in her voice as her lips quirk upwards.

The more the day unfolds, the more I understand why Rani thinks so highly of Carmen. Carmen puts on a front, a wall of impenetrable steel, to hide the genuinely kind and pleasant person beneath. We all do what we do to survive.

Wow. That's a development.

MARIANNE RETURNS a moment later with a blood bag, a first-aid kit, and a portable IV stand. Casual household objects for a woman like her. She gestures for us to step aside before hooking up the bag and fixing the line and needle, pulling back the blanket to find the crook of Arlo's left arm. We watch as she wipes the skin with alcohol and then inserts the needle, holding it in place with skin tape.

She flicks her gaze towards me when she takes a step back, seeming to read the question in my eyes.

Yes. This is vampire blood.

He needs to replenish his own blood, to counteract whatever is —or was—inside him. He can feed after.

She's saving him from himself.

"He needs to rest properly. One of us can stand guard, but we can't disturb him. He needs to wake on his own, naturally, when his body is ready."

We all nod and Rani insists she will take the first shift. We don't protest.

BARELY TWO HOURS LATER, Rani bursts into the kitchen to frantically announce Arlo has woken and he's panicking. I rush after her into the living room to see Arlo sitting up and aggressively rubbing his arm where he'd ripped out the IV, breathing heavily.

I'm wearing his gloves in a second and reach for his bare shoulders to steady him. I force his eyes to focus on mine. "Breathe, Arlo. You're okay. You're safe."

He calms a little as his eyes wander over my shoulder to Rani. The sight of her seems to calm him completely.

"Am I dreaming?" he asks and looks like he wants to smile but won't allow himself to in case none of this is real.

"You're not dreaming." Rani drops to his side, and I move out of the way so they can take a good look at each other. "You're safe." She beams.

Coughing, Arlo leans forward to hold Rani's bare hand. He grips it so tight his sharp nails nearly pierce her skin, but she doesn't pull away. She stares intently at his face.

"He's coming," Arlo whispers to her, but it's not a threat, and Rani knows that.

"But he's not going to win, Arlo. He needs you, and he's not having you." Carmen wanders into my eye line and grips Rani's shoulder from behind. "We're not going to let that happen."

Arlo's brows tense as he looks up at Carmen in bewilderment. Releasing Rani's hand, he sits back, processing Carmen's words. "Yes, I've had a change of heart. Thanks to your best friend." She rolls her eyes with a smirk and nudges Rani gently.

Arlo seems too overwhelmed, so I try to capture his focus again. "What do you want? Do you need anything? Can we get you anything?"

I watch his eyes flutter, unsure where to look. It's too much for him. I turn to ask Carmen to leave, and she does, closing the door behind her. I'm in half a mind to leave him, too, but he reaches for me when I stand, urging me to sit back down. I do.

Arlo doesn't speak again, only rubs his thumbs over both our hands in a synchronised motion.

"We've been looking for you for months." *I have.* "We travelled the country, but you hid really well. You're running from him, aren't you? You're yourself now, and you ran," I start.

Arlo takes a deep breath, rocking slightly before whispering, "He's coming," again.

I want him to speak to us, but I can't push him. Everything he's been through and all that he's seen has burned a hole in him. This isn't a quick fix, not this time.

"Would you like some tea?" Rani offers. "Earl grey? No milk. No sugar."

Arlo flicks his attention to her before slowly nodding. I hear Rani's heart flutter when she stands. "I'll make you some, then I'll be back." She squeezes Arlo's hand before leaving us alone.

I reach into his bag to find something for him to cover himself with, but he only has his scarf. The one I swore I wore for a while.

"Would you like me to wrap this around you, or would you like to do it yourself?" I ask, unfolding the large square of material. He reluctantly takes it from me and rubs his fingers over the fabric. He shakes his head. *Not the right fabric for your bare skin. Okay. I'm learning.*

"I'll get you a nice soft t-shirt in a bit then. Are you okay like this for now?" *I'm not leaving you alone.*

Arlo nods, but his next words are louder, and filled with more fear. "He's coming."

"I know, I know. He can't touch you, Arlo. I promise. Your mind will be yours alone from now on." A bold statement. I want it to be true, though. I will do everything in my power to make it true.

"Do you know where he is now?" I ask.

Arlo shakes his head quickly, his hair falling into his face. He looks so much older, especially with the light beard on his chin. Yet he's still so innocent looking. Someone I will always protect, no matter what. *Because I love him. In more ways than one.*

I have to close my eyes for a moment to think of something—*anything*—else.

"He wants to control the world."

Said every supervillain ever. "I know."

Arlo shakes his head again and leans closer, lowering his voice an octave. "No. No. He wants *our* minds. He thinks he can use our minds."

I know, but hearing Arlo confirm it makes it even more real and frightening.

"He's not getting our minds," I insist firmly. *He won't win.*

Arlo looks at me like I'm not understanding the gravity of the situation. Maybe I don't understand. Maybe I never will.

"He has mine," Arlo adds, before Rani reappears with a mug of Earl Grey. We both look at her as she passes it to Arlo, insisting he rest it on the blanket over his lap. There's too much energy in this room, but when Rani sits back down, I ask Arlo to elaborate, despite the discomfort it may cause.

Arlo bites his lip, his eyes wide. Behind him, his wings twitch, having stretched out to drape over the back of the chair.

"What he put inside you... it's gone, right?" I push.

Arlo looks at Rani in a way that makes me think he doesn't want her to know, like he doesn't want to scare or anger her. I'm not sure.

"Arlo, you know you can tell me everything. It won't change my opinion of you, I promise. That's what friends are for—we're here to talk to and be there for one another. I know what Marianne hid from me. I know everything. I'm not afraid of you. I never was and never will be."

He sits back and considers, squeezing the skin on his arm like rubber. "You'll hate me."

"I won't." Rani insists firmly, gritting her teeth. "*I won't.*"

Arlo stares down at his tea for a prolonged moment before glancing up at the pair of us. He straightens his back. "Okay," he says. Then, he confidently adds, "I want to tell you everything, but I need her to listen."

Marianne. He remembers how he got here then. What he said.

"Okay." I nod and stand. "I'll bring her in."

Chapter Twenty Eight

Arlo
Now

When I see her, I'm flooded by anger. Carmen follows close behind, but I focus only on Marianne—her bright blue eyes and wild hair. *Liar,* my brain says. But I want to talk. I need to talk. And I want her to hear everything. Then she can explain herself.

It took a while for my body to wake up properly and for my mind to catch up, but I'm fully present now. It's time. If I don't speak now, I might never get the chance again.

He's coming.

I wait for everyone to sit. Then I begin.

I TELL THEM EVERYTHING. Every single detail I can remember from the moment Michael placed The Star inside me to the moment I found them in the street. I tell them of the months I served him, the minds I took, and the lives I stole. How I fed my father to him, then ran away. Marianne flinches when I bring him up, but I don't want her to turn away, she needs to hear everything. I tell them about the months I spent running and hiding, and how my father found me and told me everything he'd done. I watch Marianne's face twist and contort at every word I say regarding Jerome, and then I go further. I tell them about meeting Casper and finding out about Ben. I'm crying when I revisit that part.

When they're all caught up on how I got here, how my father made me and Casper run, and how I don't know if he's alive, I realise everyone is crying. Maybe they had been for a while. I'd heard their gasps and noticed their movements, but everything was a blur as I retold the tale. I disassociated from reality and just spoke and spoke until my throat grew dry.

I don't know how long it took, but I'm exhausted now. I just want to curl back into a ball and sleep. But then warm arms reach for me. Things touch and scrape my body as all four bodies in the room engulf me with affection. *I can't breathe.*

"Please," I gasp, until I realise no one has moved an inch. I'd imagined it. My chest feels so tight. It's too much. *I said too much.*

No one speaks. Rani sniffs and wipes her nose with her sleeve, her heart beating erratically in her chest. Carmen's eyes remain fixed on me, while Mars rubs their eyes. Marianne stands from her chair in the corner of the room and steps forward. Then she crumbles to her knees. Back hunched, and face practically touching the floor, arms gripping her stomach as if she's in pain.

Still, no one says a word. Then, "Nicholas."

Marianne.

Carmen crouches to console The Thorns' leader and tries to pull her up.

I'm out of words.

"He's alive," Mars says slowly, looking at Marianne.

Rani doesn't take her eyes off me, though. "Ben," she says, and I nod, holding back tears. It's all I can do.

"Can I hug you, Arlo?" she asks, her voice barely audible.

"Please," I say. I don't want the feeling, but I want to let her hold me. The room feels strange now. I don't know what to think or do or say.

Rani stands and moves over to me, pulling the blanket up and over my body. Pressing her head against my chest, she wraps her arms around me, glancing at my wings briefly. I lower my arm around her and clock Mars staring between me and Marianne, looking confused about who to go to. I can't process anything at the moment. I'm exhausted.

"I'm so sorry, Arlo. It all makes sense, and I'm sorry. I know that means nothing, but I just want you to know I'm never leaving your side," Rani mutters into my chest. "Nothing you said changed my mind, I told you."

I rest my chin on her head. "I'm sorry," I say.

Then she pulls back and glares at me, and I can hear her in my head. I nearly cry again when my mouth forms into a smile. She knows I know. Marianne sits up and looks at me. "Arlo, I... I promise you I never lied. I..."

A desperate plea enters her tone, but I can't figure out if I believe her or not. How could she have forgotten?

"She thought he was dead. Michael took her memories. She honestly didn't know," Mars says, backing her up. I don't know what to believe. They're taking her side.

Michael took her memories.

"I believe her," Rani says, and I want to scream. Why do I... why? I can't think. I don't know what to do.

Michael took her memories.

"Why..." I croak before slumping backwards in defeat, my shoulder blades aching under the pressure.

"Everything you've told me, Arlo... there's no way I can make it right. I don't know how to get you to understand, but I never meant to hurt you. I had no memory of this. It was taken from me. I know it sounds like the perfect excuse, but so much was taken. I only ever wanted to help you. Always. From the moment I met you, when Mars and Casper dragged you down the halls and sat you down before me, I wanted to help. You are like a child to me, Arlo. A son. I would move the earth for you."

Listen to her. Think about what Jerome did to her. You forgave him, *didn't you?*

Michael took her memories.

I feel like giving up. I've stopped running, hit a wall, and now I'm here. There's nothing I can do.

"Nicholas was dead in my mind. He's even more so now." Marianne stares at me with fire in her eyes. "I lost my brother over a century ago. Nothing will change that fact."

And what about my dad?

"I want to save my dad," I admit in a hurry, glancing at them all. I swallow. Hard. I need them to understand. It's all I can say. The only words left in my script before the page runs out and the ink runs dry.

Marianne looks exhausted, but she nods after a moment and squeezes her eyes shut, tears falling to the carpet. It's like she's processing the last two hundred years of her life all at once.

Julian.

Manipulation.

Lies. Lies. Lies. Over a century of her life.

They both took her memories.

"We will," she chokes. "We'll save Jerome."

Chapter Twenty Nine

Arlo
Now

A weird few days follow. I can't help but look over my shoulder wherever I go, but he's still not found me. No one brings up the stories I shared, even though they want to. I can feel the words lingering like corpses in every room we're in. *Give it time.* They will ask eventually, and I will be ready when they do.

I'm slowly reintroduced to the remaining Thorns. Some faces remain bitter as they see my wings and claws, the battlefield playing out before their eyes again. I don't expect them to like me, but I hope they'll help when the time comes. And it's coming, I can feel it. I've always been able to feel it.

Rani keeps her word and insists she'd rather be in danger than not know what's going on. She takes me to our favourite coffee shops, and we go for walks around the riverside. Carmen even joins us on one occasion and reiterates the fact she doesn't hate me. I listen and forgive her, offering an apology of my own. I always apologise for everything, even before I know what I've done wrong. It's easier that way. I'm normally in the wrong, or at least, I used to think I was.

Mars lets me stay with them in their apartment, forcing me to take their bed while they inflate an airbed for themself. Casper calls Mars twice: once to tell us he'd returned to America without recalling why, and the second to tell us he remembered. He remembered what Jerome did to save us. He warned them I was in serious danger, which we already knew, of course, yet the reality hits me all the same.

When he rings again, Mars informs him I'm with them before he can speak. Casper sighs deeply before asking to speak to me. He asks how I am, and if I know what happened to my dad. I answer him, and he apologises. Why is everyone always apologising to me?

I finally have the courage to call my mum. Marianne gives me my phone back, explaining she'd been softly Manipulating her over the past few months to make sure she didn't worry, explaining the trip she fabricated for me and the stories she made up to keep my mother's mind at ease. Before, I would have been mad about Marianne Manipulating my mother. But I am thankful now. Things could have been far worse.

"Mum?" I say the second she picks up.

"Oh, Arlo. It's so good to hear your voice. I'm so proud of you for this year and everything you've done. You've pushed yourself so hard. I just needed you to call. You've not overworked yourself, have you? Are you coming home soon? Why did you never call back?"

I squeeze my eyes shut and hope the feelings don't resurface. "I'm sorry I didn't call. I'm sorry." It's all I can say.

"It's okay, baby. I'm just your mother, and I worry. How has your trip been? Surely you're coming home soon? I miss you. Bess misses you."

Don't cry.

"I know, mum. I'll be home soon, I promise. I love you."

"I love you too, sweetheart. Look after yourself, please."

I hang up.

I know Mars was listening to the whole thing.

"She'll want to hug you so tight when she sees you," they say from the doorway, their arms folded.

I know. I almost laugh.

Mars comes to join me on the bed, yet my wings keep an unnatural distance between us. *I wish I could saw them off.* I want them gone. I'm not The Star, so why are they still attached to me?

"Does she know about your dad yet?" they ask.

"No." I lower my gaze to my knees. *We almost got there.*

"Are you going to tell her?" Mars' tone is warm and gentle.

"I want to. It's just not safe. I don't want to get her involved." *We were so close. We nearly did.*

"I understand." Mars turns to look out of the window. "It's probably for the best."

They grip the sides of the bed, allowing their legs to swing. It's their tell-tale sign they're about to ask me something.

"Everything okay?" I ask.

"Hmm?" They turn back to face me, zoning back in. "Oh, no. Yeah. I'm fine."

"Are you sure?"

When they smile, their whole face smiles too. They're still holding something back, though. I see it in the shine of their eyes. "Yeah, of course. I'm always okay." They wink.

I don't believe them.

ANOTHER DAY PASSES, and Marianne invites me to her house for lunch, along with Rani. It's just the pair of us.

I shave and dress myself as nicely as I can—I want to look presentable.

I've spent the past few days in a daze, unable to think past the clouds stuffed in my brain. I don't want to talk to her anymore, but I know I must. Is that not why I ran back here in the first place?

With a warm welcome, she ushers us into her dining room and offers us a drink while she finishes preparing the meal. I stay focused on Rani to keep grounded. I need something familiar to tether my mind to. Rani was always that some*one*. She's been so nice to me since I returned. She's never once looked afraid or confused with the things I tell her, just listening and nodding along in understanding.

"You're staying for good now, right?" she's asked multiple times. I wish I could give her the answer she wants.

"I won't be far," was the closest thing I can say to the truth. I don't want to leave, but life will never return to normal until Michael is dealt with. He is the last obstacle between me and the world.

I know I can't wait any longer to find my father again, but my body still needs rest. I hate the waiting. The moment he sent me away, I knew I couldn't do this without him. None of us could. The Thorns need my father.

WE'RE sat at the dining table in the back room before a wall of windows overlooking the back garden. A grand piano sits in the far corner, with a freshly displayed vase of brightly coloured flowers atop it, the scent filling the room. This house feels different from the one I woke up in days ago, despite it not being.

"You know." Rani adjusts herself on the chair beside me and brushes her hair behind her ear. I like her new hair. It's pretty. "When I was ten, my brother lent me his copy of Dracula and said it was a gothic masterpiece. I took it to school and showed it off, trying to act like I was superior because everyone else was reading Twilight, obsessing over what I deemed were 'unrealistic' characters. In reality, I hated Dracula and ended up losing it. But anyway, my point is, a few years down the line, I read Carmilla and *loved* it." Rani laughs, blushing with embarrassment. "Look, it's got its issues, but I thought I was straight then and that book made me... *question* myself. I read into it a lot. And now, after everything I've learned, I wonder if these authors genuinely met real life vampires. But I suppose we'll never find out." She rambles then lets her eyes wander to the surrounding bookcases, taking in the scope of the room. I know her story is her way of trying to compartmentalise everything that's happened to her. I empathise with her stress. I'm not sure what to expect from this meeting either.

"Maybe they did—maybe a lot of people did, but they just didn't know how to explain it," I add.

Rani looks at me, or rather, her eyes wander just behind me... to my wings. I could never hide them from her. "I wonder if there are any stories of angels who could actually just be people like..."

"Like me?"

Rani nods. "What if this has all happened before, and this is just a natural cycle of evolution?"

I scowl. "You believe that?"

Rani shakes her head. "I don't want to, but I can't help but wonder. I mean, think of the age of the earth. It feels ignorant to think this is the first time this has happened. I mean, why now? Why *only* now? What if this has happened many times before every few centuries? Would we ever be able to prove it *didn't* happen?"

I don't know.

"I don't *want* it to happen, it's terrifying just knowing that it *could*, but you know I love my conspiracies, and yeah, I've been digging. I spent most of my teen years looking through history to find answers for things we can't explain. You know, I believe everyone on earth has been given a purpose, and having my faith brings me so much comfort, but I can't help but wonder what could be beyond the universe—out there, in the vast depths of space. There's so much we don't understand and perhaps never will. Just look at the pyramids! They're so scarily perfect that people have speculated for centuries about the involvement of higher beings or beings not of this world. There's been sightings, too! Myths and tales. UFO sightings! Ninety nine percent of the time they're just hoaxes, but what if..."

"I'm not a higher being, Rani." My brow remains tense, and my palms are sweating.

Rani's shoulders drop when she sighs with pity in her eyes. "I know you're not, I know. I just... I wish I had some answers. There're no scriptures or documents for anything I've seen in the past year, and I'm so lost. I hate it."

"I hate it too. I hate it so much, Rani." I clear my throat and rest my chin on the backs of my hands. Rani's thunderous heart pounds loud in my brain, radiating her fear and confusion. I wish I had answers for her, more than I've been able to give. I wish everything made sense. But it just... doesn't.

"Oh, Arlo. I'm..."

I close my eyes, the corners of my lips turning up as I exhale. "You're not allowed to say sorry, that's the rule," I say. I hope she senses my tone.

She does. Of course she does.

"Hey! That's my line!" She mildly slaps the table and giggles from the back of her throat. "I'm the one who has to tell you to stop bloody apologising left, right, and centre for things you literally have no control over! I... I feel cheated out of my own game." She theatrically grabs her chest in a gasp, and her eyes twinkle. "How dare you one up me!"

"Well, for that, I'm not sorry," I joke, then a tidal wave of nostalgia hits me and I gulp down a lump that made its way into my throat. I think I calm her, though.

Rani looks at me again, like there's just me and her in a vast empty space. "I missed you, Arlo. I missed you like you wouldn't believe."

Oh, Rani.

"I missed you too. A lot. I thought you'd never want to see me again."

"Never? Oh, no. No, Arlo. You know how seriously I take the title of best friend? That's a life-long commitment. You're stuck with me *forever.*"

I lean down close to her, drooping my head. "Rani, I..."

I let her press her forehead against mine; I even invite it. The warmth of her skin... calms me. I rarely feel this.

"Never let me go, Arlo. Never again," she breathes. I know she's not just talking about herself.

After what feels like an eternity, she pulls back. "And I didn't want to bring it up too soon, but when you're ready, we could... we can talk about..."

Her mouth forms a 'B', and I'm about to say his name when Marianne enters the room with a plate in her hands. It's like the lighting in the room shifts. We both straighten and look up at her. I didn't even sense her coming.

"Rani, you'll have to forgive me. I'm not the best vegetable chef in England, but I promise I really tried with this dish." Her tone is fluffy and high as she places the casserole dish before us and lifts the lid. Steam billows from the centre. It smells delicious. I wish I could eat more than I should. I miss the flavours of food, it's not the same now, never will be.

Beaming, Rani stares down at what seems to be a vegetarian dish. I spy lentils.

"I'm actually not a chef at all," Marianne jests. "This is the first proper meal I've made in years. But please, help yourself."

Rani reaches for the large spoon, serving herself a small portion before offering the spoon to me. I hold it, reluctantly, and gulp hard. I sense Marianne's eyes on me.

"You can eat as much or as little as you want, Arlo. I've got some blood for you for after if you think you need it."

I had some this morning, though only a tiny amount. It should be enough. I don't like discussing feeding around Rani, even though she understands. It feels too wrong and unnatural.

We eat in silence, apart from Rani's compliments about the

meal and Marianne's attempts at small talk. When we're finished, I sense Marianne has a lot more to say.

"Thank you for coming today," she begins, stacking the plates together and pushing them to the corner of the table. "I feared at least one of you wouldn't turn up."

Which one of us?

"I presumed you wanted to talk," I surmise, forcing confidence into my voice.

"That probably wasn't hard to guess." Marianne smiles, then leans both elbows onto the table. "I didn't want to force everything on you at once, but I know how little time we may have left, and I didn't want anything to happen before I spoke with you both." She looks between us and clears her throat. "Your father. Jerome. You believe he's still alive, yes?" Her blue eyes burn into me.

After what I saw with Nicholas, I want to say I'm not sure—but he must be alive. Michael needs him. His body will be alive. I just hope my father remains in there somewhere.

"Yes. He is. Of course. He's... oh." Words fail me again. Rani reaches for my hand under the table, and my fingers yearn to connect with hers. This much contact or personal intimacy isn't normal for me, but I take it, using it as the weight to keep me afloat.

"You know all about Julian, about our work and who we set out to be. Everything that came after? Michael finding us, my memories..." She abruptly shakes her head to clear her thoughts. "The moment I saw the monster—*Michael*—with you, I knew I could not stand against it alone. That night, everything came flooding back, like a key had turned in my brain and unleashed decades—*centuries,* in fact—of lies I'd told myself about my brother and what he did. I'd convinced myself he was dead, his bones buried beneath the earth. All I could ever think about was our childhood and the happy memories we shared. I would deliberately tear my mind away from anything bad that happened between us because I couldn't physically go there... and it was all Michael's doing. He did that." Marianne's face is sour and Rani tenses beside me. She's heard this before I think, I can read it clearly on her face.

"The moment I saw him at that damn festival, I brushed him off and thought nothing of his weirdness, but he'd planned everything so meticulously from that day, I never would have known anything had changed. But giving me it all back at that point... oh, that was cruel. But I had no time to dwell on it. I spent the whole of the last six months trying to figure out ways to bring you home. Now, here you are, having done it all on your own. God, I have no words for how much I admire you, Arlo." I don't know what to say, and neither does Rani, it seems. Marianne's breathing returns to normal as she sits back in her chair. "You are a force to be reckoned with."

"It's all been set out right from the start, hasn't it? There was no escaping this fate," I say, tears brimming in my eyes.

"Ever since Nicholas died, and I brought him back. I couldn't stand the idea of losing him, so I turned him. I gave him this life, and he came back wrong."

"Just like me."

"Oh no, not—" Rani starts.

"I did, though, but it's no one's fault. I didn't mean it like that. I know that now; no one could have known. We all came back wrong: me, my dad, Nicholas, even Michael. That was our fate." This is something I now understand. Mars saved my life, but the entities got there first. Marianne saved her brother's life, but the entities got there first. What Jerome said about the phenomenon in the sky makes sense. We were the unlucky few, with our origins forever unknown, but destiny already set.

It's up to us to change that, to change fate.

"Nicholas is working with Michael. They probably have my dad, and I know they can't be far. But nothing will take my mind ever again. I promise."

"So as long as you stay with us, nothing can happen, right?" Rani tries. I admire her optimism, but nothing is ever that simple.

"They'll be coming for me." *He always will.*

"Well, we'll be ready this time. We know what we're up against." Marianne sounds just as naïve. After everything she had to face, does she think it will be that easy? I want to scream. "We will save Jerome, and get him on our side. Then it's two against two, and we have humanity amongst us." Marianne clenches her fists around the oak table.

"And family," Rani mumbles. I peer at her expression. She's right.

Family. The reason I've done everything I've let myself do has been for family, blood or not. For my mum, my dad, Rani, Mars, Casper... everyone who welcomed me into their lives.

Ben.

I became what I am for Ben, and then he freed me.

"For Ben." The words slip out. He was just there, at the front of my brain, his name on the tip of my tongue. My brother in my heart.

Marianne lowers her gaze, almost closing her eyes entirely. "Yes. For Ben."

If I die, bury my body beside his.

"For Ben, for humanity," Rani adds into the silence.

MARIANNE SPENDS the next half an hour informing us of her plan to get my father back without Michael knowing. An impossible task, of course, but she cares too much for me to stop her. I'm not trying to be negative; I know this story all too well now. I know how it goes. It won't work. Despite everything I've said, promised, or led people to believe, I know the only way to end this is if I unite with them. However it happens, the three of us must be together for any of this to be worth it. But it will be extremely dangerous, and there's a high likelihood everything could go wrong.

I don't disregard everything she says, though.

"Jerome was entirely himself for a while with you, yes? The way he acted as your father, how long would it take for him to lose that? You know him far more than I ever did. This new Jerome, that is. I'm not quite sure I know how to separate the two, though I know I must."

It's clear it took a lot for her to say that. And I don't blame her. He's still a villain in her eyes. A cold-blooded, manipulative murderer. A monster.

"I wish I had an answer to that, but I can only hope a part of him remains."

Marianne shakes her head, her own words finally sinking in. "You know, for such a long time, even until the last few days, I wished I'd killed him that day. At the site of Julian's grave. I believed it would have been the right thing to do. To save anyone else from a fate such as mine, because no one deserved to go through what I did. I was oblivious to it all until his confession. I believed he deserved to die, and that I was a coward for running instead. I formed the Thorns because of him. I met Isiah and travelled the world with him, putting everything in its rightful place, all because I told myself I was too weak to deal with Jerome. Isiah was everything Jerome used to be, but better, or so I thought. Just look at how that turned out.

"But if I could go back now, after everything I've learned, killing him would have been the worst thing I ever could have done. To erase you and your brother from existence, what a great evil that would have made me." Marianne inhales sharply, not quite meeting my eyes. "The father you speak of now is not the man I knew. And I'll never be able to trust my gut fully, ever again, but I do trust *you*, Arlo, and I know wholeheartedly what your father means to you. I believe—oh god, I just *hope*—he was telling you the truth. Because if you're right, then we just might be able to bring him back. What he did to save you, that's not the Jerome I knew, my centuries old vampire companion. That's Jerome Mair, father to two beautiful sons, who realised his mistakes because of his children and fought hell for them."

Two beautiful sons.

"I'd quite like to meet him. This new man," she says, tendons twitching in her neck.

Really?

"I really do."

WE LEAVE Marianne an hour or so later after ending the conversation on a happier note, despite the weight lingering in our minds. I insist on walking Rani back to Carmen's flat, but she forces me in the direction of Mars' apartment and tells me to get some rest. There's no arguing with her, so I promise to see her tomorrow before parting ways.

I pick up my pace when it begins to rain, using my wings as a shield from the storm. I keep my head down and focus on hiding myself from view, but as I reach the bottom of the street and approach the door, I immediately sense something is off.

My gut sinks. Everything feels wrong.

Please, not now.

I let myself into the complex with the spare key Mars lent me and run up the stairs two at a time without taking a proper breath. I have to scrape my gut from the floor as I realise Mars' door isn't locked. It's slightly ajar, and all I can think is: *He's found me. Found us. Game over.*

But at the commotion and the sound of my panting, Mars pulls the door open and looks at me with confused worry.

"Arlo! Skies, are you okay?" They don't seem in danger, but when they step back, I see him.

There, sat at Mars' kitchen table, wearing baggy, nondescript clothes, is my father. His hair is tied back, exposing a fresh scar leading from his jaw all the way past his collarbone.

Oh.

"Yeah. Oh, sorry." Mars' brow tenses as they look between us. "I should really keep this apartment under a false name."

20th August 1931

Jerome took me to a puppet show in Vienna this weekend. It was directed for children but adults experienced just as much enjoyment.

It was the first time I thought about Nicholas in a while. Not the man I left but the boy I watched grow up.

My brother.

We once created a story about a brother and sister who ran away to a forest and encountered different weird and wonderful creatures in the woods, each who told them a story about life and how it should be lived to maintain happiness. It was never intended to represent us but I always believed it did, in a way.

And we did run away, just never towards true happiness.

I think Jerome sensed my melancholy as the performance came to a close. He squeezed my shoulder and ensured me I was safe and nothing would ever harm me. He always made sure of that.

He bought me a bouquet of flowers then we shared a rich man as the sun set.

Nicholas is probably long dead. The village got him. I need to move on.

28th August 1969

Is it normal for headaches to last this long?

27th November 1987

I don't know what woke me first, the dream or Jerome banging the door open at 4am after having just come back from the club. I heard him falling around downstairs, hopefully alone, it was hard to tell. Nothing surprises me these days.

But the dream. It was not quite a terror, but it may have turned that way if I hadn't startled awake in a sweat. The more he stared at me.

It was Nicholas, but as a grown man, face full and merry. What he may have looked like if the fever hadn't taken him at seventeen.

He didn't do much, just sat at the end of my bed, smiling. That's not quite what made me scared though. My baby brother could never have scared me, no, what frightened me was the fact this wasn't the first time this has happened. I should have noted this earlier but I've had this dream before.

This exact same dream.

And it felt too real.

—Taken from the diaries of Marianne Ashtown

CHAPTER THIRTY

Mars
Now

I must admit, I didn't expect this to happen. I mean, ever since Arlo came back, I'd considered the threat of *The Sun* and knew it could strike at any moment. I'd thought about Jerome, too, and his role in all of this, especially after what Marianne had told me.

But I didn't expect him to turn up at my door.

And not only that, I didn't expect him to be this *frightened*.

"Mars?" was the first thing he said. It was as if he knew me, like I was an old friend. He was panting, and I squinted at his strange inhuman heartbeat. He wasn't a vampire anymore, but he also wasn't fully human.

The fresh scar across his face and his wandering eyes cemented the doubt that he was dangerous, though. Call it instinct. But then when he didn't even attempt to enter, I looked at his face more closely to really drink him in. My shoulders slumped. Maybe I saw Arlo in him, or maybe I was just scared and confused too, given the last few days. I wanted to help him.

I let him inside after rushing to the conclusion that I needed to hear him out. And then once he sat himself down, his wings trailing over the chair behind him, I began to worry I'd made a huge mistake.

Then he spoke. And I knew it was him talking.

He told me everything, corroborating everything Arlo had already said. He even mentioned things I wouldn't have known, stuff only he'd done, seen, and experienced.

I do not like this man, but he's Arlo's father, and they're both in serious danger. I told myself a while ago that I'd do anything for Arlo, which means supporting his father, regardless of my feelings. It's a very odd thing to come to terms with. Having a hatred for someone you've never met, but then having no choice but to change your mind after hearing them out. Not once did he ask for forgiveness. I admired that, at least.

I'm about to ask where we go from here—I even think about offering him a place to say, since he probably isn't ready to announce himself to Marianne just yet—but I don't get a chance because Arlo is beside me in a matter of seconds, landing me in the very awkward situation of: 'Oh, hello, here's your dad.'

"DAD?" Arlo says, wide-eyed and frankly confused.

Jerome stands in an instant, his reddish wings knocking over the fruit bowl. I'm that spaced out, I almost laugh.

I have to remind myself I don't really believe in angels, despite the two very angelic beings embracing each other before my eyes.

Again, I'm spacing out. This is completely beyond me.

I've never seen Arlo relax into a hug like this before. Though it's not just a hug, it's an *embrace.* They hadn't known each other for long, but the bond they've developed is something I don't think I'll ever be able to comprehend. They'd lost and found themselves in ways so unimaginable it almost makes me dizzy trying to understand it.

"You got away," Arlo says, and Jerome nods against his son's shoulder. Seeing them side by side, their relation is obvious. He is the perfect mix of his mother and father. Arlo James Everett.

My gut sinks even lower. I love him so much it hurts.

They break apart, then carefully, Arlo raises his hand to ghost his fingers over the scar on his father's face.

He apologises, of course he does. He will never change. Jerome gently lowers Arlo's arm. "Not your fault. Never your fault. I promise." His voice is solid and protective.

I feel like I probably shouldn't be here until Jerome turns to me and dips his head, like he's aware I'm staring. "Forgive me, Mars. I didn't mean to intrude like this. I didn't know where else to go."

He sounds so *old*. He is so old.

I gulp hard as I speak. "It's okay, honestly." I say far too casually.

"Mars," Arlo's voice is as soft as ever. "Thank you."

Why is he thanking me? For opening the door? I've really done the bare minimum lately, and yet he's *thanking* me. Oh. Oh *damn*. I want to kiss him. I really want to kiss him and hold him and—

Skies, Mars. Calm. Down. You know none of this is going to happen. It can't happen.

I don't know what to do. This giant grey cloud is taking space in my chest and brain and it's panicking me.

"Michael is close, isn't he?" I know he is. Jerome told me so, detailing the parts Arlo couldn't. How he sent Casper away and told Arlo to run as he left himself to fight Nicholas. Nicholas would have told Michael everything. It was genuinely only a matter of days now.

A matter of days before the end.

I'm going to be sick.

Instead, I just pass out. It's embarrassing to say the least. I pass out on my own kitchen floor. Oh well, it could have been worse.

At least I was in the comfort of my own home surrounded by angels.

Ha ha.

Oh, skies.

WHEN I COME AROUND, I'm staring at the flaking paint on my ceiling. *I really should get that sorted*, I think.

After a few moments of watching floating dust particles, a chair creaks, and I jerk my head towards the sound, focusing on Arlo's slim frame in a chair by my side, relaxed. He has a book in his lap, something from my shelves surely, even though I read little. I think to myself *hmm, I hoped he picked up something interesting.*

His eyes flick up when I clear my throat and pull myself to a seating position.

"Mars. Good. Hi," he says, his Adam's apple bobbing as he swallows. He slams the book shut. *Shakespeare for dummies.* Oh, shit. I bought that book after I heard him and Rani talking about how much they loved Shakespeare. And I just *know* he's figured that out, too.

"Please don't test me," I say, hoping my assumption was correct.

Arlo's mouth quirks upwards into a smile, his eyes grinning just as strongly. Butterflies erupt in my chest. "How are you feeling?" he asks.

I'm fine. Honestly couldn't be more grand. "Splendid."

"Are you sure?" His brow tenses. Every single detail in his face moves and contorts. I analyse every single crease and line and dusting of hair over his soft skin. The rise and fall of his chest as he breathes. The rhythmic movement of his fingers when he concentrates. He's freshly shaved, and he smells *so good.*

I love you, Arlo. I always will. In any way you will have me.

"I promise I'm fine. Just got a bit overwhelmed for a bit. Where is your dad?"

Arlo flinches before smiling. "He's still in the kitchen, planning what he's going to say to Marianne." He says it so seriously.

I want to laugh again. "Oh. Right..." *Don't make a joke, Mars. Seriously. Grow up. This is adult business. You're high from fear, and you just don't want to admit it.*

"We won't stay here long. We need to speak to Marianne, and then we're going to go after him."

"What?" *Arlo isn't running anymore? After everything?* "You're going after him? Michael? As in, you're going to run *towards* him?" I need clarification.

Arlo is surprisingly calm when he responds. "Better that then wait for him to come to us and hurt anyone else. I know what I promised, and what The Thorns promised, but we need to end it, and we can now—now we're both ourselves."

He's been speaking to Jerome; he must have been. They've planned it out already.

"I don't want you to get hurt, though. We really need to think about this logically. You're going to need as many of us as possible. Both of you can't do this alone." *Don't do anything stupid, Arlo. Please. I'll never forgive myself.*

Arlo leans forward, and I shuffle down the bed slightly so we're both incredibly close.

"We'll talk to Marianne first, but we started it, Mars. We must end it."

"But..." *What if something goes wrong?*

"Mars, I..."

Something clatters outside, cutting off Arlo's words and severing the building tension.

A distant mumble of an apology follows, and I hope our conversation hasn't been cut short. I need to talk to Arlo like this. I've missed him being himself. By my side.

He sits back in his chair again, his eyes wandering.

I try to draw him back to me. "I really care about you, Arlo. I hope you know that. When you found me, I nearly started believing in God again because I thought it was a miracle. And now I'm worried I'm going to lose you. Again. I don't want that, I—"

Arlo fixes his eyes on me again, chewing the inside of his mouth. He's playing with his fingers, his breathing shallow.

"You're scared," I observe.

Of course, he's terrified. There's nothing that would calm *me* right now if I was in his position. In fact, I'd be worse. I'd do the silly thing. I'd be the fool. The fool I'm literally asking Arlo not to be. I'm such a hypocrite.

Arlo swallows a few times before taking a deep breath. "I'm losing my mind with fear, Mars."

His honesty shatters my heart. I can feel it in his voice and sense it in his body language. I know Arlo—I know him so well; I know I do. That felt like the most honest he'd ever been with me. He always hides everything away. Not now.

"Wait for us, then. We can help." I extend my arm, so it's less than an inch away from his skin. I stop myself, my fingers trembling. Arlo looks sad; his features droop, and pain blooms in his eyes.

"I don't want him to hurt you."

His words punch my gut. Oh, god. I can't deal with this. "He won't. He won't hurt us," I lie, and he sees right through it.

"Don't say that. Stop promising things you can't be sure of. He's not of this world. The things inside me and my father are not of this world. We're like him, except we're just vessels. I think the only way to end him is to end..."

"Shut up!" I scream, and he flinches, his eyes wide in horror. "Please," I beg, my tone settling ever so slightly. "Don't say that. Don't you dare—"

"It's the only way." He sounds so small.

"And you've talked about that with your father?"

"Well, no. Not properly. Not yet, but..."

"Arlo? Really? Please tell me you've thought about other ways."

I'm going to cry. I want to scream. He can't seriously be implying he's going to *kill* himself.

"There are no other ways."

'There are! Fran! She's immune, she can't be Manipulated. There have to be others like her too. They could solve this!"

Arlo looks at me, clearly learning this information for the first time. "She's immune?"

I nod frantically, pressing my lips tightly together. I sigh when a plan refuses to form on my tongue. "She can't be affected by the Manipulation we use, and what Michael uses... This could be the key!" I'm shaking.

"You've found others?"

I sink into myself. "Well, no... but surely if this happens, there will be enough people to break and reverse it!" I'm talking faster than my thoughts can process.

Arlo's brows lower. "So, you want to let it happen? And take that risk hoping a few people around the entire world are unaffected by this and will somehow find each other to turn the world back to the way it was? Is that what you think it will cost?"

I know it's silly. We could never risk that, and I never thought about risking that. I just want there to be another way. There has to be something else we can do. *There are other ways. Right?*

My mind is blank.

I know Arlo realises this too. A tear drips from his eye and onto the book on his lap. He swipes at it and tries to distract himself by looking away, but there's nowhere else to look.

Look at me. We can figure this out. It doesn't have to be this way.

"I'm going to check on my father. We'll go and speak to Marianne this afternoon." His tone is so *dead* and cold, it's like he's shutting down everything we just spoke about.

I watch him silently as he stands and leaves the room.
I won't let him go through with this.
I won't.
Tell him what he means to you—to all of you. Make him stay.
I clench my fists into the duvet and collapse backwards.
Find another way.

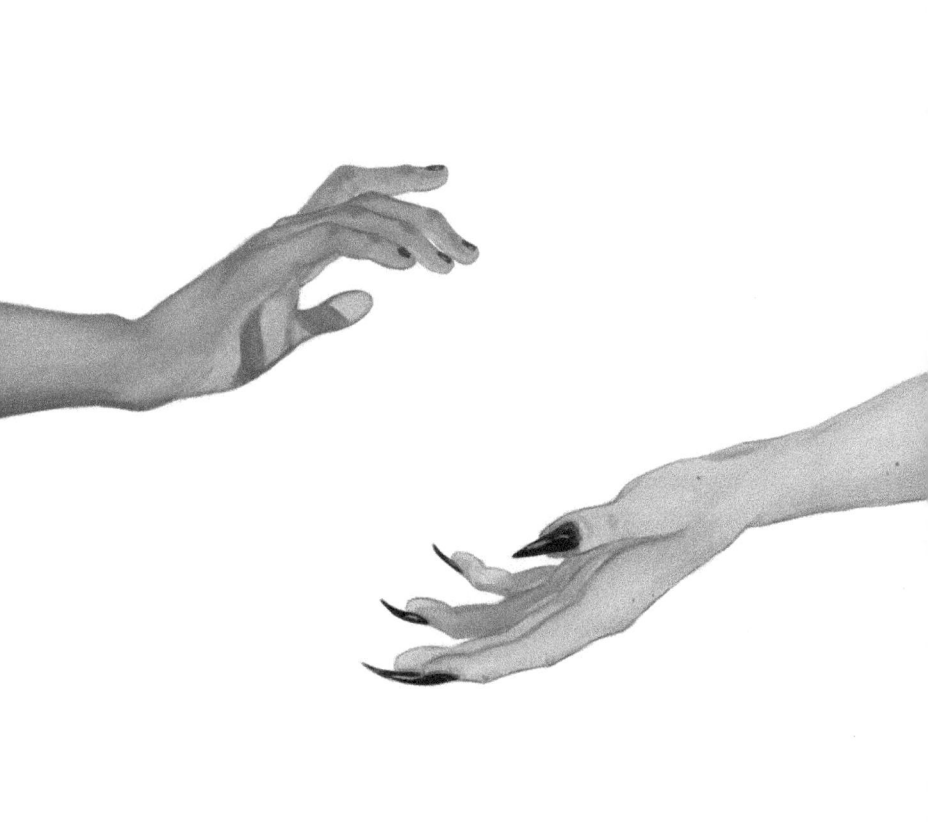

CHAPTER THIRTY ONE

Arlo
Now

I listened to everything Mars said and observed their reaction to my admission. I wasn't planning on divulging my full plan yet, especially after just learning my father was on my side. But after seeing Mars again, and spending time with Rani, I concluded the plan I'd brushed off before may actually be the only one that works. Finding out Fran was immune changes things and gives me hope for the future, but there isn't time to work with that. This is the best shot we have. A permanent conclusion. I just need to get my father on board. And everyone else.

It's a long shot, but trying is the only way to figure that out and see if it works. These entities need a vessel to survive on this earth, which surely means when they take on a host, they have to abide by the rules of the body they take on, which makes them vulnerable to any acts enacted upon the vessel. They may be from the same point of origin as vampires, but they're not the same. The parasites for vampires reanimate a dead host without truly impacting who they once were as living people, but these entities are different. They reanimate the host, but live alongside it before taking over entirely. From what my father has told me, Michael can bleed and suffer. He's seen it—he's *caused* it, which means he's not invincible. He's only human, despite the wings and what's inside. If we can get close enough to him, both me and my father, and we...

I'm so scared.

"How are they?" asks my father, looking up from his writing. His wings drape over the back of the chair, trailing across the tiles. He's actually writing out what he's going to say to Marianne. Rehearsing it.

I blink, clearing my throat. "They're okay."

My father sucks in his lips and waves the sheet of paper. "I'm such an idiot," he sighs.

"Is that?"

"It's exactly what you think it is. Only I was in half a mind to just mail it and not have to face the consequences of my actions. I've not changed as much as I'd hoped." He half laughs, but it's bitter.

"We're going to speak with her today. We need to."

My dad just nods, his throat bobbing. He rubs his finger under his bottom lip. "I figured you might have said something like that."

"You know we don't... you..." I look away, trying to find the right words. I stare at his side, imagining the thick, stretched scar on his chest, the one Nicholas used to weaken him. "How did you get away again?" I have to ask.

My dad turns in his chair to face the room fully and drops his hands onto his lap. "I may have caused some damage." I almost detect a faint smile on his lips.

"Did you hurt anyone? Did you..." I step closer, lowering my voice. "Did you *kill* anyone?"

Jerome closes his eyes and lowers his head. That answers enough.

"Dad..." I clench my fists. *He promised he'd changed.*

"I did what I had to. Nicholas is strong. He has a part of Michael in him still, and he knows how to use it to his advantage. He tried to wake The Moon and nearly succeeded, but I overpowered him and I, well, I killed his henchmen. Followers. Vampires. *Turned,* you call them. I used that as a distraction to escape." He holds a hand over his heart instinctively. Yet the way he uses the word *Turned* sparks a horrible thought. That's what my father was. Before all this. He *Turned.* He let the monster within take over.

Will he follow along with my plan? Or has he lived too long to risk sacrificing everything?

How well do I really know him?

"You're looking at me funny. Arlo, I need you to know I wouldn't have dreamed of killing an innocent. I've not killed anyone who did me no harm since..." He trails off, which makes me even more frustrated. He's not a good man.

Julian. Say his name.

"Arlo, I wouldn't. You must believe me. This was all self-defence. I would never harm anyone deliberately. I'm not who I once was. I don't know how to prove it, but please believe me." He's standing now and stepping over to reach me.

I have to speak my mind. I step back, out of his reach. "I just don't want anyone else to get hurt. No matter which side. I want no more deaths, pain, or suffering. I want to end him, and then we can all be free. Is that too much to ask for?" *Don't cry.*

I hear the breath leave his nostrils. He tilts his head slightly. "Possibly. The world isn't that simple, but I wish for the same. I know we need to end him, and I've thought about how, but he's not the only ego to crush or evil to destroy. He's not human; never was, and never will be. He thinks he can control us all and turn this world into some utopia, using the entities inside us to assist. But does pain and suffering not already occur? Are we not already sheep to the world we're fed through screens? Are we not already cogs in the machine that keep the very world turning? We can try to save the world from *him*, but it will never just end at that. We'll all destroy ourselves eventually. We're already halfway there."

I'm silent for a moment, knowing full well what he means. Yet it makes me feel so sick, so small. I'll never be able to do enough.

"This is the least we can do, though, and we have the power to do it. We can stop him. I'll do whatever it takes. Will you help me?" My hands are shaking.

His voice is serious when he says, "You know I will. And I mean that from the bottom of my soul and my pathetic little heart. We will stop him, Arlo. This is the home of the human race, and while we may never understand what else is out there, we have our chance to prove our humanity and do the right thing."

I have to say it. "I'm so scared, dad."

"I know. Me too, son. Me too."

I finally step closer, exhausted once again from my own racing thoughts.

When my father pulls me close, he lowers his chin onto my shoulder, his voice almost inaudible as he says, "I know where he is."

The words strike me like a knife. It's happening then.

"We're going after him now then. We're doing it," I say, awaiting confirmation.

"I speak with Marianne, then we go. First thing tomorrow."

I nod. I know why he needs to speak to her first. I know why, and it makes me want to vomit, but it's the way it must be.

My father has come to the same conclusion as me.

We may not be coming back from this.

This is it.

27th April 2019
Save Arlo. Avenge Ben. Remember Julian.
Save. Avenge. Remember.

Remember.
Remember.
Remember.

—Taken from the diaries of Marianne Ashtown.

CHAPTER THIRTY TWO

Mars
Now

I can't look at him. It feels pathetic, but I can't. The clawing sensation at the back of my mind lingers as I follow them out of the apartment. The pair stand close beside each other, as if whatever had transpired between them has brought them closer than before.

It's wild seeing Arlo so... *sure* of himself. So set on what he must do. I can't fathom it. Or more, I can, but I refuse to acknowledge it. He's going to kill himself to save us all. It aches and burns in my chest, and the gnawing realisation consumes me whole. I can't let him do it. After everything, this can't be the only way.

"Do I look presentable?" Jerome asks, turning to his son and adjusting the collar of the fresh shirt I'd given him. Arlo hasn't made eye contact with me, either, and has opted for walking ahead with the expectation I'd follow. It hurts, but I can't find the words to tell him how much. I think of the wound in his side and wonder if it's fully healed, despite already knowing it has. Seeing him so vulnerable and exposed and afraid less than a week ago, makes it all more difficult to fathom. He's a completely different person. Arlo reborn yet again.

He's still in there, though. That boy you knew. The man you saved more than once. Arlo. He's still there.

"You look fine." Arlo flaps his hand out quickly, as though he were about to dust the creases on his father's shirt before thinking better of the sensation. But he's not quick enough to hide the tremor in his inhuman hands, with the blackened claws curling over every tip, like talons. Sharp, yet gentle. I remember how they felt against my hands, how careful he had been not to hurt me.

Oh, Arlo.

We're walking towards the hideout. The sky is overcast and grey, despite the humidity. I wonder how Marianne will react. Will she kill him there and then out of sheer anger? Or is she expecting him?

"Mars, walk beside me." Arlo turns to face me, bringing me out of my daze. He signals with his arm for me to join him.

What? I almost say, but I don't give myself time to dwell on it. I pick up my pace until our arms almost brush. Almost. Jerome stands on Arlo's right, yet he's looking elsewhere, as if he understands it's not his place to listen to whatever Arlo might say to me. Another sudden swell of dizziness washes over me, and I try to stay calm.

"I want you to stay close when we speak. I don't know how she'll react, but I need you near to... to keep us safe."

I gulp down the lump in my throat. I don't know what else I expected him to say, but it wasn't this. This pleading for protection, as if I was on their side against my leader, as if I would raise a hand to Marianne if it came to it. As if I approve of what they're about to do. But I cannot lie to him, not after everything. I cannot lie to the one person I swore to protect until my dying breath.

"I'll be there. I'll make sure nothing bad happens. I promise."

A ghost of acknowledgement dusts Arlo's cheeks as he lowers his head slightly. "Thank you, Mars. I knew I could trust you."

Why does he sound so old suddenly? So wise and confident? Why is he acting so brave? Some heroic knight readying for his final battle.

No.

I can't help it. I reach for his hand and squeeze. I squeeze so tight I can almost feel his bones cry out. His head flashes up to me in a panic as his nails bite into my flesh, but he knows I won't let go. He doesn't fight it; my grip is so harsh it's burning. He lets it happen, his breath hitching.

Silent words fly between us. *Don't do this. Please. We can figure out another way together. With The Thorns. We can do this. Together, we can fight him off once and for all.*

You know we can't.

"Is this it? Are we close?"

I'd forgotten Jerome was only inches away from us. I wonder if he watched what just transpired. We're getting close now. The alleyways are empty as we turn the last corner to the main door, ever closer to the end.

"It's just through here." Arlo strides forward, pulling his hand from my grip and scrapes his nails against his palm. He crouches under the archway and hurries down the steps, not waiting to see if we follow.

I glance briefly at the man I want to hate. He looks at me with sorrow in his eyes. "Arlo mentioned you a lot, even in his sleep," he whispers.

He did?

"Thank you," he says, before stepping in front of me and following Arlo down the dingy steps.

I'm left stunned for a moment, watching as they both disappear from sight, their wings brushing against the damp stone above.

I take in a deep breath, then follow.

Thank you for what?

. . .

The halls are as eerily silent as ever when we enter, despite there being more of us now. I often forget the sheer size of this place: corridor after corridor, winding and arching beneath the light. Perfectly hidden—our home. The place where we have always felt safe.

And here I am, bringing in one of the few men still alive I know Marianne despises.

I'm doing this for Arlo, I remind myself.

I make sure the pair of them stay quiet as I stand in front of them, adamant to lead the way now we're closer. I haven't planned what to say, but I still think I can provide a better explanation than them.

Thankfully, the halls are empty all the way to Marianne's office, where I'm sincerely hoping she'll be at this time.

As luck would have it, there she is, sitting at her desk in deep concentration. I signal for the angels to hang back and insist on speaking to her first before springing Jerome upon her.

Jerome lowers his gaze in understanding, and Arlo nods. He rubs his flat palms frantically against his sides.

"Marianne," I say. My voice goes all harsh and croaky as I make my way across the room to face her. She startles as if she hadn't heard me coming. Maybe she hadn't. She seemed engrossed with whatever she was reading.

"Do you have a moment?"

"Is everything okay? Is it Arlo? Is he—"

"It's not—"

"It's me." He doesn't even give me a second to respond. He enters, with Arlo close behind him. Marianne's chair legs screech across the floor and I flick my focus back to her to catch her reaction as she leaps to her feet, her face gaunt and white—deathly so. I grab my face in frustration, popping my eyes back in their sockets. You could cut the tension with a knife, something I'm sure Marianne wishes she had right now.

"Please, we need to talk—" Jerome raises his hands in surrender. He visibly stiffens, as if only now registering her existence after their decades-long separation, then he's cut off as Marianne appears before him and smacks him hard across the face. He stumbles back, reaching for his jaw to wipe the spittle off his lips.

He could have waited, the bloody bastard. I had this under control!

Marianne looks like she's readying for another slap, her eyes unnaturally wide with rage. Arlo steps from the shadows of his father's wings, his voice ever so soft as he says, "Marianne, he's himself. We came to talk."

At Arlo's words, Marianne's shoulders drop. She exhales and steps back.

"I know," she says, her tone devoid of anger. It's one of defeat. "I expected you. It was only a matter of time. After all Arlo told us, I just knew you'd be close behind. You were always so loyal to those you claimed you loved." A soft bitterness laces her words as she addresses Jerome. I don't dare move. "I just needed to do that. You understand." Then she turns and slumps against the table, folding her arms. "I wanted to kill you, if I ever saw you again. I would think long and hard about how I'd do it, too. Poison was the only way, of course. Poetic justice." She sounds almost like she's laughing, but her features don't show it. She fixes her gaze on her old friend. "But I know I would have only made things worse. You are The Moon, are you not?" She gestures to his wings.

Jerome just stares at her, wide eyed. "I am," he says eventually.

"Then you have a part in this, and we need you. I don't want to trust you, but I must, for my Thorns and everyone else in this god-damn world. Can we help everyone this time?"

The heat in the room rises once again. Even Arlo is lost for words, cowering behind his father.

"I'll never expect your full trust. I know I don't deserve that. But yes. We will. I should have never stopped you."

. . .

AFTER LOCKING the door to her office, Marianne forces us all into chairs before sitting at her rightful place behind her desk. The mountain of paper either side acts like a shield.

I'm going to be honest. I expected a lot worse. I thought I would have to step in to stop Marianne from decapitating Jerome right there on the spot, but I'm glad it didn't come to that.

Arlo hasn't spoken a word since Jerome started talking, and I keep to myself, slumping down into my chair to chew my nails. I glimpse Arlo's tense expressions every now and again as Jerome and Marianne discuss 'next steps'. He never voices the plan Arlo suggested to me, so I conclude they haven't discussed it with each other yet. Ergo, Jerome may have been planning another way to end this all. But as I continue listening, I realise the conversation is leading straight to that conclusion.

Then Arlo finally sits up and voices his thoughts. "We're going to end this. This whole thing is so much bigger than any of us, and we need to make our move *now*."

Marianne's head snaps to him, while Jerome slowly turns. Marianne is the first to speak. "You have a real plan?" Her gaze flicks to Jerome for a second before returning to Arlo.

"We do," Arlo admits, his voice clogged before he lowers his gaze. Jerome tenses to my left, his unusual pulse is more notable now. *What is he, really?*

"Arlo," Jerome says in warning. I forget to breathe.

"Well?" Marianne's brows are tense.

Please don't say it.

"We're going to take the fight straight to him. Both of us." Arlo straightens slightly, his wings fluttering out behind him.

Marianne relaxes back into her chair, playing with the pen in her hands. "Okay. I suppose that is an option."

"We have to. We can't wait around putting off the inevitable," Arlo says, sighing and glancing at his father, whose eyes are wide. Jerome bites his top lip. Arlo doesn't look at me, but I want him to. I need him to.

"You know where he is? Michael?"

"We—" Jerome starts before his son cuts him off.

"We do. We're leaving tomorrow."

Jerome looks as if he's about to stand up in protest, but he relaxes after a moment, not uttering a word.

Oh, Arlo.

He wants us to follow. He wants us to be there to help and—

"Tell us your plan and we can gather everyone tonight. We'll help you end this."

My chest is filling. I'm struggling to release a full breath.

We're doing this. We're going to help. It doesn't have to end that way. I'll make sure of it.

"We destroy the vessels, we get close enough to him to let him believe we've returned to him, then we strike." His hazel eyes are dead.

Arlo no, NO!

"And you're so sure this will work?" Marianne purses her lips in concentration, twisting her chair slightly. How can she react like this? Like she doesn't care about what will happen to Arlo. Does she truly grasp what they're saying?

"We're sure. It's the only way." Still, Arlo is distant when he speaks.

Marianne only nods. *Please, don't let them do this!*

Jerome then claps his hands together, raising to his feet. "Okay then. We leave tomorrow. For Edinburgh."

Edinburgh. That's where he is.

The centre of it all. So close. *What is he going to do?*

But that's it. Nothing else is said.

Jerome knows where Michael is, and tomorrow, we end it all.

OF COURSE, we summon everyone immediately after. I'm bricking it. I don't want to see the reaction on the Thorns' faces when they finally meet the two angels at the centre of this whole mess. Arlo will hopefully be forgiven, but Jerome will definitely earn some strange looks.

I'm just trying to keep my head clear. The entire situation is a mess. I want to scream. *This is it.*

I focus so hard on staying calm, even though I worry about Arlo's inevitable recklessness. The words he still won't say out loud —he's not going to survive this.

He's too selfless and always has been. Rani obviously walks straight over to him, with Carmen in tow, but as she gets closer to the centre of the hall and notes Jerome sitting against one of the front benches, she jumps, her entire body flushing red.

Jerome's confidence fades, and he stands in a panic. The tension only lifts when Arlo turns to face him, and Carmen puts her arm around Rani's shoulders.

"You're Jerry," Rani says matter-of-factly, feigning confidence.

"And you must be Rani." Then Jerome smiles, and he looks *exactly* like Arlo. It's uncanny... it's...

Why are there tears in my eyes?

Marianne stands between them, her face unreadable. "Rani will kill you if you step an inch out of line." It's clear she's addressing Jerome, despite her neutral gaze. Rani opens her mouth to speak but thinks better of it and grins.

"And this is Carmen, my daughter. She will burn your body and hide the evidence."

Carmen curtsies sarcastically, holding an invisible skirt. Despite his height, Jerome shrinks into himself. Marianne finally looks at Jerome and squints. "I'm just laying out the facts. If you do anything that makes me question your intentions, we'll make sure you can never be reborn again—in any world."

Well, at least it's all out on the table. Marianne marks her territory by setting the ground rules. Jerome has enough sense not to contest anything.

Thankfully, the rest of The Thorns react placidly when they arrive. I suppose they had enough time to contemplate where they stood with it all; those left have no choice but to accept whatever is thrown at them.

"We're bringing the fight to Michael. We're putting an end to him before he has a chance to lay a finger on the rest of humanity." Marianne continues to speak, but I'm zoning out, focusing on Arlo beside Rani. I'm taking in every individual feather on his back, every slight curl to his white-blond waves, analysing how they shape around his neck. I imagine him breathing, experiencing life... living.

I can't lose him. I can't.

"Is that understood? Feel free to leave the room now. I won't stop you. But if you stay, I want you to understand I'll do everything in my power to protect you, but this is for the safety of the human race. We must do all we can."

I'm not fully listening, but she doesn't mention what Arlo is planning on doing to himself. She deliberately withholds that fact. *In case anyone tries to stop him.*

Because they will try to stop him. Rani, the band, even Carmen.

One Thorn rises to leave, and my eyes follow them in a daze. While I'm not entirely present, I feel the blood boiling in my body, and a sweat breaking out down my back.

I wish it didn't have to be this way.

I CATCH Arlo on the way out, reluctantly pulling himself away from Rani and his father. If I don't do this now, I'll regret it every day for the rest of my very, *very* long life.

Rani tells him where she'll be after and asks him to come and talk with her, smiling sadly. *Does she understand what's going to happen?* She nods at me as I approach.

Jerome looks a little lost, but he claims he won't be leaving the hideout until we all leave tomorrow morning. "I didn't think there was this many of us," he mutters proudly.

Us. Our family.

I let Arlo follow me down the hall to his Thorns bedroom, which isn't far. It's the best place I can think of.

"Are you okay, Mars?" he asks as I shut the door behind us and get a little too close for his liking. I step back and apologise under my breath. "Mars? Is this about the plan?"

"No, it's..." Who am I kidding? It's the whole truth or nothing right now. "Of course it is, you idiot."

He flinches at the shift in my tone, like I've hit him.

My heart breaks for him. I let my eyes consume every inch of his existence. "Arlo, I can't let you go through with this." I pace to the other end of the room.

"Mars..." He holds his hands up in protest, but I stop him, shutting my eyes.

"No, no. Please. Let me say this. Let me get this off my chest before I explode."

"Okay," he murmurs, shrinking.

I step away, throwing myself onto the bed with a sigh. I look away from him now. Seeing his face will be the death of me.

"Arlo, you were the first person I saved. The first human being I brought back from the verge of death, and ever since the moment you woke up, I've sworn to never let anything happen to you. I failed you so many times, and you can tell me it's not my fault all you want, but you have to let me shoulder some of the blame—I need you to let me do that." I still don't look up at him, but I know he's stepped closer. His feet appear in my eye-line, the ends of his wings trailing against the stone floor.

"My sister Poppy died a few years ago, and I tried to bring her back. When I realised I was too late, I could never forgive myself.

When you breathed in again and your eyes opened, I saw her. I saw her in the corner of my eye, and she smiled. She smiled so wide. I felt her presence all over my soul, and her invisible hands on my back. The warmth of her hug enveloped me, and I finally knew it wasn't my fault. It wasn't my fault she died, and she would hate to think I ever thought that. You were my chance, Arlo. I know I sound so selfish, but I—"

Arlo stoops to his knees before me, forcing me to look into his eyes. The green and gold flecks in his pretty amber eyes stand out more than they ever have. His unkempt hair curls over his shoulders like silk, and I feel the warmth of his breath on my skin.

"You're not being selfish," he says. "You've never been selfish."

His voice sounds different, more firm. More honest and real.

I swallow hard. "I can't let you die again," I admit, my voice cracking in a whisper. I'm holding back the dam of tears welling up. I'm trying to burn his presence into my mind forever, so I can *see* him forever.

"The entities inhabit dead bodies. I'm a vampire, but I'm also dead. As are you. We all died. That is how our lives turned out." Arlo takes a deep breath, adjusting his feet and catching his balance on the mattress beside me, trapping me in with his arms on either side. "The entities need a vessel, so we need to remove them in order to drive the entities out once and for all. We just need to make sure there are no other potential vessels in the room when we do it."

I really thought I was getting through to him, but then he loses me again. He didn't listen to a word I said, or he disregarded it if he did. He's so set on his plan.

"You're going to kill yourself," I say bluntly.

"I'm going to terminate the vessel."

"You..." My breath hitches, and I choke on a sob, leaning back to get away from him. "What happened to you, Arlo? What happened to the boy who wanted to write poetry and drink hot chocolate from his favourite café as he studied Shakespeare? The boy who went home and listened to Fleetwood Mac or The Velvet Underground and made his bed with his teddy bear always front and centre? Who rang his mum every night and went on walks with his best friend in his silly little jumpers and laughed hysterically every time someone brought up scenes from his favourite film before going off on tangents about all his interests and passions? What happened?"

Arlo doesn't back away. It's so unlike him, except this time, I know it really is him. That's what hurts the most. "You know what happened to him," he says after a beat, his eyes falling to the floor.

I can't take this. "Arlo, I'm so sorry."

"That's all we ever do, isn't it? Apologise to each other for not being good enough." He looks back up at me, *grinning*. I want to scream and cry and laugh all at once. I'm suffocating. Then he reaches up to cup my face with his bare hands, skin to skin. I can only imagine the toll this must be taking on him.

I don't pull away. I never want to.

"We're going to save the world, Mars." His voice is so delicate, like he's whispering into my soul.

"How can you be so sure?" I want to hold on to his wrists, but I know that would push the boundary. I never want his touch to dissipate.

"We will. I'm sure of it. It has to work. We have no choice."

There it is again, that word. *Choice.* A thing we're all meant to have, but never really do.

"I love you, Arlo," I say it. I vomit out the words. If I held it in any longer, my lungs would explode in my chest and I would have made an awful mess.

My words visibly hit him, but his smile doesn't falter. I don't expect him to respond. In fact, I worry he might. The words linger in the air for far too long. Then:

"I love you too, Mars."

I squeeze my eyes shut. It stings.

"But not..."

"Not in that way," I finish. "Not the same way."

"No. Not the same way."

I knew this, and I knew it would hurt, regardless. But I'm happy I finally brought it up.

"I'm sorry I didn't read the signs, when we... when I—"

He stops me and pulls our foreheads so close they're almost touching. "I didn't hate what we did. I let it happen. You did nothing wrong. I've had a lot of time to think about that night, and I regret nothing. I just don't make the connections the same way other people do. I could never share that with anyone, so it would never have been fair to you. But I love you, Mars. I really do. I hope my way counts enough to mean something."

"It means the world." I mean it. Knowing he sees me the way he does is enough to calm my mind, body, and soul. In fact, it means more.

Never let go of me, Arlo.

"Let me try this, Mars." He lets his hands slip from my face, but he stays just as close, looking into my eyes.

I can't. I know I need to. I hate that I know that, but I can't.

"You have to let me come with you. I need to be by your side all the way."

"I know. That's why I..."

I was right. He wants us. He needs us.

"You can't stop us. When the time comes, just keep everyone else alive."

I'm speechless, but I have to give him my word, even if it kills me.

I close my eyes and nod, a tear falling onto my lap. I'm not embarrassed, though.

I think Arlo may be on the verge of crying too. When I finally open my eyes, I see the redness around the whites of his beautiful eyes, and I know he feels the same.

"Being terrified is good, right? It's human," he says; the tremble finally comes through his voice.

I nod so fast. I need to hold him and let him know it's okay.

"Can I hug you, please?" I ask. When he nods, I wrap my arms around his neck so tightly I worry I may snap it.

He tenses and relaxes in the space of a second before his arms close around my back. I feel so small in his embrace, yet so protected. I feel safe in his arms. Just like in my dreams. He's home.

"Mars... you." He pulls back slightly, his eyes erratic, his breathing uneven.

"What?"

"You. You can kiss me, if you want."

I don't process his words right away, but I drop my arms when I do. He's just saying that; he's saying what he thinks I want to hear... *He's right. I do want to hear it, but...*

"You know I can't do that." I don't think I've ever had to say something so painful. But I know I made the right decision, and I know Arlo knows it as well.

He closes his eyes and nods before standing back to his full height.

"I'll see you tomorrow," he says, as though this entire conversation never happened. Maybe that's for the best.

"I'll see you tomorrow, Arlo."

I don't look at his face to see his reaction. I simply stand and head towards the door.

"No one else has to suffer," I say as I unlock it, fixing my eyes on the ground.

"I promise," he says, and then I leave.

I sit on my bed, alone, braiding small strands of my hair then pulling them out just as something to do. I think back to what Marianne told me about Julian. I never met him, and I suppose nothing Marianne could ever tell me will enable me to fully understand what she had with him, but I can't help but relate it to me and Arlo. What we are to each other. What he is to me. We're not lovers, not just friends, but a rare third thing that we haven't quite invented a word for yet. Maybe there's a language out there that could truly explain it. It is beyond just love in what we understand it as, but it's *everything*.

I cry myself to sleep. I knew I would.

Chapter Thirty Three

Arlo
Now

I'm startled awake by a loud pounding at my door. I thought it was thunder at first, but when it doesn't stop, I realise someone is trying to get in—desperately.

I jump up and head towards it. My thoughts drift back to earlier, and I hope it's Mars coming back to talk. I don't want them to reconsider my offer, I don't know why I even said it, I just wanted to see them smile, yet their reaction left me feeling lost. Confused.

I want to see them again, alone, before we end this. I need them to know how much they mean to me. How I want nothing more than to spend the rest of my life by their side.

I want to speak with Rani again, too. We only got to briefly talk this evening, nowhere near as long as I'd hoped. I need to apologise again for dragging her into all of this mess—I need to know she *really* knows that. I want to remind her of when we first met, and all the fun things we did together: our trip last year, when she invited me to stay with her family for Diwali, and how loved I felt with them all. I want to talk about the dog walk trips we took to Buttermere, the fish and chip shop we went to on our first night in the city. I need to give her bomber jacket back, though I don't even know where it is. I don't want her to be mad at me.

I couldn't tell her about my plan. I just... She deserves to be happy. Free. *She'll try to stop me.*

I want her to know how much she changed my life. Have I ever told her that? I must remember to do that in the morning...

I bat the thoughts away when I'm at the door. Muffled cries reach me, and I have no choice but to swing the door open and—

"Arlo, run!" My father is on his knees, his knuckles bloody and pupils burst wide. But in the space of a second, he collapses onto the ground as the attacker bluntly hits his skull and stands right behind him. Right in my eye-line.

Michael.

"Hello, my darling boy." His voice is as smooth as ever, his teeth as sharp as his grin.

He doesn't have to speak again for me to freeze on the spot; my vision zooms out, and blackness swarms my mind.

No. Not possible.

"Come on, now." Stepping over my father's body, he crosses the threshold into my room, catching both my shoulders in his grip and forcing himself into my space. "Did you really think you'd be able to hide from me? Did you think running for all those months did anything to help you? Surely you know how much I need you, and how important you are."

I don't have room in my mind to think of anything other than *this is it. This is the end of old time.*

I feel the Star crawling back. How could I have been so stupid to think it had gone forever? Of course, it was always lying dormant, waiting for a trigger to bring it back out into the open. We were so close to doing this our way, to having the power in our own hands. I'm never that lucky, though.

I'd never felt Michael this strongly before, even in my darkest times with him.

He is using all the power he has to get through to me—*The Star*.

He presses his cold hands all over my face, his blackened thumbs squeezing the spot just above my eyes, between my brows, rendering my whole body slack.

"Wake, my Star. The end is now, it is time. We are ready."

And he has me—mind, body, and soul.

Act 4

History Has
A Habit

CHAPTER THIRTY FOUR

Michael
Now

Millions of years ago, I opened my eyes. I began to exist in the boundless expanse of nothing and everything all at once. It took a millennium to figure out my purpose. *Our* purpose, but once we did, everything fell into place.

Earth, turning away from its problems, became my project. Our project. I observed the way humans interacted, how they lied and fought and killed and lied and lied and lied so much until their very sky gave in. It was something to fix—something we could turn into a paradise.

They have their gods and deities, and whilst our work may seem like that of an omnipotent power, we only seek to correct. A mild intervention, so to speak. We're only using the power we were granted and putting it to good use. Earth is not our first project, and it will not be our last. But is *has* been the most fun.

The others took a little longer to bring around, but we came together in the end. Over time, I planted the seeds, and once we found our vessels, the thrill of it all came flooding over me, over us, like nothing I've ever felt before.

The fragment of my soul, buried deep in the Ashtown boy, meant I could bring this plan so much closer to fruition. And then, as if this project couldn't get any more fun, the world changed rapidly, and I couldn't have been more overjoyed at what I had to work with.

We are going to bring about the new world, leaving our mark, and restarting humanity. When it happens, they will all understand, and they will thank us for it.

And Nicholas has done a remarkable job at readying us for the end. I must not be so harsh with him; after all, I never could have done it without him. But I'm wasting too much time now... the longer I stay amongst humanity as it is, the more it seeps into my being and warps my perception. They're all parasites, overruled by emotion and sentiment. Letting it dictate their lives. It's such a waste of everything.

But it won't have to bother me for much longer.

Of course, I always knew where they ran off to. I don't understand how they have become so foolish. Surely, they should have figured out I'm always one step ahead? We're connected, the four of us. No matter how much they try to fight it, or even believe they've won, I always have the upper hand.

I always did, even before.

Because let's face it, it really was my plan all along.

Having them by my side again, and knowing they'll stay, is the best feeling in the world.

Here we go.

5th December 1947

It bothers me sometimes that I never found out what happened to Nicholas. Maybe I should have gone back to see if he made it out. Did I want him to make it out?
Of course I wish he was still alive.
I do. I really do. I could have saved him.
I could have. I believe.

6th April 1994

I met a man today and he looked so much like Julian. Same height and build and manner! It was uncanny at first, and it upset me. He's not left my mind since he returned to it. It's nearly five years since—
Oh, I'm never going to get over this, am I? It's going to eat at me forever.

Sorry, I got carried away. But yes, this man! We bumped into each other in St. James' Park whilst I was admiring the pelicans and not paying attention to where I was walking. I do that a lot, always up in my head, but he stopped me and made sure I was okay and it was then that I realised that not only did he look so familiar, but he was also like me. A vampire.
It always feels weird to call us that, maybe we're not quite like the myths, but we are undead. Immortal.
Look, maybe it was just the nostalgia of the location but I really did see Julian in him. And I felt as if this was fate. I know it sounds so stupid really, I'm not sure I believe a whole lot in fate but yeah, he was like me, and he smiled at me in such a friendly manner, and I just saw Julian. With slightly more reddish hair—oh listen to me!
Julian was my best friend. The only best friend I've ever really had. I sometimes feel like I'm doomed to lose everyone

around me, nothing ever works out well, so yeah, maybe it was just the circumstances of the situation clouding my brain or whatever, but I've arranged to meet this man again, to see if he is truly as nice as he originally seemed. Then perhaps I can start my life again. Let go of the past.
Start doing good again.

His name is Isiah Dumont, French of origin I believe, though he's travelled around a lot. I can't wait to learn more about him.

—Taken from the diaries of Marianne Ashtown

CHAPTER THIRTY FIVE

Mars
Now

I'm stood as still as a statue. Staring. Just staring. Voices chorusing behind me, beside me, all around. Shouting. Crying. Anger, so much of it.

"Right, well, they didn't leave, because they promised they wouldn't. Arlo was just down the hall in his room. We all planned to leave this morning. They—" More shouting cuts off Rani's words as Fran and Carmen argue. Carmen insists we never should have trusted him (Jerome, she made that clear) while Fran retaliates, arguing that there was no Manipulation involved. Yet Carmen bites back with the point that real human manipulation is still a thing. And some people, clearly, are very good at it.

Arlo's room is empty, and Jerome is nowhere to be seen, either. Everyone thinks they just left, but I know that's not the case, and Rani knows it, too.

Arlo's room was left in a fashion to suggest he wasn't expecting to leave. Sheets crumpled, rug crooked and slightly folded on the floor. Arlo is very particular with precision and tidiness, so something feels *off* about it. He always leaves things pristine.

"Arlo didn't leave," I say to whoever wants to listen. I stare blankly into his cold room, picturing where we sat mere hours before. Then the shouting stops, and I realise people actually are listening to me.

"What are you suggesting? He was taken?" Fran asks, crossing her arms.

Carmen responds first. "That deceitful bastard Jerome did it. I knew he was lying. I knew there was something off about him. This was all a trap. He wasn't himself, but he let us all believe that he was, and—"

Fran cuts her off. "Carmen, I swear that wasn't it."

"Oh, for the love of god, if I have to say it one more time—"

"Carmen, please. I believe Fran. He wasn't lying," Lawrence interferes, and I'm surprised at his tone.

"Arlo trusted his father. Arlo doesn't trust many people," Rani adds, rubbing her hands over her biceps as if she were cold. Yet it's clear by her body language that's not the case. She's spacing out. Like me.

Something happened last night.

"Michael," Rani finally says, joining my side. "Do you think he..."

"I do." I didn't until she said it, but it makes perfect sense. He always needed to have one up on us, to mislead us into thinking we're ahead. He probably knew where they both were the whole time. A chill shatters my spine, and I want to be sick. I must hold it together. I need to. For Arlo. For all of us.

"He has to have taken them to Edinburgh. That's where he plans on enacting his plan, isn't it? Isn't that what you said?" Rani's words are erratic and shaky, her eyes searching mine.

"I hope to the skies that's where they've gone, because that's where we're all going. Right now."

No one moves when I do until I feel Rani's presence behind me, and then I sense two more heartbeats and a wave of cigarette smoke. Everyone is coming. I think about praying to a god I don't believe in, because I need all the hope I can get if I'm dragging everyone to hell with me. Only a handful of other Thorns are currently in the building, so we're already setting off with fewer people than we wanted.

I leave Casper a voicemail telling him to be in Edinburgh as soon as he can. He won't make it today but he'll want to be with us.

After Marianne returns from her search of the grounds, she nods along with my decision, and by lunchtime, we're all on the train up to Scotland.

It all happens so fast; I barely have time to process it, yet my brain keeps reminding me: *you can't leave him alone in this, you promised*. And I hate breaking promises.

I will kill Michael if I have to. I will tear his body apart limb from limb and I won't stop until I know there's no chance of him ever coming back. I'll do anything to protect Arlo. If he has him... god, I can't even bring myself to think about it. I can't lose him again. I refuse.

Arlo will do whatever it takes to save the world. I know he will, but I won't let him sacrifice himself to do so. Am I being selfish? I feel like I am.

Skies, *save the world*. He's just one innocent man.

"This is it, isn't it?" Rani asks me at some point, possibly when we're getting on the train, I don't know.

"It is," I reply too late. She's not beside me when I say it.

I stare out of the window for most of the journey, allowing my focus to blur with the trees as I try to clear my mind.

Marianne is opposite me, and Lawrence is beside me. He keeps exposing his palm on his knee, as if inviting me to hold it. I briefly do, but it doesn't help at all. His hand is clammy and firm.

I think of the softness of Arlo's skin, his warm breath across my face, and his soulful, wandering eyes.

My angel.

MARIANNE DOESN'T SPEAK a word the entire way. She rests her hands against the table and plays with the rings on her fingers, chewing her mouth, but keeping her gaze on the green hills. Our reflections meet a few times, but she doesn't react.

I think she knows it's the end, too. I don't know how she feels about it, but I could take a good guess. Nicholas will be there, Michael's right-hand man. I don't know what he'll do when he meets his sister again. I don't know anything. We might not even be going to the right place.

Or maybe we're too late...

EVERYTHING ELSE HAPPENS IN FLASHES.

We exit the station amongst the masses of tourists. Lawrence lights up the second we hit the afternoon light, vintage shades on. Someone hits Carmen in the shins with a suitcase.

I'm blinded by my fear.

Fran squeezes my shoulder and swings in front of me, smiling. I don't remember what she says.

"Follow any and all signs." Marianne finally speaks up.

"Arthur's Seat?" Rani.

"Old or New Town?" Carmen.

"Anywhere you're compelled to avoid. He'll be keeping us away deliberately."

Fran makes a half-arsed joke about feeling like a superhero, but her voice is quickly drowned out by the surrounding crowds and the bagpipes and car horns.

"Split into two groups," Lawrence suggests.

"Fran, Elise, and Lawrence, go with Mars. Everyone else, with me." Marianne looks at Rani and Carmen and the other two Thorns with us and speaks with a deeper voice than normal.

We all silently agree. They split to the right, and we turn left, heading through the park.

More memories flash: Fran putting her hands in her pockets, chains dangling from her studded belt. Elise clearing her throat. Lawrence tying his hair back. *Arlo cupping my cheeks, whispering to me. Arlo. Arlo. Arlo.*

"Anything feel off to you yet?" I realise a little too late that Fran is speaking to me directly.

"What? Oh." *Everything.* "No."

"Everything seems so normal, doesn't it? What if we're miles away? Did you get a response from Casper?"

"Casper used to love bringing Ben here. It was their safe place," Lawrence says, staring straight ahead while lighting up another cigarette.

"Everything will seem normal, that's the point." I ignore the sting of Lawrence's statement.

"No one is acting any different. Maybe we're not too late," Elise says, squinting up at the sun. "We'd feel it, right? If it's started."

"I bet they're at the castle. It would make so much sense." Fran looks up at the old building on the cliff face on our left. Still, there's nothing out of the ordinary, but you can never tell from this distance. I can't see anyone. Can you normally see people from that distance? From any point at this angle? I try to think back to the last and only time I went there.

I almost walk into a dog. I feel guilty, but I don't acknowledge the owner's comment.

"Look, there are people up there. Maybe I'm wrong then."

Fran points up at a few figures in the distance. It feels completely normal for a second until the chill hits me.

Tourists can't stand there. Something's wrong.

My vision focuses on the figures. They're not moving and are equidistant from each other.

"They're not tourists, are they," Lawrence says, but it's not a question.

Fran swears at the same time I realise one figure is waving at us. A slow, robotic wave.

I turn to scan my surroundings. Not a single person is looking up at the castle. No one takes pictures; no one is looking up at all. It's almost as if they're *avoiding* looking at it.

"Okay guys. You're creeping me out," Elise mutters. I think.

"You ever been up to the castle before?" Lawrence is already on it, pulling a passer-by to the side. The man pulls out his earphones and asks Lawrence to repeat the question. He's nowhere near as fazed as someone would normally be if they were manhandled in public by a stranger.

"The castle? You ever been? Edinburgh Castle, up there." He points up to clearly indicate what he's talking about, but the man doesn't even follow his finger.

Instead, he shrugs and says in a strong Glaswegian accent, "What castle?"

The world spins.

"Marianne," Lawrence says.

"On it." Fran pulls out her phone.

Then we're running, and I look back one final time to answer the nagging, possibly insane, question I just asked myself. When I notice the waving figure has gone, I find my answer.

They're expecting us.

Now.

We reach the royal mile before the others, but it doesn't matter, because the second we turn the corner, we sense it. The Manipulation. You can *smell* it. And every single person in front of us is walking away, like characters from a video game. No one looks up or speaks.

I've never seen anything this intense before—the power to command an entire city.

But that's just the starter. The teaser, if you will.

"We don't have much time, like *at all*," I say, striding forward without checking if the three of them are beside me.

We push past the mindless bodies, rerouting their destinations without even questioning it. I feel like I'm in a fun house, where the endpoint keeps getting further and further away. The Manipulation is so strong it makes me want to vomit.

Lawrence collapses onto his knees beside me, groaning. "What the fuck."

Fran continues striding forward, unfazed.

She really is immune, and Lawrence was never very strong. I wonder again how many other people are immune to this. How many people close by even. I can't see anyone else trying to fight it now, though. I've never come across anyone else in my undead life who is like Fran, and right now, it feels as though we're the only four people on earth with minds still our own. Fran's the only one immune here, but it doesn't matter how many of them there are out there, does it? Because humans can never overpower this alone. Arlo was right. They will be so far in the minority, and so far apart —not prepared, the wave would be too much. They... *God*, how is she so unaffected by it? It's choking me.

Fran takes the lead, shouting and turning back to face us as she continues walking backwards. "Come on!" she shouts. "We're nearly there."

Elise topples forward and vomits blood onto the floor, groaning and kicking her feet into the ground in frustration. "Oh, fuck this," she growls. I step down to reach for her hand, but she shakes her head. "Go," she gags. "Leave me. I'm done."

I sigh, but force myself forward. One down then. I focus on Fran ahead, neither stopping nor slowing.

I turn back once I taste blood in the back of my throat. I reach for Lawrence, who manages to keep up with me, but stumbles again until he's practically crawling on his hands and knees. He grabs at my arm, gripping on tight and dragging himself up from the ground. Blood drips down his nose, and his eyes are bloodshot. "Fucking hell," he grumbles, struggling.

Then I see them: the five figures walking towards us. I soon realise it's Marianne in front with the other Thorns, collectively dragging Carmen and Rani forwards as they try to turn away.

They won't make it.

"Mars! Come on!"

I turn back to Fran with gritted teeth. "They're not going to make it," I say.

Fran shakes her head and bites her lip. "I know. I know. We don't have time, though. We need to get to the castle. This can't be for nothing."

She's right, but it hurts all the same.

"Just go!" Lawrence shouts. "I'll follow, just give me a minute..." Then his eyes roll back, and he topples to the ground, his grip slipping from my hand.

I can't waste another second.

We continue up towards the castle, with Fran clinging to my hand as I try my best to clear my mind and force my guards up like I've never had to before. Lucy was nothing compared to this.

A lot of minds are at play here. *The cult.*

We're struggling up, our legs working slowly, but we're almost there.

"Mars!" someone shouts from behind. It's not Lawrence, but Marianne.

We turn back around to see Marianne. Alone.

"I had to leave them. I wasn't strong enough. Even the Thorns weren't prepared for this." There's sorrow and guilt in her eyes. "Rani will kill me."

"She will, but if it means Arlo lives, and we can stop Michael from literally turning the world into 1984 on steroids, it's a sacrifice we're going to have to make," Fran says matter-of-factly.

She's only human. She attended none of our training sessions, she...

I want to laugh at the absurdity of it all, but my brain is too occupied for that. I can only think about reaching Arlo before anything else happens. The other six are scattered down the street, too far away to catch up. I force myself to turn away.

"I'm sorry I couldn't help you all more," Marianne says, her throat bubbling with rage. "I don't even know how I could have prepared you for this though. It's so much stronger than I ever imagined."

We're nearly at the top now, and I feel the blood drip from my nostril. A single drip onto the pavement. It lessens as we get closer, but these final steps sap all my strength.

This is it.

We reach the summit: the stone walkway leading up to the grounds. And in a sudden wave, like hitting the eye of the storm, the Manipulation fades, and I can breathe again. The force releases.

I see them then, despite my blurred vision. I make out their outlines. Vampires, a lot of them, donning maroon robes—almost holy garments. They all join hands and surround the perimeter of the grounds.

A figure emerges, dressed head to foot in a black, tailored suit. He adjusts the cuffs while striding forward.

Marianne tenses beside me, gritting her teeth with her fangs on show.

"Ahh, sister!" Nicholas Ashtown grins, his voice deep and teasing. "So wonderful to see you alive, after all these years. And you brought friends! You always struggled to make those, didn't you?" He drops his hands behind his back and tilts his head slightly. "You know I can't let you in, though, don't you?"

His grin is like ice, shooting daggers into all our chests.

Chapter Thirty Six

Arlo
One Hour Ago

When I wake, I don't know who I am.

I'm lying on a cold, wooden floor, facing a grand fireplace. The room would be bare, if not for my presence.

I take three breaths before I realise there are wings on my back. I reach over for them in confusion, trying to grasp at any memory from *before*.

I take another two breaths before I turn on my side and see a man—no, an angel—lying in a peaceful slumber. Red wings cover his entire body, and his long auburn hair spreads across the ground, circling him like a halo.

One more breath. Something pulls me back by the neck, choking me and lifting me off the ground, dragging my feet across the floor. A cry escapes me.

"It took you long enough to wake," says the voice in my ear while I grab at its hands around my throat.

"Help!" I shout, banging my heel into the wood. But it's no use. There's no one else here.

The figure shoves its hand over my mouth, and I feel the bite of claws on my cheek.

Help me, I think. I don't know who or where I am. What's happening?

The angel beside me rouses and sits up slightly, his features morphed with confusion as he rubs the back of his head.

"What—" His eyes widen at his surroundings before our eyes lock, yet his gaze flits quickly to whatever is behind me, holding me tight against its body. One arm clutches my ribs, while the other is pressed on my lips.

"Get off him!" The angel staggers to a stand and dives forward to pull me away. He almost succeeds, loosening my captor's grip as he grabs hold of my body. Yet the thing from behind drops me entirely, and my back hits the floor, impacting my wings with a thunderous crack. A horrific shooting pain bursts through my spine, and black dots cloud my vision.

Slowly, I turn to watch as the figure behind me reveals itself to be another winged creature—this one with long white hair and a pinstripe suit. Grey feathered wings elegantly follow his movements as he reaches for the chin of the red angel and thrusts him against the stone wall, holding him up. I can't move—I'm paralysed—but I can read the panic on the red angel's face. He claws for the white angel's shoulders. My saviour successfully grabs for the attacker's neck, but then I watch as the white angel slips a hand under the other's shirt to poke a nail into its chest. The red angel's eyes bulge as he cries out and drops his hands. The white angel releases him then, knocking my saviour to his knees, who looks up, pleading with his eyes.

The white angel has his back to me, but I hear his words clearly. "There, there. You were always easier to control. I only need to see your eyes. Will you let me look into your eyes?"

The red angel stays silent, clutching his chest and directing his gaze to the ground. The white angel pulls at the other's hair, dragging it back and forcing his head up, leaving him with no choice but to face his attacker, his eyes clenched shut.

"Will you let me look in your eyes?" The white angel growls now, growing frustrated. When he does not respond, the white angel reaches for the red angel's chest again, where a dark patch of blood has now formed. Seemingly out of fear, the red angel finally gives in with a whimper.

"Good." The attacker says, holding the red angel's chin tightly, and tilting his face to meet his own. "Oh good. It's still there. That's a relief." The white angel scoffs, then drops the red angel, letting him fall onto his hands and knees until he's almost kissing the ground.

Then he turns to me.

I try to scramble back, but my back burns. It's no use. He holds me by the fabric of my shirt and presses one knee over my ribcage, crushing my airways.

"Will you be a good boy too?" he says, grinning. He's too close to my face now. I think I'm going to pass out. "It's time."

Time for what?

With tense brows, he brushes the hair from my face and stares directly in both of my eyes. He relaxes before pulling away, releasing the pressure from my sternum and stepping back.

"That will do. I'll be back in a bit, and then we begin."

I watch him stride away with painful confidence, leaving the room through one of two giant archways.

I'm stunned, completely unaware of *everything*. *What's going on?* But then the red angel beside me groans and tries to stand, clutching his injured chest.

He limps over to me. I want to move away, but as he bends down gently to my side, I see his bloodshot, green eyes and suddenly feel calm.

"Arlo?" he says, worry painting his features. "Arlo, are you still in there? Am I speaking to my son or The Star?"

And just like that, as he turns to slump beside me, tipping his head back in pain, I remember everything.

WE DON'T SPEAK for a while. After about five minutes, my father's breathing settles, and the wound in his chest closes up again, returning to its former scar. The scar, from when he was turned. *Both times.* His weakness. Something I very quickly concluded was probably used many times by Michael to get him to stay loyal. By his side. To keep Jerome at bay and The Moon shining through.

A few moments later, two figures appear in each entrance way, robed from head to foot in dark red fabric. They don't speak—they don't even look armed—but I know why they're there. To keep us from trying to escape while Michael readies his plan.

The end of old time.

"Moon," I whisper, fixing my eyes on both guards.

My father hastily pulls himself up, most likely worried he'd lost me again. But I can almost hear the cogs turning in his head when he replies, his voice monotone. "Star."

I know they can hear every word, but what I don't know is how smart they truly are. I must tread carefully.

"He's coming back for us, right?" I ask, quizzical.

"I hope so. I feel like a prisoner."

We keep our voices quiet to not come across as too theatrical.

"Do you think they know what we are?" My dad leans slightly towards me with a fake egotistical smirk.

I forge a laugh. "I doubt they understand."

The guard to the left sways slightly, an indication they very much can hear us.

I've never had to act like this before. It takes all my strength to keep calm and collected.

"How long will he be? I'm impatient," Jerome says, standing and wandering over to the giant window behind us. He holds himself with an air of confidence, the embodiment of a ruler looking over his kingdom. He's good at this.

I stand to figure out where we are. A stately home of some sort. When I reach the window, my stomach drops.

Edinburgh Castle. But the only people I can see are robed guards.

Then I spot him. Both of them. Michael and Nicholas, conversing in the sunlight, like a painting from a stained-glass window. Michael, an angel incarnate. Nicholas, a loyal and devoted disciple.

"It must be time soon. The humans have scurried away already," scoffs my father. I feel a prickle of worry then. Perhaps he isn't acting; perhaps I misread this whole situation.

But then he shifts his right wing, so it brushes mine, and reaches for my hand. I tug at his sleeve to ground myself.

"We're going to win," he whispers, almost too quiet.

That's the only confirmation I need to know he's himself. We've managed, by some miracle, to maintain the autonomy of our bodies. What Michael did to us didn't work this time.

We won. *Ha.*

Jerome turns away abruptly and strides into the empty room.

"Are you keeping us hostage?" he asks the guards, turning their attention to him. "Well?"

I come up close beside him. Now it's time to really act.

"We're impatient. Is he nearly ready? We've waited too long for this. Let us out, will you? We need to speak with him," I say. I don't even sound like myself.

The two guards, youthful in appearance but aged by vampirism, step forward to look at each other, as if they were unprepared for this situation.

"We're under strict orders to—" The far guard speaks, but Jerome raises a fist in a demand for silence. The guard obeys, nearly choking.

"A-A-Ahh. You'll listen to us." Dad's Manipulation is toxic, even to my own senses, but he's doing the best he can. "We're going to walk past you both. You're going to remain here, and we're going to speak with The Sun. You know who we are, don't you?"

They both nod, slowly but clearly.

"Good. Well. That didn't have to get messy."

And then we're both walking down the ornate hall, quickening our paces. Once we're sure we're out of earshot, my father turns to me and grips my shoulders, despite my discomfort.

"We're sticking to the plan, yeah?" he says. His odd heartbeat races.

I nod, a ball lodging in my throat. "Yes. It's the only way."

I want to see my friends one last time to tell them I love them.

My dad straightens and lessens his grip but keeps his hands on my shirt-covered shoulders. "We're not. We..." He gulps, making a frustrated 'hmm' sound before clearing his throat. "I will not get to tell your mother how sorry I am. She'll be okay, won't she?"

Without us.

I can't speak. No words even come close to forming on my lips. If I do this, my mother will be alone. She will come home to police at her door telling her I was involved in some freak accident. That it was quick, and I didn't suffer. They'll apologise and take off their hats, pressing it to their chests out of respect. She'll fall to her knees, refusing to believe it. Bess will be barking, not understanding why she's screaming.

But if I don't do this, she'll never be my mother again. Either way, I've lost her. I've lost Rani. Mars. I've lost every single person who ever smiled at me or helped me or did all they could to be good people.

This might not work. We're all out of our depth here, but I would never forgive myself for not trying.

I need to do this.

Forgive me, Rani. Mum. Mars. I'm sorry. I'm sorry. I'm sorry.

Ben, I'm doing this for you. Casper, I'm sorry for the pain you live with. I'm doing this for you all. Please, please forgive me.

"I just hope it works," I say. My father kisses my forehead and pulls me close. I hug him and feel the pounding of his heart against my chest. It's at a human pace now—a sound I hated feeling all my life and was glad to never hear again. Now, it heals me. It calms me. It's life.

And this is how I'm choosing to live mine.

I choose life.

"I love you, Arlo."

"I love you too, dad."

Then we step out into the midday sun to see Michael, almost as if he was expecting us. He reaches out a hand for us to follow him across the courtyard.

"Are we ready?" He smiles.

I really hope this works.

7ᵗʰ *May 2019*

Nicholas, if you're out there, would you leave a sign for me?
Would you have left anything for me to find?
You may not want to speak to me, and honestly, if we ever
met again, I'm not quite sure I'd know what to say to you.
But would you—

Actually no. I know what I'd say. I'd tell you I love you. And
I miss you. I lost you more than once but you never left my
mind, even when all I could remember of you was your
smile.

I was made to forget you.
I can only hope you died before anything got to you.
I'm sorry that I mean that. It would just be for the best. I
don't want you to have lived only to suffer through what is to
come.

8ᵗʰ *May 2019*

Dorabella. Dorabella. Dorabella.
I will see you again. Save some flowers for me.

9ᵗʰ *May 2019*

~~I should have killed you, Jerome.~~
~~But then Arlo wouldn't exist.~~
~~But he also would have never had to suffer.~~
What am I doing?

18ᵗʰ *June 2019*

I wonder if I'd tried harder, I might have truly been able to
save you, Jerome.
We did so many great things. We helped hundreds of people.
Where did I go wrong?

You had good in you.
I'll never forgive you, but if you truly are Arlo's father like I
suspect, then there still is good in you. You just maybe can't
see it.

12th June 2019
My name is Marianne Ashtown and the devil may have
followed me once but not anymore.

—Taken from the diaries of Marianne Ashtown

CHAPTER THIRTY SEVEN

Mars
Now

"Oh, for fuck's sake!" Fran shouts, barging past myself and Marianne to storm straight up to Nicholas, smacking him in the face with her spiked wrist cuffs, aiming and hitting home. He's too stunned to stop it.

Nicholas staggers back, clutching his bloody cheek and laughing as he processes what just happened. A few of his followers break the circle and hurry to his aid, but he raises a hand and they stop in sync. "No need. They brought a human, how... *pathetic*," he says with his back to them, wiping his cheek with his free hand and licking the blood from his fingers.

Fran stands, panting, with a disgusted scowl on her face.

"That's your brother?" She turns her nose up and points between Marianne and Nicholas.

He responds first. "Yes, we're related. Can't you tell?" He flashes a cartoonish grin, spinning beside Marianne as if trying to prove something. "And how do you know my lovely sister? Because you're sure not meant to know what we are. Do you know what we are? Truly?" He flicks his head to the side with an annoying confidence I want to slap straight out of him. My fists clench, and I grit my teeth together in frustration.

Step back, Fran, I want to say, but I don't. She doesn't even seem the slightest bit afraid.

"Oh my *god*. Seriously? You're making me cringe at how hard you're trying right now." Fran covers her mouth to stifle a laugh. Then she looks over at the distant followers and shouts, "You seriously follow this guy? Have you got nothing better to do with your lives?"

No one reacts, and I'm suddenly aware of how silent everything is. I can't even hear the birds.

"Honey." Fran steps closer to Nicholas, squaring right up to him. There's barely a few inches of height between them. Marianne steps forward to pull Fran back, but Fran bats her hand away and meets the vampire's eye-line, reaching out to straighten his tie. "Do you think I would have made it all the way up here if I didn't know what you were?" Then she grins.

"Fran, stop it. Step back," Marianne successfully pulls Fran back this time, but the human's eyes never leave his as distance is put between them again.

"It's impressive, mind you," Fran continues. "Did it take all of you to do this? Aww, and I still got through?"

"Fran. Please. Stop antagonising him." Marianne stands between the pair, but I note how Nicholas steps back slightly. He's trying not to show it, but Fran really found the crack in his façade. And she knows it. She wasn't meant to slip through. Had he considered this variable at all? That immune humans exist?

Does Michael know? He must do... it can't have fazed him. But still, it works its magic on Nicholas.

"No, no, sister. Let the human continue. I enjoy a challenge." He smirks to hide his discomfort.

"Shut up. I'm not your sister. I've not been your sister for a very long time," Marianne spits, closing the gap between them.

Nicholas only looks down at her, seemingly unbothered again. "Oh, but I thought we were about to play happy families again!" His sarcasm stinks. "Mummy and daddy would be so proud of us. Look how far we've come!"

"Where is he?" she snaps, pulling out a knife and pressing it under his jaw.

"Who?" The blade does not frighten him. He doesn't even blink.

"Don't play with me. Where's the kid? Tell me, and I won't kill you all."

"What, do you want me to pick who I care about the least or?"

Marianne growls. "Tell me. Now."

The blade draws blood and only then does Nicholas flinch. She'll push it in all the way. I know she will.

"Oh." He sounds genuinely surprised now. "Your eyes. You're letting it—"

She presses the blade in deeper, and Nicholas has no choice but to tilt his head back and choke.

What can he see in her eyes? I think back to that day in the woods. The things she confessed. She was preparing for this, even before she knew he still lived.

At his exposed vulnerability, I decide it's time to strike.

But just as I'm about to step forward, I feel a presence behind me then—

"Right. Where are we up to?" *Lawrence.*

I turn around, and there he stands, blood coating his hands, arms, and...

Carmen and Rani let out a huge gasp for air as they collapse onto the ground, peeling themselves from his grip before slowly finding their feet again. Their brows remain stern as their eyes adjust. Finally, the pair of them stand and take in their surroundings. Rani has a streak of blood on her lips, a nauseous pull to her mouth, and I try to piece together what I'm witnessing. Blood? They drank his blood? They... I nearly pounce on Lawrence as furious hatred floods my veins at the thought of him turning them. How could he? After everything?

But then I sense them... Their heartbeats. He didn't turn them. He just...

"I genuinely didn't think it would work, but they're stubborn girls, and apparently that's enough to overcome *anything*," Lawrence says, the corners of his mouth quirking upwards. "Just a temporary beverage to tide us over this mess. Well worth a try. Can't believe we never thought of this sooner!" He raises his bloody hands, exposing the not-quite healing scars on each arm as he catches his own breath and sways on his feet.

He dragged the pair of them up here? By himself?

I always seem to underestimate him, time and time again...He always does the most surprising selfless acts. Carmen gags and turns away. While the pull of the field is weak now in the centre, the strength it would have taken to get here is enormous. I don't know how they managed it on his blood alone. I nearly passed out myself. But leaving Arlo is the last thing Rani would do, and now we're witnessing what love really is. The strength it holds.

Months ago, the thing inside Arlo nearly convinced Rani to tear her very face off. Now she's standing beside her loyal partner before some of the strongest forces we've ever witnessed in our lives, and the pair of them rule the moment. No one speaks, not even Nicholas.

Then Lawrence collapses with a thud, and for a moment, I actually think he's dead until Carmen flips him over. His eyes roll back under his long, matted waves. His mouth seems fixed with permanent smugness as his head flops to one side.

Nicholas clears his throat comically. "Are we finished?" He raises a brow, looking around at his followers. "Please, someone spare me. Tell me where the cameras are. I want to collect my two hundred and fifty pounds!' He claps slowly then, surveying the scene before him. "It's impressive, honestly. I'll give you that, sis, but..." He takes a deep breath, holding back another laugh.

"Really? This is all you brought with you? Are you saving the best until last or is this truly the group of saviours you settled on?" He lets out a high-pitched laugh behind his fist as he presses it against his mouth. "Oh look! Here they come now! Can we start the party?" He looks out down the street to the three remaining Thorns, who have finally caught up, the slight break in the circle having given them a boost.

He looks as if he's about to hurl more insults at us, though I can read deep down that he's surprised by not only one human, but *three* getting past his wards. He didn't expect it—none of us did. But he's the only person this could scare. And I know it does. Because he doesn't even see it coming when Rani strides forward with rage in her eyes. She wipes the excess blood from her chin and thrusts her knee hard between Nicholas's legs. Marianne staggers back as Nicholas collapses to his knees with an uncontrollable cry.

"Show us where Arlo is or I'll end you," she spits on his fallen body without giving him a chance to even look up at her.

Everyone else seems stunned, rooted to the spot, but I take advantage of this distraction and *run*. I clocked the figures the second she marched up to him, and I had about three seconds to decide. It was all I could think to do.

I'm charging up to the castle, colliding with three bodies at once. I push, but they overpower me, chucking me to the ground like a rock and thrashing out with their arms and fangs. But before they close the gaps in my line of sight, all three humans run past me without looking back; they sprint like never before, heading straight for the castle grounds.

With a scream, I kick and push with all my might, knocking out one of my attackers and opening up a gap for me to sit. I kick the second captor to my left, stunning them enough to free my arm and press my thumb into the jugular of my last attacker, just as their teeth latch onto my arm and they bite out a chunk of my flesh. They cry out at the same time I do, but I win. I stumble upright, my arm throbbing. But I know it will heal. I don't have time to think about anything else. I need to get further in.

The rest of the Thorns hurl past me, and I realise everyone has made it past. We're doing this... we're getting through.

They're trying so hard—there's at least two for every one of us —which means Arlo is close. This is the centre of it all.

One Thorn wails at my side as he's thrown to the floor, dislocating his arm with a resounding crack. I throw off two more attackers who advance after my brief distraction, and I pull out a pocket blade to maim them.

Once I regain my balance, a pair of glasses shatter on the ground. I blindly hurl myself at the tall vampire that pins a squinting Rani against the wall, their fangs bared. She kicks and pulls, her eyes squeezed shut as I snap their neck in a heartbeat and watch them collapse to the ground. She takes two breaths to open her eyes, but then we're running again. No looking back. We never look back.

I can't see the others. I don't know where they've gone. There are robes everywhere, and a chorus of screams and growls emerge from all corners of the grounds. I don't know where I'm going.

I pull Rani alongside me to make sure she's okay. She may have vampire blood in her system for now, but I don't know how long it will last. It won't turn her, but it could also be fought off in a matter of minutes, and then she'd be dead. No doubt about it. They all will be, even Fran. This is nothing like the battlefield that day.

I might die before we even reach Arlo.

It's carnage.

My bloody arm stings like there's no tomorrow as another one pounces on my back from behind. I make quick work of throwing them off, pulling out my pocketknife again and slashing out wildly. I've never felt a violent streak like this before, but I don't care. I'll do whatever I have to. Whatever it takes.

I've lost Rani again. No, no, no...

Screams. Cries. Shouts.

I can smell so much blood.

Human.

I'm around the corner in seconds. Fran staggers back from four attackers, clutching her left eye as blood streaks from it. I run over to help, and then *Lawrence* is at my side, his fangs wide and exposed. *Lawrence?* He bites down hard on one of the attacker's necks and rips away what flesh he can, his eyes almost *glowing* red.

How did he..?

There's no time for questions. I just need to keep everyone alive long enough to see the end. *Leave no potential vessels.*

I race over to catch Fran as she slides down the stone wall, clenching her face in agony. I try to reach out to her injury, but she bats me away. "No, no. Go, Mars. Go! I'll be fine!"

I hesitate until I realise there's no one else coming for us. Obeying, I whirl back around and finish the two attackers ahead. It's then when I notice Elise on the ground, her head unnaturally bent with wide, glassy eyes. One of her arms is entirely gone, and a huge, deep slit runs vertically down her neck to her chest exposing shattered cartilage.

She's dead. No doubt about it. *No vessels. How long is a fully dead body a suitable vessel? Surely it can't be more than a minute or so? Right? Vampires are still alive in a way, our brains are alive so we're not vessels unless we're truly dead... right? They'd still need a fresh host... I hope. Are we safe? Arlo was dying, Nicholas was dying, they were all almost dead... but not quite...*

I'm sorry, Elise.

I...

"Mars, look out!" Lawrence shouts. Before I can turn, I feel a heavy weight on my back as a body falls, robes torn and soaked, then slumps off my back onto the ground. I turn, panting. Blood covers Lawrence from head to toe, matching the crimson surrounding the whites of his eyes. His hair is plastered to his face with sweat and blood and...

He's wielding a *sword*.

"Where the fuck..." *Where did he get that from?*

Lawrence shrugs, panting, then points to the corpse at his feet.

Again, there's no time to process. Another wave of the cult runs at us, all armed with varying types of medieval weapons, and that's when I *feel* it. The Manipulation.

It's coming from the Great Hall.

The *weapons* room.

Lawrence turns on them and fights with all his might. I clock Rani being slowly surrounded by easily five or six members. She, too, wields a sword, one far too heavy and large for her to hold. Even from this distance, I can tell it's blunt, but she tries anyway; it's her only form of defence.

I run to her aid, but then Carmen appears out of nowhere with a scream. She dives in front of Rani to cage her just as the attackers pounce, and all seven of them begin slashing, ripping, and tearing at her back.

It's a massacre.

I can't even think straight—

But the *pull* of energy from the weapons room. The epicentre.

That's it.

I have to follow it.

I fix my eyes on my destination and run faster than I've ever run in my life. With unyielding force, I push past everyone in my way. In seconds, someone appears beside me, and I *know* it's Marianne. She's alone.

As we arrive at the entrance to see the armed guards, we exchange one glance to signal our next move—*attack*. Our strength, mixed with Marianne's Manipulation, makes quick work of the guards, running the three of them straight into the stone ground. We step over their bodies to get through.

And there, in the centre of the Great Hall...

The Sun, The Moon, and The Star.

Arlo.

The three of them hold hands, with their eyes closed and heads lowered. I can't *see* anything, but the strength of the power flowing between them is nauseating. My head is splitting, and my vision blurs.

Michael's head shoots up, and his eyes open. Two black coals stare right at me.

We're too late.

Arlo and Jerome don't budge, their chests slowly rising and falling concurrently. They are one.

We're too late.

Then Michael grins, taking a deep breath and stretching his back out. "Ahh, friends. You came to join us. Are you ready for the end?"

Footsteps pound behind us, and I turn as Nicholas stumbles through the doorway, panting; his dark brown hair is stuck to his forehead with blood. *I never saw him.*

"Master!" he shouts. "I tried to..."

"Shut up!" Michael shrieks. The power wavers slightly, a missing link in his armour.

I can't physically move any closer to them without feeling the pressure squeeze behind my eyes, obscuring my vision. I focus my eyes on Arlo, as if just looking at him will wake him up. But we're too late. It's already started.

"We came to end this. Once and for all," Marianne bites.

"Empty words." Michael's blackened eyes roll and his face becomes one of mocking pity.

Then, the first wave hits. It washes over my body, knocking me to the ground. My mind blanks for a moment, and I feel drunk. I can't think straight.

I can't think *at all. I...*

This is it.

"Not good enough," Marianne spits. The next few moments seem to happen in slow motion. Reaching for the wall at her side, she pulls down a long sword and strides into the circle—and *swings.*

Michael staggers back, breaking the connection and dropping both Arlo and Jerome's hands. They collapse, unconscious, as Michael clutches his bloodied, open throat, oozing blackness. He coughs up a spray of tar, his eyes returning to cold silver.

Marianne throws the heavy sword to the side and screams in sheer rage, but all Michael does is laugh. He stands back up, laughing.

"It's going to take a lot more than that to end me, darling." His neck already looks like it's closing up. "I didn't appreciate the distraction, though."

I know he's in her head now when her shoulders relax and her panting ceases.

No. He's got her. He's too strong. I...

I can't do anything.

I can't do anything.

THE NEXT MINUTE that follows will be burned into my brain for as long as I live.

MICHAEL REACHES for the sword and swings hard towards Marianne. She ducks at first, winning back her own strength and I reach out my hands from where I'm still lying on the floor as I watch the second swing catch her shoulder, forcing her backwards. Nicholas is visible in the very corner of my eye, and I can just about make out his face.

He's shocked, but he doesn't move... I don't even think he can.

"I did enjoy messing with you, darling, but all good things must come to an end." Michael grins then the third swing comes with inhuman force and slashes straight across her scarred neck. He steps forward to grab her hair, yanking her head up and lifting her feet from the ground. She grasps at her throat in gargled panics. She's defenceless. She's...

The fourth swing is aimed so precisely, so perfectly, that no one could have done it more accurately. The final swing takes her head clean off, and her body falls back with a thud. Blood spills from the cavity, spraying the side of my body.

I vomit onto the floor.

She's dead. Just like that. Gone.

"NO!" Someone shouts—*Nicholas.*

Michael does not let go of the sword while he admires his handiwork. But Nicholas dives over the body and sinks to his knees, wailing.

Michael throws the head to the side, away from the body like it's nothing.

Michael throws *her* head.

Marianne. I. Oh.

She's gone.

Nicholas wails again and pulls the body up to his chest. There's blood everywhere.

His sister.

Her younger brother was still in there somewhere all along.

"Why? Why did you?" he cries, begging Michael for answers. The man who confronted us only moments ago is long gone. His façade is dead and buried in the blink of an eye. "You said we were fixing the world? No more lies, no more murder and destruction. A haven. What did she ever do to you?"

Michael is fast with his response. "She was a weed. We can't begin again if there's ivy in our walls."

That's it. That's his answer.

"You hypocrite! You bastard fool, you..." Nicholas caves in, weeping into his sister's cold shoulders.

I wonder briefly what he's really thinking, if he suddenly regrets everything he's done, and if the veil has finally been lifted from his eyes after all these years.

I hope he does.

Is that mean?

I don't think it is.

The hell angel doesn't care for the scene, though. He kicks her head further away like a football, and it bounces off the wood-panelled walls like a piece of rotten fruit.

She's dead.

She's gone.

Just like that.

Marianne is gone.

Chapter Thirty Eight

Arlo
Now

Go along with it for as long as you can, my dad had said. *Make him believe he's winning.*

So, that's what I did. It's what we both did.

He took us into the Great Hall, a chapel-like building wallpapered with battle swords and armour. He ushers us to kneel in the heart of the room.

I glance briefly at my father as Michael pulls his hands behind his back. *Don't be scared,* his eyes seem to say.

I'm not scared anymore, I think.

I can't be. For everyone.

My father bites out a cry as Michael slashes his skin before pulling out my dad's left hand. I see the blood, still too dark to be human. It trickles and spills onto the ground.

Then, Michael makes his way around to me and does the same to my right hand.

"Excellent. I knew you would come willingly in the end. I'm good at that, don't you think?" he says, taking both our injured hands in his. Immediately, I feel the power coursing through my veins.

I've felt nothing like it. Nothing even close. During the months and months of The Star being inside me, I have never felt so much like...

Like a god.

"Close your eyes, and call your strength, my Moon and Star. You are strong enough now, just like I taught you to be. At one with your bodies at last. Call it, bring it forward, and *command.*"

Then the pain starts.

It's subtle at first, like a tired headache behind my eyes, but then it reaches its tendrils through every crevice of my brain, and Arlo is sucked back into the void. Black creeps in around my eyes.

The Star. No.

Fight it, Arlo. Fight it. This can't all be for nothing.

I hear my dad cry out, gritting his teeth. Michael is pushing too much of himself into us. We can't... it's overpowering.

Let go.

I can't.

I won't.

No.

Not now.

Never again.

My eyes close on Michael's second command, and I'm drowning. Suffocating. The Star is too strong. I can't breathe. I think I'm crying, but I feel no tears. But Arlo is inside, still fighting. Fighting with every ounce of strength he has left.

It's not going to work. The plan. We're not strong enough. We went too far.

I sense a commotion and hear voices on my left, but my eyes won't open. I'm too far down, sinking to the bottom of the lake. Michael's iron grip bites into the flesh on my hand.

"Ahh, friends. You came to join us. Are you ready for the end?" he says.

Friends. Friends. Focus on them. Keep them close to you.

More footsteps.

"Master! I tried to..."

Nicholas.

Then, "We came to end this. Once and for all." *Marianne.*

They came.

But then a shock strikes through me, and I feel invincible, fixed in place like a statue. My body was just a vessel, as it always has been. I'm too big for this room; how am I still here? I'm expanding inside out like a burning star. Because that's what I am.

The *Star.*

Burning up and exploding into a blinding wave of light. Shattering the galaxy.

The darkness takes over, but then I'm falling. My body hits the floor, the connection shattering.

I open my eyes again, regaining consciousness. My vision takes a moment to adjust, my body electric and charged. My cheek is pressed firmly against the rough floor. Before me lies my father, with his eyes still closed. His energy is calm, too, and the connection is broken.

I see it just when a cry echoes out into the room. A headless body strewn across the floor behind my father.

Marianne.

No.

Nicholas leaps over to the corpse and cradles it, weeping.

Mars comes into view then as I tilt my head back. They're on the floor, propping themself up by their elbows while their eyes, wide with horror, stare at the scene before them. More movement sounds from the doorway, and I blink to clear my vision, my arm crushed beneath me.

But I see them.

My friends.

They came.

Rani appears at the door first, with Carmen's arm over her shoulder; the taller, blood-covered girl burdens her partner with most of her weight as she limps forward. Lawrence stumbles in behind, closely followed by Fran, whose left eye is smothered by thick blood and torn flesh. But they're all alive.

They came.

I'm so sorry, everyone. I wish it didn't have to be this way.

Nicholas is shouting at Michael, but Mars clocks me, and our eyes lock.

It's me, Mars. I'm me, I mouth.

They nod subtly. Slowly.

"I'm sorry," I whisper.

"Oh, I love an audience. I'm impressed at the lengths you've gone through! Do stay where you are though. We're very busy over here, if you can't already tell." Michael speaks with foul confidence. I want to scream.

Michael strides back across the room, with his arms held behind his back. As if he hasn't just murdered someone.

Not someone.

Marianne.

He killed her.

Come on, dad. Wake up.

I jerk out a leg, hoping to rouse him without drawing too much attention.

"Oh, you're awake! Good." Michael.

Shit.

But then my dad's eyes open, and he focuses on my face.

I flick my eyes to the discarded weapon near us. It's time.

Now. I mouth. My father nods.

Please work.

I dart up, ignoring the shooting pain in my arm. Without even gaging my surroundings, I leap up and throw my full weight onto Michael. Something clatters around us as we collide and fall.

Noting the healing wound on his neck, I pull his hair back and split it. The skin pulls like melting plastic as I tug as hard as my fists allow, pinning him to the ground.

"NOW!" I scream, louder than I've ever screamed in my life.

IT'S FUNNY. I never thought I'd be so content and at peace with dying again. I used to spend so much of my time thinking about the end of life and how it might feel. It would frighten me, and I'd hate myself for wasting so much of my time thinking about things beyond my control.

But I'm in control now.

And I'm happy.

As I feel the weight of the blade against my back, and the sharp sting of silver shoot through my chest, I smile. Blood rises in my throat, and I spit it out onto Michael beneath me, whose eyes widen. He feels it too.

I force all my weight onto him. He can't get out of this one. I hold his neck until my strength fades. As the light leaves his eyes, and the sword twists and slices our bodies, his brow relaxes and shifts into one of confusion.

"Is er iets mis met mijn schilderij? Vind je het niet mooi?" he says, his voice calm and innocent.

I'm staring into the eyes of the real Michael, and my smile widens.

We did it, I think.

Then I take my final breath.

23rd June 2019

Happy Birthday Benjamin. I couldn't quite remember the flowers you liked, I don't think I ever asked you. Well, I hope you like them. They're meant to stand out from far away, like you did!

I'm sorry I only come when it's dark, I'm trying to fix things, it just takes so much of my time and I get carried away and lost and—

You don't need to hear all that. Have a lovely day, Ben. I'll never forget you.

—Taken from the diaries of Marianne Ashtown

CHAPTER THIRTY NINE

Mars
Now

My throat burns when Jerome reaches for the long sword, throwing his body over Arlo's and shoving the blade into his son's back with brute force. He thrusts it in at an angle to hit its intended target—deep inside Michael's heart beneath. He wails with a roar of energy as his trembling hands twist the blade down, cracking bones. Blood trickles onto the floor.

I can only see the top of Arlo's head, and the loose arms of Michael's body, but I know. I just know.

Holding Rani back is the hardest thing I've ever had to do. Her screaming his name will haunt me forever.

Jerome turns and slumps to the floor as the struggle ceases beneath him. Reaching into his trouser pocket, he pulls out something so small I can't make it out. He doesn't look at any of us, but I see the streak of tears against his cheeks as he turns away and tips whatever he's holding into his mouth, swallowing it instantly. His eyes close.

Then I realise.

He's always been waiting for this moment.

As his body convulses and he slumps back onto the floor, foam frothing at his mouth. No one moves to help or stop him. He reaches out so his hand lands an inch away from Arlo's. Then he stops moving and his legs straighten out.

The three of them ending together.

The energy in the room shatters almost immediately as their force collapses and evaporates with them. The hall fills with the remaining breaths of everyone who remains. I finally let her go.

Rani scrambles over to Arlo and pulls the giant, bloodied sword from his back with adrenaline-fuelled strength, trying and failing to catch his heavy body as it slumps to the floor with a thud. She scoops her arms under his and drags him away as far as she can as the whole room witnesses the mess of his body. I don't want to look at his face. I stare into nothingness. My limbs don't work.

Carmen comes stumbling into view to help, and I see the blood painting her back, the fabric of her top shredded to pieces. She shouts for Rani before reaching her partner's side, helping to get Arlo's body away from Michael.

Then they all run to him.

I still don't move.

I can't.

But I know why.

There's something missing. It's not over. I still feel a smidge of power from before.

Nicholas.

He has part of The Sun in him. A small part, but it's enough.

We just need to make sure there are no other potential vessels in the room when we do it.

Will this be enough? They can't reach far, surely. This has to be...

My head flicks to him, where he kneels beside his sister's head-less corpse, whose skin is already grey. *He never even tried to stop us...*

He must sense me, because he turns to face me with understanding in his eyes.

He doesn't grin or smile or give any indication of his former pride, influenced by The Sun. It doesn't matter, though. Arlo can't have died for nothing.

Arlo is dead.

"You don't want to do this," he says, holding up his hands in surrender while slowly rising to his feet.

I don't think. I don't care. *Finish it,* my mind says.

I flick out my pocket-knife, it's all I have on hand.

I stand and edge towards him like a predator.

"Hey, kid. You really don't want to do that. I'll leave; I'll never show my face again. You don't have to worry about me anymore. I'm done."

I ignore him.

"I'm not."

I thrust the blade straight through his chest, twisting and pulling, rendering him helpless. As he falls, I push the whole thing inside his chest cavity and step down onto his ribs, reaching for one of the smaller swords strewn behind us. I bring it home, straight through the cartilage in his neck. He doesn't even struggle. He doesn't seem to try. The blade blunts at the floor, severing his spine. The light in his eyes dies almost instantly as a fountain of dark red blood gushes beneath my hands.

I straighten, panting over his body and pushing my boot down hard onto his chest one last time, leaving the blade buried deep. And only then does that last bit of energy dissipate.

We did it. We won.

Arlo saved the world.

Then the tears fall.

I back away from the body, dropping the weapon.

I just killed a man.

"Mars! Please, you have to help!" Rani shouts for me.

Did no one see what I just did?

I turn to face them all. Rani sits with Arlo's head in her lap, and Carmen by her side. The other two are at his other side, surrounded by his wings, which have turned almost powdery, as if they're rotting away. Rani's cheeks are streaked with tears as she looks up at me. They all do.

"There has to be something you can do?" Fran says, reaching out to squeeze the fabric of Arlo's jeans. Her eye is sealed shut with blood, but it no longer seems to concern her.

Despite the blood on his lips—the *red* blood—and the giant patch staining the entire front of his shirt, he looks restful.

His blond lashes sleep delicately over his eyes. I lower myself to my knees to join them, watching Arlo.

"Is there really nothing you can do?" Fran asks again.

"Surely that can't have..." Lawrence leans forward and rips open Arlo's shirt to expose his chest. We stare at the giant bloody, open wound across the entirety of his sternum. The blood sticks to the fabric of his shirt. Jerome aimed perfectly.

I gag.

"No! Everyone, step back!" Rani shouts, flaying out her hands to shoo Lawrence away. She pulls Arlo's body towards her with her jumper sleeves before shuffling away from everyone. The wings on his back make a sound, like a snapping branch, as they detach from his body and crumble to ash. She lets out a loud sob. "He doesn't like people touching his skin like this. It's too abrupt. Please, he doesn't like it... he doesn't." Rani's voice trails off, and she slumps inwards on herself, tears dripping onto Arlo's face. "He doesn't like touch."

Every interaction I ever had with him hits me at once. Everything from the moment I found him lying in that alleyway.

"Are you sure there's nothing you can do? Can't we at least try? Your blood is fast healing, surely it can..." Carmen's voice is calm and collected, but she holds on tightly to Rani's right arm, rubbing her thumb over Rani's wrist. She looks drained, almost corpse-like. She needs to get to a hospital. Fast.

I shake my head. "He was already dead. We all are." I'm about to gesture to us all, but then I realise in that moment, me and Lawrence are the only vampires left in the room.

"Vampires. We die to become who we are. Arlo died last year; I can't—"

I didn't want to choke up, but my throat closes entirely.

"But what about Jerome? He came back. He—"

I glance over at Jerome's body. "I'd need a... No. Even if we had someone willing, I can't even guarantee it would work. It's virtually unheard of..."

"I could—"

"Rani! Don't you dare!" Carmen slaps Rani's arm. "I can't believe you'd say that!"

She doesn't mean it. She's just desperate. We all are.

Rani bites her fist. "But what Lawrence did to us? Could we not force him to drink some vampire blood to help with the healing? Is that not how it works? When Marianne gave him..."

"He's gone," I announce, standing and stepping away.

My voice may have sounded too harsh. Too blunt. But if I don't shut away my emotions now, I don't know how I'll go on. Everyone tracks me with their eyes.

"Mars!" Rani shouts, and I look down at her, and Arlo's eternally sleeping head in her lap. Our eyes lock, and she sucks in her lower lip. "You knew he was going to do this, didn't you? They planned to sacrifice themselves all along. That's what they meant by bringing the fight to Michael. They... You knew!"

I can't lie, not to her. Not ever.

I swallow, aware of every eye sewn into my skin. "I did."

"Why didn't you..." Rani stops herself. I think she knows now, deep down. There was nothing else we could have done. Arlo did this for everyone, not just for her or me or The Thorns. This was so much bigger than all of us, and he had made his decision. Nothing I could have done or said would have changed his mind.

I harshly brush under my nose with my arm to wipe away my emotion. No one else speaks.

What now?

There's over a dozen bodies outside. Most will recover soon, and the survivors will want revenge. Or they'll run once they realise the scale of what happened. I need to take charge. To lead. Just like Marianne asked of me.

The image of her body falling to the ground crashes through my mind over and over, even as I close my eyes. When I finally step towards Jerome's body, no one follows. His wings have detached and crumbled to dust beneath him; his skin is purple. I reach to brush the hair from his face; his veins protrude from his temples, his eyes bloody and void from suffocation.

The colour of Ben's. Green.

I reach out to close his eyelids and lower my head, closing my own eyes momentarily.

A soft, cold touch lowers over my hand, and I look up slowly. There's no one there, but I'd like to think it's Arlo or Ben, or maybe both of them, in whatever form spirits really exist in. A cold whisper of their souls—barely there, maybe not even there at all. It may just all be in my head. I'm feeling what I want to feel. Closure.

"Thank you," I breathe to whoever is listening. But when I blink, the sensation leaves me.

A final goodbye.

I stand again, brushing out my trousers and taking a deep breath before stepping over to Michael's body. I've only ever known him as the embodiment of evil, but now, jewellery and claws aside, all I can see is that black-and-white photograph of Michael van der Meer and his family.

The artist who went missing in 1967 and was never seen again.

There's no known living relatives, but I can only hope they're watching down and know that he is finally at peace. Closure, finally, after decades.

I reach down to close Michael's eyes, placing my hand over his chest and saying a silent prayer.

The entities won't be gone forever. It would be naïve to believe they'd never return. After all, their hosts might be dead, but their essence—their existence—will live on out there. Recovering, waiting, regathering.

But we'll be waiting. They've seen the fight we give. We know enough now. We'll travel the globe to make sure *everyone* is prepared.

They will *never* win.

But for now, and perhaps for a very long time, it's over.

It's all over.

July 2019

Hello Mars! This is probably going to be my last entry, if not, you'll have given me the key back anyway and you won't have to suffer through another one of my ramblings. I am aware 90% of my entries are extremely tedious.
But if this is my last entry, I just wanted to get some final words off my chest!

Is immortality real? Is it really possible to never die?
I don't think so. In fact, at this point, I know so.
This parasite, it just extends our lives, doesn't remove the end date entirely.
I wonder if they will ever study us. Use this infection for good. For humanity.

I wonder why it chose Nicholas. That thing. I don't care what it wants to be called. I spent decades believing what happened to my brother was all my fault. That the infection had tainted him, used him. Turned him wrong. Then my memories were stolen, my brain mashed around, and when they came back, I worried even more.
But it was never me.
I saved my brother because I could, and any sister would. If it was any other night, perhaps this would have all been different.
But would it have been? It could have been me instead. Or anyone else. This all would have still happened, I would have just been oblivious to it. If I hadn't been turned that night, Nicholas would have died, then I would have not long after, and that would have been it.
But I have a chance to fix things.
One final time.

And I won't mess it up.

I do regret a lot I did in my life, if I could take it all back, I would. I should have never abused my power, whether I was conscious of it or not, but I did those things, and I hope all the good I tried to do counts towards something.

Protect The Thorns. I know you will, but I wouldn't be an annoying mother if I didn't say it! I know you will always do the right thing.

I feel like I'm missing something, something else I want to say.

Oh! This won't mean anything to you if you haven't read any of my other diaries yet but my answer to Julian is yes. It was always yes.

—*Taken from the diaries of Marianne Ashtown*

CHAPTER FOURTY

Mars
Three Weeks Later

It's been an odd month, but that's a very light way of putting it. *Odd*, as if it's just been a little unusual, not a series of funerals and a changed world.

A year ago, I was happy and my life was on track. I had a good relationship with my friends and family, and everything was relatively normal.

Normal.

I don't even know what that means anymore. Ha. Skies.

Up until yesterday, I would have wanted nothing more to return to that life and live in ignorant bliss. To not only paint, but to manage my four silly liabilities, going for drinks with them and travelling the world.

I suppose I can still do that. I can travel the world and all the places on my list, just like I've always wanted to, but I have a job to do while I'm there. The remaining cult members will have spread themselves far and wide; we won't get away with things that easily, but we *will* keep them in check.

I've got some large boots to fill, but I'm ready now.

I'm finally ready to live my life *after.*

We'll all be ready. Whether it be in ten years, a hundred, or even a thousand.

Whatever the immortal life throws at me, I'll deal with it. I'm still so *young.* And knowing what I've achieved at this age, I'm not afraid of what's to come. I'll know what to do.

WHEN CASPER ARRIVED in Edinburgh the afternoon after the end, he broke down to his knees. He'd lost his husband, and now his newly realised brother-in-law. I often wonder, if there *is* a higher power, why is it so unbelievably harsh on some people? Why do some people have to suffer and endure so much? What did they do to deserve it? Nothing, clearly nothing, so why must it be this way?

We wept as one. We exchanged guilt and 'what ifs', but ultimately, we did all we could.

Fran's eye couldn't be saved, but she made a quick and healthy recovery, having already picked out four different coloured eyes she wanted to try before she was even discharged.

Of course, Carmen was rushed straight to hospital once the world woke up. She was treated for severe lacerations to the back and arms, but she healed a lot faster than expected. Maybe the remnants of Lawrence's blood had something to do with it, or maybe she really is just *that* stubborn. Rani stayed by her side the whole time, until she was discharged before the funerals.

We buried Marianne first as her funeral was to be held entirely amongst The Thorns. We buried her amongst all the fallen Thorns who had outlived all family—deep in the heart of the hideout, for their souls to hold up the walls for centuries to come.

We buried Nicholas too. Nicholas Ashtown. Marianne's baby brother. The puppeteer turned puppet.

I read her diaries. Every single one. He meant so much to her.

. . .

MAYBE I SHOULDN'T HAVE DONE what I did next, but something so strong compelled me to, justifying my decision. I hope I did the right thing.

I had Julian's body legally exhumed, along with his two sisters, and I moved them away from the family plot in Highgate. I had them reburied in a fresh patch, commissioning new tombstones to replace the false and toxic spewings on the original graves.

I never knew them in person, but the way Marianne wrote about them was enough for me to want to help them, even long after death. Maybe now they can finally rest, knowing someone remembers them for who they really were, not what documents made them out to be. They weren't just pawns in the family business. They were so much more.

WE HAD to wait a few weeks to bury Arlo and Jerome together, but we decided it was for the best. In the time between, Rani moved into her second-year accommodation, with Carmen joining her in her third year. The pair soon settled into their new routine and I've kept a close eye on them. I'll forever feel like a guardian to them, but I will leave them in peace eventually. I will. They want nothing more to do with our world now, which I understand. I expected nothing less. Carmen lost a mother—*again*. The world gave her two, then took them both away. It's not fair. Why must it be this way?

Rani's only connection to us was only ever Arlo, really. She was a good friend to me, but I know she was doing it all for him. She deserves to live away from it all now. To have a normal life. Ha, there's that word again. *Normal.*

. . .

A FEW DAYS AGO, I found Casper, Francesca, and Lawrence in the studio. The last place I expected them to be, but it wasn't an accident or a spur of the moment thing; I knew as soon as I met their eyes what they were doing. And they'd been sorting it for a while.

A laptop sat open with a list of recordings pulled up. Old mixes. Unreleased material.

Casper silently handed me a set of headphones, and a ball formed in my throat.

Months ago, before we found Lucy, the band dragged Arlo into the studio to record some piano samples. They didn't know what to put them to at the time, but they decided to save them for potential future projects. But as Lawrence hit play, and the sound played into my ears, I heard what they created.

Ben left behind enough samples and snippets of his voice, singing through both released and unreleased lyrics, and the three of them reworked all of these tracks into something...

Well, there's no other way to put it.

It was magic.

I cried almost as soon as Arlo's keys started, and Ben's voice sounded over the top. We held one another for a long time. No words needed to be shared.

After playing it for the seventh time, I finally removed the headphones and thanked them. Thanked them for everything. Casper sniffled, and Fran caught a tear with her thumb.

"We've talked about returning," Lawrence said, swinging his legs awkwardly on the table.

"Maybe one day we will; it's not entirely off the table, but..." Fran's voice wandered off as she cleared her throat and looked away from us.

"Not yet. Not as Forever Red. That story has ended, and I think we're slowly learning to be at peace with that." Casper puffed out his chest to hold back his emotions.

"We maybe want to release this piece once it's mastered, with

Katerina and Melissa's approval, of course. We wouldn't just go ahead with—"

I cut Fran off. "Yeah. No, yeah. I think that would be nice." And it would be. It would be hard, an emotion-fuelled piece, but it would be for them. The brothers.

Before I left them, they shared their working title, which brought yet another tear to my eye.

I DIDN'T SLEEP that night, but to be honest, I've not slept much since that day. It will take some time. A long time. I'll manage, though. I'll do it.

TODAY, we bury Arlo, with Jerome at his side, and Ben on the other.

A family.

It rained overnight, and I woke up and cried into my morning blood, for I worried the soil would be too damp or wet, or just not the right condition.

Then I banged my knee against the table leg and kicked the kitchen chair across the room in frustration.

Rani knocked on my door a few minutes later, and I had to look at myself in the mirror and tell myself to get it together. I opened the door to Rani and Carmen in beautiful black dresses and invited them in while I finished getting ready.

I panicked the whole time about being late or forgetting to do something, but Rani reassured me everything had been properly organised. I don't know how she manages to keep everyone calm. Her kohl-lined eyes had smudged a little under her smile, but it didn't change anything.

She handed me a folded, handwritten note but told me not to open it until after the funeral. The way Carmen squeezed her shoulder indicated she already read its contents. I nodded in thanks, slowly processing it all.

We're the first ones there, except for Melissa. I'd offered to meet her so we could go together, but she insisted she'd make her own way. Maybe it might have been a bit too much for her.

I knew she would have wanted him to have been buried close to their house in the Lakes, but after learning about Ben, she made no protest to him being buried beside his brother.

Jerome's would be lowered first, that's what they told us, then Arlo second.

Only a handful of people actually knew Jerome existed. Katerina and Edith are there, as well as Melissa, but most other people who turn up—and there's a lot of people—come for Arlo.

I wonder if he knew how many people really loved him.

I watch them lower both coffins in a trance. I even sway a few times, having to keep my legs from giving way.

He did this for everyone. For all of us.

A few days ago, Melissa asked me if I wanted to say a few words, but I told her I wouldn't know what to say. She looked back at me, stunned.

I didn't mean it like that. I could talk about Arlo for days. But in the moment, and even now, I can't form the words.

I just want him back.

And I know that can never happen.

He saved the world.

They both did.

I hold Melissa's hand as the first shovels of soil are thrown over Jerome's grave. To my side, Katerina squeezes Casper's hand and leans into his shoulder.

Maybe, in another world, he called her back and travelled over to start a life with her.

Maybe, in another, he never left Melissa and Arlo grew up with his father alongside him.

But those worlds don't exist. And The Sun is to blame for that.

Not Michael, not the real Michael. He was as much of a victim as the rest, if not more. He didn't even get a choice. But it was never a choice really though, was it?

Arlo never chose this.

A cold wind whirls through us all, and I close my eyes, focusing on Melissa's warmth beside me. I've decided I'm going to tell her the truth. And Katerina. Once this is over. It will be hard, but they need to know. I can't have them live the rest of their lives believing they lost all these people to just *accidents*. I'll just have to stop them from being able to tell anyone else.

Rani comes up beside me and reaches for my free arm. She briefly glances at my side, and we share a million words through our minds. Then, we watch them cover up Arlo's resting place.

I DON'T GO to the wake. I hate wakes. I just can't stomach it.

I promise Melissa I'll visit her before she leaves the city. I thank my Thorns, but then I go home.

ARLO IS FINALLY AT PEACE.

Maybe I will be, one day.

I will. It's just hard.

I love you, Arlo. Always.

THE NOTE SITS on my bedside table, the one Rani handed me earlier. It's something she clearly wanted me to read. I stare at it for a while as the clock ticks behind me in my kitchen.

I finally lean over to open it, the edges slightly creased. I hold the paper in my hands for a while and rub my fingers over the grains, unable to focus on the words until I see the handwriting.

It's a poem.

Arlo's.

. . .

Our minds in orbit
So close, too far
Run t'wards infinity
A planet like my own.
Our minds in orbit
Un-beating hearts, undying souls
Run t'wards home
They found life there, you know.

EPILOGUE

Mars
Day After Funeral

I wake suddenly during the night, my head pounding. It took me forever to get to sleep, my head still spinning from yesterday. Arlo's funeral.

I did not cry then. I don't know why—I thought I would—but I had to be strong for everyone else.

It wasn't until I went home and broke down with the poem between my fingers.

He's really gone.

Now, I'm sitting in bed with the strangest feeling I've been awoken by something. But my room is silent.

I feel compelled to get up to chase the imaginary sound. Something feels wrong, like I'm missing something. As if I've awoken from a dream that reminded me to do something. Like I awoke with a purpose.

I throw on some jeans and tie my hair up, moving without thinking.

What's going on?

I walk over to grab my coat and decide to take a walk. Clear my head, maybe.

IT'S 3AM. The streets are eerily silent, not a soul about.

I walk and walk with no real destination in mind and shiver at the chill.

My feet take me to the cemetery, and my stomach sinks.

The memories from the day before are still so fresh in my mind: the coffin lowering, the dazzling sun peeking through the trees, Melissa and Katerina holding hands, despite having only met days prior. Mothers holding each other up.

I try to shake it off, yet my feet carry me forward.

I'm even more afraid as I round the corner to see the graves. A figure stands beside...

Beside Arlo's grave.

I pick up my pace, carefully weaving through the rows of gravestones until the figure hears me and peers up in my direction.

It's Rani.

And she's standing over Arlo's grave.

The soil entirely disturbed, and...

"He's gone," she says when she notices it's me.

How did you know to be here?

"What?" I come up beside her to look at it from her angle. The soil is all over the place, but the hole is still relatively filled. She can't know that...

"How could someone..." Rani sounds as if she's about to cry, and not for the first time this evening either.

How did you know to be here?

Rani lowers herself to her knees and grabs at the soil, leaning against the entrance. I reach out on instinct to stop her from leaning too far in, just in case it *is* hollow in places. It's so dark, it's hard to tell.

"Careful," I shout-whisper.

"How could anyone..."

I rub her back, glancing at Ben's undisturbed grave beside us, and Jerome's equally untouched grave on the other side.

"How did you know to be here?" I ask aloud this time. Because I'm not feeling the same emotions.

"What?" Rani's head snaps up to me. "What do you mean?"

"How did you know to come here? Now, at this time?" My tone does not falter.

"I... I just... I don't know." Even in the dark, I watch her tense brow loosen, while her mind tries to come up with a reason.

"Did you just wake up and decide to go for a walk?" I ask.

"I... yes. I did." I don't say anything. "What? What does that mean?" Panic laces her voice.

But I'm not scared. I'm not afraid or worried or concerned.

"I think... I think we're here for a reason," I say.

Rani stands up to face me. "What? Why? To catch whoever did this? After everything, why can't he just rest?"

"Rani, how do you know he's gone?" I point at the grave.

"I..." But then she looks at me blankly, the words dying on her lips. Something stirs behind us—the snap of a twig.

We both startle around, and Rani grips my arm with force.

But there's nothing to be afraid of.

The water ripples, babbling against the pebbles and stones.
Cotton clouds roll over each other gently as a ray of white peers
through and turns the lake to glass. A picture of tranquillity.
Miles and miles of green and ochre giants watch down in a huddle,
holding up the sky.
A single car drives past on the winding road embedded in the chest of
the hillside, and the dog barks in shock.
A puddle of water glides over the owner's boots as they bend down to
brush the golden fur with a smile.
They throw a twig into the water and the dog bounds in after it with
glee.
The owner breathes in and looks up.
It's paradise.

FOREVER RED

If you enjoyed this duology and want to read more about Ben and Casper's story, Forever Red is out now! A prequel companion story I wrote to be read in between or after the duology! It's available in paperback and ebook and features a lot of familiar faces from the duology!

Rising Ashes Playlist

'Follow The Voice' by Kraków Loves Adana
'Acid Eyes' by Paolo Nutini
'Sam, A Dream' by Black Belt Eagle Scout
'Neptune' by Daughter
'In Cold Light' by Vanbur
'how do you feel' by strawbey
'Maine' by hey, nothing
'Pavane for Summer' by You'll Never Get to Heaven
'Marble Eyes' by Labyrinth Ear
'my angel' by Adrianne Lenker
'Drag Me Under' by Sleep Token
'Suburban War' by Arcade Fire
'Bad Kingdom - (Lulu's Version)' by Apparat
'Ivy' by Robin Guthrie
'Thatorchia' by Ethel Cain
'Teenage Exorcists' by Mogwai
'Nothing Stirs' by The Body
'Love Fade' by Tamaryn
'Wilderness' by Bat For Lashes
'everything to die for' by mui zyu

A Note on Locations

I love reading books where I can vividly picture locations, especially ones that I've been to, so I thought it would be fun for me to tell you what was going on in my brain when I wrote these books.

This series is mainly set in Durham, England and most of the places mentioned are real. Vennel's Café in the centre of Durham is the setting for most coffee shop scenes in this series. Arlo meets Lucy on their date in The Boathouse right by the riverside and then the alley that Arlo dies in is Moatside Lane, a very narrow alley between Pizza Express and The Shakespeare Pub that does actually lead you down a long and winding path and spits you out close to the riverside but definitely not a recommended night walk. (Silly, Arlo!)

The Thorns' hideout does not exist unfortunately... or maybe it does, and we humans just can't find it...

The abandoned swimming pool is still there as of 2025 though the entrance Arlo and Mars take has since been blocked off for any urban explorers out there!

Somewhere in the woodland parts of Durham, there is a small

abandoned chapel that my friend stumbled across many years ago, and whilst I've never seen it myself, it was the inspiration for the abandoned church featured in this duology. I can only hope nothing awful has ever happened there...

With regards to Rising Ashes, I took a few liberties with building placements just for convenience. The room Arlo and his father wake up in in Edinburgh Castle doesn't actually exist (at least not to my knowledge, nor would the view actually be the view they have) but the Great Hall is real, as is every other location mentioned in Edinburgh.

The church Arlo hides out in in Lancashire is inspired by the still standing St John's Church, formerly attached to the since demolished Whittingham Hospital. One of my special interests as a teen was Victorian architecture, specifically hospital and 'public buildings' architecture so Whittingham was at the forefront of my brain when I thought of the location. I've never seen the church in person but I do know that there have been plans to renovate it!

And finally! Arlo and Rani are from around the Kendal area of the Lake District but enjoyed a few trips up to Buttermere as in my mind, it is one of the most beautiful areas in the UK and definitely a stunning place for a peaceful dog walk...

A Note from Harvey

My debut series is over and I'm not quite sure how to feel. I'm happy, of course. Happy that I had enough support to release these books in the first place and that they resonated with so many more people than I ever would have expected! But I'm also sad, inevitably. Arlo popped into my head in the summer of 2021 when I was staying in a converted chapel in the Lake District (Yes, the same converted chapel Arlo lives in) and at first he was just an idea, like most of my other stories I'd created up until that point. But I very quickly realised he was different. His story needed to be told. And now it has been! But that's that... it's over! It will be very hard for me to say goodbye and I think the only way I can do that is to continue writing little shorts that I'll probably start posting over the summer into autumn of 2025. A slow and gradual goodbye...

This series is a lot, I'm aware it's a bit out there and a lot of the plot lines went through many different iterations during the writing process, but at it's core, it's a story of love and acceptance and family in all forms. I hope the ending I finally settled on has shown that!

Oh, and don't worry too much, this may be the end of THIS story, but not the end of this world. I've got many more stories to tell from different points in time following completely different characters.

How about a novella following two vampires and a human over the course of one night in a Manor House?

Or the story of what happened to the cult follower who ran into the village?

Or the story of the orphaned son of Marianne's first victim after she ran from her brother?

'Drink Up, Darling' - Coming Winter 2025

'A Cautionary Tale for Village Boys' - Coming Spring 2026

'Death in C Minor' - Coming Summer/Autumn 2026

;)

Acknowledgments

So here it is! The Fallen Thorns series is finally over! I've come a long way since I began drafting this in mid 2021 and my main thank you goes to everyone who supported my journey to make this sequel even possible!

Thank you once again to my wonderful editor Eden Northover and to my beta readers (Syd, Elpida, Thy, Alyssa, Karnam, Joe and Katrina) for helping me make this book the best it can be!

Thank you to Elliot for double checking my Spanish, and to Archer for translating my Dutch!

I also wanted to thank Bri, Yves, Lex, Katrina, Annabel and Caden for being my writing buddies over the past year, your friendships and support mean the world to me! (And a special thanks to Katrina for standing over me with an epipen whilst I poisoned myself.)

And as always, a massive shout out to Maia and Sy for putting up with me on the daily in our All For The Gays group chat and to everyone in Sunderland Waterstones Café for keeping me fed and watered for hours on end.

ABOUT THE AUTHOR

Harvey Oliver Baxter is an author and illustrator from the North of England. They are the author of the *Fallen Thorns* duology as well as the spin-off prequel *Forever Red*.

instagram.com/lastvanillasmile

tiktok.com/authorhobaxter

9 781739 520854